About the Authors

USA *TODAY* bestselling author, **Trish Morey**, just loves happy endings. Now that her four daughters are (mostly) grown and off her hands having left the nest, Trish is rapidly working out that a real happy ending is when you downsize, end up alone with the guy you married and realise you still love him. There's a happy ever after right there. Or a happy new beginning!

Trish loves to hear from her readers – you can email her at trish@trishmorey.com

Abby **Green** spent her teens reading Mills & Boon romances. She then spent many years working in the film and TV industry as an Assistant Director. One day while standing outside an actor's trailer in the rain, she thought: *there has to be more than this.* So she sent off a partial to Mills & Boon. After many rewrites, they accepted her first book and an author was born. She lives in Dublin, Ireland and you can find out more here: www.abby-green.com

Nikki **Logan** lives amongst a string of wetlands in ...alia with her partner and a menagerie of animals. ... full of romance in descriptive, natural ... ss and danger ... and risk of ... nce on a ... shed by ... 10, her

By the Sea

COLLECTION

August 2019
Second Chance at Sea

September 2019
Seduced at Sea

February 2020
Escape by the Sea

April 2020
Married by the Sea

Escape by the Sea

TRISH MOREY

ABBY GREEN

NIKKI LOGAN

MILLS & BOON

First Published in Great Britain 2020
By Mills & Boon, an imprint of Harper*CollinsPublishers*
1 London Bridge Street, London, SE1 9GF

ISBN: 978-0-263-28082-1

0220

FIANCÉE FOR ONE NIGHT

TRISH MOREY

This book is dedicated to you, the reader,
the person this book was written for.
Please enjoy FIANCÉE FOR ONE NIGHT.
Much love, as always,
Trish x

CHAPTER ONE

LEO ZAMOS loved it when a plan came together.

Not that he couldn't find pleasure in other, more everyday pursuits. He was more than partial to having a naked woman in his bed, and the more naked the woman the more partial he was inclined to be, and he lived for the blood-dizzying rush from successfully navigating his Maserati Granturismo S at speed around the sixty hairpin turns of the Passa dello Stelvio whenever he was in Italy and got the chance.

Still, nothing could beat the sheer unmitigated buzz that came from conceiving a plan so audacious it could never happen, and then steering it through the ensuing battles, corporate manoeuvrings and around the endless bureaucratic roadblocks to its ultimate conclusion—*and his inevitable success.*

And right now he was on the cusp of his most audacious success yet.

All he needed was a wife.

He stepped from his private jet into the mild Melbourne spring air, refusing to let that one niggling detail ruin his good mood. He was too close to pulling off his greatest coup yet to allow that to happen. He sucked in a lungful of the Avgas-flavoured air and tasted only success as he headed down the stairs to the waiting car. The Culshaw Diamond Corporation, owner and producer of the world's finest pink diamonds and a major powerhouse on the diamond market, had been in the hands of the one big Australian diamond dynasty for ever. Leo had been the one to sense a change in the dynamic of those heading up the business, to detect the hairline cracks that had been starting to show in the Culshaw brothers' management team, though not even he had seen the ensuing scandal coming, the circumstances of which had made the brothers' positions on the board untenable.

There'd been a flurry of interest from all quarters then, but Leo had been the one in pole position. Already he'd introduced Richard Alvarez, head of the team interested in buying the business, to Eric Culshaw senior, an intensely private man who had been appalled by the scandal and just wanted to fade quietly into obscurity. And so now for the first time in its long and previously unsullied history, the Culshaw Diamond Corporation was about to change hands, courtesy of Leo Zamos, broker to billionaires.

Given the circumstances, perhaps he should have seen this latest complication coming. But if Eric Culshaw, married nearly fifty years to his childhood sweetheart, had decreed that he would only do business with people of impeccable family credentials and values, and with Alvarez agreeing to bring his wife along, clearly Leo would just have to find himself a wife too.

Kind of ironic really, given he'd avoided the institution with considerable success all these years. Women did not make the mistake of thinking there was any degree of permanence in the arrangement when they chanced to grace his arm or bed.

Not for long anyway.

But a one-night wife? That much he could handle. The fact he had to have one by eight p.m. tonight was no real problem.

Evelyn would soon find him someone suitable.

After all, it wasn't like he actually needed to get married. A fiancée would do just fine, a fiancée found after no doubt long years of searching for that 'perfect' soulmate—Eric Culshaw could hardly hold the fact they hadn't as yet tied the knot against him, surely?

He had his phone in hand as he nodded to the waiting driver before curling himself into the sleek limousine, thankful they'd cleared customs when they'd landed earlier in Darwin to refuel, and already devising a mental list of the woman's necessary attributes.

Clearly he didn't want just any woman. This one had to be classy, intelligent and charming. The ability to hold a conversation desirable though not essential. It wouldn't necessarily matter if she couldn't, so long as she was easy on the eye.

Evelyn would no doubt be flicking through her contacts, turning up a suitable candidate, before she hung up the phone. Leo allowed himself a flicker of a smile and listened to the burr of a telephone ringing somewhere across the city as his driver pulled effortlessly into the endless stream of airport traffic.

Dispensing with his office two years ago had been one of the best decisions he had ever made. Now, instead of an office, he had a jet that could fly him anywhere in the world, a garage in Italy to house his Maserati, lawyers and financiers on retainer, and a 'virtual' PA who handled everything else he needed with earth-shattering efficiency.

The woman was a marvel. He could only applaud whatever mid-life crisis had prompted her move from employment in a bricks and mortar office to the virtual world. Not that he knew her age, come to think of it. He didn't know any of that personal stuff, he didn't have to, which was half the appeal. No more excuses why someone was late to work, no more hinting about up-coming birthdays or favourite perfumes or sultry looks of availability. He had to endure none of that because he had Evelyn at the end of an email, and given the references she'd proffered and the qualifications and experience she'd quoted in her CV, she'd have to be in her mid-forties at least. No wonder she was over life in the fast lane. Working this way, she'd be able to take a nanna nap whenever she needed it.

The call went to the answering-machine and a toffee butler voice invited him to leave a message, bringing a halt to his self-congratulations. He frowned, not used to wondering where his PA might be. Normally he'd email Evelyn from wherever he happened to be and not have to worry about international connections or time differences. The arrangement worked well, so well in fact that half the time he'd find her answering by return email almost immediately, even when he was sure it must be the middle of the night in Australia. But here in her city at barely eleven in the morning, when she'd known his flight times, he'd simply expected she'd be there to take his call.

'It's Leo,' he growled, after the phone had beeped for him to leave his message. Still he waited, and kept waiting, to see if that announcement would make his virtual PA suddenly pick up. When it was clear no one would, he sighed, rubbed his forehead with his other hand and spat out his message. 'Listen, I need you to find me a woman for tonight...'

'Thank you for your call.'

Leo swore under his breath as the butler terminated the message. Come to think of it, there was a damn good reason he usually emailed.

Eve Carmichael dropped the third peg in as many pairs of leggings and growled in frustration as she reached down to scoop up the offending article and fix the final item on the line. She'd been on tenterhooks all day. *All week more like it*. Ever since she'd known *he* was coming to Melbourne.

She looked up at the weak sun, willing it to dry her washing before Melbourne's notoriously fickle weather suddenly changed seasons on her, and shivered, a spidery shiver that descended down her spine and had nothing to do with the weather and everything to do with the fact Leo Zamos was coming.

And then she glanced down at her watch and the spider ran all the way up again.

Wrong. Leo Zamos was *here*.

It made no difference reminding herself that it was illogical to feel this way. She had no reason, no reason at all, to feel apprehensive. It wasn't like he'd asked her to meet his plane. In fact, it wasn't like he'd made any arrangements to see her at all. Logically, there was no reason why he should—she was his virtual PA after all. He paid her to run around on his behalf via the wonders of the world wide web, not to wait on him hand and foot.

Besides, there was simply no time to shoehorn her into his busy schedule even if he did have reason. She knew that for a fact because she'd emailed him the latest version this morning at six, just before she'd got into the shower and worked out her hot water service had chosen today of all days to die, not twenty-four hours after her clothes line had turned up its toes. A sign? She sure hoped not. If it was, it wasn't a good one.

No wonder she was edgy.

And no wonder this strange sense of foreboding simmered away inside her like a pot of soup that had been on the boil so long that it had thickened and reduced until you could just about stand a spoon in it.

Damn.

She shot a warning look at a cloud threatening to block out the sun and gave the old rotary clothes hoist a spin, hoping to encourage a breeze while cursing the fact that right now she probably had more hope of controlling the weather than she did reining in her own illogical thoughts, and there was no chance of controlling Melbourne's changeable weather.

And then she stiffened her jittery spine and headed back to the house, trying to shake off this irrational urge to do a Rip Van Evelyn and go to sleep until Leo Zamos was safely and surely out of her city.

What the hell was her problem?

Simple, the answer came right back at her, catching her so unawares she forgot to open the back door and almost crashed into it instead.

You're afraid of him.

It stopped her for a moment. Stilled her muscles and cemented her bones with the certainty of someone who had good reason to fear.

Ridiculous, she chided, her mind swiftly writing off the possibility, her breath coming short as she finally forced her fingers to work enough to turn the door handle and let herself in. Leo Zamos was nothing to her but the best hourly rate she'd ever been paid. He was a meal ticket, the ticket to renovating her late-nineteenth-century bungalow she affectionately referred to as the hovel, a ticket to something better in her life and getting it a hell of a lot sooner than it would ever happen otherwise. She just wished she didn't have to spend her renovation money on appliances now, before she even had an idea of what she'd need when the final plans came in.

She glanced upward at the strips of paint shredding from the walls of the laundry and the ivy that was creeping inside through the cracks where sixty years ago her grandfather had tacked it onto the back of the bungalow, and told herself she should be grateful for Leo's business, not a jittery bundle of nerves just because he was in town. Their arrangement worked well. That was all that mattered. That's what she had to concentrate on. Not some long-ago dusty memory that she'd managed to blow out of all proportion.

After all, Leo Zamos certainly wasn't wasting any time fretting about her. And in less than forty-eight hours he'd be gone. There was absolutely nothing at all to be afraid of.

And then she pulled open the creaking laundry door and heard a deep rich voice she recognised instantly, if only because it instinctively made her toes curl and her skin sizzle, "*...find me a woman for tonight...*" and the composure she'd been battling to talk herself into shattered into a million pieces.

She stood there, rooted to the spot, staring at the phone as the call terminated, emotions warring for supremacy inside her. Fury. Outrage. Disbelief. All of them tangled in the barbed wire of something that pricked at her skin and deeper, something she couldn't quite—*or didn't want to*—put a name to.

She ignored the niggling prickle. Homed straight in on the fury.

Who the hell did Leo Zamos think he was?

And what did he think she was? Some kind of pimp?

She swooped around the tiny kitchen, gathering dishes and piling them clattering into the sink. Oh, she knew he had his women. She'd arranged enough Tiffany trinkets and bottles of perfume to be sent to his countless Kristinas and Sabrinas and Audrinas over the last two years—and all with the same terminal message—

Thanks for your company.
Take care.
Leo

—to know he'd barely survive a night without a bed-warmer. But just because he was in her home town it didn't mean he could expect her to find him one.

Pipes groaned and hammered as she spun the hot water tap on fruitlessly, until she realised she needed to boil the kettle first to have any hope of hot water. But finally the sink was filled with suds and the tiny room was full of steam. She shoved her hands into rubber gloves and set upon attacking the stack of dishes and plastic cups, all but hidden under the froth and bubbles.

It had been lucky the machine had cut him off when it had or she might have been forced to pick up the receiver and tell him exactly what he could do with his demands—and that would be one sure way to terminate an income flow she had no way of replacing any time soon.

But, then, did she really want to work with a man who seemed to think it was perfectly acceptable asking his PA to organise him a night-time plaything? Maybe she should just call him herself. Remind him of the duties she had agreed to undertake.

Except that would require talking to him…

Oh, for heavens sake! On impulse she swiped at a tea towel and dried her gloves as she crossed the small living area towards the answering-machine, jabbing at a button before she could change her mind, her brain busy being rational. She dealt with his correspondence all the time, even if mostly by email. Surely she wasn't about to go weak at the knees at the sound of his voice?

And then the message replayed and she heard the weight of expectation in his pause as he waited for her to pick up—expected her to pick up—before his message. *"Listen, I need you to find me a woman for tonight…"*

And this time her outrage was submerged in a tremor that started in a bloom of heat that radiated across her chest and down her belly, tingling as it shot down her arms and legs. Damn. She shook her hands as if to rid herself of the unwelcome sensations, and headed back to finish the dishes.

So nothing had changed. Because his voice had had the same unsettling effect on her from the very first time she'd heard him speak more than three years ago in a glass-walled boardroom fifty floors above Sydney's CBD. She recalled the way he'd swept out of the lift that day, the air shifting in currents around him in a way that had turned heads and caused more than one woman to stumble as she'd craned her head instead of looking where she was going.

He'd seemed oblivious to his impact, sweeping into the boardroom like he owned it, spicing the air with a mix of musk and wood and citrus and radiating absolute confidence in himself and his role. And no wonder. For whether by sheer force of his personality or acute business acumen, or maybe the dark chocolate over gravel voice that had soothed everyone into submission, he'd successfully brought that deal to a conclusion that day, bringing together an over-eager buyer and a still unconvinced seller, and had had them both smiling as if they'd each got the better part of the deal.

She'd sat in the far corner of the room, taking minutes for her lawyer boss, while another part of her had been busy taking inventory of the man himself even as his rich voice had rippled through her and given birth to all kinds of wayward thoughts she had no business thinking.

Was there anything the man lacked?

Softness, she'd decided, drinking in the details, the thick black hair, the dark-as-night eyes, the strong angles of jaw and nose and the shadowed planes and recesses of his face. No, there was nothing soft about his looks, nothing at all. Even the lips that gave shape to that smooth-as-sin voice were fiercely masculine, a strong mouth she'd imagined as capable of both a smile as a cruel twist.

And then she'd looked up from her notebook to see him staring at her, his eyes narrowing, assessing as, without a move in his head, their focus moved down, and she'd felt his gaze like the touch of his long-fingered hand down her face and throat until with burning cheeks she'd wrenched her eyes away before she felt them wander still lower.

The rest of the meeting had passed in a blur and all she remembered was that every time she had looked up, it had seemed as though he was there, waiting to capture her eyes in his simmering gaze. And all the while the discussions had gone on around her, the finer points of the agreement hammered out, and all she'd been able to think about was discovering the sinful pleasures promised in his deep, dark eyes.

And when she'd gone to help organise coffee and had met him on the way back, she'd felt warmth bloom in her chest and pool in her belly when he'd smiled at her, and let him draw her gently aside with no more than a touch of his hand to her elbow that had almost had her bones melt.

'I want you,' he'd whispered, shocking her with his savage honesty, thrilling her with his message. 'Spend the night with me,' he'd invited, and his words had poured into all the places that had been empty and longing all her life, even the tiny crevices and recesses she'd never known existed until then.

And she, who had never been noticed in her life by anyone with such intensity, let alone a powerhouse of masculine perfection like this man, had done the only possible thing she could do. She'd said yes, maybe a little too breathlessly, a little too easily, for he'd growled and pulled her into a room stacked high with row upon row of files, already pulling her into his kiss, one hand at her breast, another curving around her behind even as he manoeuvred her to the furthest corner of the room.

Blown away by the man, blown away by the red-hot magma of sensations surging up inside her, she hadn't made a move to stop him, hadn't entertained the possibility until, with one hand under her shirt and his hard thighs wedged between hers, the door had opened and they'd both stilled and waited while whoever it was searched a row of files, pulling one out with a swish and exiting the room. And he'd pulled her shirt down and pushed the hair back from her face from where he'd loosened it from the coil behind her and asked her name, before he'd kissed her one more time. 'Tonight, Eve,' he'd said, before he'd straightened his tie and gone.

Cups clunked together under the suds and banged into the sides of the tiny sink, a sound reassuringly concrete right now. For this was her reality—a ramshackle bungalow it would cost a fortune to tear down and rebuild and probably more if she decided to renovate and try to preserve what original features might be worth saving.

She finished up the dishes and pulled the plug, letting the water go. She had commitments now. Obligations. A glimpse at her watch told her that her most important obligation would be waking up any minute now.

Would her life be any different if she had spent the night with Leo that night, if he hadn't been called away with barely a hurried goodbye to sort out a hiccup in the next billionaire deal he had been brokering somewhere halfway around the world, and if they'd actually finished what they'd started in that filing room?

Or given how she'd been incapable of saying no to him that day, maybe her child might simply have been born with skin even more olive, hair a little thicker?

Not that Leo would make those kind of mistakes, she was sure.

No, it was better that nothing had happened that night. He wouldn't be her client now if it had.

Besides, she knew what happened to the women Leo bedded. She could live without one of those terse thank-you notes, even if it did come attached to some pretty piece of bling.

The room darkened and she looked out the window in time to see the first fat drops fall from the dark clouds scudding across the sky and splatter against the glass.

'I thought I warned you,' she growled at the sky,

already making for the back door and forgetting all about Leo Zamos for one short moment.

Until the phone rang again.

CHAPTER TWO

SHE stood there, one hand on the door handle, one thought to the pattering rain growing louder on the tin lean-to roof, and yet Eve made no move towards the clothesline as the phone rang the requisite number of times before the machine cut in, inviting the caller to leave a message.

'Evelyn, it's Leo.'

Redundant really. The flush of heat under her skin told her who it was, and she was forced to admit that even when he sounded half-annoyed, he still had the most amazing voice. She could almost feel the stroke of it across her heated skin, almost feel it cup her elbow, as his hand once had.

'I've sent you an email,' Leo continued, 'or half of one, but this is urgent and I really need to speak with you. If you're home, can you pick up?'

Annoyance slid down her spine. Of course it was urgent. Or it no doubt seemed urgent to Leo Zamos. A night without a woman to entertain him? It was probably unthinkable. It was also hardly her concern. And still the barbed wire prickling her skin and her psyche tangled tighter around her, squeezing her lungs, and she wished he'd just hang up so she could breathe again.

'Damn it, Evelyn!' he growled, his voice a velvet

glove over an iron fist that would wake up the dead, let alone Sam if he kept this up. 'It's eleven a.m. on a Friday. Where the hell are you?'

And she realised that praying for the machine to cut him off was going to do no good at all if he was just going to call back, angrier next time. She snatched the receiver up. 'I didn't realise I was required to keep office hours.'

'Evelyn, thank God.' He blew out, long and hard and irritated, and she could almost imagine his free hand raking through his thick wavy hair in frustration. 'Where the hell have you been? I tried to call earlier.'

'I know. I heard.'

'You heard? Then why didn't you pick up? Or at least call me back?'

'Because I figured you were quite capable of searching the *Yellow Pages* yourself.'

There was a weighted pause and she heard the roar of diesel engines and hum of traffic, and she guessed he was still on the way to the hotel. 'What's that supposed to mean?'

'I mean, I'll do all manner of work for you as contracted. I'll do your correspondence and manage your diary, without issue. I'll set up appointments, do your word processing and I'll even flick off your latest girlfriend with some expensive but ultimately meaningless bauble, but don't expect me to act like some kind of pimp. As far as I recall, that wasn't one of the services I agreed to provide.'

This time the pause stretched so long she imagined the line would snap. 'Is something wrong?'

God, everything was wrong! She had appliances to replace that would suck money out of her building fund, she had a gut that was churning so hard she couldn't think straight, and now she was expected to find this man a sleeping partner. 'You're the one who left the message on my machine, remember, asking me to fix you up with a woman for the night.'

She heard a muttered curse. 'And you think I wanted you to find me someone to go to bed with.'

'What else was I supposed to think?'

'You don't think me perfectly capable of finding my own bedtime companions?'

'I would have expected so, given…' She dropped her forehead in one hand and bit down on her wayward tongue. Oh, God, what was she thinking, sparring with a client, especially when that client was almost single-handedly funding her life and the future she was working towards? But what else could she do? It was hard to think logically with this churning gut and this tangle of barbs biting into her.

'Given what, exactly?' he prompted. 'Given the number of "expensive but ultimately meaningless baubles" I've had you send? Why, Evelyn, anyone would think you were jealous.'

I am not jealous, she wanted to argue. *I don't care who you sleep with*. But even in her own mind the words rang hollow and she could swear that the barbed wire actually laughed as it pulled tighter and pressed its pointed spines deeper into her flesh.

So, okay, maybe she had felt just a tiny bit cheated that nothing had happened that night and she hadn't ended up in his bed, but it was hardly wrong to wonder, surely? It was curiosity, more than anything. Naturally she'd had plenty of time since then to count herself lucky she had escaped that fate, after seeing how efficiently and ruthlessly he dispensed with his women, but it didn't stop her wondering what it would have been like…

She took a deep, calming breath, blew it out slowly and cursed whatever masochistic tendencies had made her pick up the phone in the first place when it would have been far more productive to rescue her washing than risk losing the best client she was ever likely to have. 'I'm sorry. Clearly I misunderstood your message. What is it that I can do for you?'

'Simple.' His liquid voice flowed down the line now she was so clearly back on task. 'I just need you to find me a wife.'

'Are you serious?'

So far this call was going nothing like he'd anticipated. It wasn't just her jumping to the wrong kind of conclusion about his earlier call that niggled at him, or her obvious disapproval of his sleeping habits—most PAs he'd met weren't that openly prudish; in fact, most he'd encountered had been too busy trying to get into his pants—but there was something else that didn't sit right about his indignant PA. She didn't sound at all like he'd expected. Admittedly he was out of practice with that demographic, but since when did middle-aged women—any woman for that matter—ask their employer if they were serious?

'Would I be asking if I weren't? And I need her in time for that dinner with Culshaw tonight. And she probably doesn't have to be a pretend wife—a pretend fiancée should do nicely.'

There was silence on the end of the line as the car climbed the sweeping approach to the Western Gate Bridge and for a moment he was almost distracted by the view of the buildings of Melbourne's sprawling CBD to his left, the port of Melbourne on his right. Until he realised they'd be at his hotel in Southbank in a matter of minutes and he needed to get things moving. He had to have tonight's arrangements squared away before he got tied up with his lunchtime meeting with the government regulators due to sign off on the transfer of ownership when it went ahead. He'd dealt with those guys before and knew it was likely to be a long lunch. 'Evelyn?'

'I'm here. Although I'm still not quite sure I understand.'

He sighed. What was so hard to understand? 'Culshaw's feeling insecure about the deal. Wants to be sure he's dealing with solid family people and, given the circumstances, maybe I don't blame him. Culshaw and Alvarez are both bringing their wives to dinner tonight, and I don't want to do anything to make Culshaw more nervous by having me turn up alone, not when we're so close to closing the deal. So I want you to increase the number at dinner to six and find me someone who can play my fiancée for a night.'

'I can certainly let the hotel know to cater for six,' she said, sounding like she meant to go on before there the line went quiet again and he sensed a 'but' coming.

'Well?' he prompted, running out of time and patience.

'I can see what you're trying to do.' Her words spilled out in a rush. 'But is taking along a pretend fiancée really wise? I mean, what if Culshaw finds out? How will that look?'

Her words grated on both his senses and his gut. Of course it was a risk, but right now, with Culshaw feeling so vulnerable, so too was turning up alone. 'Choose the right woman,' he said, 'and that won't be an issue. It's only for a night after all. Are you anywhere near your email? I sent you an idea of what I'm looking for.'

'Look, Mr Zamos—'

'Leo.'

'Okay, so, Leo, I appreciate that I got the wrong end of the stick before, but finding you someone to play fiancée, that's not exactly part of the service I offer.'

'No? Then let's make it part of them.'

'It's not actually that simple.'

'Sure it is. Find an acting school or something. Tell whoever you find that I'm willing to pay over the odds. Have you got that email yet?'

'I'm opening it now,' she said with an air of resignation, her Australian accent softened with a hint of husky sweetness. He decided he liked it. Idly he wondered what kind of mouth it was attached to. 'Charming,' she read from the list of characteristics he'd provided, and he wondered. Surprisingly argumentative would be a better way to describe his virtual PA right now.

'Intelligent. Classy.' Again he mused. She was definitely intelligent, given the calibre of work she did for him. Classy? Maybe so if she'd worked as a corporate PA for several years. It wasn't a profession where you could get away with anything less than being impeccably groomed.

'And I've thought of something else.'

'Oh, goodie.'

Okay, so maybe charm wasn't her strong point, but so long as she got him the perfect pretend fiancée, he would overlook it for now. 'You might want to brief her on both Culshaw and Alvarez. Only the broad-brush stuff, no details. But it would be good if she wasn't completely ignorant of the players involved and what they do and can at least hold a conversation. And, of course, she'll need to know something about me as well. You know the kind of stuff…'

And then it suddenly occurred to him what had been bothering him. She said stuff like 'Are you serious?' and 'goodie' in a voice threaded with honey, and that put her age years younger than he'd expected. A glimmer of inspiration told him that if she was, maybe his search for the perfect pretend fiancée was already over...

'How old are you, Evelyn?'

'Excuse me?'

'I had you pegged for middle-aged, but you don't sound it. In fact, you sound much younger. So how old are you?'

'Is that entirely relevant right now?'

'It could be.' Though by the way she was hedging, he was pretty certain his question was unnecessary. At a guess he'd say she wasn't a day over thirty-five. It was perfect really. So perfect he was convinced it might have occurred to him earlier if he hadn't assumed his virtual PA was a good ten years older.

'And dare I ask...?' Her voice was barely a whispered breath he had to search for over the sounds of the city traffic. 'Why would that be?'

And he smiled. 'Because it would be weird if my fiancée looked old enough to be my mother.'

There was silence on the end of the line, a silence so fat with suspicion that it almost oozed out of the handset. Then that husky, hesitant Aussie drawl. 'I don't follow you.'

'It's quite simple,' he said, his blood once again fizzing with the heady buzz of a plan coming together beautifully. 'Are you doing anything for dinner tonight?'

'No. Leo—Mr Zamos. No!' This could not be happening. There was no way she was going to dinner with Leo Zamos and pretending to be his fiancée. No way!

'Excellent,' she heard him say through the mists of her panic. 'I'll have my driver pick you up at seven.'

'No! I meant yes, I'm busy. I meant no, I can't come.'

'Why? Is there a Mr Carmichael I need to smooth things over with? '

'No, but—'

'Then what's the problem?'

She squeezed her eyes shut. Tried to find the words with which to give her denial, words he might understand, before realising she didn't have to justify her position, didn't have to explain she had an infant to consider or that she didn't want to see him or that the idea simply sat uncomfortably with her. She simply had to say no. 'I don't have to do this. And neither do you, for that matter. Mr Culshaw knows you've only just flown in from overseas. Will he really be expecting you to brandish a fiancée at a business dinner?'

'But this is why it's so perfect, Evelyn. My fiancée happens to be Australian and she's already here. What could be better?'

She shook her head. For her own benefit maybe, but it made her feel better. 'It won't work. It can't. This is artifice and it will come unstuck and in grand style.'

'Evelyn,' he said measuredly, 'it can work and it will. If you let it.'

'Mr Zamos—'

'One evening, Evelyn. Just one dinner.'

'But it's not honest. We'd both be lying.'

'I prefer to think of it as offering reassurance where reassurance is needed. And if Culshaw needs reassurance before finalising this deal, who am I to deny him that?'

But making out we're engaged? 'I don't know.'

'Look, I haven't got time for this now. Let's cut to the chase. I said I was willing to pay someone above the odds and that goes for you too. This dinner is important to me, Evelyn, I don't have to tell you how much. What do you think it's worth for a few hours' work?'

'It's not about the money!'

'In my experience, it's always about the money. Shall we say ten thousand of your Australian dollars?'

Eve gasped, thinking of new clothesdryers and new hot water services and the cost of plumbers and the possibility of not dipping into her savings and still having change left over. And last but by no means least, whether Mrs Willis next door might be able to babysit tonight…

'You're right,' he said. 'Let's make it twenty. Would that be enough?'

Eve's stomach roiled, even as she felt her eyes widening in response to the temptation. 'Twenty thousand dollars,' she repeated mechanically, 'For one evening.'

'I told you it was important to me. Is it enough, do you think, to entice you to have dinner with me?'

Twenty thousand dollars enough? It didn't matter that his tone told her he was laughing at her. But for someone who had been willing to spend the night with him for nothing, the concept that he would pay so much blew her away. Did tonight really mean so much to him? Was there really that much at stake?

Really, the idea was so bizarre and ridiculous and impossible that it just might work. And, honestly, what were the chances he would recognise her? It had been almost three years ago and in a different city, and beyond heated looks they'd barely communicated that day and she doubted he even remembered her name, let alone what she looked like. And since then he'd met a thousand women in a thousand different cities, all of them beautiful, plenty of whom he'd no doubt slept with.

And since then she'd let her coloured hair settle back closer to its natural mousy colour and her body had changed with her pregnancy. Now she had curves that hadn't been there before and maybe wouldn't be there if she'd returned to work in that highly groomed, highly competitive office environment. One of the perils of working from home, she mused, was not having to keep up appearances.

Which also meant she had one hell of an afternoon in front of her if she was to be ready before seven. A glance at the wall clock told her she had less than eight hours to find a salon to squeeze into on the busiest day of the week, and find an outfit somewhere. Still assuming her neighbour could babysit tonight.

A thud came from the nursery, followed by a squeal and gurgles of pleasure, and she swung her head around. Sam was awake and busy liberating his soft toys from the confines of the cot. That meant she had about thirty seconds before he was the last man left standing and demanding to be released from jail the way he knew best. The loud way.

'There's a couple of things I have to square away,' she said, anxious to get off the phone before Sam decided to howl the place down. 'Can I call you back in a few minutes to confirm?'

'Of course,' he said, in that velvet-rich voice that felt like it was stroking her. 'Call me. So long as it's a yes.'

Leo slipped his phone into his pocket as the car came to a smooth halt outside his hotel. A doorman touched his gloved fingers to his hat as he pulled open the door, bowing his welcome. 'We've been expecting you, Mr Zamos.' He handed him a slim pink envelope that bore his name and a room number on the front. 'Your suite is ready if you'd like to go straight up.'

'Excellent,' he said, nodding his thanks as he strode into the hotel entry and headed for the lifts, feeling more and more confident by the minute. He'd known Evelyn would soon have that little problem sorted, although maybe he hadn't exactly anticipated her sorting it so quickly and efficiently.

What was she like? he wondered as the lift whisked him soundlessly skywards. Was he wrong not to insist on a photo of her to be safe? Originally he'd had looks on his list of requirements, on the basis that if he had to act as someone's fiancé, he'd expected it would be one hell of a lot easier to be act the part if he didn't have to force himself to smile whenever he looked at her or slipped his arm around her shoulders. But maybe someone more ordinary would be more convincing. Culshaw didn't strike him as the sort of man who went for looks over substance and, given his circumstances, he'd be looking for a love match in the people he did business with. In which case, some nice plain girl might just fit the bill.

It was only for one night, after all.

The lift doors whooshed open on the twenty-fourth floor onto a window with a view over the outer city that stretched to the sea and air faintly scented with ginger flower.

Other than to get his bearings, he paid scant attention to the view. It was success Leo Zamos could smell first and foremost, success that set his blood to fizzing as he headed for his suite.

God, but he loved it when a plan came together!

CHAPTER THREE

EVE had some idea of how Cinderella must have felt on her way to the ball. Half an hour ago she'd left her old world behind, all tumbling-down house and broken-down appliances and baby rusks, and was now being whisked off in a silken gown to a world she had only ever dreamt of.

Had Cinderella been similarly terrified on her way to the ball? Had she felt this tangle of nerves writhing in her stomach as she'd neared the palace on that fairy-tale night? Had she felt this cold, hard fear that things would come terribly, terribly unstuck before the night was over? If so, she could well empathise.

Not that her story was any kind of fairy-tale. There'd been no fairy godmother who could transform her into some kind of princess in an instant with a touch of her magic wand for a start. Instead, Eve had spent the afternoon in a blur of preparations, almost spinning from salon to boutiques to appliance stores, in between packing up tiny pots of yoghurt and Sam's favourite pasta so Mrs Willis wouldn't have to worry about finding him something to eat. There had been no time for reflection, no time to sit down and really think about what she was doing or why she was even doing it.

But here, sitting alone against the buttery-soft

upholstery of an entire limousine, she had no distractions, no escape from asking herself the questions that demanded to be answered. Why was she doing this? Why had she agreed to be Leo's pretend fiancée, when all her instincts told her it was wrong? Why hadn't she insisted on saying no?

Sure, there was the money. She wouldn't call herself mercenary exactly, but she was motivated at the thought of getting enough money together to handle both her renovations and taking care of Sam. And how else would she so quickly gather the funds to replace a hot water service that had inconsiderately died twelve months too early and buy a new clothesdryer so she could keep up with Sam's washing in the face of Melbourne's fickle weather?

What other reason could there be?

Because you're curious.

Ridiculous. She thrust the suggestion aside, determined to focus on the view. She loved Melbourne. After so many years in Sydney, it was good to be home, not that she got into the city too often these days.

But the annoying, niggling voice in her head refused to be captivated or silenced by the view.

You want to see if he has the same impact on you that he had three years ago.

You want to know if it's not just his voice that makes your stomach curl.

You want to know if he'll once again look at you with eyes filled with dark desire and simmering need.

No, no and no! She shuffled restlessly against the leather, adjusting her seat belt so it wasn't so tight across her chest and she could breathe easier.

Dark desire and simmering need were the last things she needed these days. She had responsibilities now. A child to provide for. Which was exactly what she was doing by coming tonight, she acknowledged, latching onto the concept with zeal. She was providing for her child. After all, if she didn't, who would? Not his father, that was for sure.

She bit down on her lip, remembering only then that she was wearing lipstick for a change and that she shouldn't do that. It had been harder than she'd imagined, leaving Sam for an evening—the first time she'd ever left him at night—and it had been such a wrench she'd been almost tempted to call Leo and tell him she'd changed her mind.

But she hadn't. And Sam had splashed happily in an early bath and enjoyed dinner. She'd read him a story and he'd already been nodding off when she'd left him with Mrs Willis, his little fist clenched, his thumb firmly wedged between cupid bow lips. But what if he woke up and she wasn't there? What if he wouldn't settle back down for Mrs Willis?

God, what the hell had she been thinking, agreeing to this?

Outside the limousine windows the city of Melbourne was lighting up. It wasn't long after seven, the sky caught in that time between day and night, washed with soft shadows that told of the coming darkness, and buildings were preparing, showing their colours, strutting their stuff.

Just like she was, she thought. She wore a gown of aqua silk, which had cost her the equivalent of a month's salary in her old office job, but she figured the evening called for something more grand than her usual chain-store purchases. Leo would no doubt expect it, she figured. And she'd loved the dress as she'd slipped it over her head and zipped it up, loved the look of it over her post-baby curves and the feel of it against her skin, and loved what it did to accentuate the colour of her eyes, but the clincher had been when her eighteen-month-old son had looked up at her from his pram, broken into an enormous grin and clapped his pudgy hands together.

And she must look all right in her new dress and newly highlighted hair because her neighbour had gasped when she'd come to the door to deliver Sam and insisted she cover herself with an apron in case she inadvertently spilled anything on it before she left.

Dear Mrs Willis, who was the closest to a grand-parent that Sam would ever know, and who had been delighted to babysit and have Eve go out for a night for a change, no doubt in the hope that Eve would find a nice man to settle down with and provide a father to Sam. And even though Eve had explained it was a work function and she'd no doubt be home early, her neighbour had simply smiled and taken no notice as she'd practically pushed her out the door to the waiting car. 'Have a lovely evening and don't rush. If it's after ten when you get home, I'll no doubt be asleep, so you can come and pick Sam up in the morning.'

And then they were there. The driver pulled into a turnaround and eased the car to a stop. He passed her a keycard as a doorman stepped forward to open her door. 'Mr Zamos says to let you know he's running late and to let yourself in.' She smiled her thanks as he recited a room number, praying she'd manage to remember it as the doorman welcomed her to the hotel.

Deep breath.

Warily she stepped out of the car, cautious on heels that seemed perilously high, where once upon a time she would have thought nothing of sprinting to catch a bus in even higher. Strange, what skills you forgot, she thought, when you don't use them. And then she sincerely hoped she hadn't forgotten the art of making conversation with adults because a few rounds of 'Open, shut them, open, shut them,' was going to get tired pretty quickly.

And then she stepped through the sliding doors into the hotel and almost turned around and walked straight back out again. It was little more than the entrance, a bank of grand elevators in front of her and a lift lobby to the left, but it was beautiful. A massive arrangement of flowers sat between the escalators, lilies bright and beautiful, palm leaves vivid green and all so artfully arranged that it looked too good to be real.

Just like her, she thought. Because she did so not belong here in this amazing place. She was a fake, pretending to be something she was not, and everyone would see through her in an instant.

She must have hesitated too long or maybe they recognised her as a fraud because someone emerged from behind the concierge desk and asked if she needed assistance. 'I'm to meet Mr Zamos in his suite,' she said, her voice sounding other-worldy in the moneyed air of one of Melbourne's most prestigious hotels, but instead of calling for Security, like she half expected, he simply led her to the lift lobby and saw her safely inside a lift, even smiling as he pressed Leo's level on the floor selection so she could make no mistake.

Oh, God, she thought, clutching her shawl around her as the lift door pinged open on the chosen floor, the keycard clenched tightly in her fingers, this is it.

One night, she told herself, it's just one night. *One evening*, she corrected herself, *just a dinner*. Because in just a few short hours she would be home and life could get back to normal and she could go back to being a work-from-home mum in her trackpants again.

She could hardly wait.

She stepped out into the lift lobby, drinking deeply of the hotel's sweetly spiced air, willing it to give her strength as she started on the long journey down the hall. Her stomach felt alive with the beating of a thousand tiny wings, giving flight to a thousand tiny and not so tiny fears and stopping her feet dead on the carpet.

What the hell was she doing? How could she be so sure Leo wouldn't recognise her? And how could she bear it if he did? The shame of knowing how she'd acted—like some kind of wanton. How could she possibly keep working for him if he knew?

Because she wasn't like that. Not normally. A first date might end with a kiss if it had gone well, the concept of a one-night stand the furthest thing from her mind, but something about Leo had stripped away her usual cautiousness, turning her reckless, wanting it all and wanting it now.

She couldn't bear it if he knew. She couldn't bear the aftermath or the subsequent humiliation.

Would he terminate her contract?

Or would he expect to pick up where he'd left off?

She shivered, her thumping heart beating much too loud for the hushed, elegant surroundings.

Lift doors pinged softly behind her and she glanced around as a couple emerged from the lift, forcing her to move both her feet and her thoughts closer to Leo's door.

Seriously, why should he remember her? A rushed grope in a filing room with a woman he hadn't seen before or since. Clearly it would mean nothing to a man with such an appetite for sex. He'd probably forgotten her the moment he'd left the building. And she'd been Eve then, too. Not the Evelyn she'd reverted to when she'd started her virtual PA business, wanting to sound serious and no-nonsense on her website.

And it's only one night, she told herself, willing herself to relax as she arrived at the designated door. Just one short evening. And then she looked down at the keycard in her damp hand and found she'd been clenching it so tightly it had bitten deep and left bold white lines across her fingers.

Let herself in when it was the last place she wanted to be? Hardly. She rapped softly on the door. Maybe the driver was wrong. Maybe he wasn't even there…

There was no answer, even after a second knock, so taking a fortifying breath she slid the card through the reader. There was a whirr and click and a green light winked at her encouragingly.

The door swung open to a large sitting room decorated in soft toffee and cream tones. 'Hello,' she ventured softly, snicking the door closed behind her, not game to venture yet beyond the entryway other than to admire the room and its elegant furnishings. Along the angled wall sat a sofa with chairs arranged around a low coffee table, while opposite a long dresser bore a massive flatscreen television. A desk faced the window, a laptop open on top. Through the open door alongside, she could just make out the sound of someone talking.

Leo, if the way her nerves rippled along her spine was any indication. And then the voice grew less indistinct and louder and she heard him say, 'I've got the figures right here. Hang on…'

A moment later he strode into the room without so much as a glance in her direction, all his focus on the laptop that flashed into life with just a touch, while all her focus was on him clad in nothing more than a pair of black silk briefs that made nothing more than a passing concession to modesty.

He was a god, from the tips of his damp tousled hair all the way down, over broad muscled shoulders that flexed as he moved his hand over the keyboard, over olive skin that glistened under the light, and over the tight V of his hips to the tapered muscular legs below.

And Eve felt muscles clench that she hadn't even known she'd possessed.

She must have made some kind of sound—she hoped to God it wasn't a whimper—because he stilled and glanced at the window in front of him, searching the reflection. She knew the instant he saw her, knew it in the way his muscles stiffened, his body straightening before he slowly turned around, his eyes narrowing as they drank her in, so measuredly, so heatedly she was sure they must leave tracks on her skin.

'I'll call you back,' he said into the phone, without taking his eyes from her, without making any attempt to leave the room or cover himself. 'Something's come up.'

She risked a glance—*there*—and immediately wished she hadn't, for when she looked back at him, his eyes glinted knowingly, the corners creasing, as if he'd known exactly what she'd been doing and where she'd been looking.

'Evelyn?'

He was waiting for an answer, but right now her tongue felt like it was stuck to the roof of her mouth, her softly fitted dress seemed suddenly too tight, too restrictive, and the man opposite her was too big and all too obviously virile. And much, much too undressed. The fact he made no attempt to cover himself up only served to unsettle her even more.

He took a step closer. 'You're Evelyn Carmichael?'

She took a step back. 'You were expecting someone else?'

'No. Nobody else—except...'

'Except what?' she whispered, wondering if spiders' eyes glinted the same way his did as they sized up their prey.

'I sure as hell wasn't expecting anyone like you.'

She felt dizzy, unbalanced and unprepared, and there was absolutely no question in her mind what she had to do next, no wavering. She turned, one hand already fumbling for the door handle, her nails scratching against the wood. 'Clearly you're not ready,' she said, breathless and panicky and desperate to escape. 'I'll wait outside.'

But she'd barely pulled it open an inch before a hand pushed it closed over her shoulder. 'There's no need to run away.'

No need? Who was he trying to kid? What about the fact a near-naked man was standing a bare few inches away from her and filling the air she breathed with a near-fatal mix of soap and citrus and pure, unadulterated testosterone? A man she'd once been prepared to spend the night with, a lost night she'd fantasised about ever since. A man standing so close she could feel his warm breath fanning the loose ends of her hair, sending warm shivers down her neck. What more reason did a girl need to flee?

Apart from the knowledge that it wasn't the beast she had to be afraid of after all. It wasn't the beast she couldn't trust.

It was her own unquenched desires.

'Stay. Help yourself to something from the minibar while I get dressed next door. I promise I won't be long.'

'Thanks,' she whispered softly to the door, not sure if she was thanking him for the offer of a drink or for the fact he was intending to put some clothes on. But she was sure about not turning around before he removed his arm from over her shoulder and moved away. Far, far away with any luck. 'I'll do that.'

And then the arm withdrew and she sensed the air shift and swirl as he departed, leaving her feeling strangely bereft instead of relieved, like she'd expected. Bereft and embarrassed. God, she must seem so unsophisticated and gauche compared to the usual kind of woman he entertained, practically bolting from the room with her cheeks on fire like some schoolgirl who'd wandered into the wrong loos by mistake!

She could actually do with a stiff drink right now, she mused, still shaky as she pulled open the minibar fridge, assuming she could open her throat wide enough to drink it. Then again, tonight would be a very good night not to drink alcohol, and not just because she probably had no tolerance for it these days. But because drinking anything with anaesthetic qualities in this man's presence would be a very, very bad idea.

Especially given she was already half-intoxicated just being in his presence.

True to his word, he was already returning from the room beyond by the time she'd made her selection, a pair of slim-fitting black trousers encasing those powerful-looking legs and a crisp white shirt buttoned over his broad chest. Even dressed, he still looked like a god rather than any mere mortal, tall, dynamic and harshly beautiful, and yet for one insane, irrational moment her eyes actually mourned the loss of naked skin to feast upon, until he joined her at the minibar and it occurred to her that at least now she might be able to speak coherently.

'Did you find something?' he asked, as she moved aside to give him room as he pulled a beer from the fridge.

'Yes, thanks,' she said, twisting the cap from a bottle of mineral water and grabbing a glass, still discomfited by his presence. Then again, it was impossible to see him clothed and not think about those broad shoulders, the pebbled nipples and the cluster of dark hair between them that swirled like storm fronts on a weather map, before heading south, circling his navel and arrowing still downwards…

She sucked in a rush of air, cursing when it came once again laced with his tell-tale scent. Distance was what she needed and soon, and she took advantage of his phone ringing again to find it. She did a quick risk assessment of the sitting room and decided an armchair was the safest option. She needed to stop thinking about Leo Zamos with no clothes on and start thinking about something else. Something that didn't return the flush to her skin and the heat to her face.

Like the decor. Her eyes latched onto a triptych set above the sofa. Perfect. The three black and white prints featured photographs of Melbourne street-scapes from the Fifties and Sixties, their brushed gold frames softening their impact against the cream-coloured wall. Understated. Tasteful. Like the rest of the furnishings, she thought, drinking in the elegant surrounds of the sitting area and admiring how the decorator had so successfully combined a mix of fabrics, patterns and textures. Maybe she should try for something similar…

And then Leo finished the call and dropped onto the sofa opposite, scuttling every thought in her head.

He stretched one arm out along the top of the cushions, crossed one long leg over the other and took a swig from his beer, all the while studying her until her skin prickled with the intensity of his gaze and her heart cranked up in her chest till she was afraid to breathe.

'It's a pleasure to meet you, Evelyn Carmichael, my virtual PA. I have to say I'm delighted to find you're very much real and not so virtual after all.' And then he shook his head slowly and Eve's lungs shut down on the panicked thought, *He knows*! Except his mouth turned up into a wry smile. 'Why did I ever imagine you were middle-aged?'

And breath whooshed from her lungs, so relieved she even managed a smile. 'Not quite yet, thankfully.'

'But your credentials—your CV was a mile long. What did you do, leave school when you were ten?'

The question threw her, amazed he'd remembered the details she'd supplied when he'd first sent his enquiry through her website. But better he remember those details rather than a frenetic encounter in a filing room with a PA with a raging libido. 'I was seventeen. I did my commercial degree part time. I was lucky enough to make a few good contacts and get head-hunted to a few high-end roles.'

His eyes narrowed again and she could almost see the cogs turning inside his head. 'Surely that's every PA's dream. What made you leave all that and go out on your own? It must have been a huge risk.'

'Oh, you know…' she said, her hands fluttering around her glass. 'Just things. I'd been working in an office a long time and…'

'And?'

And I got pregnant to one of the firm's interstate consultants…

She shrugged. 'It was time for a change.'

He leaned forward, held out his beer towards her in a toast. 'Well, the bricks and mortar office world's loss is my gain. It's a pleasure meeting you at last after all this time, Evelyn. You don't know how much of a pleasure it is.'

They touched drinks, her glass against his bottle, his bottomless eyes not leaving hers for a moment, and now she'd reeled in her panic, she remembered the heat and the sheer power of that gaze and the way it could find a place deep down inside her that seemed to unfurl and blossom in the warmth.

'And you,' she murmured, taking a sip of her sparkling water, needing the coolness against her heated skin, tempted to hold the glass up to her burning cheeks.

Nothing had changed, she thought as the cooling waters slid down her throat. Leo Zamos was still the same. Intense, powerful, and as dangerous as sin.

And it was no consolation to learn that after everything she'd been through these last few years, everything she'd learned, she was just as affected, just as vulnerable.

No consolation at all.

She was perfect. Absolutely perfect. He sipped his beer and reflected on the list of qualities he'd wanted in a pretend fiancée as he watched the woman sitting opposite him, trying so hard to look at ease as she perched awkwardly on the edge of her seat, picking up her glass and then putting it down, forgetting to drink from it before picking it up again and going through the same nervous ritual before she excused herself to use the powder room.

She'd been so reluctant to come tonight. What was that about when clearly she ticked every box? She was intelligent, he knew that for a fact given the calibre of the work she did for him. And that dress and that classically upswept hair spoke of class, nothing cheap or tacky there.

As for charming, he'd never seen anything as charming as the way she'd blushed, totally mortified when confronted by his state of undress before she'd tried to flee from the room. He'd had no idea she was there or he would never have scared her like that, but, then, how long had it been since a woman had run the other way when they'd seen him without his clothes on? Even room service the world over weren't that precious, and yet she'd taken off like the devil himself had been after her. What was her problem? It wasn't like he was a complete stranger to her after all. Then again, she'd made plain her disapproval of his long line of companions. Maybe she was scared she might end up on it.

Now, there was a thought…

He discounted the idea as quickly as it had come. She was his PA after all, even if a virtual one, and a rule was a rule. Maybe a shame, on reflection, that he'd made that rule, but he'd made it knowing he might be tempted from time to time and he'd made it for good reason. But at least he knew he wouldn't have to spend the night forcing himself to smile at a woman he wasn't interested in. He found it easy to smile at her now, as she returned from the powder room, coyly avoiding his eyes. She was uncannily, serendipitously perfect, from the top of her honey-caramel hair to the tips of the lacquered toenails peeping out of her shoes. And he had to smile. To think he'd imagined her middle-aged and taking nanna naps! How wrong could a man be? He would have no trouble at all feigning interest in this woman, no trouble at all.

He rose, heading her off before she could sit down, her eyes widening as he approached and blocked off the route to her armchair so she was forced to stop, even in heels forced to tilt her head up to look at him. Even now her colour was unnaturally high, her bright eyes alert as if she was poised on the brink of escape.

There was no chance of escape.

Oh no. His clever, classy little virtual PA wasn't going anywhere yet. Not before he'd convinced Culshaw that he had nothing to fear from dealing with him, and that he was a rock-solid family man. Which meant he just had to convince Evelyn that she had nothing to fear from him.

'Are we late?' she asked, sounding breathless and edgy. 'Is it time to go?'

He could be annoyed at her clear display of nerves. He should be if her nervousness put his plans at risk. But somehow the entire package was so enticing. He liked it that he so obviously affected her. And so what that she wasn't plain? She wasn't exactly classically pretty either—her green eyes were perhaps too wide, her nose too narrow, but they were balanced by a wide mouth that lent itself to both the artist's paintbrush and to thoughts of long afternoons of lazy sex.

Not necessarily in that order.

For just one moment he thought he'd noted those precise details in a face before, but the snatch of memory was fleeting, if in fact it was memory at all, and flittered away before he could pin it down to a place or time. No matter. Nothing mattered right now but that she was there and that he had a good feeling about tonight. His lips curved into a smile. A very good feeling.

'Not yet. Dinner is set for eight in the presidential suite.'

She glanced at the sparkly evening watch on her wrist and then over her shoulder, edging ever so slightly towards the door, and as much as he found her agitation gratifying, he knew he had to sort this out. 'Maybe I should check with the staff that everything's good with the dinner,' she suggested. 'Just remind them that it's for a party of six now...'

He shook his head benevolently, imagining this was how gamekeepers felt when they soothed nervous animals. 'Evelyn, it's all under control. Besides, there's something more important you should be doing right now.' He touched the pad of his middle finger, just one finger, to her shoulder and she jumped and shrank back.

'And what might that be?' she asked, breathless and trembling and trying to mask it by feigning interest in the closest photographic print on the wall. A picture of the riverbank, he noticed with a glance, of trees and park benches and some old man sitting in the middle of the bench, gazing out at the river. That wouldn't hold her attention for long. Not when he did this...

'You're perfect,' he said, lifting his hand to a stray tendril of hair that had come loose and feeling her shudder as his fingertips caressed her neck. 'I couldn't have asked for a better pretend fiancée.'

Her eyelids fluttered as he swore she swayed into his touch until she seemed to snap herself awake and shift the other way. 'I sense a "but" coming.'

'No buts,' he said, pretending to focus on the print on the wall before them. 'We just have to get our stories straight, in case someone asks us how we met. I was thinking it would make sense to keep things as close to the truth as possible. That you were working as my PA and one thing led to another.'

'I guess.'

'And we've been together now, what, two years? Except we don't see each other that often as I'm always on the move and you live in Australia.'

'That makes sense.'

'That makes perfect sense. And explains why we want to wait before making that final commitment.'

'Marriage.' She nodded. 'We're taking our time.'

'Exactly,' he said, slipping a tentative arm around her shoulders, feeling her shudder at the contact. 'We want to be absolutely sure, which is hard when we only get to see each other a few snatched times a year.'

'Okay. I've got that.'

'Excellent.' He turned towards her. Put a finger under her chin and lifted it so that she had no choice but to look into his eyes. 'But there's one thing you don't get.'

'I knew there was a but coming,' she said, and he would have laughed, but she was so nervous, so on edge, and he didn't want to spook her. Not when she was so important to him tonight.

'This one's simple,' he said. 'All you have to do is relax with me.'

'I'm perfectly relaxed,' she said stiffly, sounding more like a prim librarian than any kind of lover.

'Are you, when my slightest touch...' he ran a fingertip down her arm and she shivered and shied away '...clearly makes you uncomfortable.'

'It's a dinner,' she said, defensively. 'Why should you need to touch me?'

'Because any red-blooded man, especially one intending to marry you and who doesn't get the chance to see you that often, would want to touch you every possible moment of every day.'

'Oh.'

'Oh, indeed. You see my problem.'

'So what do you suggest?'

Her eyes were wide and luminous and up close he could see they were neither simply green nor blue but all the myriad colours of the sea mixed together, the vibrant green where the shallow water kissed the sand, the sapphire blue of the deep water, and everything in between. And even though she was supposed to be off limits, he found himself wondering what they'd look like when she came.

'I find practice usually makes perfect.'

She swallowed, and he followed the movement down her slender throat. 'You want to practise touching me?'

Fascinated, his thumb found the place where the movement had disappeared, his fingers tracing her collarbone and feeling her trembling response, before sliding around her neck, drawing her closer as his eyes settled on her too-wide lips, deciding they weren't too wide at all, but as close to perfect as they could get.

'And I want you to practise not jumping every time I do.'

'I...I'll try,' she said, a mist rolling in over her eyes, and he doubted she even realised she was already swaying into his touch.

He smiled as he tilted her chin with his other hand, his thumb stroking along the line of her jaw. 'You see, it's not that hard.'

She blinked, looking confused. 'I understand. I...I'll be fine.'

But he had no intention of ending the lesson yet.

Not when he had such a willing and biddable pupil. 'Excellent,' he said, tilting her chin higher, 'and now there's just one more thing.'

'There is?' she breathed.

'Of course,' he said, once again drawing her closer, his eyes once again on her lips. 'We just need to get that awkward first kiss out of the way.'

CHAPTER FOUR

SHE barely had time to gasp, barely had time to think before his lips brushed hers, so feather-light in their touch, so devastating in their impact that she trembled against him, thankful for both his solidity and his strength.

More thankful when his lips returned, this time to linger, to play about her mouth, teasing and coaxing and stealing the air from her lungs.

She heard a sound—a mewl of pleasure—and realised it had emanated from the depths of her own desperate need.

Realised she was clinging to him, her fingers anchored in his firm-fleshed shoulders.

Realised that either or both of these things had triggered something in Leo, for suddenly his kiss deepened, his mouth more punishing, and she was swept away on a wave of sensation like she'd only ever experienced once before. He was everywhere, his taste in her mouth, his hot breath on her cheek, his scent filling the air she breathed.

And the feel of his steel-like arms around her, his hard body plastered against her, was almost too much to comprehend, too much to absorb.

It was too much to think. It was enough to kiss and be

kissed, to feel the probing exploration of his tongue, the invitation to tangle and dance, and accept that intimate invitation.

How many nights had she remembered the power of this kiss, remembered what it felt like to be held in Leo's arms? It had been her secret fantasy, fuelled by one heated encounter with a stranger, but even she had not recalled this utter madness, this sheer frantic expression of need.

It was everything she'd ever dreamed of and more, that chance to recapture these feelings. And then he shifted to drop his mouth to her throat and she felt him, rock hard against her belly, and she shuddered hard against him, a shudder that intensified as he skimmed his hands up her sides and brushed peaked nipples in achingly full breasts with electric thumbs.

She groaned as his lips returned to her mouth, a feather-light kiss that lasted a fraction of a second before the air shifted and swirled cold around her and he was gone.

She opened her eyes, breathless and stunned and wondering what had just happened. 'Excellent,' he said thickly. 'That should do nicely. Wait here. I've got something for you.' He turned and disappeared into the other room. She slumped against the credenza behind her, put her hands to her face and tried not to think about how she'd responded to his kiss exactly like she had the first time. Drugged stupid with desire, shameless in her response to him.

Excellent? Hardly. Not when in another ten seconds he could have had her dress off. Another twenty and she would probably have ripped it off herself in desperation to save him the trouble. And all because he didn't want her to be nervous around him! God, how was she supposed to be anything but, especially after that little performance? Had she learned nothing in the intervening years?

She'd barely managed to catch her breath when Leo returned, a tie looped loosely around his collar, a jacket over his arm, and an expression she couldn't quite read on his face. Not the smug satisfaction she'd expected, but something that looked almost uncomfortable. When she saw the two small boxes in his hand, she thought she knew why and she didn't feel any better.

'Try these on,' he said, offering the boxes to her. 'I borrowed them for the night. Hopefully one should fit well enough.'

'You borrowed them?' she said, considering them warily, knowing what came in dangerous-looking little blue boxes like those. And if his words were a hint that whatever sparkly bauble she would wear on her finger wouldn't be hers to keep, it wasn't terribly subtle. But that wasn't what bothered her. Rather, it was the artifice of it all, like they were gilding the lie, layering pretence upon pretence. 'Is this strictly necessary?'

He lifted her hand, dropped the boxes on her palm. 'They'll notice if you don't wear an engagement ring.'

'Can't I simply be your girlfriend?'

'Fiancée sounds much better. All that added commitment.' He winked as he shrugged into his jacket. 'Besides, I've already told them. Go on, try them on.'

Reluctantly she opened the first. Brilliant light erupted from the stone, a huge square-cut diamond set in a sculpted white-gold band, inlaid with tiny pink diamonds. She couldn't imagine anything more stunning.

Until she opened the second and imagination took a back seat to reality. It was magnificent, a Ceylon sapphire set with diamonds either side. She had never seen anything so beautiful. Certainly had never imagined wearing anything as beautiful. She put down the box with the white-gold ring, tugged the other ring free and slipped it on her finger, hoping—*secretly praying*—that it would fit, irrationally delighted when it skimmed over her knuckle and nestled perfectly at the base of her finger.

She looked down at her hand, turning it this way and that, watching the blue lights dance in the stone. 'They must be worth a fortune.'

He shrugged, as if it was no matter, using the mirror to deftly negotiate the two ends of his tie into a neat knot. 'A small one, perhaps. It's not like I'm actually buying them.'

'No. Of course not.' He was merely borrowing them for a night to help convince people he was getting married. Just like he was borrowing her.

But even his ruthless designs couldn't stop her wondering what it must be like to be given such a ring, such an object of incredible beauty, by the man you loved? To have him slide that ring on your finger to the sound of a heartfelt 'I love you. Marry me,' instead of, *'Go on, try them on'*.

The sapphire caught the light, its polished facets throwing a dozen different shades of blue, the diamonds sparkling, and she felt her resistance wavering.

With or without the ring, she was already pretending to be something she was not. Could she really make the lie worse than it already was?

'Very nice,' he said, lifting her fingers. 'Have you tried the other one?'

She looked down at the open box, and the pale beauty that resided there. 'No real need,' she said, trying to sound like she didn't care as well as make out that she wasn't bothered by his proximity, even though her fingers tingled and her body buzzed with his closeness. 'This one fits perfectly.'

'And it matches your eyes.'

She looked up to see him studying her face. 'You know you have the most amazing eyes, every shade of the sea and more.'

'Th-thank you.'

He lifted a hand to her face and swiped the pad of his thumb at the corner of her mouth. 'And you have a little smudge of lipstick right here.' He smiled a knowing smile. 'How did that happen, I wonder?'

Instinctively she put a hand over her mouth, backing away. 'I better repair my make-up,' she said, sweeping up her evening purse from the coffee table and making for the powder room. How had that happened indeed. She really didn't need to be reminded of that kiss and how she'd practically given him a green light to do whatever he wanted with her. It was amazing it was only her lipstick that had slipped. Well, there would be no more smudged lipstick if she had any say in it. None at all.

He watched her go, his eyes missing nothing of her ramrod-straight spine or the forced stiffness that hampered her movements. She hadn't been stiff or hampered a few moments ago, when she'd all but rested her cheek against his hand. She hadn't been stiff or hampered when he'd held her in his arms and kissed her senseless.

'Evelyn,' he called behind her, and she stopped and turned, gripping her purse tightly in front of her chest. 'Something that might make you feel more relaxed in my company...'

'Yes?' She sounded sceptical.

'As much as I enjoyed that kiss, I have a rule about not mixing business with pleasure.'

She blinked those big blue eyes up at him and he could tell she didn't get it. 'I don't sleep with my PA. Whatever I do tonight, a touch, a caress, a kiss, it's all just part of an act. You're perfectly safe with me. All right?'

And something—he'd expected relief, but it wasn't quite that—flashed across her eyes and was gone. 'Of course,' she said, and fled into to powder room.

There. He'd said it. He blew out a breath as he picked up the leftover ring from the coffee table, snapped the box shut and returned it to the safe. Maybe it was, as he had said, to put her at her ease, but there'd also been a measure of wanting to remind himself of his golden rule. Because it had been hard enough to remember which way was up, let alone anything else in the midst of that kiss.

He hadn't intended it to go so far. He'd meant to tease her into submission, give her just a little taste for more, so she'd be more malleable and receptive to his touch, but she'd sighed into his mouth and turned molten and turned him incendiary with it.

And if he hadn't frightened her away by the strength of his reaction, he'd damned near frightened himself. He'd had to leave the room before she could see how affected he was, and before he looked into her ocean-deep eyes and decided to finish what he'd started.

He ached to finish what he'd started.

Why did he have that rule about not sleeping with his PAs? What had he been thinking? Surely this was a matter that should be decided on a case-by-case basis.

And then he remembered Inge of the ice-cool demeanour and red hot bedroom athletics and how she'd so neatly tried to demand a chunk of ice for her finger by nailing him with her alleged pregnancy.

There was good reason for his self-imposed rule, he reluctantly acknowledged. Damn good reason.

If only he could make himself believe it.

She didn't recognise herself in the powder-room mirror. Even after repairing her make-up and smoothing the stray wisps of her hair back into its sleek coil, she still looked like a stranger. No amount of lipstick could disguise the flush to her swollen lips. And while the ring on her finger sparkled under the light, it was no match for the lights in her eyes.

Not when all she could do was remember that kiss, and how he had damn near wrenched out her mind if not her soul with it.

It was wrong to feel excited, even though its impact had so closely mirrored that of the first. But he'd simply been making a point. He'd been acting. He'd said as much himself. It had meant nothing. Or else why could he so easily have turned and walked away?

Yet still she trembled at the memory of his lips on hers. Still she trembled when she thought of how he'd felt, pressing hard and insistent against her belly, stirring secret places until they blossomed and ached with want.

Want that would go unsatisfied. Cheated again. Just an act. *'I don't sleep with my PA.'*

And part of her had longed to laugh and tell him that he'd had his chance, years ago, and blown it then. Another part had wanted to slump with relief. While the greater part of her had wanted to protest at the unfairness of it all.

Damn. She'd known this would be difficult. She'd known that seeing him again would rekindle all those feelings she had been unable to bury, unable to dim, even with the passage of time.

She dragged air into her lungs, breathed out slowly and resolutely angled her chin higher as she made one final check on her appearance. For surely the worst was over. And at least she knew where she stood. She may as well try to enjoy the rare evening out.

How hard could it be?

'Remember,' Leo said, as they made their way to the presidential suite, 'keep it light and friendly and whatever you do, avoid any talk of family.'

Suits me, she thought, knowing Leo would be less than impressed if she started telling everyone about Sam. 'What is it exactly that their sons are supposed to have done?'

'You didn't see the articles?'

She shook her head. 'Clearly I don't read the right kind of magazine.'

'Or visit the right websites. Someone got a video of them at a party and posted it on the web.'

'And they were doing something embarrassing?'

'You could say that. It was a wife-swapping party.'

'Oh.'

'Oh, indeed. Half the board were implicated and Culshaw couldn't stand seeing what he'd worked for all his life being dragged through the mud.' He stopped outside the suite. 'Are you ready?'

As ready as I'll ever be. 'Yes.'

He slipped her hand into his, surprising her but not so much this time because it was unexpected but because it felt so comfortable to have his large hand wrapped around hers. Amazing, given the circumstances, that it felt so right. 'You look beautiful,' he whispered, so close to her ear that she could feel his warm breath kiss her skin, setting light to her senses and setting flame licking at her core.

It's make-believe, she warned herself as he tilted her chin and she once more gave herself up to his kiss, this time a kiss so tender and sweet that the very air seemed to shimmer and spin like gold around her. She drew herself back, trying to find logic in a sea of sensation and air that didn't come charged with the spice of him.

It meant nothing, a warning echoed as he pressed the buzzer. It was all just part of the act. She could not afford to start thinking it felt right. She could not afford to think it was real.

She had just one short evening of pretending this man loved her and she loved him, and then the make-believe ended and she could go home to her falling-down house and her baby son. Alone. That was reality. That was her life.

She should be grateful it was so easy to pretend…

A butler opened the door, showing them into an impressive mirror-lined entry that opened into the massive presidential suite, Eve's heels clicked on the high gloss parquet floor. Floor-to-ceiling mirrors either side reflected their images back at them, and Eve was struck when she realised that the woman in that glamorous couple, her hand in Leo's and her eyes still sparkling, was her. Maybe she shouldn't feel so nervous. Maybe they could pull this off. It had seemed such a crazy idea, and questions remained in her mind as to the ethics of the plan, but maybe they could convince his business colleagues they were a couple. Certainly she had twenty thousand good reasons to try.

'Welcome, welcome!' An older man came to meet them and Eve recognised him from the newspapers. Eric

Culshaw had aged, though, she noticed, his silvering hair white at the temples, his shoulders a little stooped as if he'd held the weight of the world on them. Given the nature of the scandal that had rocked his world, maybe that was how he felt. He pumped Leo's hand. 'Welcome to you both,' he said, smiling broadly.

'Eric,' Leo said, 'allow me to introduce my fiancée, Evelyn Carmichael.'

And Eric's smile widened as he took her hand. 'It is indeed a pleasure, Evelyn. Come over and meet everyone.'

Eve needed the few short seconds to get over the scale of the suite. She'd arranged the bookings for all the rooms, similar corner spa suites for Leo and the Alvarezes, and the presidential suite for the Culshaws, but she'd had no idea just how grand they were. Leo's suite had seemed enormous, with the separate living area, but this suite was more like an entire home. A dining room occupied the right third of the room, a study opposite the entry, and to the left a generous sitting area, filled with plump sofas and welcoming armchairs. Doors hinted at still more rooms, no doubt lavish bedrooms and bathrooms and a kitchen for the dining room, and all along one side was a wall of windows to take in the view of the Melbourne city skyline. The others were sipping champagne in the living room, admiring the view, when they joined them.

Eric made the introductions. Maureen Culshaw was a slim sixty-something with a pinched face, like someone had pricked her bubble when she wasn't looking. Clearly the scandal had hurt both the Culshaws deeply. But her grey eyes were warm and genuine, and Eve took to her immediately, the older woman wrapping her hands in her own. 'I'm so pleased you could come, Evelyn. Now, there's a name you don't hear terribly often these days, although I've met a few Eves in my time.'

'It was my grandmother's name,' she said, giving the other woman's hands a return squeeze, 'and a bit of a mouthful, I know. Either is perfectly fine.'

Maureen said something in return, but it was the movement in Eve's peripheral vision that caught her attention, and she glanced up in time to see something skate across Leo's eyes, a frown tugging at his brow, and for a moment she wondered what that was about, before Eric started introducing the Alvarezes, snagging her attention.

Richard Alvarez looked tan and fit, maybe fifteen years younger than Eric, with sandy hair and piercing blue eyes. His wife, Felicity, could have been a film star and was probably another ten years younger than he, dark where he was fair, exotic and vibrant, like a tropical flower in her gown of fuchsia silk atop strappy jewel-encrusted sandals.

Waiters unobtrusively brought platters of canapés and more glasses of champagne, topping up the others, and they settled into the lounge area, Leo somehow managing to steer them both onto the long sofa where he sat alongside her, clearly part of the act to show how close they were.

Extremely close apparently.

For he stretched back and looped an arm around her shoulders, totally at ease as he bounced the conversation between Eric and Richard, though Eve recognised it for the calculated move it was. Yet still that insider knowledge didn't stop her catching her breath when his fingers lazily traced a trail down her shoulder and up again, a slow trail that had her senses humming and her nipples on high alert and a curling ribbon of desire twisting and unfurling inside her. A red ribbon. Velvet. Like the sound of Leo's voice…

'Evelyn?'

She blinked, realising she'd been asked a question that had completely failed to register through the fog of Leo's sensual onslaught. She captured his wandering fingers in hers, ostensibly a display of affection but very definitely a self-defence mechanism if she was going to be able to carry on any kind of conversation. 'Sorry, Maureen, you were asking about how we met?' She turned to Leo and smiled, giving his fingers a squeeze so he might get the message she could do without the manhandling. 'It's not exactly romantic. I'm actually his PA. I was handling all his paperwork and arrangements and suddenly one day it kind of happened.'

'That's right,' Leo added with his own smile, fighting her self-defence measures by putting a proprietorial hand on her leg, smoothing down the silk of her gown towards her knee, bringing his hand back to her thigh, giving her a squeeze, setting up a sizzling, burning need. It was all Eve could do to keep smiling. She put her glass down and curled her fingers around the offending hand, squeezing her nails just a tiny bit too hard into his palm, just a tiny warning.

But he only looked at her and smiled some more. 'And this was after I'd sworn I'd never get involved in an office romance.'

Maureen clapped her hands together, totally oblivious of Eve's ongoing battle. 'Did you hear that, Eric? An office romance. Just like us!'

Eric beamed and raised his glass. 'Maureen was the best little secretary I ever had. Could type a hundred and twenty words a minute, answer the phone and take shorthand all at the same time. I could hardly let her go, could I?'

'Eric! You told me you fell in love with me at first sight.'

'It's true,' he said, with a rueful nod. 'Her first day in the job and the moment I walked in and saw the sexy minx sitting on her little swivel chair, I was toast. I just can't have that story getting around business circles, you understand.'

The men agreed unreservedly as Maureen blushed, her eyes a little glassy as she reached across and gave Eric's hand a squeeze. 'You're an old softie from way back, Eric Culshaw, and you know it.' She dabbed at her eyes with a lace handkerchief, and Eve, thinking she must look like she was shackled to Leo, shifted away, brushing his hand from her leg as she reached for her champagne. He must have got the message, because he didn't press the issue, simply reached for his own drink, and part of her wondered whether he thought he'd done enough.

Part of her hoped he did.

The other part already missed his touch.

'Felicity, how about you?' she said, trying to forget about that other wayward part of her. 'How did you and Richard meet?'

'Well…' The woman smiled and popped her glass on the table, slipping her hand into her husband's. 'This might sound familiar, but I'd been out with a friend, watching the sailing on Sydney Harbour. It had been a long day, so we stopped off to have a drink in a little pub on the way home, and the next thing I know, this nice fellow came up and asked if he could buy us both a drink.' She turned to him and smiled and he leaned over and kissed her delicately on the tip of her nose. 'And the rest, as they say, is history.'

'That's just like Princess Mary and Prince Frederik of Denmark,' said Maureen. 'Don't you remember, everyone?' Eve did, but she never had a chance to say anything because Leo chose that precise moment to run his finger along the back of her neck, a feather-light touch that came with depth charges that detonated deep down inside her as his fingertips drew tiny circles on her back.

'It wasn't the same hotel, was it?' Maureen continued.

'No. But it's just as special to us. We go every year on the anniversary of that first meeting.'

'How special,' said Maureen. 'Oh, I do love Sydney and the harbour. I have to say, the warmer weather suits me better than Melbourne's, too.'

And Eve, lulled by the gentle touch of a master's hand, and thinking of her never-ending quest to get the washing dried and not looking forward to cold showers and boiling kettles so Sam could have a warm bath, couldn't help but agree. 'Sydney's wonderful. I used to work there. I spent so many weekends at the beach.'

The fingers at her neck stilled, a memory flickering like the frames of an old black and white movie in the recesses of his mind. Something about Sydney and a woman he'd met years ago so briefly—too briefly—*a woman called Eve.*

CHAPTER FIVE

WHAT was it Maureen had said? *'Most people would shorten it to Eve.'* And she'd said something like, *'Either is fine.'* The exchange had niggled at some part of him when he'd heard it, although he hadn't fully understood why at the time, but then the mention of Sydney had provided the missing link, and suddenly he'd realised that there could be no coincidence—that bit had provided the missing piece and the jigsaw had fitted together.

He thought back to a day that seemed so long ago, of flying into Sydney in the early morning, recalling memories of a whirlwind visit to rescue a deal threatening to go pear-shaped, and of a glass-walled office that had looked over Sydney Harbour and boasted plum views of both the Harbour Bridge and the Opera House. But the view had faded to insignificance when his eyes had happened upon the woman sitting in the opposite corner of the room. Her hair had been streaked with blonde and her skin had had a golden tan, like both had been kissed by the sun, and her amazing eyes had looked deeper and more inviting than any famous harbour.

And endless meetings and time differences and jet-lag had all combined to press upon him one undeniable certainty.

He'd wanted her.

'Eve,' she'd told him when he'd cornered her during a break and asked her name. Breathless Eve with the lush mouth and amazing eyes and a body made for sin, a body all too willing to sin, as he'd discovered in that storeroom.

And he'd cursed when he'd had to leave all too suddenly for Santiago, cursed that he'd missed out on peeling her clothes from her luscious body, piece by piece. He'd had half a mind to return to Sydney after his business in Chile concluded, but by then something else had come up. And then there'd been more business in other countries, and other women, and she'd slipped from his radar, to be loosely filed under the-ones-that-got-away.

It wasn't a big file and as it happened she hadn't got away after all. She'd been right there under his nose, answering his emails, handling his paperwork, organising meetings, and she'd never once let on. Never once mentioned the fact they'd already met.

What was that about?

His hand drifted back to his pretend fiancée's back, letting the conversation wash over him—something about an island the Culshaws owned in the Whitsundays—his fingertips busy tracing patterns on her satiny-soft skin as he studied her profile, the line of her jaw, the eyes he'd noticed and should have recognised. She was slightly changed, the colour of her hair more caramel now than the sun-streaked blonde it had been back then, and maybe she wasn't quite so reed thin. Slight changes, no more than that, and they looked good on her. But no wonder he'd thought she'd looked familiar.

She glanced briefly at him then, as the party rose and headed for the dining area, a slight frown marring an otherwise perfect brow, as if she was wondering why he'd been so quiet. He smiled, knowing that the waiting time to meeting her again had passed; knowing that her time had come.

Knowing that for him the long wait would soon be over. She'd been like quicksilver in his arms that day, so potent and powerful that he hadn't been able to wait the few hours before closing the deal to sample her.

There was no doubt in his mind that the long wait was going to be worth it.

So what, then, that he had a rule about not sleeping with his PA? Rules were made to be broken after all, some more than others. He smiled at her, taking her arm, already anticipating the evening ahead. A long evening filled with many delights, if he had anything to do with it. Which of course, he thought with a smile, he did.

Maybe it was the fact everyone so readily accepted Evelyn as his fiancée. Maybe it was the surprising realisation that playing the part of a fiancé wasn't as appalling or difficult as he'd first imagined that made the evening work.

Or maybe it was the thought of afterwards, when he would finally get the opportunity to peel off her gown and unleash the real woman beneath.

But the evening did work, and well. The drinks and canapés, the dinner, the coffee and dessert—the hotel catering would get a bonus. It was all faultless. Culshaw was beaming, his wife was glowing and the Alvarezes made such entertaining dinner companions, reeling out one amusing anecdote after another, that half the time everyone was laughing too much to eat.

And Evelyn—the delectable Evelyn—played her part to perfection. Though he frowned as he caught her glancing at her watch again. Perfect, apart from that annoying habit she had of checking the time every ten minutes. Why? It wasn't like she was going anywhere. Certainly not before they'd had a chance to catch up on old times.

Finally coffee and liqueurs had been served and the staff quietly vanished back into the kitchen. Culshaw stifled a yawn, apologising and blaming his habit of going for a long early walk every morning for not letting him stay up late. 'But I thank you all for coming. Richard and Leo, maybe we can get those contract terms nutted out tomorrow— what do you think?'

The men drew aside to agree on a time to meet while the women chatted, gathering up purses and wraps. They were nice people, Eve thought, wishing she could have met them in different circumstances, and not while living this lie. She knew she'd never meet them again, and maybe in the bigger scheme of things it made no difference to anything, as they would all go their separate ways in a day or so, but that thought was no compensation for knowing she'd spent the evening pretending to be someone and something she was not.

'Shall we go?' Leo said, breaking into her thoughts as he wrapped his big hand around hers and lifted it to his mouth, and Eve could see how pleased he was with himself and with the way things had gone.

The final act, she thought as his lips brushed her hand and his eyes simmered with barely contained desire. A look filled with heated promise, of a coming night filled with tangled limbs in tangled sheets. The look a man should give his fiancée before they retired to their room for the night. The final pretence.

No pretence necessary when her body responded like a woman's should respond to her lover's unspoken invitation, ripening and readying until she could feel the pulse of her blood beating out her need in that secret place between her thighs, achingly insistent, turning her thoughts to sex. No wonder everyone believed them to be lovers. He acted the part so very well. He made it so easy. He made her body want to believe it.

A shame, she thought as they said their final goodbyes and left the suite. Such a shame it was all for nothing. Such a waste of emotional energy and sizzling intensity. Already she could feel her body winding down, the sense of anticlimax rolling in. The sudden silence somehow magnified it, the hushed passage devoid of other guests, as empty as their pretend relationship.

'Will the car be waiting for me downstairs?' she asked, glancing at her phone as they waited in the lift lobby. No messages, she noticed with relief, dropping it back into her purse. Which meant Mrs Willis had had no problems with Sam.

'So anxious to get away?' the man at her side said. 'Do you have somewhere you're desperate to get to?'

'Not really. Just looking forward to getting home.' And she wasn't desperate. There no point rushing now, Eve knew. She'd been watching the time and chances were Mrs Willis was well and truly tucked up in bed by now, which meant no picking up Sam before morning. But equally there was nothing for her here. She'd done her job. It was time to drop the make-believe and go home to her real life.

'No? Only you kept checking your watch every five minutes through dinner and you just now checked your phone. I get the impression I'm keeping you from something—or someone.'

'No,' she insisted, cursing herself for being so obvious. She'd gone to the powder room to check her messages during the evening, not wanting to be rude or raise questions. She hadn't thought anyone would notice a quick glance at her watch. 'Look, it's nothing. But we've finished here, haven't we?'

'Aren't you forgetting something?'

'What?' He took her hand and lifted it, the sapphire flashing on her finger. 'Oh, of course. I almost forgot.' She tried to slip her hand from his so she could take it off, but he stilled her.

'Not here. Wait till we get to the suite.' And she would have argued that it wasn't necessary, that she could give it to him in the lift for that matter, only she heard voices behind them and the sound of the Alvarezes approaching and knew she had no choice, not when their suites were on the same floor and it would look bizarre if she didn't accompany Leo.

'Ah, we meet again,' Richard said, coming around the corner with Felicity on his arm as the lift doors whooshed open softly behind them. 'Great night, Leo, well done. Culshaw seems much more comfortable to do business now. He agreed to call to arrange things after his walk in the morning.'

Leo smiled and nodded. 'Excellent,' he said, pressing the button for the next floor as they made small talk about the dinner, within seconds the two couples bidding each other goodnight again and heading for their respective suites.

And, really, it wasn't a problem for Eve. Leo had told her his rule about not mixing business with pleasure. So she knew she had nothing to fear. She'd give him back the ring, make sure the coast was clear, and be gone. She'd be in and out in two minutes, tops.

He swiped a card through the reader, holding the door open so she could precede him into the room. She ignored the flush of sensation as she brushed past him, tried not to think about how good he smelt or analyse the individual ingredients that made up his signature scent, and had the ring off her finger and back in its tiny box before the door had closed behind her. 'Well, that's that, then,' she said brightly, snapping the box shut and setting it back on the coffee table. 'I think that concludes our business tonight. Maybe you could summon up that car for me and I'll get going.'

'You said you didn't have to rush off,' he said, busy extracting a cork from what looked suspiciously like a bottle of French champagne he'd just pulled from an ice bucket she was sure hadn't seen before, and felt her first shiver of apprehension.

'I don't remember that being there when we left.'

'I asked the wait staff to organise it,' he explained. 'I thought a celebration was in order.'

Another tremor. Another tiny inkling of…*what*? 'A celebration?'

'For pulling off tonight. For having everyone believe we were a couple. You had both Eric and Maureen, not to mention Richard and Felicity, eating out of your hand.'

'It was a nice evening,' she said warily, accepting a flute of the pale gold liquid, wishing he'd make a move to sit down, wishing he was anywhere in the suite but standing right there between her and the door. Knowing she could move away but that would only take her deeper into his suite. Knowing that was the last place she wanted to be. 'They're nice people.'

'It was a perfect evening. In fact, you make the perfect virtual fiancée, Evelyn Carmichael. Perhaps you should even put that on your CV.' He touched his glass to hers and raised it. 'Here's to you, my virtual PA, my virtual fiancée. Here's to…us.'

She could barely breathe, barely think. There was

no *us*. But he had that look again, the look he'd had before they'd left the presidential suite that had her pulse quickening and beating in dark, secret places. And suddenly there was that image back in her mind, of tangled bedlinen and twisted limbs, and a strange sense of dislocation from the world, as if someone had changed the rules when she wasn't looking and now black was white and up was down and nothing, especially not Leo Zamos, made any kind of sense.

She shook her head, had to look away for a moment to try to clear her own tangled thoughts.

'Oh, I don't think I'll be doing anything like this again.'

'Why not? When you're so clearly a natural at playing a part.' He nodded in the direction of her untouched glass. 'Wine not to your taste?'

She blinked and took a sip, wondering if he was ever going to move away from the minibar and from blocking the door, moving closer to the wall at her back in case he was waiting for her to move first. 'It's lovely, thank you. And the Culshaws and Alvarezes are lovely people. I still can't help but feel uncomfortable about deceiving them that way.'

'That's something I like about you, Evelyn.' He moved at last, but not to go past her. He moved closer, touching the pad of one finger to her brow, shifted back a stray tendril of hair, a touch so gentle and light but so heated and powerful that she shivered under its impact. 'That honest streak you have. That desire not to deceive. I have to admire that.'

Warning bells rang out in her mind. There was a calm, controlled anger rippling through the underbelly of his words that she was sure hadn't been there before, an iron fist beneath the velvet-gloved voice, and she wasn't sure what he thought he was celebrating but she did know she didn't want to be any part of it.

'I should be going,' she said, searching for the nearest horizontal surface on which to deposit her nearly untouched drink, finding it in the credenza at her side. 'It's late. Don't bother your driver. I'll get myself a cab.'

He smiled then, as lazily and smugly as a crocodile who knew that all the efforts of its prey were futile for there was no escape. a smile that made her shiver, all the way down.

'If you'll just move out the way,' she suggested, 'I'll go.'

'Let you go?' he questioned, retrieving her glass and holding it out to her. *When she was so clearly leaving.* 'When I thought you might like to share a drink with me.'

She ignored it. 'I had one, thanks.'

'No, that drink was a celebration. This one will be for old times' sake. What do you say, Evelyn? Or maybe you'd prefer if I called you *Eve*.'

And a tidal wave of fear crashed over her, cold and drenching and leaving her shuddering against the wall, thankful for its solidity in a world where the ground kept shifting. *He knew*! He knew and he was angry and there was no way he was going to move away from that door and let her calmly walk out of here. Her tongue found her lips, trying valiantly to moisten them, but her mouth was dry, her throat constricted. 'I'm good with either,' she said, trying for calm and serene and hearing her voice come out thready and desperate. 'And I really should be going.'

'Because I met an Eve once,' he continued, his voice rich and smooth by comparison, apparently oblivious to her discomfiture, or simply enjoying it too much to put an end to it, 'in an office overlooking Sydney Harbour. She had the most amazing blue eyes, a body built for sinful pleasures, and she was practically gagging for it. Come to think of it, she *was* gagging for it.'

'I was not!' she blurted, immediately regretting her outburst, wishing the shifting ground would crack open and swallow her whole, or that her pounding heart would break the door down so she could escape. Because she was kidding herself. Even if it hadn't been how she usually acted, even if it had been an aberration, he was right. Because if that person hadn't interrupted them in the midst of that frantic, heated encounter, she would have spread her legs for him right there and then, and what was that, if not gagging for it?

And afterwards she'd been taking minutes, writing notes, even if she'd found it nearly impossible to transcribe them or remember what had actually been said when she'd returned to her office because of thoughts of what had almost happened in that filing room and what would happen during the night ahead.

He curled his fingers under her chin, forced her to look at him, triumph glinting menacingly in his eyes. 'You've been working with me for more than two years, sweet little Miss Evelyn don't-like-to-deceive-anyone Carmichael. When exactly were you planning on telling me?'

She looked up at him, hoping to reason with him, hoping that reason made sense. 'There was nothing to tell.'

'Nothing? When you were so hot for me you were practically molten. And you didn't think I might be interested to know we'd more than just met before?'

'But nothing happened! Not really. It was purely a coincidence that I came to work for you. You wanted a virtual PA. You sent a query on my webpage. You agreed the terms and I did the work you wanted and what did or didn't happen between us one night in Sydney was irrelevant. It didn't matter.' She was babbling and she knew it, but she couldn't stop herself, tripping over the words in the rush to get them out. 'It wasn't like we ever had to meet. If you hadn't needed a pretend fiancée tonight, you would never have known.'

'Oh, I get it. So it's my fault, is it, that all this time you lied to me.'

'I never lied.'

'You lied by omission. You knew who I was, you knew what had so very nearly happened, and you failed to tell me that I knew you. You walked in here and hoped and prayed I wouldn't recognise you and you almost got away with it.'

'I didn't ask to come tonight!'

'No. And now I know why. Because you knew your dishonesty would come unstuck. All that talk about not deceiving people and you've happily been deceiving me for two years.'

'I do my job and I do it well!'

'Nobody said you didn't. What is an issue is that you should have told me.'

'And would you have contracted me if I had?'

'Who knows? Maybe if you had, we might be having great sex right now instead of arguing.'

Unfair, she thought as she sucked in air, finding it irritatingly laden with his testosterone-rich scent. So unfair to bring up sex right now, to remind her of what might have been, when she was right here in his suite and about to lose the backbone of her income because she'd neglected to tell him about a night when nothing had happened.

'Let me tell you something, Evelyn Carmichael,' he said, as he trailed lazy fingertips down the side of her face. 'Let me share something I might have shared with you, if you'd ever bothered to share the truth with me. Three years ago, I was aboard a flight to Santiago. I had a fifty-page report to read and digest and a strategy to close a deal to work out and I knew what I needed to be doing, but hour after hour into the flight I couldn't concentrate. And why couldn't I concentrate? Because my head was filled with thoughts of a blonde, long-limbed PA with the sexiest eyes I had ever seen and thinking about what we both should have been doing right then if I hadn't had to leave Sydney.'

'Oh.' It had never occurred to her that he might have regretted his sudden departure. It had never occurred to her that she hadn't been the only one unable to sleep that night, the only one who remembered.

'I felt cheated,' he said, his fingers skimming the line of her collarbone, 'because I had to leave before we got a chance to...get to know each other.' His fingers played at her shoulder, his thumbs stroking close to the place on her throat where she could feel her pulse beat at a frantic pace. 'Did you feel cheated, Evelyn?'

'Perhaps. Maybe just a little.'

'I was hoping maybe more than just a little.'

'Maybe,' she agreed, earning herself a smile in return.

'And now I find that I have been cheated in those years since. I never had a chance to revisit what we had lost that night, because you chose not to tell me.'

She blinked up at him, still reeling from the impact of his words. 'How could I tell you?'

'How could you not tell me, when you must know how good we will be together. We knew it that day. We recognised it. And we knew it earlier when I kissed you and you turned near incendiary in my arms. Do you know how hard that kiss was to break, Evelyn? Do you know what it took to let you go and take you to dinner and not take you straight to my bed?'

She shuddered at his words, knowing them to be true, knowing that if he'd taken her to bed that night, she would have gone and gone willingly. But he'd left her confused. He'd been angry with her a moment ago, yet now the air vibrated around them with a different tension. 'What do you want?'

'What I have always wanted ever since the first time I saw you,' he said, his eyes wild with desire and dark promises that kept those dark, secret places of her humming with sensation and aching with need. 'I want you.'

CHAPTER SIX

'THIS won't work,' she warned weakly, her hands reaching for the wall behind her as his mouth descended towards hers. 'This can't happen.'

He brushed her lips with his. 'Why not?'

'You don't sleep with your PAs. You don't mix business with pleasure. You said so yourself.'

'True,' he agreed, making a second pass over her mouth, and then a third, lingering just a fraction longer this time. 'Never mix business with pleasure.'

'Then what are you doing?' she asked, her senses buzzing. He slipped his hands behind her head, his fingers weaving through her hair as he angled her mouth higher.

'Unfinished business, on the other hand,' he murmured, his eyes on her mouth. 'That's a whole different rule book.' He moved his gaze until dark eyes met her own, gazing at her with such feverish intensity that she felt bewitched under their spell. 'Do you want to open that book, Evelyn? Do you want to dip into its pages and enjoy one night of pleasure, one night of sin, to make up for that night we were both cheated out of?'

This time he kissed her eyes, first one and then the other, butterfly kisses of heated breath and warm lips that made her tremble with both their tenderness and their devastating impact on her senses. 'Or do you still wish to leave?'

He kissed her lips then before she could respond, as if trying to convince her with his hot mouth instead of his words, and she could feel the tension underlining his movements, could tell he was barely controlling the passion that bubbled so close below the surface as he tried to be gentle with her. He was offering her a night of unimaginable pleasure, a night she'd thought about so many times since that ill-fated first meeting.

Or he was offering her escape.

She was so, so very tempted to stay, to stay with this man who'd invaded her dreams and longings, the man who'd taken possession of them ever since the day they'd first met. The man who had made her want and lust and feel alive for the first time in her life. She wanted to stay and feel alive again.

But she should go. The sensible thing would be to go. She was no longer a free agent, able to do as she pleased when she pleased. She had responsibilities. She was a mother now, with a child waiting at home.

His kisses tortured her with their sweetness while her mind grappled with the dilemma, throwing out arguments for and against. The decision was hers and yet she felt powerless to make it, knowing that whatever she decided, she would live to regret it.

But it was just one night.

And her child was safely tucked up in bed, asleep.

But hadn't her child resulted from just one such night? One foolish wrong decision and she would live with the consequences for ever. Did she really want to risk that happening again? Could she afford to?

Could she afford not to?

Did she really want to go home to her empty bed

and know that she'd turned her back on this chance to stop wondering what if, the chance to finally burn this indecent obsession out of her system?

And didn't she deserve just one night? She'd worked hard to make a success of her business and to provide for Sam. Surely she deserved a few short hours of pleasure? Maybe then she could stop wondering, stop imagining what it would have been like to have made love that night, to have finished what they'd started. And maybe he was a lousy lover and this would cure her of him for ever, just like one night with Sam's father had been more than enough.

Hadn't she already paid the price?

His mouth played on hers, enticing her into the dance, his tongue a wicked invitation, his big hands skimming her sides so that his thumbs brushed the undersides of her breasts, so close to her aching nipples that she gasped, and felt herself pushing into his hands.

A lousy lover? *Not likely.*

'What's it to be?' he said, pulling back, his breathing ragged, searching her eyes for her answer. 'Do I open the book? Or do you go? Because if you don't decide now, I promise you, there will be no going anywhere.'

And his words were so hungry, the pain of his restraint so clearly etched on his tightly drawn features, that she realised how much power she really held. He wanted her so much, and still he was prepared to let her walk away. Maybe because he sensed she was beyond leaving, maybe because he knew that his kisses and touches had lit a fire inside her that would not be put out, not be quenched until it had burned itself to ash. But he was giving her the choice.

When really, just like that first time, there was none.

'Maybe,' she ventured tentatively, her voice breathy as she wondered whether in wanting to make up for a lost opportunity she was making the mistake of her life, 'we could at least check out a page or two.'

He growled his approval, a sound straight from the Stone Age, a dark, deep sound that rumbled into her very bones and shook them loose. She would have fallen then, if he hadn't pulled her into his kiss, his hot mouth explosive on her lips, on her throat, as he celebrated her acquiescence, his arms like steel crushing her to him, his hands on her back, on her shoulders, capturing a breast and sweeping his thumb over her peaked nipple, sending sensation spearing down to that hot place between her thighs and making her mewl into his mouth.

'God, I want you,' he said, echoing the only words she was capable of thinking, as she pushed his jacket off his shoulders and he shucked off his shoes. He released her for only a moment, shrugged the jacket off and let it drop to the floor while she worked desperately at his buttons and his tie, and he turned his attentions to her zipper. She felt the slide down her spine and the loosening of fabric, the electric touch of his hands at the small of her back. Impatient to similarly feel his flesh under her hands, she ripped the last few buttons of his shirt apart, scattering them without regard.

Finally she had him, her hands on his firm chest, her fingers curling through the wiry thatch of hair, lingering over the hard, tight nubs of his nipples, relishing all the different textures of him, the hard and the hot, the wet and the insistent, and if she'd had any doubt at all that he wanted her, it was banished by the bucking welcome of that rigid column as her hand slid down to cup his length. He groaned and pushed her back hard against the wall as she grappled with his belt.

He was everywhere then, his taste in her mouth, his hands separating her from the dress, slipping the straps from her shoulders, letting it slip between them as he took her breasts, the scrap of lace no barrier against the heat from his hands. And then even that was gone, replaced by his hot mouth, devouring her, lapping and suckling at her flesh until she cried out with the agony and the ecstasy of it all. It was everything she had imagined in dreams spun in hot, torrid nights alone and more, and still it was not enough.

She clung to his shoulders as he laved her nipples, gathering her skirt as his hands skimmed up her legs, not taking his time but still taking so much longer than she wanted.

'Please,' she pleaded, clutching at his head, gasping as he cupped her mound, his long fingers stroking her through panties wet for him, needing him, hot and hard, inside her. Needing him now, before she came with just one more touch. *'Please!'*

'God, you're so hot,' he said, dispensing with her underwear, pulling free his belt with damn near the same frenetic action.

She saw him then. Her first glimpse of him unleashed and hungry and pointing at her, a compass needle finding true north. Once she might have wanted to believe it. But she was wiser than to believe such fantasies these days, and much wiser to the consequences. Which reminded her…

'Protection,' she muttered through the fog of need, but he was already ripping open a sachet with his teeth, rolling it on before pulling her back into his kiss. Her breasts met his chest, the feel of skin against skin taking her breath away, or maybe it was what he was doing with his hands and clever fingers.

Her dress bunched at her waist, his hands kneading her behind, fingers teasingly close to the centre of her, driving her insane with need, as he lifted her, the wall at her back, still kissing her as he urged her legs around him until she felt him, thick and hard, nudging, testing, at her entrance.

She cried out, something unintelligible and primal, lost in an ocean of sensation, drowning under the depths. It was almost too much and yet it was nowhere near enough and she only knew that if she didn't get him inside her she would surely die of need.

He didn't keep her waiting. With a guttural cry of his own he lowered her, meeting her with his own thrust, until he was lodged deep inside her.

A moment in time. Just a moment, a fraction of a second perhaps, but Eve knew it for a moment about which she would always remember every single detail, the salt of his skin and the smell of his shampoo, the feel of his big hands paused at her hips, and the glorious feeling of the pulsing fullness inside her.

Could it get any better than this?

And then he moved, and it did, and flesh against flesh had never felt so good, every new moment giving her treasures to secrete away, to add to a store of memories she would take from this night, of sensations she would never forget. Sensations that built, one upon another, layer upon layer, higher and higher, fed by each calculated withdrawal, each powerful thrust.

Until there was no place to go, no place higher or brighter or more wondrous as the sensation, the friction, the furious rhythm of his pounding body all melded together into a cataclysm, taking her with it.

She screamed her release, throwing her head back

against the wall, her muscles clamping down hard as he shuddered his own frenetic release.

She didn't know how long they stood together that way, she couldn't tell, too busy trying to replace the oxygen consumed in the fire of their coupling while her body hummed its way down from the peak. But slowly her feet found the floor, slowly her senses and sensibility returned. To the knowledge she was standing barely dressed between a wall and a near naked man she barely knew but with whom she'd just had mind-blowing sex.

'Wow,' she said, embarrassed in the aftermath as he dispensed with the condom and she remembered her own wantonness. Had she really pulled his shirt apart in her desperation to get inside it? Had she really cried out like a banshee?

And he laughed, a low rumble in a velvet coat. 'Evelyn Carmichael,' he told her with a chaste kiss to her lips, 'you are just one surprise package after another.'

He didn't know the half of it. She found the straps of her dress, pulling it up to cover herself before she started looking for her underwear.

'Leave it,' he said, his hand around her wrist. 'There's no point. It's only coming off again.'

'Again?'

His eyes glinted. 'This book I was telling you about. It's a long book,' he said. 'That was only chapter one.'

She blinked up at him, her dress gathered in front of her, and he pulled her arm away, letting the dress drop to her waist, then slide over her hips in a whisper of silk to pool like a lake on the floor.

And even though they'd just had sex, she felt nervous standing there before him wearing nothing more than lace-topped stockings and spiky sandals. She hadn't been with anyone since Sam's father. She didn't have the body she'd once had, her belly neat but traced with tiny silvery lines and softer than it had been before bearing a child.

She held her breath. Could he tell? Would it matter?

'You look,' he said, 'like a goddess emerging from the sea.' And some tiny, futile creature somewhere deep inside her grew wings and attempted a fluttery take-off.

'And you look like a pirate,' she countered, reminding herself it was just a game. It wasn't real and that pointless tiny creature inside her would soon die a rapid death, its gossamer wings stilled. 'Ruthless and swashbuckling.'

'Uncanny,' he said, his lips turning in a half-smile as he swung her into his arms. 'However did you know?'

'Know what?' she asked, feeling a secret thrill as he carried her into the next room.

'The goddess of the sea and the swashbuckling pirate.' He winked at her and he laid her gently on the king-sized bed. 'That's the title of chapter two.'

It was a long and detailed chapter. There were passages Eve found agonising going, like when the pirate sampled the goddess, tasting every last inch of her except *there*, where she craved his detailed attentions the most, and then there were the passages that moved at what felt like breakneck speed, where he feasted on her until she was bucking on the bed.

And even when she lay, still gasping, after her latest orgasm, the chapter didn't end and he joined her in savouring the final few pages together until that final breathtaking climax.

Outside the lights of Melbourne winked at her, the

skies unusually clear, a heavy full moon hanging above the bridge over the Yarra.

Inside the suite, Eve's breathing slowly returned to normal as she savoured the feel of Leo's arm lying proprietorially over her stomach as he lay face down alongside her, his eyes closed, his lips slightly parted, his thick black hair mussed into bed-head perfection by her own hands. He wasn't asleep, she knew, but it was a wonder given the energy he'd used tonight. Definitely a pirate, she thought. And very definitely a magic night. But it was late and magic nights had to end, just as goddesses had responsibilities too.

Oh, my, he'd actually called her a goddess! And she felt that tiny winged creature launch itself for another lurching spin around her stomach.

'I should go,' she said, with a wistful sigh for the ill-fated beast before she returned to sensible Evelyn Carmichael again and considered the practicalities of not having a functioning hot water service. 'Do you mind if I take a shower before I go?'

And his eyes blinked open, the arm around her waist shifting, scooping higher to capture a breast. A smile played on his lips while he coaxed a nipple into unexpected responsiveness. 'I've got a much better idea.'

She swallowed. Surely it wasn't possible? But still her body hummed into life at the thought. 'Chapter three?'

He nodded, his busy fingers hard at work on the other nipple, adding his hot mouth to the mix, guaranteeing the result. 'The goddess returns to the sea only to find the pirate lurking in the depths, waiting to ambush her.'

'That's a long title.'

'It's a long chapter,' he said, rolling off the bed and scooping her up into his arms. 'In which case, we should get started.'

An hour later Eve had bubbles up to her chin and warm jets massaging all those newly found muscles of hers she hadn't realised would so appreciate the attention. From the bedroom came the sound of Leo's voice on the phone as he arranged her car. In a moment she'd have to prise herself from the bath and shower off the bubbles but for the moment she lingered, her limbs heavy, feeling languorous and spoilt and thoroughly, thoroughly spent.

It was easy to feel spoilt here, she thought, quietly reflecting on her opulent surroundings, committing them to memory as part of the experience. For if the size and scale of the suites had amazed her, the sheer lavishness of the bathroom had taken her breath away.

Marble in muted tones of sun-ripened wheat and golden honey lined the floor and walls, the lighting low and warm and inviting, the spa and shower enclosure—a space as big as her entire bathroom at home—separated from the long marble vanity by heavy glass doors. It was utterly, utterly decadent.

And if there hadn't been enough bubbles, he'd found champagne and ripe, red strawberries to go with it. He'd turned what she'd intended simply as a shower into another erotic fantasy.

What a night. Three chapters of his book, all of them different, every one of them a complete fantasy. If chapter one had been desperate and frenetic, and chapter two slow to the point of torture, chapter three had showed the pirate at his most playfully erotic best. The slip of oils on skin, the play of the jets on naked flesh and the sheer fun of discovering what lay beneath the foam.

She closed her eyes, allowing herself just a few snatched seconds of imagining what it would be like if this was her life, all posh hotels with views of city lights and an attentive lover like Leo to make her feel the most special woman alive, with no worries about broken-down appliances and falling-down houses.

But then there was Sam.

And she felt guilty for even thinking of a world that didn't include him—that couldn't include him. For Sam was her life, whereas this was a fantasy that had no other course but to end and end soon.

She slipped under the water one last time, letting her hair fan out around her head, relishing the big wide bath, before she sat up, the water sluicing from her body. No regrets, she told herself as she squeezed the water from her hair, she wouldn't allow it. She'd made her choice. She would live with it. And whatever happened in her life after this, whatever her everyday suburban life might hold, she knew she would have this one secret night of passion to look back on.

'The car will be waiting in half an hour,' Leo said, returning to the bathroom, a white towel slung perilously low over his hips, and even though she knew what lay beneath, even though she knew what that line of dark hair leading down from his navel led so tantalisingly and inexorably to, she couldn't look away. *Or maybe because of it.* 'Will that give you enough time for that shower you wanted and get dressed?'

And even though she knew this moment was coming, Eve still felt a pang, the fabric of her fantasy starting to unravel, as already she started counting down the minutes. Just thirty of them to go before she turned from one-night lover to a billionaire into long-term single mother. But there was nothing else for it. She nodded. 'Plenty of time,' she said.

He offered her his hand rather than the towel she would have preferred and she hesitated, before realising that after the things they'd done together this night, there was no point in being coy. So she rose, taking his hand to prevent her slipping as she stepped out, and taking half the foam with her. Something about the way his body stilled alerted her. She was taller than him now, standing in the raised bath like this, and his eyes drank her in. 'What is it?' she said, looking down to see patches of foam sliding down her body and clinging to her breasts, the pink nub of one nipple peeping through. And she looked back to him to see him shaking his head, his dark eyes hot and heavy with desire. 'Suddenly I'm not so sure it will be anywhere near enough time.'

Something sizzled in her veins, even while her mind said no. 'You can't be serious.'

He gave a wry smile as he reached out to brush the offending nipple with the pad of one finger, sending tremors through her sensitive flesh, and he smoothed away more of the suds to reveal patches of skin, piece by agonising piece. 'It's still early.'

'Leo,' she said, ignoring the pleas her body was making to stay right where she was and stepping out to snap on the shower taps before she could take his words seriously. A torrent rained down from the cloudburst showerhead and she stepped into it, determined to be rid of the bubbles regardless of the water temperature. 'It's three o'clock in the morning. I'm going home.'

He peeled the towel from his hips, turned on his own shower. 'We have all night.'

'No. I have to go.' She turned her face away from the sight of his thickening member and up into the stream of water, relishing the drenching. It was cooler than she would normally prefer, but it was helping to clear her mind, helping cool her body down. And very definitely she needed to cool down. What kind of man could make love so many times in one night and still come back for more? When had fantasy ever collided so perfectly with reality? Well, that was apart from the reality she would no doubt be exhausted tomorrow while Sam would be his usual bundle of energy. *Today*, she reminded herself. He'd be up in a few short hours. She really needed to get home if she was to get any sleep tonight. 'Besides, you have an important deal to close.'

'So maybe I can give you a call, pick you up afterwards?'

Her heart skipped a beat and she paused, soap in hand, feeling only the pounding of the cascading water, the thudding of her heart and the flutter of those damned tiny wings. Without turning around, she said, 'I thought you were planning on leaving for London the minute you concluded the Culshaw deal.'

His mouth found her shoulder, his arms wrapping around her belly, and there was no missing that growing part of him pressing against her back, no missing the rush of blood to tissues already tender. And even though she knew his words meant nothing, nothing more anyway than him wanting a repeat performance in bed, it was impossible not to lean her head back against his shoulder just one last sweet time. 'I don't think that would be wise.' She turned off the water and peeled herself away, reaching for a towel as she exited the shower. 'We both agreed this was just one night. And while it's been good, I think, given our working relationship, that it's better left that way.'

'Only good?' he demanded, and she rolled her eyes.

Trust the man to home in on the least important detail of the conversation. He followed her from the stall, swiping his own towel from the rack and lashing it around his hips, not bothering to wipe the beads of water from his skin so that his chest hair formed scrolls like an ancient tattoo down his chest to his belly and below.

Oh, my…

She squeezed her eyes shut. Grabbed another towel and covered her head with it, rubbing her hair frantically so she couldn't see him, even if she opened her eyes. 'All right. The sex was great. Fabulous.'

The towel blinding her eyes was no defence against the electric touch of his fingers at her shoulders. 'Then why shouldn't we meet again? It's not as if I'm asking for some long-term commitment.'

That's just it, she yearned to say. There's no future in it. There's nothing but great sex and the longer that happens, the greater the risk that I start to believe it's about more than that, and I can't afford to let that happen.

Not when she had Sam…

One night of sin was one thing. But she could not contemplate any kind of affair. What Sam needed was stability, not his mother embarking on a series of meaningless one-night stands, passing him off to whoever could look after him. She shook her head, heading for the bedroom, her clothes and a return to sanity. 'I can't sleep with you and work with you at the same time.'

'So become my mistress instead of my PA.'

She blinked, blindsided once again by the night's increasingly insane developments, pulling on her underwear in a rush, slipping off the towel to fix her bra, needing the shelter of her dress.

'Are you kidding?'

'You're right,' he said, without a hint of irony. 'Who could I get to replace you? So why can't you be both?'

'Perfect.' She slipped into her dress, retrieved her stockings and sat on the end of the bed, hastily rolling them up her legs. 'I thought you'd never ask. And when you get sick of me being your mistress, you can get me to send myself one of those trinkets you're so fond of sending to your ex-playmates. I already know where to send it. How efficient would that be?'

'Evelyn?'

She was busy in her purse, searching for a comb in order to slick back and twist up her wet hair and not finding one. 'What?'

'Anyone might think you were jealous.'

'Jealous? Me?' She scooted past him back into the bathroom. Pulled a comb from the complimentary supplies boxed up on the vanity, raking it through her hair before twisting it up and securing it with a clip. It was rough but it would do until she got home. She certainly wasn't going to hang around here, styling her hair or trying to reapply make-up that would just have to come off at home anyway. 'Jealous of what?'

He leaned an arm up against the door, muscles pulling tight under his skin, making the most of the posture, and she cursed the fact he hadn't thought to put on anything more than a towel yet. Or maybe that was his intention. To remind her what she'd be missing out on. Well, tough. After tonight she knew what she'd be missing out on. Of course, he was tempting, but there came a time where self-preservation came first.

'You did make a point about having to send out those gifts to...my friends.'

'Your ex-lovers, you mean.'

'You *are* jealous.'

She shrugged. 'No. I've had my one night with you. Why should I be jealous?'

'Well, something's bugging you. What is it?'

She turned toward him then, wishing she could just walk away, sensitive to the fact that she could still be at risk of losing her contract if she angered him but still bothered enough by the riddle that was Leo Zamos to ask. 'You really want to know?'

'Tell me.'

'Okay,' she started, her eyes taking this last opportunity to drink in the glorious definition of his body, wanting to imprint all she could upon her memory before she left, because after tonight her memories would be all she had. 'What I don't understand is you.'

He laughed, a rich, deep sound she discovered she liked too much. 'What's so hard to understand?'

'Everything. You're confident and successful and ultra-rich—you have your own plane, for heaven's sake!—and you're a passionate lover and clearly have no trouble finding women willing to share your bed…' She paused for a moment, wondering if she'd said enough, wondering if she added that he was drop-dead gorgeous and had a body that turned a woman's thoughts to carnal acts, she would be saying more about herself than about him.

He smiled. 'That's it? I'm not actually sure where your problem lies.'

'No, that's not it. You know there's more. People are drawn to you, Leo, you know it. And it's just that, with everything you have going for you, I don't understand how it can be that when you feel the need to play happy families, you have to pay someone to pretend to be your fiancée.'

'You would have done it for free?' He gave a wry smile. 'I'll remember that for next time.'

'No!' she said, knowing she was making a hash of it, knowing he was laughing at her. 'That's not my point at all. I just don't understand why you're in the situation where you need to pretend. How is it that a man with clearly such great appeal to women hasn't got a wife or a fiancée or even a serious girlfriend? How is that possible?'

The smile slipped as he pushed away from the wall, moving closer, the menacing glint in his eyes putting her on sudden alert. 'Maybe,' he said, drawing near, touching his fingers to her brow, tracing a line south, 'it's because there is no lack of women willing to share my bed. What is that delightful saying? Why buy a book when you can join a library?'

She stood stock-still, resisting the tremors set off by his merest touch, hating the smug look on his face, forcing a smile to hers. 'Well, the loan on this particular book just expired. Goodnight, Leo.'

He let her go, at least as far as the door.

'Evelyn.'

She halted, put her hand on the doorframe to stop herself swaying, and without turning around said, 'Yes?'

'Something I tell all the women I spend time with. Something I thought you might have understood, although, given your questions, maybe you need to hear it too.'

She looked over her shoulder, curious about what it was he told his 'women', what he thought she needed to hear. 'Yes?'

'I like women. I like sex. But that's where it starts and finishes. Because I don't do family. It's not going to happen.'

This time she took a step towards him, stunned by his sheer arrogance. 'You think I was on some kind of fishing expedition to work out what my chances were of becoming Mrs Leo Zamos for real?'

'You were the one asking the questions.'

'And I also said I don't want to see you again. Which part of "I don't want to see you again" equates to "Please marry me" exactly?'

'I was just saying—'

'And I'm saying you needn't have bothered. I'm not in the market for a husband as it happens, but even if I were, I'm certain I'd prefer someone who didn't profess to liking women and sex quite so much!' She turned on her heel and strode through the bedroom, slipping on her heels and picking up her purse, scanning the room for anything she might have left.

'Evelyn!'

But she didn't stop until she was through the living room then, turned, one more question to be answered before she left. 'I'll understand if you no longer want to retain me as your PA.'

'Don't be ridiculous. Of course I want to keep you.'

She nodded, relieved, suddenly realising how perilously close she'd come to blowing things. 'All right. All the best with the deal tomorrow. I guess I'll be hearing from you in due course.' She offered him her hand, back to brisk, businesslike efficiency, even if she was dealing with a man wearing nothing more than a towel. 'Thank you for a pleasant evening, Mr Zamos. I'll see myself out, under the circumstances.'

One eyebrow quirked at the formality but he took her hand, squeezing it gently. 'It was my pleasure, Evelyn. My pleasure entirely.'

Minutes later, she sank her head back against the

plush leather headrest and sighed as the limousine slipped smoothly from the hotel. Better to end this way, she reflected; better that they had argued rather than agreeing to meet again. Better that it had ended now when anything else would merely have been putting off the inevitable.

For it would have ended, nothing surer, and probably as soon as their next meeting. And then Leo would take off in his jet and find another convenient Evelyn somewhere else in the world, and she would be forgotten.

But now they'd claimed their stolen night, the night they'd been cheated out of by conspiring circumstances those years ago, and it had been an amazing night and she'd managed to survive with both some degree of pride and her job intact. But it was for the best that it had ended on a sour note.

Now they could both put it behind them.

CHAPTER SEVEN

SHE grappled with the front-door key, her baby growing heavier by the minute. That or her night of sinful and unfamiliar pleasures had taken it out of her, but the child dozing on her shoulder felt like he'd doubled in size and weight overnight. Then again, maybe he'd just had one too many pancakes. She knew she had. She'd woken this morning after too few hours' sleep almost ravenous.

She was barely inside the door when the phone started ringing and she picked it up more to shut it up than any desire to talk to whoever was calling. She had less desire to talk when she found out who it was.

'Evelyn, it's Leo.'

The sound of his voice sent ripples of pleasure through her, triggering memories formed all too recently to not remember every single sensual detail. She sucked in air, but Leo was the last person she'd expected to call and there was nothing she could think of to say. Hadn't they said everything that needed to be said last night?

'Evelyn?'

She squeezed her eyes shut, trying to ignore the snatches of memory flashing through her mind, the rumble of his murmured words against her thigh, the brush of his whiskered cheek against her skin, his clever tongue…

'I…I didn't expect to hear from you.'

'I didn't expect to be calling. Look, Evelyn, there's been a development. Culshaw wants to move the contract discussions to somewhere where the weather suits Maureen better. He suggested we reconvene on his island off North Queensland.'

With the dead-to-the-world weight of her toddler on her shoulder, she battled to work out what it was Leo actually wanted. 'So you need me to make some bookings? Or do I have to rearrange your schedule?'

'Neither.' A pause. 'I need you to come.'

Sam stirred on her shoulder, his head lolling from one side to the other, and she kissed his head to soothe him. 'Leo, you know that's not possible.'

'Why isn't it possible?'

'You said our deal was for one night only and I already told you I wouldn't meet you again.'

'But that was before Culshaw came up with this idea.'

'That's too bad. I did what we agreed.' And then, thinking he might better understand it in business-speak, 'I fulfilled the terms of the contract, Leo, and then some.'

'So we make a new deal. How much this time, Evelyn?' he asked, sounding angry now.

'I told you before, it's not about the money.'

'Fifty thousand.'

'No. I told you, they're nice people. I don't want to lie to them any more.'

'One hundred thousand.'

She looked up at the ceiling, cursing under her breath, trying not to think about what a sum like that would mean to the timing of her renovation plans. She could engage a decent architect, get quotes, maybe landscaping so Sam had a decent play area outside. But it was impossible. 'No!'

'Then you won't come?'

'Absolutely not.'

'So what am I supposed to tell Culshaw?'

'It's your lie, Leo. Tell him what you like. Tell him it's family reasons, tell him I'm sick, tell him I never was and never will be your fiancée. It's your call.' On her shoulder her son grew unsettled, picking up on the vibe in the air, butting his head from side to side against her shoulder, starting to grizzle.

'What was that?' Leo demanded.

'Me about to hang up. Are we finished here? Only it's not really a convenient time to call.' Please, God, can we be finished here? she prayed as her muscles burned under Sam's weight.

'No. I need…I need some documents to take with me!'

'Fine,' she said, sighing, wondering which documents they could possibly be when she was sure she'd provided him with everything he needed already and in triplicate. 'Let me know which ones and I'll email them straight away.'

'No. I need them in hard copy. All originals. You have to bring them to the hotel, as soon as you can.'

If she'd had a free hand, it would have gone to her head. 'I've always emailed documents to you before. It's never been a problem.'

'I need those documents delivered to me personally this afternoon!'

She sucked in a breath. 'Okay. I'll get them couriered over as soon as I can.'

'No. Definitely not couriered. You need to deliver them personally.'

'Why?'

'Because I need them immediately and they're commercial-in-confidence. I'm not about to entrust them to someone else, not at this crucial stage. You'll have to bring them yourself.'

When she made no response, she heard, 'You did say you wanted to keep working with me.'

Bastard! She could take a veiled threat just as well as she could take a hint. She was damned if she'd take more of Leo's money to pretend to be his fiancée, but right now she couldn't afford to ditch him as a client. 'Of course. I'll bring them over myself.'

'Good. I'll be in my suite.'

'Not there.'

'What?'

'I won't bring them to your suite. I won't go there again. Not after...'

'You think I'd try something?'

Hardly, after the way they'd parted last night. But she didn't trust herself not to be tempted, there in that room where they'd done so many things... How could she be in that room and see that wall and know how it felt to have her back to it and have him between her legs and driving into her? How could she calmly pretend nothing had happened? How could she not want it to happen again?

She swallowed, trying not to think of all the reasons she didn't want to be in that room. 'I just don't think it would be wise.'

She heard his rushed expulsion of air. 'Okay,' he said. 'Let's play it your way. Culshaw's taking Maureen out to visit friends so we should be safe to meet in the bar. I'll buy you a coffee—is that permissible?'

She nodded into the phone, relieved at least they'd

be meeting somewhere public. Sam settled back on her shoulder. 'A coffee would be fine.'

He clicked off his phone, cursing softly. So she wouldn't come to the room. But she had agreed to come. Of course she could have emailed the documents, but then he'd have no way of convincing her to come to the island with him. He could convince her, he had no doubt. Look at how she had all but melted in his arms last night with just one kiss! And once she was back in his bed, she'd get over whatever hang-up she had about coming with him. He was already looking forward to it.

Because while sex was easy to come by, great sex wasn't, and last night had definitely registered right up there with the best. And while he'd been content for it to end last night the way it had—it would have ended some time anyway—the opportunity to have her in his bed for another couple of nights held considerable appeal. He could do much worse than sharing his bed with Evelyn.

He'd soon make it happen. Once she was here, he'd just have to come up with a way to get her up to his suite and convince her how much she wanted to come with him. He'd think of something.

His phone rang, a glance at the caller ID assuring him it wasn't Evelyn calling back to change her mind about meeting him.

'Eric,' he said, relieved, his mind already working on a plan to get Evelyn up to his suite. 'What can I do for you?'

But relief died a quick death as Culshaw explained how Maureen was looking to book a day in the island resort's spa for the women and wanted to know if Evelyn might be interested. Leo knew he had to say something now, in case she refused to change her mind.

'Look, Eric, about Evelyn, you might want to warn Maureen. It seems there's a slight chance she might not be able to make it after all…'

'I wish I could help, lovey,' Mrs Willis said, when Evelyn nipped over to ask if she would mind babysitting again, this time only for an hour or so, 'but my brother Jack's just had an episode and I promised to go and help Nancy with him. He gets terribly confused, poor love. I was going to pop by and tell you, because I might be away for a few days.' She stopped folding clothes for a moment, her creased brow folding along time worn lines. 'I hate leaving you, though, with the hot water not working and no family to help out. Such a tragedy to lose your parents so young and then your granddad. They've all missed out on so much, watching you grow up and now Sam.' She shook her head. 'Such a pity.'

'I know,' Eve said softly, feeling a pang of sadness for her grandfather and for parents she could barely remember. 'But don't worry. You do too much for me as it is. We'll be fine. I'll call Emily down the street. She's always on the lookout for some extra cash.'

Except when she called it was to hear Emily was already working a shift at the local supermarket. Which left Evelyn with only one option.

Not such a bad option, she reflected as she turned onto the freeway and pointed her little city commuter towards the city, wondering why it hadn't occurred to her earlier. She hadn't wanted to tell Leo about her child, figuring it was none of his business and that it might prejudice his opinion of her as someone able to handle his workload, but neither did she trust him not to try to change her mind by fair means or foul. And then there was the matter of not trusting her own wayward desires. Look where they'd landed her last night—right in Leo Zamos's bed. Not to mention his spa bath…

She shivered, unable to suppress either a secret smile or the delicious shimmy at the memories of his mouth seeking her breasts as he raised her over him, of his hungry mouth at her nipples as he probed her entrance, of the long, hard length of him filling her as he pulled her down on him inch by glorious inch, a shimmy that radiated out from muscles tender and sore and clearly still far too ready to party.

Oh, no, there was no way she could trust herself with him.

And if there was one certain way to ensure that there would be no repeats of last night's performance, it was to take her child along. Leo didn't do family, and clearly didn't want one. He'd made that abundantly clear and she was grateful he had. For it had put paid to that tiny creature that insisted on fluttering around inside her despite what she'd known in her head all along to be true. That his interest in her began and finished with sex. There could be no future with him. There was no future for them.

And with just one look at Sam he'd forget all about wanting to play make-believe with her. One look at Sam and he'd never want to see her again. Which suited her just fine.

It was foolproof!

Forty minutes later the doorman helped her unload both her baby stroller and a sleeping Sam startled into wakefulness from the car. She settled him, watching his eyelids flutter closed again, still sleepy from the journey, lowering the back and tucking his favourite bear by his side so he would feel secure and snooze on as long as possible. Soon enough he'd be demanding to get out and explore this new world—she just prayed he'd last until she got him out of the hotel. Not that the meeting should take longer than ten minutes when it was only documents she had to hand over. Probably less, she thought with a smile, doubting Leo would stick around long enough for coffee when he saw what else she'd brought with her.

She could hardly wait to see his face.

The subtly lit lounge wasn't busy, only a few tables occupied this time of the day, couples sharing coffee and secrets, family groups gathered around tables enjoying afternoon tea.

She found a hotel phone, asked Reception to let Mr Zamos know she was there, and stopped a while in awe to admire, over the balcony, the amazing sweeping stairway that rose grandly from entry level and the water feature that spilled and spouted between levels of the hotel. She must commit this to memory, she thought. It was the place of fairy-tales, of princes and princesses, and not of the real world, and of ordinary people like her who had blown hot water services and frazzled appliances to replace.

She settled into a booth that offered some degree of privacy, gently rocking the stroller. Sam wasn't buying it, jerking into wakefulness, this time taking in the unfamiliar surroundings with wide, suspicious eyes.

'It's okay, Sam,' she said, reaching for the stash of food she'd brought and had tucked away in the baby bag. 'We're visiting, that's all. And then I'll take you for a walk along Southbank. You'll like that. There's a river and lots of music and birds. Maybe we might even spot you a fish.'

'Fith!' He grinned, recognising the word as she handed him his favourite board book and he reached for a sultana with the other. 'Fith!'

He'd been waiting on the call, all the while working out a strategy that would get her out of the lounge and up into his room. At last he'd hit on the perfect plan, so simple it couldn't fail. He'd play it cool, accept the documents she'd brought without mention of the trip away and without trying to change her mind, and see her to her car, remembering once they'd got to the lifts something he'd meant to bring down for her—it wouldn't take a moment to collect it from his suite…

He hit the second floor with a spring in his step. Oh, he loved it when a plan came together.

He scanned the lounge for her, skipping over the groups and couples, searching for a single woman sitting no doubt nervously by herself. Had she been able to forget about last night's love-making yet? He doubted it. Even though the night had ended on a sour note, those flashbacks had kept him awake thinking about it half the night. When Culshaw had mooted this idea of going away for the weekend, he'd initially been appalled. It was bad enough that the closing of the deal had been held up by last night's dinner, without having to endure still more delays while Culshaw soothed his wife's wounded soul with an impromptu holiday. Until he'd worked out that he could easily endure a couple of more nights like the last. Very easily.

And then he saw her sitting with her back to him in a little booth off to one side, her hair twisted high behind her head, making the most of that smooth column of neck. Just the sight of that bare patch of skin sent such a jolt of pure lust surging through him, such a heady burst of memories of her spread naked on his sheets, that it was hard to think over the pounding of the blood in his veins, other than to want to drag her to his room and prove why she needed to come with him until she begged him not to leave her behind.

In another time, maybe even in another part of this world, he would do exactly that, and nobody would stop him, nobody would think twice.

But there was more reason than the mores of the so-called civilised world that stilled his savage urges. For he knew what he might become if he let the animal inside him off the leash.

Never had he felt so close to that beast. Why now? What was it about her that gave rise to such thoughts? She was the means to an end, that was why he needed her. Nothing more. Great sex was just a bonus.

She turned her head to the side then, her lips moving as if she was talking to someone, but there was nobody there, nothing but a dark shape in the shadowed recess behind the sofa, a dark shape that had him wondering if he'd found the wrong woman the closer he got. Because it made no sense…

She looked around at the exact time his brain had finally come to terms with what his eyes were telling him, at the precise moment the cold wave of shock crashed over him, washing away his well-laid plans and leaving them a tangled and broken mess at his feet.

'Hello, Leo,' she said, closing the picture book she was holding in her hands. 'I've brought those documents you asked for.'

She'd brought a hell of a lot more than documents! In the dark shape he'd worked out was a pram sat a baby—a child—holding onto the rail in front of him and staring wide-eyed and open-mouthed up at Leo like he was some kind of monster. It didn't matter that the kid was probably right. He looked back at Evelyn. 'What the hell is this?'

'Leo, meet my son, Sam.' She turned toward the pram. 'Sam, this is Mr Zamos. If you're very nice, he might let you call him Leo.'

'No!' Sam pushed back in his stroller and twisted his body away, clearly unimpressed as he pushed his face under his bear and began to grizzle.

'I'm sorry,' she said, one hand reaching out to rub him on the back. 'He's just woken up. Don't worry about coffee, it's probably better I take him for a walk.' She picked up a folder from the table and stood, holding it out for Leo. 'Here's all the documents you asked for and I've flagged where signatures are required. Let me know if there's anything else you need. I promised Sam a walk along the river while we're here, but we'll be home in a couple of hours.'

He couldn't say anything. He could barely move his hand far enough to accept the folder she proffered. All he could think of was that she had a child and she hadn't told him. What else hadn't she told him? 'You said there wasn't a Mr Carmichael.'

'There's isn't.'

'Then whose is it?'

'His name is Sam, Leo.'

'And his father's name?'

'Is none of your business.'

'And is that what you told him when he asked you where you were all night?'

She shook her head, her eyes tinged with sadness. 'Sam's father doesn't figure in this.'

His eyes darted between mother and child, noticing for the first time the child's dark hair and eyes, the olive tinge to the skin, and he half wondered if she was bluffing and had borrowed someone else's baby as some kind of human shield. He would have called her on it but for noticing the angle of the child's wide mouth and the dark eyes stamped with one hundred per cent Evelyn, and that made him no happier.

Because someone else had slept with her.

He thought of her in his arms, her long-limbed body interwoven with his, he thought of her eyes when she came apart with him inside her, damn near shorting his brain. And now he thought of her coming apart in someone else's arms…

'You should have told me.'

'Why?'

'Damn it, Evelyn! You know why!'

'Because we spent the night together?' she hissed. Sam yowled, as if he'd been on the receiving end of that, and she leaned over, surprising Leo when she didn't smack him, as he'd half expected, but instead delicately stroked the child's cheek and calmed him with whispered words. Something twisted inside him, something shapeless and long buried, and he had to look away lest the shape take form and he worked out what it was. His gut roiled. What was happening to him? Why did she have this effect on him? She made him feel too much. She made him see too much.

She made him remember things he didn't want to remember.

And none of it made sense. None of it he could understand.

'I'm sorry you feel aggrieved,' she said, and reluctantly he turned back to see her unclipping the child's harness and lifting the child into her arms, where he snuggled close, sniffling against her shoulder as she rubbed his back. 'But what part of our contract did I miss that said I should stipulate whether I should have children or what number of them I should have?'

'Children? You mean there's more?'

She huffed and turned away, rubbing the boy's back, whispering sweet words, stroking away his hiccups, and the gentle sway of her hips setting her skirt to a gently seductive hula.

'Ironic isn't it?' she threw at him over her shoulder. 'Here you are, so desperate to prove to Eric Culshaw that you're some kind of rock-solid family man, and you're scared stiff of a tiny child.'

'I'm not—'

She spun around. 'You're terrified! And you're taking it like some kind of personal affront. But I wouldn't worry. Sam's a bit old for anyone to believe he was conceived last night, so there's no reason to fear any kind of paternity claim.'

'You wouldn't dare!'

'Oh, you do flatter yourself. A woman would have to be certifiably insane to want to shackle themselves to you!'

'Clearly Sam's father was of the same mind about you.'

He knew he'd hurt her. He recognised the precise moment when his words pierced the fighting sheen over her eyes and left them bewildered and wounded. He almost felt regret. Almost wanted to reach out and touch her cheek like she'd touched her child's, and soothe away her pain.

Almost.

But that would mean he cared. And he couldn't care about anyone. Not that way.

And just as quickly as it had gone down, the armour

was resurrected and her eyes blazed fire at him. 'I have a child, Mr Zamos. It's never affected the quality of my work to date and it's my intention that it never will, but if you can't live with that then fine, maybe it's time we terminated our agreement now and you found someone else to look after your needs.'

Bile, bitter and portentous, rose in the back of his throat. She was right. There was no point noticing her eyes or the sensual sway of her hips. There was no point reliving the evening they'd had last night. She couldn't help him now and it was the now he had to be concerned with. As to the future, maybe it was better he found someone else. Maybe someone older this time. It wasn't politically correct to ask for a date of birth, but he'd never been any kind of fan of political correctness. Especially not when it messed with his plans. He huffed an agreement. 'If that's what you want.'

She stood there, the child plastered against her from shoulder to hip, his arms wound tightly around his mother's neck, the mother so fierce he was reminded of an animal fighting to protect its litter that he'd seen on one of those television documentaries that appeared when you were flicking through the channels on long-haul flights. The comparison surprised him. Was that how all mothers were supposed to be?

'In that case,' she said, 'I'll burn everything of yours onto disk and delete it from my computer. I'll send it to you care of the hotel. You can let them know your forwarding address.'

His hands clenched at his sides, his nails biting into his palms. 'Fine.'

'Goodbye, Mr Zamos.' She held out her hand. 'I hope you find whatever it is you're looking for.' Her words washed over him, making no sense as he looked down at her hand. The last time he would touch her. The last time they would meet skin to skin.

How had things gone so wrong?

He wrapped his hand around hers, her hand cool against his heated flesh, and he felt the tremor move through her, saw her eyelids flutter closed, and despite the fact she represented everything he didn't want in this world, everything he hated and despised and had promised himself he would never have, still some strange untapped part of him mourned her loss.

Maybe that was how it started, though, with this strange want, this strange need to possess.

Maybe it was better to let her go now, he thought, while he still could. While she was still beautiful.

But still it hurt like hell.

Unable to stop himself, unable to let her go just yet, his other hand joined the first, capturing her hand, raising it to his mouth for one final kiss.

'Goodbye Evelyn,' he said, his voice gravel rich, tasting her on his lips, knowing he would never forget the taste of her or the one night of passion they'd shared in Melbourne.

'Leo! Evelyn!' came a voice from over near the bar. 'There you are!'

CHAPTER EIGHT

EVE gasped, tugging to free her hand, the fight-or-flight instinct telling her to get out while she still could, but Leo wasn't about to let her go, his grip tightening until she felt her hand was encased in steel. 'This is your fault.' He leaned over and whispered in her ear as Eric Culshaw bounded towards them, beaming from ear to ear. 'Remember that.' And then he straightened and even managed to turn on a smile, although his eyes were anything but relaxed. She could almost hear the brain spinning behind them.

'Eric,' Leo said, his velvet voice all charm on the surface, springloaded with tension beneath. 'What a surprise. I thought you were taking Maureen out.'

He grunted. 'She spotted some article in a woman's magazine—you know the sort of thing—and grew herself a headache.' He shook his head. 'Sordid bloody affair. You'd think the reporters could find something else to amuse themselves with by now.' And then he huffed and smiled. 'Which makes you two a sight for sore eyes.' His eyes fell on the dozing child in her arms. 'Although maybe I should make that three. Who's this little tacker, then?'

Almost as if aware he was being discussed, Sam

stirred and swung his head round, blinking open big dark eyes to check out this latest stranger.

'This is Sam,' Eve said, her tongue feeling too big for her mouth as she searched for things she could tell him that wouldn't add to the lie tally. 'He's just turned eighteen months.'

Culshaw grinned at the child and Sam gave a wary smile in return before burying his head back in his mother's shoulder, which made the older man laugh and reach out a hand to ruffle his hair. 'Good-looking boy. I thought you two were playing things a bit close to the chest last night. When were you going to tell us?'

Eve felt the ground lurch once more beneath her feet. Eric thought Sam was *theirs*? But, then, of course he would. They were supposed to have been a couple for more than two years and Sam's father was of Italian descent. It would be easy to mistake Sam's dark eyes and hair for Leo's. Why would they question it?

But she couldn't let them keep thinking it. Weren't there enough lies between them already?

'Actually,' she started, 'Sam—'

Her efforts earned her a blazing look from Leo. 'Eve doesn't like to give too much away,' he said, smiling at Eric, glancing back in her direction with a look of cold, hard challenge.

Suddenly Maureen was there too, looking pale and strained, her mood lifting when she saw Sam, clucking over him like he was a grandchild rather than the child of someone she'd only just met.

'You didn't tell us you had such an adorable little boy,' she admonished, already engaging Sam in a game of peek-a-boo before holding out her hands to take him.

'Some people wouldn't approve,' Eve offered stiffly, ignoring Leo's warning glare as she handed Sam over, then adding because of it, 'I mean, given the fact we're not married and all.'

'Nonsense,' Eric said, pinching Sam's cheek. 'There's no need to rush things, not these days.'

Leo smiled, his eyes glinting triumphantly as Maureen settled into a chair and jogged Sam up and down on her knees, making him chuckle.

'So,' said Eric, following his wife's lead and pulling up a chair, and soon demanding equal time with Sam, 'I assume Sam explains the "family reasons" you weren't going to be able to join us on the island?'

Eve dropped into a chair, feeling like she was being sucked deeper and deeper into a web of deceit. Leo must have warned them she might not be coming and used one of the excuses she'd suggested.

'That was my fault, Eric,' he said coolly. 'I figured that a toddler was hardly conducive to contract deliberations.'

'He can be very disruptive,' she added. 'Especially when he's out of his routine. You wouldn't believe what a handful he can be.'

'What, this little champion?' Bouncing the laughing toddler on his knee with such delight until it was impossible to work out who was laughing the most, Eric or Sam, as the toddler got the horsy ride of his life. 'You must come,' he said, slowing down to take a breather.

'More,' demanded Sam, bouncing up and down. 'More!'

Culshaw laughed and obliged, though at a much gentler pace. 'You will come, won't you? After all, it's hardly fair to keep you two apart when you barely get to see each other as it is. You will love it, I promise. Tropical island paradise. Your own bungalow right on the beach. We'll organise a cot for Sam and a babysitter to give you a real break. I imagine you don't get too many of those, working for Leo and looking after this little chap. How does that sound?'

Eve tried to smile, not sure she'd succeeded when the ground beneath her felt so unsteady. 'It does sound lovely.' And it did. A few days on a tropical island paradise with nothing more to do than swim or read or sip drinks with tiny umbrellas. The bungalow probably even had hot running water. Except she'd be sharing that bungalow with *him*. 'It's just that—'

'Oh, please,' Maureen added, putting her hand on Eve's arm. 'Last night was the best time I've had for ages. I know it's asking a terrible lot of everyone and disrupting everyone's schedules, but right now it would mean so very much to me.'

'Of course they'll come,' she heard Leo say, 'won't you, Eve?'

And finally the unsteady ground she'd felt shifting under her feet the last few days opened up and swallowed her whole.

A smiling flight attendant greeted them, cooing over Sam, as Eve carried him on her hip into the jet. Eve just nodded in return, weariness combining with a simmering resentment. As far as she was concerned, this was no pleasure trip and she certainly wasn't happy about how she'd been manipulated into coming.

And then she stepped into the plane and found even more reason to resent the man behind her. It looked more like a luxury lounge room than any plane interior she'd ever seen before, the cabin filled not with the usual rows and rows of narrow seats and plastic fittings and overhead lockers but a few scattered wide leather armchairs with timber cabinet work trimmed with bronze. Beyond the lounge area a door led to what must be more rooms and Eve caught a glimpse of a dining table with half a dozen chairs in a recessed alcove.

So much wealth. So much to impress. Leo Zamos seemed to have everything.

Everything but a heart.

Maybe that's how you got to be a billionaire, she mused as another attendant showed her to a pair of seats where someone had already fitted her child restraint to buckle Sam in more securely. She helped settle the pair in and to stow their things, chattering pleasantly all the time while Eve stewed as she stashed books and toys close by and missed every word.

It all made sense. No wonder Leo Zamos was the success he was. Being ruthless in business, ruthless in the bedroom, taking what you wanted when you wanted—a heart would surely get in your way if you had one.

And while Eve simmered, Sam, on the other hand, was having the time of his tiny life, relishing the adventure and the attention, his dark eyes filled with glee as he pumped his arms up and down and made a sound like a war cry.

'I think someone approves,' Leo said from the seat alongside when the attendants had gone to fetch pre-flight drinks.

'His name is Sam,' she hissed, her resentment bubbling over at how she'd been trapped into this weekend away, a weekend of continued pretence with people who didn't deserve to be lied to. The only bright spots she could see were that the Culshaws and the Alvarezes were travelling together on the Culshaws' jet, and that they would all have private quarters, which meant she didn't have to pretend being madly in love with Leo twenty-four seven. She couldn't have stood the strain of it all if she had. As it was, she didn't know now how she was going to keep up the charade.

The attendant brought their drinks, advised there were two minutes until departure and discreetly disappeared.

What a mess. Eve poured a box of juice into a two-handled cup and passed it to a waiting Sam, along with a picture book to occupy him for a few minutes. How was she expected to act like Leo's loving fiancée now? It had been so much easier last night when there had been so much sexual tension and simmering heat sparking between them. Now the tension and the heat had more to do with anger.

All to do with anger, she corrected herself with a sigh. She was over him, even if he did have a velvet voice and the body of a god.

Across the aisle, the subject of her dark thoughts raised his drink. 'You sound like you have a problem.'

'Funny you should mention that.'

'You could have said no.'

'I did say no, remember? And then you turned around and said yes, of course we would come!'

He shrugged, as if it didn't matter, and if they'd been on any normal kind of plane, Eve could have given in to the desire to smack him. 'What can I say? Maureen likes you. It means the world to her that you can go.'

'You don't care about Maureen,' she said, keeping her voice low so she didn't alarm Sam. 'You don't care about anyone. All you care about is yourself and what you want, and you'll do anything to keep this deal from going off the rails, even if it means lying to people.'

'You don't know anything.'

'I know you made the right decision to never get married. Because I understand you now, and I understand what makes you tick, and you might have a fortune and a private jet and do okay in the sack with women, but you have a stone where your heart should be.'

His dark eyes glinted coldly, his jaw could have been chiseled from the same hard stone from which his heart was carved. 'Thank you for that observation. Perhaps I might make my own? You seem very tense, Evelyn. I think you might benefit from a couple of days relaxing on a tropical island.'

Bastard! Eve turned away, checking on Sam as the cabin attendant collected their glasses and checked all was ready for take-off.

The jet engines wound up as the plane taxied to the runway and Sam looked up in wonder at her, excited but looking for reassurance at the new sounds and sensations. She stroked his head. 'We're going on a plane, Sam. We're going on a holiday.'

And Sam squealed with delight and the plane raced down the runway and lifted off. *Good on you, Sam,* Eve thought, finding the book she'd hoped to read a few pages of as the plane speared into the sky, *at least one of us might as well enjoy the weekend.*

She must have dozed off. Bleary eyed, she found her book neatly placed by her side, while beside her Sam was grizzling softly but insistently, unable to settle.

'What's wrong?' Leo asked, putting aside the laptop he was working on as she unbuckled Sam from his seat and brought him against her chest.

'It's his nap time. He might settle better on my lap.' She searched for the chair's controls, although it was hard to manoeuvre with Sam's weight on her chest. 'Does this seat recline?'

'I've got a better idea. There's still a couple of hours'

flight time to go. You might both be more comfortable in the bedroom. Let me show you the way.'

And the idea of a real bed in which to cuddle up and snooze with Sam sounded so wonderful right now, she didn't hesitate.

Maybe if she hadn't been so bone-weary. Maybe in an ordinary airline seat, by holding onto the back of the seat in front of her to pull herself up, she could have managed it. Then again, she realised, maybe if she'd thought to undo her seat belt she could have done it. Damn.

'What is it?' he said, when she didn't follow him.

'Can you take Sam for a moment? My seat belt's still done up.'

Leo turned into a statue right before her eyes, rigid and unblinking as he stared down at her restless child. And if she wasn't mistaken, that look she saw in his eyes was fear.

'Take him?'

'Yes,' she said, her hands under his arms, ready to hand him over. 'Just for a second. I just need to undo my seat belt.'

'I…'

'I'll give you a hand,' said one of the cabin attendants, slipping past the stunned Leo. 'I've been secretly hoping for a cuddle of this gorgeous boy.'

She took Sam from her and swung him around, jogging him on her hip so that he stopped grizzling, instead blinking up at her with his big dark eyes, plump lips parted. 'You are gorgeous, aren't you? You're going to be a real heartbreaker, I can tell.' And then to Eve, 'How about I carry him for you? I'm probably more used to the motion of the plane.' Eve smiled her thanks, retrieving Sam's bear from the seat as Leo remembered how to move and led the way.

'There you go,' the attendant said a few moments later, as she peeled back the covers and laid the drowsy child down. 'Press this button,' she said, pointing to a console on the side table, 'if there's anything else I can help you with.' And with a brisk smile to them both and one last lingering look at Sam, she was gone.

'Thank you for thinking of this,' Evelyn said, sitting down alongside her son and tucking his bear under his arm. And then, because she felt bad about the things she'd said to him earlier and without taking her eyes from Sam, she said, 'I'm sorry for what I said earlier. I had no right.'

'Forget it,' he said, his velvet voice thick with gravel. 'For the record, you were probably right. Now, there's an en suite through that door,' he continued, and she looked over her shoulder, surprised to see a door set so cleverly into the panelling that she'd missed it as she'd looked around.

'Oh, I thought that was the bathroom we passed on the way. Next to the galley.'

'That serves the other suite.'

'Wow,' Eve said, taking it all in—the wide bed, the dark polished timber panelling and gilt-edged mirror and adding it to what she'd already seen, the dining table and spacious lounge. 'Incredible. A person could just about live in one of these things, couldn't they?'

'I do.'

Her head swung back. 'When you're travelling, you mean?'

'You know my diary, Evelyn. I'm always travelling. I live either in the plane or in some hotel somewhere.'

'So where's home?'

He held out his arms. 'This is home. Wherever I am is home.'

'But you can't live on a plane. Everyone has a home. You must have family somewhere.' She frowned, thinking about his voice and the lack of any discernable accent. Clearly he had Mediterranean roots but his voice gave nothing away. 'Where do you come from?'

Something bleak skated across his eyes as he looked at his watch. 'You're obviously tired and I'm keeping you both. Have a good sleep.'

He turned to leave then, turned back, reaching into his pocket. 'Oh, you'd better have this back.' He set the tiny box on the bedside table. Eve blinked at it, already knowing what it held.

'They extended the loan?'

He gave a wry smile. 'Not exactly. But it's yours to keep afterwards.'

'You bought it?'

'It looks good on you. It matches your eyes.'

She looked from the box to the man, still stroking her son's back, aware of his soft breathing as he settled into a more comfortable sleep. Thank heavens for the reality of Sam or she could easily think she was dreaming. 'What is this?' she said, mistrustful, the smouldering sparks of their earlier confrontation glowing brightly, fanned by this latest development. 'Some kind of bribe so I behave properly all weekend?'

'Do I need it to be?'

'No. I'm here, aren't I? And so I'm hardly likely to make a scene and reveal myself as some kind of fraud. But I'm certainly not doing it for your benefit, just like I'm not doing it for any financial gain. I just don't want to let Maureen down. She's had enough people do that recently, without me adding to their number.'

'Suit yourself,' he said, his voice sounding desolate and empty. 'But if you change your mind, feel free to consider it your parting trinket. And just like you said, you won't even need to post it to yourself. So efficient.'

And then he was gone, leaving only the sting of his parting words in his wake. She kicked off her shoes and crawled into the welcoming bed, sliding her arm under Sam's head and pulling him in close. She kissed his head, drinking deeply of his scent and his warm breath in an attempt to blot out the woody spice of another's signature tones.

She was so confused, so tired. Sleep, she told herself, knowing that after a late night of sexual excesses followed by today's tension, what she really needed was to sleep. But something tugged at her consciousness and refused to let go as his words whirled and eddied in her mind, keeping her from the sleep she craved so much as she tried to make sense of what Leo had said.

A heart of stone she'd accused him of, and when she'd apologised, he'd told her she was probably right. She shivered just thinking how forlorn he'd looked. How lost.

A man with a stone for a heart. A man with no home.

A man with everything and yet with nothing.

And a picture flashed in her mind—the photographic print she'd seen in Leo's suite before dinner last night.

She'd been looking for a distraction at the time, looking for something to pretend interest in if only so she didn't have to look at him, so her eyes would not betray how strongly she was drawn to him. Only she hadn't had to feign interest when she'd seen it, a picture from the 1950s, a picture of a riverbank and a curving row of trees and a park bench set between.

Something about the arrangement or the atmosphere

of that black and white photograph had jagged in her memory at the time, just as it struck a chord now. It was the old man sitting all alone on that park bench, hunched and self-contained, and sitting all alone, staring out over the river.

A lonely man.

A man with no family and nowhere to call home.

A man with nothing.

And it struck her then. Twenty or thirty years from now, that man could very well be Leo.

It was just a hiccup, Leo told himself as he considered the task ahead, just a slight hitch in his plans. Only a weekend, three nights at most, and the deal would be wrapped up once and for all. After all, Culshaw knew that even though they all called the shots in their respective businesses, none of them could just drop everything and disappear off the face of the earth—not for too long anyway. Neither could he risk them walking away. It had to be tied up this weekend.

He sighed as he packed up his laptop. He'd got precious little done, not that he'd expected to, with a child running riot. Only this one he'd barely seen and still he'd got nothing done.

Maybe because he couldn't stop thinking about her.

What was it about the woman that needled him so much? She was so passionate and wild in bed, like a tigress waiting to be unleashed, waiting for him to let her off the chain. Wasn't that enough? Why couldn't she just leave it at that? Why did she have to needle him and needle him and lever lids off things that had been welded shut for a reason? All her pointless questions.

All working away under his skin. And why did she even care?

Two days. Three nights. So maybe extending his time in her presence wasn't his preferred option, but he could survive being around Evelyn that long, surely. After all, he'd had mistresses who'd lasted a month or two before he'd lost interest or moved cities. Seriously, what could possibly happen in just a weekend?

Hopefully more great sex. A sound sleep would do wonders to improve her mood, and a tropical island sunset would soon have her feeling romantic and back in his arms. Nothing surer.

And in a few short days he'd have the deal tied up and Evelyn and child safely delivered home again.

Easy.

'Mr Zamos,' the cabin attendant said, refreshing his water, 'the captain said to tell you we'll be landing in half an hour. Would you like me to let Ms Carmic [illegible] know?'

He looked at his watch, rubbed his brow, [illegible] how long she'd slept. If his theory was right [illegible] should be very much improved already. 'Th [illegible] he said, 'but I'll do it.'

There was no answer to his soft knock, so he turned the handle, cracked open the door. 'Evelyn?'

Light slanted into the darkened room and as his eyes adjusted he could make her out in the bed, her caramel hair tumbling over the pillow, her face turned away, her arm protectively resting over her child's belly.

Mother and child.

And he felt such a surge of feeling inside him, such a tangle of twisted emotions, that for a moment the noise of that blast blotted everything else out, and there was nothing else for it but to close his eyes and endure the rush of pain and disgust and anger as it ripped through him.

And when he could breathe again, he opened his eyes to see another pair of dark eyes blinking up at him from the bed. Across the sleeping woman, the pair considered each other, Leo totally ill equipped to deal with the situation. In the end it was Sam who took the initiative. He pulled his teddy from his arms and offered him to Leo. 'Bear.'

He looked blankly at the child and immediately Sam rolled over, taking his toy with him, then promptly rolled back and held his bear out to Leo again. 'Bear.'

And Leo felt—he didn't know how he felt. He didn't know what was expected of him. He was still reeling from the explosion of emotions that had rocked through him to know how to react to this.

'Bear!'

'Mmm, what's that, Sam?' Eve said drowsily, and she [illegible] around and saw Leo. 'Oh.' She pushed herself [illegible] over her hair. 'Have I overslept?'

[illegible] was red where it had lain against the [illegible] hair was mussed and there was a smudge of [illegible] under one eye, but yet none of that detracted from her fundamental beauty. And he felt an insane surge of masculine pride that he was the one responsible for her exhaustion. And a not-so-insane surge of lust in anticipation of a repeat performance in his near future.

'We'll be landing soon. You don't want to miss the view as we come in. It's pretty spectacular, they tell me.'

It *was* spectacular, Eve discovered after she'd freshened herelf up and changed Sam before joining Leo back in the cabin. The sea was the most amazing blue, and she could make out in the distance some of the islands that made up the Whitsunday group. From here they looked like jewels in the sea, all lush green slopes and white sand surrounded by water containing every shade of blue. The sun was starting to go down, blazing fire, washing everything in a golden hue.

'That's Hamilton Island,' he said, indicating a larger island as they circled the group for their approach. 'That's where we'll land before transferring to the helicopter for Mina Island.'

'It's beautiful,' she said, pointing over Sam's shoulder. 'Look, Sam, that's where we're going for a holiday.' Sam burst into song and pumped his arms up and down.

It did look idyllic, she thought. Maybe a couple of days relaxing on a tropical island wouldn't be such a hardship. She glanced over at the man beside her, felt the familiar sizzle in her veins she now associated with him and only him, and knew she was fooling herself.

With Leo around things were bound to get complicated. They always did.

Which meant she just had to establish a few ground rules first.

CHAPTER NINE

'I'M NOT sleeping with you.'

They'd landed on Hamilton Island and made the helicopter transfer to Mina without incident, arriving to be greeted by Eric just as the sun was dipping into the water in a glorious blaze of gold. Eric had laughed, secretly delighted she could tell, when they'd all stood and watched the spectacle, telling them they'd soon get used to 'that old thing', before dropping them off at their beachside bure to freshen up before dinner.

And now, after a tour of the timber and glass five-star bungalow, their eyes met over the king-sized bed. The *only* bed, aside from the cot set up for Sam in the generous adjoining dressing room.

She wasn't about to change her mind. 'You'll just have to find yourself somewhere else to sleep.'

'Come on, Evelyn,' he said, sitting down on the bed and slipping off his shoes, peeling off his socks, 'don't you think you're being just a little melodramatic? It's not like we haven't slept together before.'

'That was different.'

He looked over his shoulder at her, one eyebrow raised. 'Was it?'

Her arms flapped uselessly at her sides. From outside she could hear Sam laughing as Hannah, the young woman who had been sent to be his babysitter, fed him his dinner. At least that part of the arrangements seemed to be going well.

'I'm not sharing a bed with you,' she said. 'And I certainly don't have to sleep with you just because we happen to be caught in the same lie.'

He stood, reefing his shirt from his pants as he started undoing the buttons at his cuffs. 'No? Even though you know we're good together?'

She blinked. 'What are you doing?'

He shrugged. 'Taking a shower before dinner,' he said innocently enough, although she saw the gleam in his eyes. 'Care to join me?'

'No!'

But she couldn't resist watching his hands moving over the buttons, feeling for them, pushing them through the holes. Clever hands. Long-fingered hands. And as he tweaked the buttons she was reminded of the clever way he'd tweaked her nipples and worked other magic… She looked away. Looked back again. 'There's no point. No point to any of it.'

'It's only sex,' he said, finishing off the rest of the buttons before peeling off his shirt. 'It's not like we haven't already done it—several times. And I know for a fact you enjoyed it. I really don't know why you're making out like it's some kind of ordeal.'

'It was supposed to be for just one night,' she said, trying and failing not to be distracted by his broad chest and that line of dark hair heading south. 'A one-night stand. No strings attached.'

'So we make it a four-night stand. And I sure as hell don't see any strings.'

She dragged her recalcitrant eyes north again, wondering how he could so easily consider making love to a person like they had for not one but four nights, and not want to feel some kind of affection for the other party. But, then, he had a head start on her. He had a heart of stone. 'It was nice, sure. But that doesn't mean we have to have any repeat performances.'

'There's that word again.' His hands dropped to the waistband of his pants, stilled there. '"Nice". Tell me, if you scream like that for nice, what do you do for mind-blowing? Shatter windows?'

She felt heat flood her face, totally mortified at being reminded of her other wanton self, especially now when she was trying to make like she could live without such sex. 'Okay, so it was better than nice. So what? It's not as if we even like each other.'

'And that matters because…?'

She spun away, reduced to feeling like some random object rather than a woman with feelings and needs of her own, and crossed to the wall of windows that looked out through palm trees to the bay beyond. It was moonlit now, the moon dusting the swaying palm leaves with silver and laying a silvery trail across the water to the shore, where tiny waves rippled in, luminescent as they kissed the beach. It was beautiful, the air balmy and still, and she wished she could enjoy it. But right now she was having trouble getting past the knowledge that she'd spent an entire night, had bared herself, body and soul, to a man who treated sex as some kind of birthright.

And if it wasn't bad enough that he'd not so subtly pointed out she'd been vocally enthusiastic, now he'd as much as agreed that he didn't even like her. Lovely.

And that was supposed to make her happier about sleeping with him?

Fat chance.

She felt his hands land on her shoulders, his long fingers stroking her arms, felt his warm breath fan her hair. 'You are a beautiful woman, Evelyn. You are beautiful and sexy and built for unspeakable pleasure. And you know it. So why do you deny yourself that which you so clearly desire?'

Self-preservation, she thought, as his velvet-coated words warmed her in places she didn't want warmed and stroked an ego that wanted to be liked and maybe, maybe even more than that.

'I can't,' she said. *Not without losing myself in a place I don't want to be. Not without risking falling in love with a man who has no heart.* 'Please, just believe me, I'll pretend to be your fiancée, I'll pretend to be your lover. But, please, don't expect me to sleep with you.'

The big house, as the Culshaws referred to it, was exactly that. Not flashy, but all spacious tropical elegance, the architecture, like that of the bures, styled to bring the outside in with lots of timber and glass and sliding walls. Outside, on an expansive deck overlooking the bay and the islands silhouetted against the sky, a table had been beautifully laid, but it was the night sky that captured everyone's attention.

'I don't think I've ever seen so many stars,' Eve confessed, dazzled by the display as they sat down for the meal. 'It's just magical.'

Eric laughed. 'We think so. This island takes its name from one of them but don't ask me to point out which one.'

Maureen continued, 'When we first came here for a holiday about thirty years ago, we got home to Melbourne and wanted to turn right back round again.

We've been coming here every year since. Hasn't been used much lately, not since—'

Eric cut in, saving her from finishing. 'Well, it's good to have guests here again, that's for sure. So I'd like to propose a toast. To guests and good friends and good times,' he said, and they all raised their glasses for the toast.

'Now,' Eric said, from alongside Leo, 'how's that young man of yours settling in?'

'He's in his element,' Eve replied. 'Two of his favourite things are fish and boats. He can't believe his good fortune.'

'Excellent. And the babysitter's to your satisfaction? Did she tell you she's hoping to study child care next year?'

'Hannah seems wonderful, thank you.'

Maureen distracted her on the other side, patting her on the hand. 'Oh, that reminds me, I've booked the spa,' she started.

But Eve didn't hear the rest, not when she heard Eric ask Leo, 'How old did you say Sam was again?'

She froze, her focus on the man beside her and how he replied to the question, the man stumbling with an answer, seemingly unable to remember the age of his own supposed child.

'Ah, remind me again, Eve?' he said at last. 'Is Sam two yet?' Eve excused herself and smiled, forcing a laugh.

'You go away much too much if you think Sam's already had his birthday. He's eighteen months old. How could you possibly forget?'

Leo snorted and said, 'I never remember this milestone stuff. It's lucky Evelyn does,' which earned agreement from Eric at least.

'It must be hard on you, though, Evelyn, with Leo always on the move,' Maureen said. Eve wanted to hug the woman for moving the conversation along, although a moment later she wished she'd opted for a complete change of topic. 'Do you have family nearby who help out?'

She smiled softly, looking up at the stars for just a moment, wondering where they were amidst the vast array. Her grandfather had held her hand and taken her outside on starry nights when she hadn't been able to stop crying and had told her they were up there somewhere, shining brightly, keeping her grandmother company. And now her grandfather was there too. She blinked. 'I have a wonderful neighbour who helps out. My parents died when I was ten and—I hate to admit it—I don't remember terribly much about them. I lived with my grandfather after that.'

'Oh-h-h,' said Felicity. 'They never got to meet Sam.'

'No, and I know they would have loved him.' She took a breath. 'Oh, I'm sorry for sounding so maudlin on such a beautiful night. Maybe we should change the topic, talk about something more cheerful.'

'I know,' said Eric jovially. 'So when's the happy day, you two?'

Eve wanted to groan, until she felt Leo's arm around her shoulders and met his dazzling smile. 'Just as soon as I can convince her she can't live without me a moment longer.'

Somehow they made it through the rest of the evening without further embarrassment but it was still a relief to get back to their bure. The long day had taken its toll, the stress of constantly fearing they would be caught out weighing heavily on Eve, and even though she'd slept on the plane, she couldn't wait to crawl into bed. *Her bed*, because after their earlier discussion, Leo had offered to sleep on the sofa. Hannah was sitting on it now, watching music television on low. She stood and clicked the remote off as they came in.

'How was Sam?' Eve asked, looking critically at the sofa, frowning at its length. Or lack of it. How the hell did Leo think he was going to fit on that?

'Sam's brilliant. I let him stay up half an hour longer, like you suggested, and he went down easy as. I checked him the last time about five minutes ago, and he hadn't stirred. I don't think I've ever looked after such a good baby.'

Eve smiled, relieved. 'Lucky you didn't meet him last week when he was teething—you might have had a different opinion.' She opened her purse to find some notes and Hannah waved her away. 'No. It's all taken care of. It's my job to look after Sam while you're here.' She headed for the door, gave a cheery wave. 'I'll see you in the morning, then.'

Eve met Leo coming out of the bedroom with an armful of pillows and linen. 'Goodnight,' he said, heading for the sofa maybe a little too stoically.

She watched him drop it all on the sofa, measured the height and breadth of man against length and width of sofa and realised it was never going to work. It should be her sleeping on the sofa. Except Sam's room was beyond the bedroom and it would be foolhardy if not impossible to move him now.

She watched him for a while try to make sense of

the bedding, as if he was ever going to be comfortable there.

And suddenly she was too tired to care. It wasn't like they were strangers after all. They had made love and several times. And even if they didn't like each other, surely they could share two sides of a big wide bed and still manage to get a good night's sleep?

'Stop it,' she said, as Leo attempted to punch his pillow into submission at one end, one bare foot sticking out over the other. 'This is ridiculous.'

'You don't say.'

'Look, it's a big bed,' she said reluctantly, gnawing her lip, trying not to think of the broad, fit body that would be taking up at least half of it. 'We can share it.' Then she added, 'So long as that's all we share. Is that a deal?'

He sat up on a sigh, clearly relieved. 'It's a promise. I promise not to share anything, so long as you don't jump me first.'

'Ha. And I thought you were awake. Now I know you're dreaming. I'm going to have a shower—alone. You'd better be in bed and asleep when I get there, or it's straight back to the sofa for you.'

And he was asleep when she slipped under the covers, or he was good at pretending. She clung close to her edge of the bed, thinking that was the safest place, yet she could still feel the heat emanating from his body, could hear his slow, steady breathing, and tried not to think about what they'd been doing twenty-four hours ago, but found it hard to think of anything else. Especially when she was so acutely aware of every tiny rustle of sheets or shift in his breathing.

Twenty-four hours. How could so much have happened in that time? How could so much change?

Outside the breeze stirred the leaves in the trees, set the palm fronds rustling, and if she listened hard, she could just hear a faint swoosh as the tiny swell rushed up the shore. But it was so hard to hear anything, so very hard, over the tremulous beating of her heart…

It was happening again. He buried his head under the blanket and put his hands over his ears but it didn't stop the shouting, or the sound of the blows, or the screams that followed. He cowered under the covers, whimpering, trying not to make too much noise in case he was heard and dragged out too, already dreading what he'd find in the morning at breakfast. If they all made it to breakfast.

There was a crash of furniture, a scream and something smashed, and the blows continued unabated, his mother's cries and pleas going unheard, until finally, eventually, he heard the familiar mantra, the mantra he knew by heart, even as his mother continued to sob. Over and over he heard his father utter the words telling her he was sorry, telling her he loved her. 'Signome! Se agapo. Se agapo poli. Signome.'

Sam! Eve woke with a mother's certainty that something was wrong, bolting from the bed and momentarily disoriented with her new surroundings, only to realise it wasn't Sam who was in trouble. For in the bed she'd so recently left, Leo was thrashing from side to side, making gravel-voiced mutterings against the mattress, rantings that made no sense in any language she knew, his body glossy with sweat under the moonlight.

He cried out in his sleep, a howl of desperation and helplessness, anguish clear in his tortured limbs and fevered brow as he twisted and writhed. Eve did the only thing she could think of, the only thing she knew helped Sam when he had night terrors. She went to Leo's side of the bed and sat down softly. 'It's okay, Leo,' she said, sweeping a calming hand over his brow, finding it burning hot. He flnched at her touch, resisting it at first, so she tried to soothe him with her words. 'It's okay. It's all right. You're safe now. Leo, you're safe.'

He seemed to slump under her hands, his body slick with sweat, his breathing still hard but slowing, and Eve suspected that whatever demons had invaded his midnight hours had now departed. She went to leave then, to return to her side of the bed, but when she made a move to leave, a hand locked around her wrist and she realised that maybe there were still some demons hanging on.

And just as she would do and had done with Sam when he needed comfort, she slid under the covers alongside the hot body of Leo, putting her arm around him, soothing him back to sleep with the gentle reassurance of another's touch and trying not to think of the heated presence lying so close to her or the thud of his heart under her hands.

Five minutes should be enough, she figured, until he had settled back into sleep. Five minutes and she'd escape back to her edge of the mattress. Five minutes would be more than enough…

Something was different. She woke to the soft light of the coming dawn, filtering grey through the shutters, and to the sound of birdsong coming from the palms outside. And she woke to the certain knowledge that she had stayed far, far too long. Fingers trailed over her back, making lazy circles on her skin through her thin cotton nightie and setting her skin to tingling, and warm lips nuzzled at her brow as the hand between them somehow managed to brush past her nipples and send spears of electricity to her core.

And she was very, very aroused.

She was also trapped, his heavy arm over her, one leg casually thrown over hers. She tried to wiggle her way out but the movement brought her into contact with a part of him that told her he was also very much aroused. He growled his appreciation, shifted closer, and she tried not to think about how good that part of him had felt inside her.

'Leo…' she said, conflicted, her mind in panic, her body in revolt, turning her face up to his, only to be met by his mouth as he dragged her into his long, lazy kiss, a kiss she had no power or intention to cut short even though she knew it was utter madness.

Utter pleasure.

Her senses soared, her flesh tingled and breasts ached for the caress of his clever hands and hot mouth, and arguments that things were complicated enough, that there was no point, that this must end and end badly made little impression against this slow, sensual onslaught.

'I see you changed your mind,' he murmured, a brush of velvet against her skin.

'You had a nightmare.'

'This,' he said, sliding one long-fingered hand up the back of her leg, kneading her bottom in his hand, 'is no nightmare.'

'Don't you—' His mouth cut her off again as his hand

captured her breast, working at her nipple, plucking at her nerve endings, making her groan into his mouth with the exquisite pleasure of his caress, emerging breathless and dizzy when it ended so that she almost forgot what she wanted to say. 'Don't you remember?'

'Maybe…' he said, rolling her under him, pinning her arms to the bed above her head as his head dipped to her throat, 'maybe right now I'd rather forget.'

She moaned with the wicked pleasure of it all, his hot mouth like a brand against her skin. But this wasn't supposed to happen. She hadn't wanted this to happen. But as he lowered his head to her breast and drew in one achingly hard nipple to his mouth, laving it with his hot tongue, blowing on the damp fabric and sending exquisite chills coursing through her, she couldn't, for the life of her, remember why. Her body was alive with wanting him, alive with the power that came from him and that she craved, and there was no way she could stop.

He let her wrists go, his hands busy at her nightie. She felt the soft fabric lifting as he skimmed his hands up her sides, before skimming down again, taking her underwear with them. 'You're beautiful,' he growled, his voice like a brush of velvet over her bare skin as he pulled it over her head. And yet he was the magnificent one, broad and dark, his erection swaying and bucking over her, a pearl of liquid glistening at its head. Transfixed, unable to stop herself, she reached out her hand and touched it with the pad of her thumb. He uttered something urgent, his dark eyes flared, wild and filled with the same dark need that consumed her as he swiped up his wallet, found what he needed and tossed the wallet away in his rush to be inside her.

He dragged in air, forced himself to slow. 'You do this to me,' he accused her softly as he parted her thighs with his hand and found her slick and wet and wanting. 'You make me rock hard and aching,' he continued, his fingers circling that tiny nub of nerve endings, a touch so delicious she mewled with pleasure, writhing as sensation built on the back of his words, fuelling her need, fuelling her desperation.

Until at last she felt him nudge her *there*, hot and hard and pulsing with life as he tensed above her for one tantalising moment of anticipation.

And then joyfully, blissfully, he entered her in one magical thrust and she held him there, at her very core, welcoming him home, tears squeezing from her eyes at the sheer ecstasy of it all.

So much to feel. So much to experience and hold precious. And still the best was to come. The dance, the friction, the delicious moment of tension when he would sit poised at her entrance, before slamming back inside.

She went with him, matched him measure for measure, gasp for gasp as the pace increased, their bodies slick and hot as the rhythm increased, faster, more furious, the climb too high until this thing building inside her felt too big for her chest, her lungs too small.

Until with one final thrust, one final guttural roar, he sent her shattering, coming apart in his arms, falling, spinning weightless and formless and satisfied beyond measure.

'So beautiful,' he said, as he smoothed her hair from her damp brow, kissing her lightly on her eyes, on her nose, on her gasping lips.

And you're dangerous, she thought as he disappeared

to the bathroom, as her brain resumed functioning and a cold and very real panic seized her heart. So utterly, utterly dangerous.

And I am so in trouble.

What should one say now? What would an army do, its defences stripped bare, the castle walls well and truly breached? Try to hastily rebuild them? Call for reinforcements?

Or surrender?

She squeezed her eyes shut, trying not to think about the sizzle under her skin where his fingers had stroked her shoulder.

As if she had a choice. She would no sooner patch up her defences and he would have them down again. One silken touch, one poignant kiss, and he would have those walls tumbling right down.

But she was kidding himself. There was no point rebuilding walls or calling for reinforcements. No point trying to save herself from attack from outside the castle walls.

Not when the enemy was already within.

Tears sprang to her eyes and she swiped them away. Damn. What was she doing? What was she risking? 'I can't afford to get pregnant again,' she said when he returned, putting voice to her greatest fear.

'I wouldn't let you.'

'But Sam's father—'

He rose over her, cutting her off with his kiss. 'I would never do that to you.'

'How do I know that? And I would have two babies from two different fathers. How could I cope with that?'

'Believe me. It won't happen but even if it did, I would not abandon you as he has done.'

'But you wouldn't marry me either.'

He searched her eyes and frowned and she thought it was at her words, until he used the pad of his thumb to wipe away the moisture there.

'I thought I heard you say any woman would be certifiably insane to want to get shackled to me.'

'I'm sorry,' she whispered, remembering the scene in the bar. 'I was angry.'

'As was I. I should never have said what I did about Sam's father thinking the same of you. But you're right. Marriage is not an option, which means the best thing for everyone is to ensure we're careful. All right?'

She wished he wouldn't be like this. She wished he could go back to being ruthless and hard, because when he was tender and gentle with her, she could almost, *almost*, imagine he actually cared.

And she could almost, *almost*, imagine that she cared for him. She couldn't afford to care for him. She couldn't afford to read anything into his apology for what he'd said about Sam's dad when it was plain he wasn't lining up to marry her himself.

But she could enjoy him.

Two more nights in Leo's bed. Why was she fighting it when it was where she so wanted to be? Why not treat it as the holiday it really was? Time spent in a tropical paradise with a man who knew how to pleasure a woman. No ties, no commitments and a promise not to let her down.

Was she mad to fight it?

And was it really surrendering, to take advantage of what she'd been offered on a plate?

His hand cupped her breast, feeling its weight, stroking her nipple and her senses until it peaked hard and plump under his fingers while his lips worked their heated way along her jaw towards her mouth. 'Evelyn?'

A woman would have to be mad to want to give this up, she reasoned, leaning into his ministrations, giving herself over to the sensations. Two nights to enjoy the pleasures of the flesh. It was more than some people had in a lifetime.

It would be enough.

It had to be enough.

'All right,' she whispered, giving herself up to his kiss.

CHAPTER TEN

SAM'S morning chatter roused them, as he tested all the sounds in his vocabulary in one long gabble, then she heard a tell-tale bump on the floor, followed by a squeal. 'That's Sam,' she said unnecessarily, locating her nightie and snatching up her balled-up underwear and a robe and making for the bathroom for a quick pit stop, wanting to ensure she looked maternal rather than wanton when she greeted her son. Not that he was old enough to notice anything amiss, she thought, giving thanks for his innocence.

Sam was hanging onto the rails and bouncing on the mattress and greeted her with a huge grin followed by 'mumumumumum', which warmed her heart. Unconditional love. There was nothing like it. She changed him on the table provided and equipped for the task before popping his wriggling body down on the floor. 'Bear!' he shouted, gleefully scooping up the toy and running with his wide toddler gait out of the room before her, looking a little bit lost at the new surroundings for just a moment, before running full pelt and colliding with the bed.

Dark eyes blinked up at Leo, openly curious. He blinked back, wondering what one was supposed to say to a child. Sam looked around at his mother, who was pulling milk from the fridge in the small kitchenette and pouring it into a jug. 'It's okay, Sam, you remember Leo,' she said reassuringly as she put the jug in the microwave, and Sam turned and careened straight into his mother's legs, hiding his face between them.

'I'm sorry,' she said, hoisting him to her hip in one efficient movement, although it wasn't so much the efficiency that impressed Leo but the unexpected way the sudden angle of her hip displayed the long line of her legs. His mouth went dry, his blood went south. Strange really, for here she was, dressed in a cheap cotton nightgown, a toweling robe sashed at her waist and with a baby at her hip, and maybe it was her tousled hair, or the jut of that damned hip, or even the fact she'd just blown his world apart in bed—twice—but suddenly he was thinking about a third time.

The microwave pinged.

'Ping,' cried Sam, holding his hands out. 'Ping!'

One-handed, she poured the milk into some kind of cup, fixing on a spout before passing it to the boy. 'Here's your ping, Sam.' Leo watched her, admiring the way she looked so at ease working one-handedly. Sam dropped his bear to clasp the cup in his pudgy hands, gulping deep. 'Sam's used to joining me in bed in the morning,' she said, bending over to retrieve the bear and giving his sex a hell of a jolt in the process. Until, through the fog of rising testosterone, it occurred to him that she was about to bring Sam back to bed.

'Although, admittedly,' she added, already on her way, 'he's not used to finding someone else there.'

He tucked that piece of information away in a file that came marked with a tick, even as he gladly took her hint and pulled on a robe to vacate the bed. He liked the knowledge she didn't often entertain at home. Sam was evidence she'd been with someone, and that wasn't something he wanted to contemplate. He didn't want to think there had been or were others.

'I didn't mean you had to run away,' she said, settling Sam between the pillows. 'It's still early.'

'I think I'll go for a run.'

'You haven't had that much to do with babies or children, have you?'

'Does it show?'

'Blatantly. You might want to do something about that if you want people to believe you're actually Sam's father. The fact you're travelling most of the year is no excuse for not knowing how to deal with the child who's supposed to be your own.'

He shrugged, knowing he'd handled things badly last night, not even remembering his supposed son's age, but uncomfortable with where the conversation was headed. 'What do you suggest?'

'Maybe you should try holding him from time to time. Even just hold his hand. Engage with him.'

'Engage with him?'

'He's a person, Leo, just like anyone else. Maybe try directing all that animal magnetism you have at him instead of every woman you happen to meet.'

He looked at the child. Looked back at her, not sure who was making him feel more uncomfortable now. 'But can he even understand what I say?'

She laughed. 'More than you know.'

He sat down awkwardly on the side of the bed, watching Sam, Sam watching him as he swigged at his milk, his teddy tucked securely once again under his arm.

And Sam guzzled the last of his milk and held out his toy. 'Bear!'

He looked on uncertainly, not sure what was expected

of him, unfamiliar with this role. 'I'm not sure I can do this.'

'He's offering it to you. Try taking it,' she suggested.

He put out his hand toward the bear and Sam immediately rolled over, giggling madly, the toy wedged tightly beneath him.

He looked over at her. 'I don't get it.'

'It's a game, Leo. Wait.' And sure enough the arm shot out again.

'Bear.'

This time Leo made a grab for it. A slow lunge, and way too slow for Sam, but he loved it anyway, squealing with glee as he hid his teddy.

The next time was nearly a draw, Sam winning by a whisker, and he was in stitches on the bed, his body curved over his prize, and even Leo was finding it amusing. 'He's quick,' he said, and he looked at Evelyn, who was smiling too, although her eyes looked almost sad, almost as if…

'I'll go take a shower,' he said, standing abruptly, not interested in analysing what a look like that might mean. He didn't do family. He'd told her that. And if the shadowed remnants of last night's nightmares had reminded him of him anything, it was that he could never do family. He dared not risk it. He was broken, and that was just the way it was.

So she could look at him any damned way and it would make no difference. Because after two more nights with her, he would let her go for ever.

He didn't want anything more.

And he definitely didn't want her pity.

They were all meeting after breakfast at the dock, ready for a day's adventure. A morning sail, and then a helicopter trip over the more far-flung sights of the islands and the reef. Hannah had already collected Sam and taken him up to the main house where there was a large playroom filled with toys and games and all surrounded by secure fences so he couldn't get into trouble if he wandered off. Which meant Eve had a rare few hours without Sam, not to work but to enjoy her beautiful if temporary surroundings, and the heated attention of a man just as beautiful and temporary, if a lot more complex.

He held her hand as they wended their way along the palm-studded sand toward the dock on the bay, the whispering wind promising a day of seductive warmth, the odd scattered white cloud offering no threat, and the man at her side promising days and nights filled with sinful pleasures.

Now that she had made her decision, and had Leo's commitment that he wouldn't abandon her if the worst happened, as Sam's father had done, she was determined to enjoy every last moment of it. Maybe she was crazy, but she trusted him, at least on that score. And there was no question that he didn't lack the means to support a child.

The morning sun kissed her bare arms where it infiltrated the foliage, the air fresh with salt and the sweet scent of tropical flowers. Ten whole degrees warmer up here than Melbourne's showery forecast, Eve had heard when she'd flicked on the weather channel while feeding Sam his breakfast. She could think of worse ways to spend the time waiting for a new hot water service to be installed.

She glanced up at the man alongside her, his loose white shirt rolled up at the cuffs, with designer stubble adding to his pirate appeal, and with one look the memories of their love-making flooded back, warming her in places the sun did not reach. Oh, no, she would have no trouble enjoying her nights with him either.

'You look pleased with yourself.'

'Do I?' Only then did she realise she'd been smiling. 'It must be the weather.'

'Good morning!' Maureen said, greeting them, looking resort elegant in linen co-ordinates in taupe and coffee colours. 'How was the bure? Did you all sleep well?'

Eve smiled. 'It's just beautiful. I love it here.'

'Everything is perfect,' Leo added, slipping an arm around Eve's shoulders, giving her arm a squeeze. 'Couldn't be better.'

'And Sam's okay with Hannah? You're not worried about leaving him, are you?'

Eve shook her head. 'Hannah's wonderful. He's having the time of his life.'

The older woman looked from one to the other and smiled knowingly. 'I hope you understand why we were so keen to drag you away from Melbourne. And there's just so much more to share with you.'

'All aboard!' called Eric, appropriately wearing a captain's cap over his silvering hair, and Leo handed both women onto the yacht where Richard and Felicity were already waiting. There was a distinct holiday mood in the air as they set off, the boat slicing through the azure waters, the wind catching in the flapping sails, the magnificent vistas ever-changing, with new wonders revealed around every point, with every new bay. 'Isn't it fabulous?' Felicity said, leaning over the railing, looking glamorous in a short wrap skirt and peasant top, and Eve could't help but agree, even though she felt decidedly designer dull in her denim shorts and chain-store tanktop. Motherhood in Melbourne, she reflected, didn't lend itself to a vast resort wardrobe.

Decidedly dull, that was, until Leo slipped an arm around her waist and pressed his mouth to her ear. 'Did I tell you how much I love your shorts,' he whispered, 'and how much I can't wait to peel them off?'

And she shuddered right there in anticipation of that very act. But first there were other pleasures, other discoveries. They discovered secret bays and tiny coves with sheer cliff walls and crystal-clear waters. They found bays where inlets carved dark blue ribbons through shallow water backed by pure white sand, a thousand shades of blue and green against the stark white beach and the lushly vegetated hills rising above.

They stopped for a swim at that beach, followed by a picnic comprising a large platter of antipasto and cold chicken and prawns, with Vietnamese cold rolls with dipping sauce all washed down with chilled white wine or sparkling water.

After lunch, the Alvarezes went for a stroll along the beach and Maureen took a snooze while Eric and Leo chatted, no doubt about business, a little way away. And Eve was happy to sit right there on the beach in her bikini, taking in the wonders of the scenery around her, the islands and the mountains, the lush foliage and amazing sea and above it all the endless blue sky. And she felt guilty for not sharing it with Sam, even though she knew that if he had come, none of them would have been able to relax for a minute. One day, when he was older, she would love to show him.

Leo dropped down on his knees behind her, picked up her bottle of lotion and squeezed some into his hand, started smoothing it onto her shoulders and neck until she almost purred with pleasure. She didn't think it necessary to inform him she'd just done that. 'You look deep in thought.'

'I was just thinking how much Sam would love this. I'll have to try to bring him one day.'

His hands stilled for a moment, before they resumed their slippery, sensual massage. 'Don't you love it?' she said. 'Can you believe the colour of that sea?'

'I've seen it before.'

'You have?' But of course he would have. Leo had been everywhere. 'Where?'

'In your eyes.'

The shiver arrowed directly down her spine. She snapped her head round. 'What?'

He squeezed more lotion, spread it down her arms, his fingertips brushing her bikini top as he looked out at the bay. 'When I first saw them, they reminded me of the Aegean, of the sea around the islands of Santorini and Mykonos, but I was wrong. For every colour in your eyes is right here, in these waters.'

And that battle scarred never-say-die, foolish, foolish creature inside her lumbered back into life and prepared for take-off once more. 'Leo…'

He looked down at her upturned face, touched one hand to the side of her face. 'I don't know how I'm ever going to forget those eyes.'

Then don't! she almost blurted, surprising herself with her vehement reaction, but he angled her shoulders and invited her into his kiss, a heart-wrenching bitter-sweet kiss that spoke of something lost before it had even been found, and she cursed a man with a stone for a heart, cursed her own foolish heart for caring.

'Come on, you two lovebirds,' Eric yelled along the beach. 'We've got a seaplane to catch!'

* * *

If the Whitsundays had been spectacular from the boat, they were breathtaking from the air in the clear afternoon light. Island after island could be explored from the air in the tiny plane, each island a brilliant green gem in a sapphire sea. And just when Eve thought it couldn't possibly get any better, they headed out over the Coral Sea to the Great Barrier Reef. The sheer scale of the reefs took everyone's breath away, the colours vivid and bright, like someone had painted pictures upon the sea, random shapes bordered in snowy white splashed with everything from emerald green and palest blue to muted shades of mocha.

And then they landed on the water and transferred to a glass-bottomed boat so they could see the amazing Technicolor world under the sea together with its rich sea life. 'I am definitely coming back one day to show Sam,' she told Maureen as they boarded the seaplane for the journey back to Mina. 'Thank you so much for today. I know I'll treasure these memories for ever.'

And from the back seat Eric piped up, 'You just wait. We saved the best till last!'

They had. They were heading back over a section he identified as Hardy Reef, one part of a network of reefs that extended more than two thousand kilometres up the north Queensland coastline, when she saw something that didn't fit with the randomness of the coral structures.

She pointed out the window. 'That looks like... Is that what I think it is?' Eric laughed and had the pilot circle around so they could all see.

'That's it. What do you think of that?'

It was incredible and for a moment her brain had refused to believe what her eyes were telling her. For in the middle of a kind of lagoon in the midst of a coral reef where everything appeared random, there sat a reef grown in the shape of a heart, its outline made from coral that looked from above like milk chocolate sprinkles on a cake, the inside like it was covered in a soft cream-cheese frosting, all surrounded by a sea of brilliant blue.

And little wonder she thought in terms of frostings and cakes, because it reminded her so much of the cake she'd made for Sam for his first birthday, knowing that as he got older he'd want bears or trains or some cartoon character or other. She figured that for his first, before he had a say, she could choose, and she'd made a heart shape, because that was what Sam meant to her.

'Look, Richard,' Felicity said, clasping his hand as they circled around. 'It's a heart. Isn't that amazing?'

'It magical,' Eve said, gazing down in wonder at the unique formation below. 'This entire place is just magical. Thank you.' The Culshaws laughed, delighted with the reactions of their guests as Leo took her hand and pressed it to his lips. She turned to him, surprised at the tenderness of the gesture, finding his eyes softly sad, feeling that sense of loss again, for something she had not yet quite gained. 'What is it?' she asked, confused.

'You are magical,' he told her, and his words shimmied down her spine and left her infused with a warm, golden glow and a question mark over her earlier accusation. A heart of stone? she wondered.

But there was definitely something magical in the air.

They dined alfresco that evening, an informal barbecue held early enough that Sam could join them, happily showing off his new toy collection to anyone who displayed an interest. Luckily nobody seemed to mind and Sam was in his element, lapping up the attention. When he yawned, there was general consensus amongst the couples. It had been a fabulous day, but exhausting, and tomorrow there was serious work to be done, an agreement to finally be hammered out between the men, a morning at the spa on a neighbouring island for the women.

And before that a night of explosive sex. Eve felt the tension change in the man alongside her, the barely restrained desire bubbling away so close to the surface she could just about smell the pheromones on the fresh night air. She sensed the changes in her own body, the prickling awareness, the mounting heat. It distracted her.

Sam, sensing the party winding up around him, found his second wind and made a dash for the toy room. Eve was too slow, caught unawares, and surprised when it was Felicity who snatched up the squirming child. 'Gotcha!' she said, swinging him in the air and tickling his tummy before, breathless and red cheeked, she passed him to his mother.

He was asleep before they reached the bure. She put Sam down, emerging from his small room to a darkened bedroom, lit only by the moonlight filtering through the glass windows. Leo had left the blinds open. She liked that; liked the way the shadows of the palms swayed on the breeze; liked the way the room glowed silver.

'Come to bed,' came the velvet-clad invitation.

And that was the part she liked best of all.

She was screaming again, crying out in pain as the blows rained down, as the bad words continued. 'Stomato to!' *he cried from his bed. 'Stop it!' But it didn't stop, and in fear and desperation he crept to the door, tears streaming down his face, afraid to move, afraid not to move, afraid of what he would find when he opened the door. So he did nothing, just curled up into a ball behind the door and covered his ears and prayed for it to stop.*

'Leo, it's okay.'

He sat bolt upright in bed, panting, desperate for air, burning up. He put his hands to his head, bent over his knees.

'You had a nightmare again.'

God, it wasn't a nightmare. *It was his life*. He swept the sheet aside, stormed from the bed, pacing the floor, circuit after circuit.

Twenty years ago he had escaped. Twenty years ago he had made his own way. But he had always known it was there, always known it was lurking. Waiting.

But it had never been this close. This real.

He felt cool hands on his back. 'What is it?'

He flinched, jumping away. 'Don't touch me! You shouldn't touch me!'

'Leo?'

'I have to go for a walk.' He pulled open a drawer, pulled out a pair of cotton pants and shoved his legs into them.

'It's two o'clock in the morning.'

'Let me go!'

The night air fanned around him, warming against his burning skin, the shallows sucking at his feet. There was a reason he didn't get close to anyone. Good reason. He was broken. Twisted. Made to be alone.

Couldn't she see that?

And yet she kept looking at him that way with those

damned blue eyes and even had him wishing for things that could never be. It was his fault. When had he stopped acting a part? When had he forgotten that this weekend was about pretence, that it wasn't real?

When she'd bucked underneath him in bed, her body writhing in its sweat-slicked release? Or when she'd talked about her parents and made him want to reach out and soothe her pain?

He stopped where the beach turned to rock, looked out over the sea to the looming dark shapes of the nearest islands.

One more day. One more night. And he would take her home before he could hurt her and there would be no more dreams.

It was as easy and as hard as that.

CHAPTER ELEVEN

SHE needed this. Eve lay on the massage table, scented candles perfuming the air, skilful hands working the knots out of her back and neck. She only wished someone would work out the knots in her mind, but that was impossible while Leo Zamos was at their core.

He'd been so desperate to get away, bursting from the bure this morning like the devil himself was after him. She'd watched him go, lit by moonlight as he'd moved through the trees towards the beach. Watched him and waited for him to come back. But eventually she'd gone back to bed and when she'd woken, he'd been sitting, having coffee on the deck.

She didn't know what it was, only that something was terribly, desperately wrong and that if he only opened up and shared what was troubling him, maybe she could help.

She sighed, a mixture of muscular bliss and frustrated mind, as the masseuse had her roll over, readying her for her facial. What was the point of wanting to help? He didn't want it and tomorrow she would go home, and all of this would be nothing more than a memory.

She couldn't afford to care. She mustn't, even when he told her she was magical. Even when he tugged on her heart and her soul with his kiss.

Even though she so very much wanted to believe it.

Thoroughly pampered after their hours at the spa, the three women enjoyed a late lunch at the big house, on the terrace overlooking the pool. The men were still in conference apparently, although Maureen suggested that might just mean they'd popped out in the boat for a spot of fishing while the women weren't looking. Not that it mattered. After they'd been massaged until their bones had just about melted, they were more than content to sit and chat in the warm, balmy air of tropical North Queensland. After all, they were going home tomorrow. Soon enough real life would intrude.

Sam was once again more than happy to provide the entertainment if they weren't up to it. He tottered between the three women, perfectly at ease with them all now, sharing around building blocks he'd taken a shine to, taking them back and redistributing them as if this was all part of some grand plan, happily chattering the whole time. Eve watched him, so proud of her little man, knowing that at least when Leo walked out of her life, she would still have Sam. He'd surprised her too. Instead of providing a disruptive force, as she'd expected, it seemed that, at least in some part, he seemed to pull them together. He definitely kept them amused.

And Felicity surprised her again, playing his games, picking him up when he passed, giving him hugs and raspberry kisses on his cheek to his squeals and giggles of delight before he scampered off on his toddler legs.

'I always wanted a child,' she said wistfully, her eyes following his escape. 'In fact, I always imagined myself surrounded by children. And when I met Richard and thought he was the one, I thought it might happen, even though it was already getting late…' Then she blinked and looked around. 'I guess things sometimes turn out differently to what we expect.'

And the other two women nodded, each wrapped in their own separate thoughts and experiences.

'It seemed easier to give up and pretend it didn't matter. But meeting you and seeing you with Sam makes me realise how much it means to me. I want to try again. At least one more time.' Tears made her eyes glassy. 'You're so lucky to be able to give Leo a child, Evelyn. I really wish I could do the same for Richard.' Her voice hitched. 'Damn! I'm so sorry.' She fled inside.

Eve felt sick, a hand instinctively going to her mouth. And all the good feelings, all the positive goodwill she'd been stashing away in her memory while she was determined to enjoy this weekend were for nothing. They meant nothing if her deceit led someone else to want what she was having. A wish based on a lie.

She rose to follow and tell her exactly that when Maureen stopped her. 'Let her go.'

'But she thinks—'

Maureen nodded. 'I know what she thinks.'

'But you don't understand.' She slumped back in her chair, feeling the weight of the lie crushing down on her, feeling her heart squeezed tight, knowing she couldn't go home without admitting the truth. 'I hate this! I hate the pretence. I'm so sorry, Maureen.' She shook her head, and still couldn't find a nice way to say it. 'Look, Leo's not really Sam's father.'

She heard a sharp intake of air, followed by an equally sharp exhalation. But then, instead of the censure she'd expected, or the outrage, she felt a gentling hand over her own. 'I wondered when you were going to feel able to share that.'

Warily, feeling sicker than ever, Eve looked up. 'You knew?'

'From the moment I met you in that bar in Melbourne. Of course, Sam could have passed for Leo's son, but it was crystal clear to anyone who had ever been a mother that Leo had no idea about being a father. And then his awkwardness at dinner, not knowing his own son's birthday, only reinforced that impression, at least to me.' She shrugged. 'Though when it comes down to it, does Sam's parentage really matter?'

'But you don't understand. It's not that simple—'

'Of course it's that simple.' Maureen said, cutting her off. 'I saw you and Leo out there yesterday in the boat and on the beach. It's clear to everyone that you love him and he loves you, so why should it matter one bit who Sam's father really is?' she insisted. 'Why should a silly detail like that matter when you are going to marry a man who clearly worships the ground you walk on? Now, I'll go check on Felicity and you stop worrying.'

How could Maureen know so much and yet be so wrong? Eve sat on the sand with Sam, watching him busily digging holes. All those hours of massaging and jet baths and a relaxing facial, all that pampering and all for nothing. Not even the magic of the island itself, the rustle of the palms and the vivid colours, none of it could dispel the tightness in her gut.

She didn't love Leo.

Sure, she was worried about him and whatever it was that plagued his dreams and turned his skin cold with sweat, and she certainly had an unhealthy obsession with the man, one that had started that fateful day three years ago, and which had only gathered momentum after mind-blowing nights of sex.

And maybe she didn't want to to think about going home tomorrow and never seeing him again.

But that was hardly the same as love.

As for Leo, no way did he love her. He was merely acting a part, plying her with attention as a means to an end, certainly not because he loved her. Ridiculous. They'd only been together a couple of days after all. What Maureen was witnessing was pure lust. Leo just had a bit more to throw around than most. He didn't do family and he didn't want her thinking he'd change his mind. Why else would he underline every endearment, every tender moment with a stinging reminder that it would soon end?

Sam oohed and pulled something from the sand then, shaking it, showing her what looked like some kind of shell, and she gave up thinking about questions she had no answers to, puzzles that made no sense. Tomorrow, she knew, she would go home and this brief interlude in her life would be over and she would have to find herself new clients and build a new fee base. And look after Sam. That's what she should be worrying about.

'Shall we see what it is, Sam?' she said to the child, a launch catching her attention for just a moment as it powered past the bay, before taking Sam's hand as they stepped into the shallows to wash this new treasure clean.

'Boat!' he said, pointing.

'It is,' she said. 'A big one.'

Her sarong clung to her where she'd sat in the damp sand, her ankles looked lean and sexy as her feet were lapped by the shallows, all her attention on her child by her side, guiding him, encouraging him with just a touch or a word or a smile, and he knew in that instant he had never seen anything more beautiful or powerful or sexy.

All he knew was that he wanted her. He wanted to celebrate, knowing the deal was finally done, but he wanted something more fundamental too. More basic. More necessary.

Except he also knew he couldn't let that happen. He'd realised that during his walk this morning and as much as he'd tried to find a way around it all day, even when he was supposed to be thinking about the Culshaw deal, he still knew it to be true. He couldn't take the chance.

He watched, as mother and son washed something in the shallows, he couldnt tell what, and she must have sensed his presence because he hadn't moved and she couldn't have heard him, yet she'd turned her head and looked up and seen him. And he'd seen his name on her lips as she'd stood and she'd smiled, only a tentative smile, but after the way he'd abandoned her this morning, he didn't deserve even that much.

And something bent and shifted and warmed inside that he could treat her so badly and still she could find a smile for him. He hoped it meant she liked him, just a little, just enough to one day find a way to forgive him for the way he had no choice but to treat her.

The wash was nothing really. No more than a ripple to any adult, and Leo had no idea it would be any different for a child, until he saw Sam pushed face first into the water with the rolling force of it.

'Sam!' he yelled, crossing the beach and pulling the child, spluttering and then squealing, from the water. 'Is he all right?' he asked, as she collected the wailing child, dropping to her towel, rocking him on her shoulder.

'Oh, my God, I took my eye off him for a second,' she said, her voice heavy with self-recrimination. 'I'm so sorry, Sam,' she said, kissing his head. 'I should have seen that coming.'

'Will he be okay?' Leo asked, but Sam's cries were already abating. He sniffled and hiccuped and caught sight of a passing sail, twisting in his mother's arms as his arm shot out. 'Boat!'

She sighed with relief. 'He sounds fine. He got a shock. I think we all did.'

Leo squatted down beside them and they said nothing for a while, all watching the boat bob by.

'You actually picked him up,' she said. 'Is that the first time you've ever held a child?'

He frowned as he considered her question, not because he didn't already know the answer but because this weekend suddenly seemed filled with firsts: the first time he'd thought a cotton nightie sexy; the first time he'd looked at a woman holding a baby and got a hard on; the first time he'd felt remorse that he'd never see a particular woman again…

But, no, he wasn't going there. What were his nightmares if not a warning of what would happen if he did?

'It's not something my job calls for much of, no.'

'Well, thank you for acting so quickly. I don't know what I was doing.'

He knew. She'd been looking at him with those damned eyes of hers. And he hadn't wanted to let them go.

Sam soon grew restless in his mother's arms and wiggled his way out, soon scouring the sands and collecting new treasure, keeping a healthy distance from the water, his mother shadowing his every movement.

'So how goes the deal?'

'It's done.'

She looked up, her expression unreadable, and he wasn't entirely certain what he'd been looking for. 'Congratulations. You must be pleased.'

'It's a good feeling.' Strangely, though, it didn't feel as good as it usually did, didn't feel as good as he'd expected it would. Maybe because of all the delays.

And then she was suddenly squatting down, writing Sam's name with a stick in the sand while he looked on, clapping. 'So we're done here.'

And that didn't make him feel any better. 'Looks like it. Culshaw is planning a celebratory dinner for tonight and tomorrow we all go home.'

'I thought you didn't have a home.'

There was a lump in the back of his throat that shouldn't have been there. He was supposed to be feeling good about this, wasn't he? He rubbed the back of his neck with his hand, watched her write 'Mum' in the sand. 'Mum,' she said to Sam, pointing.

Sam leaned over with his hands on his pudgy knees and solemnly studied the squiggles she'd made in the sand. 'Mumumumum,' sang Sam.

'That's right, clever clogs, you can read!' And she gave him a big squeeze that he wriggled out of and scooted off down the beach.

'Tell me about Sam's father,' Leo said, as they followed along behind.

She looked up suspiciously, her eyebrows jagging in the middle. Where was this coming from? 'Why?'

'Who was he?'

She shrugged. 'Just some guy I met.'

'You don't strike me as the "just-some-guy-I-met" type.'

'Oh, and you, with your vast experience of women, you'd know about all the different types, I guess.'

'Stop trying to change the subject. This is about you. How did you manage to hook up with such a loser?'

She stopped then, her eyes flicking between Leo and Sam. 'You don't know the first thing about me. And you certainly don't know the first thing about him. He just turned out not to be who I thought he was.'

'I know that he was a fool to let you go.'

Wow, she thought, forced to close her eyes for a second as the tremor rattled through her, *where did that come from*?

'Thanks,' she said, still getting over his last comment. 'But it was me who was the fool.'

'For getting pregnant? You can't blame yourself for that.'

For ever imagining he was anything at all like Leo. 'No. For believing him. He was an interstate consultant who visited every couple of weeks. Always flirting. We worked late one night, he invited me out for a drink afterwards'—*and he had sexy dark hair and olive skin and dark eyes and I wanted to pretend…*

'And?'

She shrugged. 'And the rest, as they say, is history.'

'You told him about Sam—about the pregnancy?'

'I told him. I wasn't particularly interested in seeing him again, but I thought he had a right to know. He wasn't interested as it happened. He was more interested in his wife not finding out.'

'Scum!' he spat, surprising her with the level of ferocity behind the word.

'It's not so bad. At least I've got Sam. And it got me motivated to start my own business.' She caught a flash of movement in the crystal clear water, a school of tiny fish darting to and fro in the shallows. She scooped up her son and ventured to the water's edge, careful not to disturb them. 'Look Sam,' she said, 'fish!'

And Sam's eyes opened wide, his arms pumping up and down. 'Fith!'

She laughed, chasing the fish in the shallows even as she envied her young son his raw enthusiasm. She envied him his simple needs and pleasures. Why did it have to become so hard when you were a grown up, she wondered, when the world spun not on the turns of the planet and shades of dark or light, but on emotions that made a mockery of science and fact and good sense.

Wanting Leo was so not good sense.

Loving him made even less.

Maureen was wrong. She had to be.

The mood at dinner was jovial, the conversation flowing and fun. Only Leo seemed tense, strangely separate from the group, as if he'd already moved on to the next place, the next deal. The next woman. 'Are you all right?' she asked, on the way back to their bure, his hand like a vise around hers. 'Do you want to go take a walk first?'

Hannah had taken Sam back earlier and by now he would be safely in the land of Nod. They didn't have to rush back if he had something on his mind.

He blew out in a rush. 'I'll sleep on the sofa tonight,' he said almost too quickly, as if the words had been waiting to spill out. 'It'll be better that way.'

And she stopped right where she was and refused to move on so he had no choice but to turn and face her. 'You're telling me that after three nights of the best sex of my life, on the last night we have together, you're going to sleep on the sofa? Not a chance.'

He tried to smile. Failed miserably. 'It's for the best.'

'Who says? What's wrong, Leo? Why can't you tell me?'

'Believe me,' he snorted, 'you really don't want to know.'

'I wouldn't ask if I didn't want to know. What the hell changes tonight? The fact you don't have to pretend anymore?'

'You think I ever had to pretend about that?'

'Then don't pretend you don't want me tonight.' She moved closer, ran her free hand up his chest, 'We've got just one night left together. We're good together. You said that yourself. Why can't we enjoy it?'

He grabbed her hand, pushed it away. 'Don't you understand? It's for your own good!'

'How can I believe that if you won't tell me? What's wrong? Is it the dreams you're having?'

And he made a roar like a wounded animal in distress, a cry that spoke of so much pain and anguish and loss that it chilled her to the bone. 'Just leave it,' he said. 'Just leave me.'

He turned and stormed off across the sand towards the beach, leaving her standing there, gutted and empty on the path.

Maybe it was better this way, she thought, as she dragged herself back to the bure, forcing herself to put on a bright face for Hannah who wasn't taken in for a moment, she could tell, but she wasn't about to explain it to anyone. Not when she had no idea what was happening herself.

She checked Sam, listening to his even breathing, giving thanks for the fact he was in her life, giving thanks for the gift she'd been given, even if borne of a mistake. He was the best mistake she'd ever made.

And then she dragged bedding to the sofa, knowing from the previous night Leo was more likely to disturb her if he tried to fit onto the sofa than because of any nightmare he might have. At least she knew he would fit on the big king sized bed.

She lay there in the dark, waiting for what seemed like hours, until at last she heard his footfall on the decking outside. She cracked open her eyelids as the sliding door swooshed open and she saw his silhouette framed in the doorway, big and dark and not dangerous, like she'd always seen him, but strangely sad. He crossed the floor softly, hesitating when he got to the sofa. She could hear him at her feet, hear his troubled breathing.

Come to me, she willed, *pick me up and carry me to bed like you have done before and make love to me.*

And she heard him turn on a sigh and move away. She heard the bathroom door snick closed and she squeezed her eyes shut, wondering what he would do if she sneaked into the bed before he came back; knowing it was futile because he would straightaway head for the sofa.

He didn't need her any more. Or he didn't want her. What did it matter which or both it was? They both hurt like hell. They both hurt like someone had ripped out her heart and torn it to shreds and trampled on the pieces.

Could injured pride feel this bad? Could a miffed ego tear out your heart and rip it to shreds? Or had she been kidding herself and it had been Maureen who had been right all along?

Oh god, surely she hadn't fallen in love with Leo?

And yet all along she had known it was a risk, the greater risk; had known the possibility was there, the possibility to be drawn deeper and deeper under his spell until she could not bear the thought of being without him. All along she had known he had a heart of stone and still she had managed to do the unthinkable.

She'd fallen in love with him.

She lay there in the semi-gloom, the once silvery light of the moon now a dull grey, listening to him climb into bed, listening to him toss and turn and sigh, wishing him peace, even if he couldn't find it with her.

The scream woke him and he stilled with fear, hoping he'd imagined it. But then he heard the shouting, his father's voice, calling his mother those horrible names he didn't understand only to know they must be bad, and he cringed, waiting for the blow that would come at the end of his tirade. Then it came with a thump and his mother made a sound like a football when you kick it on the street and he vomited right there in his bed. He climbed out, weak and shaky, to the sound of his mother's cries, the bitter taste of sick in his mouth.

'*Stamata,*' he cried weakly through his tears, knowing he would be in trouble for messing up his bed, knowing his mother would be angry with him, wanting her to be angry with him so that things might be normal again. '*Stamato to tora.*' Stop it now!

And he pulled the door open and ran out, to see his father's fist raised high over his mother lying prostrate on the floor.

'*Stamato to!*' he screamed, running across the room, lashing out at his father, young fists flying, and earning that raised fist across his jaw as his reward, but not giving up. He couldn't stop, he had to try to make him stop hurting his mother.

He struck out again lashing at his father, but it was his mother who cried out and it made no sense, nor the thump of a body hitting the floor and then a baby screamed somewhere, and he blinked into consciousness, shaking and wet with perspiration, and waking to his own personal nightmare.

She was lying on the floor, looking dazed, tears springing from her eyes and her hand over her mouth where he must have hit her. And Sam screaming from the next room.

And he wanted to help. He knew he should help. He should do something.

But the walls caved in around him, his muscles remained frozen. Because, oh god, he was back in his past. He was back in that mean kitchen, his father shouting, his mother screaming and a child that saw too much.

And he wanted to put his hands over his ears and block it all out.

Oh god.

What had he done?

What had he done?

CHAPTER TWELVE

SHE blnked up at him warily, testing her aching jaw. 'I have to get Sam,' she said, wondering why he just sat there like a statue, wondering if that wild look in his eyes signalled that he was still sleeping, still lost in whatever nightmare had possessed him.

'I hit you,' he said at last, his voice a mere rasp, his skin grey in the moonlight.

'You didn't mean to,' she said, climbing to her feet. 'You were asleep. You were tossing and—'

'I hurt you.'

He had, but right now she was more concerned with the hurt in his eyes. With the raw, savage pain she saw there. And with reassuring her son, whose cries were escalating. 'It was an accident. You didn't mean it.'

'I warned you!'

'I have to see to Sam. Excuse me.' She rushed around the bed to the dressing room and her distraught child, his tear streaked face giving licence for her own tears to fall. 'Oh Sam,' she whispered, kissing his tear stained cheek, pushing back the damp hair from his brow and clutching him tightly to her as she rocked him against her body. 'It's all right, baby,' she soothed, trying to believe it. 'It's going to be all right.'

She heard movement outside, things bumping and

drawers being opened, but she dared not look, not until she felt her son's body relax against her, his whimpers slowly steadying. She waited a while, just to be sure, and then she kissed his brow and laid him back down in his cot.

And then she stood there a while longer, looking down at her child, his cheek softly illuminated in the moonlight, while she wondered what to do.

What did you do when your heart was breaking for a man who didn't want family? Who didn't want your love?

What could you do?

'What are you doing?' she asked when she emerged, watching Leo stashing clothes in a bag.

'I can't do this. I can't do this to you.'

'You can't do what to me?'

'I don't want to hurt you.'

'Leo, you were in the midst of a nightmare. I got too close. You didn't know I was there.'

He pulled open another drawer, extracted its contents. 'No. I know who I am. I know what I am. Pack your things, we're leaving.'

'No. I'm not going anywhere. Not before you tell me what's going on.'

'I can't do this,' he said in his frenzied state, 'to you and Sam.'

She sat on the bed and put a hand to her forehead, stunned, while he opened another drawer, threw out more clothes. 'You're not making any sense.'

'It makes perfect sense!'

'No! It makes no sense at all! Why are you doing this? Because of a nightmare, because you accidentally lashed out and struck me?'

He walked stiffly up the bed, his chest heaving. 'Don't you understand, Evelyn, or Eve, or whoever you are, if I can do that to you asleep, how much more damage can I do when I am awake?'

And despite the cold chill in his words, she stood up and faced him, because she knew him well enough by now to know he was wrong. 'You wouldn't hit me.'

'You don't know that!' he cried, 'Nobody can know that,' giving her yet another hint of the anguish assailing him.

And Eve knew what she had to say; knew what she had to do; knew that she had to be brave. She moved closer, slowly, stopping before she reached him, but wanting to be close enough that he could see the truth of her words reflected on her face in the moonlight, close enough that she could pick up his hand and hold it to her chest so that he might feel her heart telling him the same message.

'I know it, because I've been with you Leo. I've spent nights filled with passion in your bed. I've spent days when you made me feel more alive than I have in my entire life. And I've seen the way you pulled my child from the sea when you saw him fall into the surf before I did. I know you would never harm him.'

She shook her head, amazed that she was about to confess something so very, very new; so very, very precious and tender, before she had even time to pull it out and examine it for all its flaws and weaknesses in private herself.

'Don't you see? I know it, Leo, because—' She sucked in air, praying for strength in order to confess her foolishness. Because hadn't he warned her not to get involved? Hadn't he told her enough times nothing could come of their liaison? But how else could she reach him? How else could she make him understand? 'Damn it, I know it because I love you.'

He looked down at her, his bleak eyes filled with some kind of terror before he shut them down, and she wondered what kind of hell she would see when he opened them again.

'Don't say that. You mustn't say that.' His words squeezed through his teeth, a cold, hard stiletto of pain that tore at her psyche, ripping into the fabric of her soul. But while it terrified her, at the same time she felt empowered. After all, what did she have left to lose? She'd already admitted the worst, she'd already laid her cards on the table. There was nothing left but to fight for this fledgling love, to defend it, and to defend her right to it.

'Why can't I say it, when it's the truth? And I know it's futile and pointless but it's there. I love you, Leo. Get used to it.'

'No! Saying I love you doesn't make everything all right. Saying I love you doesn't make it okay to beat someone.'

But he hadn't—

And suddenly a rush of cold drenching fear flooded down her spine along with the realisation that he wasn't talking about what had just taken place in this room. And whatever he had witnessed, it was violent and brutal and had scarred him deeply. 'What happened to you to make you believe yourself capable of these things? What horrors were you subjected to that won't let you rest at night?'

'The nightmares are a warning,' he said. 'A warning not to let this happen, and I won't. Not if it means hurting you and Sam.'

'But Leo—'

'Pack your things,' he said simply, sounding defeated. 'I'm taking you home.'

Melbourne was doing what it knew best, she thought as they touched down, offering up a bit of everything, the runway still damp from the latest shower, a bit of wind to tinker with the wings and liven up the landing and the sun peeping out behind a gilt edged cloud.

But it was so good to be home.

He insisted on driving her—or rather, having his driver drive them—and she wondered why he bothered coming along if he was going to be so glum and morose, unless it was so he could be sure she was gone.

And then they were there. At her house she had until now affectionately referred to as the hovel and never would again, because it was a home, a real home and it was hers and Sam's and filled with love and she was proud of it.

'Let me help you out,' Leo said and she wanted to tell him there was no need, that the driver would help unload and that she could manage, but there were bags and bags and a child seat and a sleeping Sam to carry inside, and it would have been churlish to refuse, and so she let him help.

Except what was she supposed to do with a billionaire in her house?

She had Sam on her hip, heavy with sleep, head lolling and clearly needing his cot while Leo deposited the last of her bags and her car seat, looking around him, looking like the world had suddenly been shrink wrapped and was too small for him. What on earth would he think of her tiny house and eclectic furniture after his posh hotels and private jet?

'Thank you,' she said, her heart heavy, not wanting to say goodbye but not wanting to delay the inevitable as clearly he looked for an exit. 'For everything.'

'It wouldn't work,' he offered, with a thumb to the place he knew he'd hurt her. 'It couldn't.'

She leaned into his touch, trying to hold it for as long as she possibly could, trying to imprint this very last touch on her memory. 'You don't know that,' she said. 'And now you'll never know.'

'There are things—' he started, before shaking his head, his eyes sad. 'It doesn't matter. I know there is no way…'

'You know nothing,' she said, pulling away, stronger now for simply being home, by being back in her own environment, with her own bookshelves and ancient sofa and even her own faded rugs. 'But I do. I know how you'll end up if you walk out that door, if you turn your back on me and my love.

'You'll be like that old man in the picture in your suite, the old man sitting hunched and all alone on the park bench, staring out over the river and wondering whether he should have taken a chance, whether he should have taken that risk rather than playing it safe, rather than ending up all alone.

'You will be that man, Leo.'

He looked at her, his eyes bleak, his jaw set. He lifted a hand, put it one last time to Sam's head.

'Goodbye, Evelyn.'

CHAPTER THIRTEEN

EARLY summer wasn't one whole lot more reliable than spring, Eve reflected, as she looked up at the patchy blue sky, determined to risk the clothes line rather than using the dryer. Any savings on the electricity bill would be welcome. She'd picked up a couple of new clients recently, but things were still tight if she didnt want to dip into her savings.

Although of course, there was always the ring…

She'd taken it off in the plane, meaning to give it back to Leo but she'd forgotten in those gut wrenching final moments and he'd always said it was hers. Every day since then she checked her emails to see if he'd sent her some small message. Every time she found a recorded message, she punched the play button hoping, always hoping.

And after two weeks when he'd made no contact, out of spite or frustration or grief, she'd taken the ring to a jewellery shop to have it valued, staggered when she found out how much it was worth.

She wouldn't have to scrimp if she sold it.

But that had been nearly a month back and she hadn't been able to bring herself to do it.

Six weeks, she thought, as she pegged the first of her sheets to the line. Six weeks since that night in his suite, since that weekend in paradise. No wonder it seemed like a dream.

'Nice day,' called Mrs Willis, from over the fence. 'Reckon it'll rain later though.'

She glanced up at the sky, scowling at an approaching bank of cloud. 'Probably. How's Jack lately?'

'Going okay since they changed his meds. Sister reckons he's on the improve.' Her neighbour looked around. 'Where's Sam?'

'Just gone down for a nap,' Eve said, pegging up another sheet. 'Should be good for a couple of hours work.'

'Oh,' the older woman said. 'Speaking of work, there's someone out the front to see you. Some posh looking bloke in a suit. Fancy car. Says he tried your door, but no answer. I told him I thought you were home though. I told him—'

Something like a lightning bolt surged down her spine. 'What did you say?' But she was already on her way, the sheets snapping in the breeze behind her. She touched a hand to the hair she'd tied back in a rough ponytail, then told herself off for even thinking it. Why did she immediately think it could be him? For all she knew it could be a courier delivery from one of her clients, although since when did courier drivers dress in posh suits and drive flash cars? Her heart tripping at a million miles an hour, nerves flapping and snapping like the sheets on the line, she allowed herself one deep breath, and then she opened the door.

There he stood. Gloriously, absolutely Leo, right there on her doorstep. He looked just as breathtakingly beautiful, his shoulders as broad, his hair so rich and dark and his eyes, his dark eyes looked different, there was sorrow there and pain, and something else swirling in the mix—hope?

And her heart felt it must be ten times its normal size the way it was clamouring around in there. But she'd had hopes before, had thought she'd seen cracks develop in his stone heart, and those hopes had been dashed.

'Leo,' she said breathlessly.

'Eve. You look good.'

She didn't look good. She had circles under her eyes, her hair was a mess and Mrs Willis had been on at her about losing too much weight. 'You look better.' And she winced, because it sounded so lame.

He looked around her legs. 'Where's Sam?'

'Nap time,' she said, and he nodded.

'Can I come in?'

'Oh.' She stood back, let him in. 'Of course.'

He looked just as awkward in her living room. 'I'll make coffee,' she suggested when he grabbed her hand, sending an electrical charge up her arm.

'No. I have to explain something first, Eve, if you will listen. I need you to listen, to understand.'

She nodded, afraid to speak.

He took a deep breath once they were sitting on the sofa, his elbows using his knees for props as he held out his hands. 'I was not happy when I left you. I went to London, threw myself into the contract negotiations there; then to Rome and New York, and nowhere, nowhere could I forget you, nothing I could do, nothing I could achieve could blot out the thoughts of you.

'But I could not come back. I knew it could not work. But there was something I could do.'

She held her breath, her body tingling. Hoping.

'I hadn't seen my parents since I was twelve. I had to find them. It took— It took a little while to track them down, and then it was to discover my father was dead.'

She put a hand to his and he shook his head. 'Don't feel sorry. He was a sailor and a brutal, violent man. Everytime he was on leave he used my mother as a punching bag, calling her all sorts of vicious names, beating her senseless. I used to cower in fear behind my door, praying for it to stop. I was glad he was dead.'

He dragged in air. 'And the worst part of it—the worst of it was that he was always so full of remorse afterwards. Always telling her he was sorry, and that he loved her, even as she lay bruised and bleeding on the floor.'

Eve felt something crawl down her spine. A man who couldn't let himself love. A man who equated love with a beating. No wonder he felt broken inside. No wonder he was so afraid. 'Your poor mother,' she said, thinking, poor you.

He made a sound like a laugh, but utterly tragic. 'Poor mother. I thought so too. Until I was big enough to grow fists and hurt him like he hurt my mother. And my mother went to him. After everything he had done to her, she screamed at me and she went to him to nurse his wounds.' He dropped his head down, wrapped his arms over his head and breathed deep, shaking his head as he rose. 'She would not leave him, even when I begged and pleaded with her. She would not go. So I did. I slept at school. Friends gave me food. I got a job emptying rubbish bins. I begged on the streets. And it was the happiest I'd ever been.'

'Oh, Leo,' she said, thinking of the homeless child, no home to go to, no family…

'I left school a year later, went to work on the boats around the harbour. But I would not be a sailor like him, at that stage I didn't want to be Greek like him. So I learned from the people around me, speaking their languages, and started handling deals for people.

'I was good at it. I could finally make something of myself. But even though I could escape my world, I could not escape my past. I could not escape who I was. The shadow of my father was too big. The knowledge of what I would become…' His voice trailed off. 'I swore I would never let that happen to me. I would never love.'

She slipped a hand into one of his, felt his pain and his sorrow and his grieving. 'I'm so sorry it had to be that way for you. You should have had better.'

'Sam is blessed,' he said, shaking his head. 'Sam has a mother who fights for him like a tigress. His mother is warm and strong and filled with sunshine.' He lifted her hand, pressed it to his lips. 'Not like…'

And his words warmed her heart, even when she knew there was more he had to tell her. 'Did you find her then? Did you find your mother?'

His eyes were empty black, his focus nowhere, but someplace deep inside himself. 'She's in a home for battered women, broken and ill. She sits in a wheelchair all day looking out over a garden. She has nothing now, no-one. And as I looked at her, I remembered the words you said, about an old man sitting on a parkbench, staring at nothing, wishing he'd taking a chance…'

'Leo, I should never have said that. I had no right. I was hurting.'

'But you were right. When I looked at her, I saw my future, and for the first time, I was afraid. I didn't want it. Instead I wanted to take that chance that you offered me, like she should have taken that chance with me and escaped. But my father's shadow still loomed over me.

My greatest fear was turning into him. Hurting you or Sam. I could not bear that.'

'You're not like that,' she said, tears squeezing from her eyes. 'You would never do that.'

'I couldn't trust myself to believe it. Until I was about to leave my mother's side and she told me the truth in her cracked and bitter voice, the truth that would have set me free so many years ago, but I never questioned what I had grown up believing. The truth that my father had come home after six months at sea and found her four months pregnant.'

'Leo!'

His eyes were bright and that tiny kernel of hope she'd seen there while he'd stood on her doorstep had flickered and flared into something much more powerful. 'He was impotent and she wanted a child and I was never his, Eve. I don't have to be that way. I don't have to turn into him.'

Tears blurred her vision, tears for the lost childhood, tears for the betrayal of trust between the parents and the child, the absence of a love that should have been his birthright. 'You would never have turned into him. I know.'

And he brought her hands to his lips and kissed them. 'You do things to me, Eve. You turn me inside out and upside down and I want to be with you, but I just don't know if I can do this. I don't know if I can love the way I should. The way you deserve.'

'Of course you can. It's been there, all along. You knew what was happening was wrong. You tried to save your mother. You tried to save me and Sam by cutting us loose. Because you didn't want to hurt us. You would never have done that if you hadn't cared, if you hadn't loved us, just a little.'

'I think...' He gave her a look that spoke of his confusion and fears. 'I think it's more than a little. These last weeks have been hell. I never want to be apart from you again. I want to wake up every morning and see your face next to mine. I want to take care of you and Sam, if you'll let me.'

She blinked across at him, unable to believe what she was hearing, but so desperately wanting it to be true. 'What are you saying?'

'I can't live without you. I need you.' He squeezed her hands, just as he squeezed the unfamiliar words from his lips. 'I love you.'

And she flew into his arms, big, fat tears of happiness welling in her eyes. 'Oh Leo, I love you so much.'

'Oh my god, that's such a relief,' he said, clutching her tightly. 'I was afraid you would hate me for how I treated you.' He tugged her back, so he could look at her, brushing the hair from her face where it had got mussed. 'Because there's something else I need to know. Eve, will you take a chance on me. Would you consider becoming my wife?'

And her tears became a flood and she didn't care that she was blubbering, didn't care that she was a mess, only that Leo had loved her and wanted to marry her and life just couldn't get any better than that. 'Yes,' she said, her smile feeling like it was a mile wide, 'Yes, of course I will marry you.'

He pulled her into his kiss, a whirlpool of a kiss that spun her senses and sent her spirits and soul soaring.

'Thank you for coming into my life,' he said, drawing back, breathing hard. 'You are magical, Eve. You have brought happiness and hope to a place where there was only misery and darkness. How can I ever repay you?'

And she smiled up at his beautiful face, knowing he would never again live without love, not if she had anything to do with it. 'You can start by kissing me again.'

EPILOGUE

LEO Zamos loved it when a plan came together. He relished the cut and thrust of business, the negotiations, the sometimes compromise, the closing of the deal.

He lived for the adrenaline rush of the chase, and he lived for the buzz of success.

Or at least he had, until now.

These days he had other priorities.

He shook Culshaw's hand, who was still beaming with the honour of walking Eve down the aisle before leaving him chatting to Mrs Willis about the weather. He looked around and found his new bride standing in the raised gazebo where they'd been married a little while ago. She was holding Sam's hand as Hannah jigged him on her hip, the sapphire ring sparkling on her finger nestled alongside a new matching plain band. Evelyn—Eve—he still couldn't decide which he liked best, had always looked more like a goddess than any mere mortal, but today, in her slim fitting lace gown, her hair piled high and curling in tendrils around her face and pinned with a long gossamer thin veil that danced in the warm tropical breeze, she was the queen of goddesses, and she was his. She laughed as her veil was caught in the breeze, the ends tickling Sam's face and making him squeal with delight. And then, as if aware he was watching, as if feeling the tug of his own hungry gaze, she turned her head, turned those brilliant blue eyes on him, her laughter faltering as their eyes connected on so many different levels before her luscious mouth turned up into a wide smile.

And it was physically impossible for his feet not to take the quickest and most direct route through the guests until he was at her side, his arm snaked around her waist pulling her in tight, taking Sam's free hand with the other.

'How is my beautiful new family enjoying today?'

And Sam pulled both hands free and pointed, 'Boat!'

'Sam is beside himself,' Eve said, as Hannah put him down and let him run to the other side of the gazebo to gaze out between the slats at the sailing boat lazily cruising past the bay.

'Culshaw's the same. Asking him to give you away has made his year, I'd say.'

'I like him,' she said, as they watched him animatedly tell Mrs Willis a story. 'He feels like family to me.'

'Canny old devil,' he said as he folded his arms around her. 'Did I tell you what he said when I tried to apologise and tell him that we hadn't really been engaged that weekend in Melbourne? He actually said, "poppycock, everyone knew you were destined to be together",' and Eve laughed.

'Maureen told me the same thing.'

'And they were right,' he said, drawing her back into the circle of his arms, kissing her lightly on the head. 'You are my destiny, Eve, my beautiful wife.'

'Oh,' she said, turning in the circle of his arms. 'Did you hear the Alvarezes' news?'

He frowned, 'I'm not sure I did.'

'Felicity is pregnant. They're both thrilled. I couldn't be happier.'

He nodded. 'That is good news, but at the risk of trying to make you happier, I have a small present for you.'

'But you've already given me so much.'

'This is special. Culshaw's agreed to sell Mina Island. It's yours now, Evelyn.'

'What?' Her eyes shone bright with incredulity. 'It's mine? Really?'

'Yours and Sam's. Everything of mine is now yours, but this is especially for you both. It's a wedding gift and a thank you gift and an I love you gift all rolled into one. And it guarantees you can bring Sam back when he's older any time you want and show him everything he missed out on now.'

'Oh, Leo,' she said, her eyes bright with tears, 'I don't know what to say. It's too much. I have nothing for you.'

He shook his head. 'It's nowhere near enough. It was here that you gave me the greatest gift of all. You gave me back my heart. You taught me how to love. How can I ever repay you for that?'

She cupped his cheek against her palm, her cereulean eyes filled with love, and he took that hand and pressed his lips upon it. 'I love you, Evelyn Zamos.'

'Oh, Leo, I love you so very, very much.'

They were the words he needed to hear, the words that set his newly unlocked heart soaring. He kissed her then, in the white gazebo covered with sweetly scented flowers, kissed her in the perfumed air as the breeze set the palm tree fronds to rustling and the sail boat gracefully cruised by.

'Boat!' yelled Sam to the sound of wobbly footsteps,

suddenly tugging at their legs, pointing out to sea. 'Boat!'

And laughing, Leo scooped the boy up in his arms and they all gazed out over the sapphire blue water to watch the passing vessel. 'How long, do you think,' he whispered to the woman at his side, 'is the perfect age gap between children?'

She looked up at him on a blink. 'I don't know. Some people say two to three years.'

'In that case,' he said, with a chaste kiss to her forehead and a very unchaste look in his eyes, 'I have a plan.'

* * * * *

THE BRIDE FONSECA NEEDS

ABBY GREEN

CHAPTER ONE

'WELL, WELL, WELL. This *is* interesting. Little Darcy Lennox, in my office, looking for work.'

Darcy curbed the flash of irritation at the not entirely inaccurate reference to her being *little* and fought against the onslaught on her senses from being mere feet away from Maximiliano Fonseca Roselli, separated from him only by an impressive desk. But it was hard. Because he was quite simply as devastatingly gorgeous as he'd always been. More so now, because he was a man. Not the seventeen-year-old boy she remembered. Sex appeal flowed from him like an invisible but heady scent. It made Darcy absurdly aware that underneath all the layers of civility they were just animals.

He was half-Brazilian, half-Italian. Dark blond hair was still unruly and messy—long enough to proclaim that he didn't really give a damn about anything, much less conforming. Although clearly along the way he'd given enough of a damn to become one of Europe's youngest 'billionaire entrepreneurs to watch', according to a leading financial magazine.

Darcy could imagine how any number of women would be only too happy to watch his every sexy move. She did notice one new addition to his almost perfect features, though, and blurted out before she could stop herself, 'You have a scar.'

It snaked from his left temple to his jaw in a jagged line and had the effect of making him even more mysterious and brooding.

The man under her close scrutiny arched one dark blond brow and drawled, 'Your powers of observation are clearly in working order.'

Darcy flushed at being so caught out. Since when had she been gauche enough to refer to someone's physical appearance? He had stood to greet her when she'd walked into his palatial office, situated in the centre of Rome, and she was still standing too, beginning to feel hot in her trouser suit, hot under the tawny green gaze that had captivated her the first time she'd ever seen him.

He folded his arms across his chest and her eye was drawn helplessly to where impressive muscles bunched against the fine material of his open-necked white shirt, sleeves rolled up. And even though he wore smart dark trousers he looked anything but civilised. That gaze was too knowing, too cynical, for *politesse*.

'So, what's a fellow alumna from Boissy le Château doing looking for work as a PA?' Before she could answer he was adding, with the faintest of sneers to his tone, 'I would have thought you'd be married into European aristrocracy by now, and producing a gaggle of heirs like every other girl in that anachronistic medieval institution.'

Pinned under that golden gaze, she regretted the moment she'd ever thought it might be a good idea to apply for the job advertised on a very select applications board. And she hated to think that a part of her had been curious to see Max Fonseca Roselli Fonseca again.

She replied, 'I was only at Boissy for another year after

you left…' She faltered then, thinking of a lurid memory of Max beating another boy outside in the snow, and the bright stain of blood against the pristine white. She pushed it down. 'My father was badly affected by the recession so I went back to England to finish my schooling.'

She didn't think it worth mentioning that that schooling had taken place in a comprehensive school, which she would have chosen any day over the oppressive atmosphere of Boissy.

Max made a sound of faux commiseration. 'So Darcy *didn't* get to be the belle of the ball in Paris with all the other debutantes?'

She gritted her jaw at his reference to the exclusive annual Bal des Débutantes; she was no belle of any ball. She knew Max hadn't had a good time at Boissy, but she hadn't been one of his antagonists. Anything but. She cringed inwardly now when she recalled another vivid memory, from not long after he'd first arrived. Darcy had come upon two guys holding Max back, with another about to punch him in the belly. Without even thinking, she'd rushed into the fray, screaming, *'Stop!'*

Heat climbed inside her at the thought that he might remember that too.

'No,' she responded tightly. 'I didn't go to the ball in Paris. I sat my A levels and then got a degree in languages and business from London University, as you'll see from my CV.'

Which was laid out on his desk.

This had been a huge mistake.

'Look, I saw your name come up on the applications board—that you're looking for a PA. I probably shouldn't have come.' Darcy reached down to where she'd put her briefcase by her feet and picked it up.

Max was frowning at her. 'Do you want a job or not?'

Darcy felt tetchy with herself for having been so impetuous, and irritated with Max for being so bloody gorgeous and distracting. *Still.* So she said, more snippily than she'd intended, 'Of course I want a job. I *need* a job.'

Max's frown deepened. 'Did your parents lose everything?'

She bristled at the implication that she was looking for work because her family wasn't funding her any more. 'No, thankfully my father was able to recover.' And then she said tartly, 'Believe it or not, I like to make my own living.'

Max made some kind of a dismissive sound, as if he didn't quite believe her, and Darcy bit her lip in order to stay quiet. She couldn't exactly blame him for his assumption, but unlike the other alumnae of their school she *didn't* expect everything in life to be handed to her.

Those mesmerising eyes were looking at her far too closely now and Darcy became excruciatingly conscious of her dark hair, pulled back into a ponytail, her diminutive stature and the unfashionably full figure she'd long ago given up any hope of minimising, choosing instead to work with what she had.

Max rapped out in Italian, 'You're fluent in Italian?'

Darcy blinked, but quickly replied in the same language. 'Yes. My mother is from just outside Rome. I've been bilingual since I learnt how to talk and I'm also fluent in Spanish, German and French. And I have passable Chinese.'

He flicked a look at her CV and then looked back, switching to English again. 'It says here that you've been in Brussels for the past five years—is that where you're based?'

Darcy's insides tightened at his direct question, as if warding off a blow. The truth was that she hadn't really had a base since her parents had split up when she was eight and they'd sold off the family home. They'd shuttled her between schools and wherever they'd been living which had changed constantly, due to her father's work and her mother's subsequent relationships.

She'd learnt that the only constant she could depend on was herself and her ability to forge a successful career, cocooning her from the pillar-to-post feeling she hated so much and the vagaries of volatile relationships.

She answered Max. 'I don't have a base at the moment, so I'm free to go where the work is.'

Once again that incisive gaze was on her. Darcy hated the insecurity that crept up on her at the thought that he might be assessing how she'd turned out, judging her against the svelte supermodel types he was always photographed with. Beside them, at five foot two, Darcy would look like a baby elephant! In weak moments over the years she'd seen Max on the covers of gossip magazines and had picked them up to read the salacious content. And it had always been salacious.

When she'd read about his three-in-a-bed romp with two Russian models she'd flung the magazine into a trash can, disgusted with herself.

He suddenly stuck out his hand. 'I'll give you a two-week trial, starting tomorrow. Do you have accommodation sorted?'

Darcy blanched. *He was offering her the job?* Her head was still filled with lurid images of pouting blonde glamazons, crawling all over Max's louche form. Reacting reflexively, she put out her hand to meet his and suddenly was engulfed in heat as his long fingers curled around hers.

He took his hand away abruptly and glanced at a

fearsome-looking watch, then back to her, a little impatiently.

Darcy woke up. 'Um…yes, I have somewhere to stay for a few days.' She repressed a small grimace when she thought of the very basic hostel in one of Rome's busier tourist districts.

Max nodded. 'Good. If I keep you on then we'll get you something more permanent.'

They looked at each other as Darcy's mind boggled at the thought of working with him.

Then he said pointedly, 'I have a meeting now, I'll see you tomorrow at nine a.m. We'll go through everything then.'

Darcy quickly picked up her briefcase and backed away. 'Okay, then, tomorrow.' She walked to the door and then turned around again. 'You're not just doing this because we know each other…?'

Max had his hands on his hips. He was beginning to look slightly impatient. 'No, Darcy. That's coincidental. You're the most qualified person I've seen for the job, your references are impeccable, and after dealing with a slew of PAs—gay and straight—who all seem to think that seducing the boss is an unwritten requirement of the job it'll be a relief to deal with someone who knows the boundaries.'

Darcy didn't like the fact that it stung her somewhere very deep and secret to think that Max would dismiss her ability to seduce him so summarily, but before she could acknowledge how inappropriate that was she muttered something incoherent and left before she could make a complete ass of herself.

Max watched the space where the door had just closed, rendered uncharacteristically still for a moment. Darcy

Lennox. Her name on his list of potential PAs had been a jolt out of the blue, as had the way her face had sprung back into his mind with vivid recollection as soon as he'd seen her name. He doubted he could pick many of his ex-classmates out of a police line-up, and Darcy hadn't even been in his year.

But, as small and unassuming as she had been, and some four years behind him, she seemed to have made some kind of lingering impact. It wasn't an altogether comfortable realisation for a man who regularly excised people from his life with little regret, whether they were lovers or business associates he was done with.

Her eyes were still seared into his mind—huge and blue, a startling contrast to that pale olive complexion, obviously inherited from her Italian mother.

Max cursed himself. *Startling?* He ran a hand through his hair, leaving it even messier. He was running on fumes of exhaustion since returning from a trip to Brazil a couple of days ago, and quite frankly it would be a relief to have someone working for him who *wouldn't* feel the need to see him as a challenge akin to scaling a sexual Everest.

Darcy Lennox exuded common sense and practicality. Dependability. The fact that she had also been in Boissy, even if her time had been cut short, meant that she knew her place and would never overstep the mark. Not like his last assistant, who had been waiting for him one morning, sitting in his chair, dressed only in one of his shirts.

He tried for a moment to conjure up a similar image featuring Darcy. but all he could see was her serious face and her smart, structured shirt and skirt, the tidy glossy hair. A sense of relief infused him. Finally an assistant who would not distract him from the deal of a lifetime.

A deal that would set him up as a serious player in the very competitive world of global finance.

Quite frankly, this was the best thing that had happened to him in weeks. Darcy would meld seamlessly into the background while performing her duties with skill and efficiency. Of that he had no doubt. Her CV was a glowing testament to her abilities.

He picked up the phone to speak to his temp and when she answered said curtly, 'Send all the other applicants away, Miss Lennox is starting tomorrow.'

He didn't even bother to reiterate the two-week trial caveat, so confident was he that he'd made the right decision.

Three months later

'Darcy, get in here—*now*!'

Darcy rolled her eyes at the bellowed order and got up from behind her desk, smoothing down her skirt as she did so. When she walked into Max's office and saw him pacing back and forth behind his desk she cursed the little jolt she always got in her solar plexus when she looked at him.

Virile, masculine energy crackled in the air around him. She put her uncomfortable reaction down to the fact that any being with a pulse would be incapable of *not* responding to his charisma.

He turned and locked that dark golden gaze onto her and snapped out, 'Well? Don't just stand there—come in.'

Darcy had learnt that the way to deal with Max Fonseca Roselli was to treat him like an arrogant thoroughbred stallion. With the utmost respect and caution and a healthy dollop of firm-handedness.

'There is no need to shout,' she said calmly. 'I'm right outside your door.'

She came in and perched on the chair on the other side of his desk and looked at him, awaiting instruction. She had to admit that, while his manners could do with finessing, working for Max was the most exhilarating experience of her life. It was a challenge just to keep up with his quicksilver intellect, and she'd already learnt more from him than she had in all of her previous jobs combined.

Shortly after starting to work for him he'd installed her in a luxurious flat near the office at a ridiculously low rent. He'd waved her protests away, saying, 'I don't need to be worrying about you living in a bad area, and I will require you to be available to work out of hours sometimes, so it's for my convenience as much as yours.'

That had shut Darcy up. He was putting her there so she was more accessible to him—not out of any sense of concern because she was on her own in a city she didn't know as well as she might, considering her mother's Italian background. Still, she couldn't complain, and had enjoyed the chance to have a central base from which to explore Rome.

Max had been true to his word. She'd found herself working late plenty of evenings and on some Saturdays for half the day. His work ethic was intimidating, to say the least.

He rapped out now, 'What was Montgomery's response?'

Darcy didn't have to consult her notes. 'He wants you to meet him for dinner when he's here with his wife next week.'

Max's face hardened. 'Damn him. I'd bet money that

the wily old man is enjoying every moment of drawing this out for as long as possible.'

Watching his hands, splayed on his slim hips, Darcy found it hard to focus for a second, but she forced her gaze back up and had to acknowledge that this *was* unusual. Most people Max dealt with knew better than to refuse him what he wanted.

His mouth was tight as he spoke almost to himself. 'Montgomery doesn't think I'm suitable to take control of his hedge fund. I'm an unknown, I don't come with a blue-blooded background, but worst of all, in his eyes, I'm not respectably married.'

No, you certainly are not, Darcy observed frigidly to herself, thinking of the recent weekend Max had spent in the Middle East, visiting his exotically beautiful lover, a high-profile supermodel. A little churlishly Darcy imagined them having lots of exotically beautiful babies together, with tawny eyes, dark hair and long legs.

'Darcy.'

She flushed, caught out. Surely working with someone every day should inure you to his presence? Not make it worse?

'It's just dinner, Max, not a test,' she pointed out calmly.

He paced back and forth, which threatened Darcy's focus *again*, but she kept her eyeline resolutely up.

'Of course it's a test,' he said now, irritably. 'Why do you think he wants me to meet his wife?'

'Maybe he just wants to get to know you better? After all, he's potentially asking you to manage one of the oldest and most illustrious fortunes in Europe and his family's legacy.'

Max snorted. 'Montgomery will have already deemed me suitable or unsuitable—a man like that has nothing left to do in life except amuse himself and play people off each other like pawns.'

He raked a hand through unruly hair, a familiar gesture by now, and Darcy felt slightly breathless for a moment. And then, angry at her reaction to him, she said with not a little exasperation, 'So take…' She stopped for a moment, wondering how best to describe his mistress and settled for the most diplomatic option. 'Take Noor to dinner and persuade Montgomery that you're in a settled relationship.'

Max's expression turned horrified. 'Take Noor al-Fasari to dinner with Montgomery? Are you *mad*?'

Darcy frowned, and didn't like the way something inside her jumped a little at seeing Max's reaction to her suggestion. 'Why not? She's your lover, and she's beautiful, accomplished—'

Max waved a hand, cutting Darcy off. 'She's spoilt, petulant, avaricious—and in any case she's no longer my lover.'

Darcy had to battle to keep her face expressionless as this little bombshell hit. Evidently the papers hadn't yet picked up on this nugget of information, and he certainly didn't confide his innermost secrets to her.

She looked at Max as guilelessly as she could. 'That's a pity. She sounds positively delightful.'

He made that dismissive snorting sound again and said, with a distinct edge to his voice, 'I choose my lovers for myriad reasons, Darcy, not one of which I've ever considered is because they're *delightful*.'

No, he chose them because they were the most beautiful women in the world, and because he could have whoever he wanted.

For a moment Darcy couldn't look away from Max's gaze, caught by something inexplicable, and she felt heat start to climb up her body. And then his phone rang. She broke the intense, unsettling eye contact and stretched across to answer it, then pressed the 'hold' button.

'It's the Sultan of Al-Omar.'

Max reached for the phone. 'I'll take it.'

Darcy stood up with not a little sense of relief and walked out, aware of Max's deep voice as he greeted his friend and one of his most important clients.

When she closed the door behind her she leaned back against it for a moment. What had that look been about? She'd caught Max staring at her a few times lately, with something unreadable in his expression, and each time it had made her silly pulse speed up.

She gritted her jaw as she sat down behind her desk and cursed herself for a fool if she thought for a second that Max ever looked at her with anything more than professional interest.

It wasn't as if she even *wanted* him to look at her with anything more than professional interest. She was not about to jeopardise the best job of her career by mooning about after him like she had at school, when she'd been in the throes of a very embarrassing pubescent crush.

Max finished his call with his friend and stood up to look out of his office window, feeling restless. The window framed an impressive view of Rome's ancient ruins—something that usually soothed him with its timelessness. But not right now.

Sultan Sadiq of Al-Omar was just one of Max's very small inner circle of friends who had given up the heady days of being a bachelor to settle down. He'd broken off their conversation just now when his wife had come into his office with their toddler son, whom Max had heard gabbling happily in the background. Sadiq had confided just before that they were expecting baby number two in a few months, and happiness had been evident in his friend's voice.

Max might have ribbed him before. But something about that almost tangible contentment and his absorption in his family had made him feel uncharacteristically hollow.

Memories of his brother's recent wedding in Rio de Janeiro came back to him. He and his brother weren't close. Not after a lifetime spent living apart—the legacy of warring parents who'd lived on different continents. But Max had gone to the wedding—more because of the shared business concerns he had with his brother than any great need to 'connect'.

If he had ever had anything in common with his brother apart from blood it had been a very ingrained sense of cynicism. But that cynicism had all but disappeared from his brother's eyes as he'd looked adoringly at his new wife.

Max sighed volubly, forcibly wiping the memory from his mind. Damn this introspection. Since when did he feel *hollow* and give his brother and his new wife a moment's consideration?

He frowned and brooded over the view. He was a loner, and he'd been a loner since he'd taken responsibility for his actions as a young boy and realised that he had no one to turn to but himself.

And yet he had to concede, with some amount of irritation, that watching his peers fall by the wayside into domesticity was beginning to make him stand out by comparison. The prospect of going to dinner with Montgomery and his wife was becoming more and more unappealing, and Max was certain that the old man was determined to use it as an opportunity to demonstrate his unsuitability.

At that moment Max thought of Darcy's suggestion that he take his ex-lover to dinner. For some reason he found himself thinking not so much of Noor but of Darcy's huge blue eyes. And the way colour had flared in her cheeks when he'd told her what he thought of that suggestion.

He found himself comparing the two women and surmised with some level of grim humour that they couldn't be more different.

Noor al-Fasari was without a doubt one of the most beautiful women in the world. And yet when Max tried to visualise her face now he found that it was amorphous—hard to recall.

And Darcy… Max frowned. He'd been about to assert that she *wasn't* beautiful, but it surprised him to realise that, while she certainly didn't share Noor's show-stopping, almost outlandish looks, Darcy was more than just pretty or attractive.

And, in fairness, her job was not to promote what beauty she did possess. Suddenly Max found himself wondering what she would be like dressed more enticingly, and with subtle make-up to enhance those huge eyes and soft rosebud lips.

Much to his growing sense of horror, he found that her voluptuous figure came to mind as easily as if she was still walking out of his office, as she'd done only minutes before. He might have fooled himself that he'd been engrossed in the conversation with his friend, but in reality his eyes had been glued to the provocative way Darcy's pencil skirt clung to her full hips, and how the shiny leather belt drew the eye to a waist so small he fancied he might span it with one hand.

His skin prickled. It was almost as if an awareness of her had been growing stealthily in his subconscious for the past few months. And as if to compound this unsettling revelation he found the blood in his body growing heated and flowing south, to a part of his anatomy that was behaving in a manner that was way out of his usual sense of control.

Almost in shock, Max sat down, afraid that Darcy might walk in and catch him in this moment of confusion and not a little irritation at his wayward responses.

It was the memory of his ex-lover that had precipitated this random lapse in control. It had to be. But when he tried to conjure up Noor's face again, with a sense of desperation, all he could recall were the shrill shrieks she'd hurled his way—along with an expensive vase or two—after he'd told her their affair was over.

A brief knock came to his door and Darcy didn't wait before opening it to step inside. 'I'm heading home now, in case you want anything else?'

And just like that Max's blood sizzled in earnest. A floodgate had been opened and now all he could see was her glossy dark brown hair, neatly tied back. Along with her provocative curves. Full breasts thrust against her silk shirt. The tiny waist. Womanly hips, firm thighs and shapely calves. Small ankles. And this was all in a package a couple of inches over five feet. When Max had never before found petite women particularly attractive.

She wasn't even dressed to seduce. She was the epitome of classic style.

He couldn't fault her—not for one thing. Yet all he could think about doing right now was walking over to her and hauling her up against his hot and aching body. And, for a man who wasn't used to denying his urges when it came to women, he found himself floundering.

What the hell…? Was he going crazy?

Darcy frowned. 'Is there something wrong, Max?'

'Wrong?' he barked, feeling slightly desperate. 'Nothing is wrong.'

'Oh,' said Darcy. 'Well, then, why are you scowling at me?'

Max thought of the upcoming dinner date with Montgomery and his wife and imagined sitting between them like a reluctant gooseberry. He made a split-second decision. 'I was just thinking about the dinner with Montgomery…'

Darcy raised a brow. 'Yes?'

Feeling grim, Max said, 'You're coming with me.'

She straightened up at the door. 'Oh.' She looked nonplussed for a moment, and then said, 'Is that really appropriate?'

Max finally felt as if he had his recalcitrant body under some kind of control and stood up, putting his hands in his pockets. 'Yes, it's highly appropriate. You've been working on this deal with me and I'll need you there to keep track of the conversation and make nice with Montgomery's wife.'

Darcy was clearly reluctant. 'Don't you think that perhaps someone else might be more—?'

Max took one hand out of his pocket and held it up. 'I don't want any further discussion about this matter. You're coming with me—that's it.'

Darcy looked at him with those huge blue eyes and for a dizzying moment Max felt as if she could see all the way down into the depths of his being. And then the moment broke when she shrugged lightly and said, 'Okay, fine. Anything else you need this evening?'

He had a sudden vivid image of ripping her shirt open,

to see her lush breasts encased in silk and satin, and got out a strangled-sounding, 'No, you can go.'

To his blessed relief, she did go. He ran both hands through his hair with frustration. Ordinarily Max would have taken this rogue reaction as a clear sign that he should go out and seek a new lover, but he knew that the last thing he needed right now in the run-up to the final negotiations with Montgomery was for him to be at the centre of headlines speculating about his colourful love-life.

So for now he was stuck in the throes of lusting after his very capable PA—an impossible situation that Max felt some god somewhere had engineered just for his own amusement.

CHAPTER TWO

A WEEK LATER Darcy was still mulling over the prospect of going to the Montgomery dinner the following evening with Max. She assured herself again that she was being ridiculous to feel so reluctant. Lots of PAs accompanied their bosses on social occasions that blurred into work.

So why was it that her pulse seemed to step up a gear when she thought about being out in public with Max, in a social environment?

Because she was an idiot. She scowled at herself and almost jumped out of her skin when Max yelled her name from inside his office. If anything, his curtness over the last week should have eased her concerns. He certainly wasn't giving her the remotest indication that there was anything but business on his mind.

She got up and hurried into his office, schooling her face into a neutral expression. As always, though, as soon as she laid eyes on him her insides clenched in reaction.

He was pacing back and forth, angry energy sparking. She sighed inwardly. This protracted deal was starting to wear on *her* nerves too.

She sat down and waited patiently, and then Max rounded on her and glared at her so fiercely her eyes widened with reproach. 'What did I do?'

He snapped his gaze away and bit out, 'Nothing. It's not you. It's—'

'Montgomery,' Darcy said flatly.

He looked at her again and his silence told her succinctly that that was exactly what it was.

'I'll need you to work late this evening. I want to make sure that when we meet him tomorrow I'm not giving him one single reason to doubt my ability.'

Darcy shrugged. 'Sure thing.'

Max put his hands on his hips, a look of determination stamped on his gorgeous features. 'Okay, clear the schedule of anything else today and let's take out everything to do with this deal. I want to go through it all with a fine-tooth comb.'

Darcy got up and mentally braced herself for a gruelling day ahead.

Much later that evening Darcy sat back on her heels in Max's office and arched her spine, with her hands on the small of her back. Her shoes had come off hours ago and they'd eaten take-out.

It had to be close to midnight when Max finally said wearily, 'That's it, isn't it? We've been through every file, memo and e-mail. Checked into the man's entire history and all his business endeavours.'

Darcy smiled wryly and reached up to tuck some escaping hair back into her chignon. 'I think it's safe to say that we could write an authorised biography on Cecil Montgomery now.'

The dark night outside made Max's office feel like a cocoon. They were surrounded by the soft glow of numerous lights. He didn't respond and she looked up at him where he stood behind his desk, shirt open at the throat and sleeves rolled up. In spite of that he barely looked rumpled—whereas she felt as if she'd been dragged through a hedge backwards and was in dire need of a long, relaxing bath.

He was looking at her with a strange expression, as if caught for a moment, and it made Darcy's pulse skip. She felt self-conscious, aware of how she'd just been stretching like a cat. But then the moment passed and he moved and went over to the bar, his loose-limbed grace evident even after the day's hard slog. Darcy envied him. As *she* stood up her bones and joints protested. She told herself she was being ridiculous to imagine that Max was looking at her any kind of which way.

He came back and handed her a tumbler of dark golden liquid. Her first thought was that it was like his eyes, and then he said with a wry smile, 'Scottish whisky—I feel it's appropriate.' He was referring to Montgomery's nationality.

Darcy smiled too and clinked her glass off Max's. 'Sláinte.'

Their eyes held as they took a sip of their drinks and it was like liquid fire going down her throat. Aware that they were most likely alone in the vast building, and feeling self-consciousness again, Darcy broke the contact and moved away to sit on the edge of a couch near Max's desk.

She watched as he came and stood at the window near her, saw the scar on the his face snaking down from his temple to his jaw.

She found herself asking impulsively, 'The scar—how did you get it?'

Max tensed, and there was an almost imperceptible tightening of his fingers around his glass. His mouth thinned and he didn't look at her. 'Amazing how a scar fascinates so many people—especially women.'

Immediately Darcy tensed, feeling acutely exposed. She said stiffly, 'Sorry, it's none of my business.'

He looked at her. 'No, it's not.'

Max took in Darcy's wide eyes and a memory rushed back at him with such force that it almost felled him: a much younger Darcy, but with the same pale heart-shaped face. Concerned. Pushing between him and the boys who had been punching the breath out of him with brute force.

He'd been gasping like a grounded fish, eyes streaming, familiar humiliation and impotent anger burning in his belly, and she'd stood there like a tiny fierce virago. When they'd left and he'd got his breath back she'd turned to him, worried.

Without even thinking about what he was doing, still dizzy, Max had straightened and reached out to touch her jaw. He'd said, almost to himself, '"Though she be but little, she is fierce."'

She'd blushed and whirled around and left. He'd still been reeling from the attack—reeling from whatever impulse had led him to quote Shakespeare.

Darcy was reaching across to put her glass on the table now, standing up, clearly intending to leave. And why wouldn't she after he'd just shut her down?

An impulse rose up within Max and he heard himself say gruffly, 'It happened on the streets. Here in Rome, when I was homeless.'

Darcy stopped. She lifted her hand from the glass and looked at him warily. 'Homeless?'

Max leaned his shoulder against the solid glass window, careful to keep his face expressionless. Curiously, he didn't feel any sense of regret for letting that slip out. He nodded. 'I was homeless for a couple of years after I was kicked out of Boissy.'

Darcy said, 'I remember the blood on the snow.'

Max felt slightly sick. *He* still remembered the vivid stain of blood on the snow, and woke sometimes at night sweating. He'd vowed ever since then not to allow anyone to make him lose control again. He would beat them at their own game, in their own rareified world.

'A boy went to hospital unconscious because of me.'

She shook her head faintly. 'Why did they torment you so much?'

Max's mouth twisted. 'Because one of their fathers was my mother's current lover and he was paying my fees. They didn't take kindly to that.'

Darcy had one very vague memory of an incredibly beautiful and glamorous woman arriving at the school one year with Max, in a chauffeur-driven car.

She found herself resting against the edge of the desk, not leaving as she'd intended to moments ago. 'Why were you homeless?'

Max's face was harsh in the low light. 'My mother failed to inform me that she'd decided to move to the States with a new lover and left no forwarding details. Let's just say she wasn't exactly at the nurturing end on the scale of motherhood.'

Darcy frowned. 'You must have had other family… Your father?'

Max's face was so expressionless that Darcy had to repress a shiver.

'I have a brother, but my father died some years ago. I couldn't go to them, in any case. My father had made it clear I was my mother's responsibillty when they divorced and he wanted nothing to do with me. They lived in Brazil.'

Darcy tried not to look too shocked. 'But you must have been just—'

'Seventeen,' Max offered grimly.

'And the scar…?' It seemed to stand out even more lividly now, and Darcy had to curb the urge to reach out and touch it.

Max looked down at his drink, swirling it in his glass. 'I saw a man being robbed and chased after the guy.' He looked up again. 'I didn't realise he was a junkie with a knife until he turned around and lunged at me, cutting my face. I managed to take the briefcase from him. I won't lie—there was a moment when I almost ran with it myself… But I didn't.'

Max shrugged, as if chasing junkies and staying on the right side of his conscience was nothing.

'The owner was so grateful when I returned it that he insisted on taking me to the hospital. He talked to me, figured out a little of my story. It turned out that he was CEO of a private equity finance firm, and as a gesture of goodwill for returning his property he offered me a position as an intern. I knew this was a chance and I vowed not to mess it up…'

Darcy said, a little wryly, 'I think it's safe to say you didn't waste the opportunity. He must have been a special man to do that.'

'He was,' Max said with uncharacteristic softness. 'One of the few people I trusted completely. He died a couple of years ago.'

There was only the faintest low hum of traffic coming from the streets far below. Isolated siren calls that faded into the distance. Everything around them was dark and golden. Darcy felt as if she were suspended in a dream. She'd never in a million years thought she might have a conversation like this with Max, who was unreadable on the best of days and never spoke of his personal life.

'You don't trust easily, then?'

Max grimaced slightly. 'I learnt early to take care of myself. Trust someone and you make yourself weak.'

'That's so cynical,' Darcy said, but it came out flat, not with the mocking edge she'd aimed for.

Max straightened up from the window and was suddenly much closer to Darcy. She could smell him—a light tangy musk, with undertones of something much more earthy and masculine.

He looked at her assessingly. 'What about you, Darcy? Are you telling me *you're not* cynical after your parents' divorce?'

She immediately avoided that incisive gaze and looked out at the glittering cityscape beyond Max. A part of her had broken when her world had been upended and she'd been split between her parents. But as a rule it wasn't something she liked to dwell on. She was reluctant to explore the fact that it had a lot to do with her subsequent avoidance of relationships.

She finally looked back to Max, forcing her voice to sound light. 'I prefer to say realistic. Not cynical.'

The corner of Max's mouth twitched. Had he moved even closer? He felt very close to Darcy.

He drawled now, 'Let's agree to call it realistic cynicism, then. So—no dreams of a picturesque house and a white picket fence with two point two kids to repair the damage your parents did to you?'

Darcy sucked in a breath at Max's unwitting perspicacity. Damn him for once again effortlessly honing in on her weak spot: her desire to have a base. A home of her own. Not the cynical picture he painted, but her own oasis in a life that she knew well could be upended without any warning, leaving her reeling with no sense of a safe centre.

Her career had become her centre, but Darcy knew she needed something more tangibly rooted.

She tried to sound as if he hadn't hit a raw nerve. 'Do I *really* strike you as someone who is yearning for the domestic idyll?'

He shook his head and took a step closer, reaching past Darcy to put his glass on the table behind her. She knew this should feel a little weird—after all they'd never been so physically close before, beyond their handshake when she'd taken the job. But after the intensity of their day spent cocooned in this office, with the darkness outside now, and after Max had revealed the origin of his scar, a dangerous sense of familiarity suppressed Darcy's normal impulse to observe the proper boundaries.

She told herself it was their shared experience in Boissy that made things a little different than the usual normal boss/PA relationship. But really the truth was that she didn't *want* to move as Max's arm lightly brushed against hers when he straightened again. The sip of whisky she'd taken seemed to be spreading throughout her body, oozing warmth and a sense of delicious lethargy.

Max looked at her. He was so close now that she could see how his eyelashes were dark gold, lighter at the tips.

'No,' he said. 'I don't think you are looking for the domestic idyll. You strike me as someone who is very focused on her career. A bit of a loner, perhaps?'

That stung. Darcy had friends, but she'd been working away so much that she only saw them if she went back to the UK. He was right, though, and that was why it stung. The revelation that she might be avoiding platonic as well as romantic relationships was not welcome.

She cursed herself. She was allowing fatigue, a sip of whisky and some unexpected revelations from Max to seriously impair her judgement. There was no intimacy here. They were both exhausted.

She straightened up, not liking the way that put her

even closer to Max. She looked anywhere but at him. 'It's late. I should get going if you want me to be awake enough to pay attention at dinner tomorrow evening.'

'Yes,' Max said. 'That's probably wise.'

Her feet seemed to be welded to the floor, but Darcy forced herself to move and turned to walk away—bumping straight into the corner of the desk, jarring her hip bone. She gave a pained gasp.

Max's hand came to her arm. 'Are you okay?'

Darcy could feel the imprint of Max's fingers, strong and firm, and just like that she was breathless. He turned her towards him and she couldn't evade his gaze.

'I… Thanks. It was nothing.' Any pain was fast being eclipsed by the look in Max's eyes. Darcy's insides swooped and flipped. The air between them was suddenly charged in a way that made her think of running in the opposite direction. Curiously, though, she didn't want to obey this impulse.

And then something resolute crossed his face and he pulled her towards him.

Darcy was vaguely aware that Max's grip on her arm wasn't so tight that she couldn't pull free. But a sense of shock mixed with intense excitement gripped her.

'What are you doing?' she half whispered.

His gaze moved from her mouth up to her eyes and time stood still. Max's other hand moved around to the back of her neck, tugging her inexorably towards him. His voice was low and seductive. 'I haven't been able to stop thinking about what this would be like.'

'What *what* would be like?'

'This…'

Before Darcy's brain could catch up with the speed at which things were moving Max's mouth came down and covered hers, fitting to her softer contours like a jigsaw piece slotting into place.

He was hard and firm, masterful as he moved his mouth against hers, enticing her to open up to him—which she found herself doing unhesitatingly. The kiss instantly became something else…something much deeper and darker.

Max was bold, his tongue exploring the depths of her mouth, stroking sensuously, making her lower body clench in helpless reaction. His body was whipcord-hard against hers, calling to her innermost feminine instincts that relished such evidence of his masculinity.

The edge of the desk was digging into Darcy's buttocks, but she barely noticed as Max urged her back so that she was sitting on it, moving his body between her legs so she had to widen them.

It was as if he'd simply inserted himself like a sharp blade under her skin and she'd been rendered powerless to think coherently or do anything except respond to the feverish call of her blood to taste this man, drink him in. It was intoxicating, heady, and completely out of character for her to behave like this.

Max's hands were moving now, sliding down the back of her silk shirt, resting on her waist over the belt of her trousers. And then he moved even closer between her legs and Darcy felt the thrust of his erection against her belly.

It was that very stark evidence of just how far over the edge they were tipping that blasted some cold air through the heat haze clouding her brain.

Darcy pulled back to find two slumberous pools of tawny gold staring at her. Their breathing was laboured and she was aware of thinking with sudden clarity: *Max Fonseca Roselli can't possibly want me. I'm not remotely his type. He's playing with me.*

She jerked back out of his arms and off the desk so abruptly that she surprised him into letting her go. Her heart was racing as if she'd just run half a marathon.

Some space and air between them brought Darcy back to full shaming reality. One minute they'd been knee-deep in the minutiae of Montgomery's life and business strategies, and the next she'd been sipping fine whisky and Max had been telling her stuff she'd never expected to hear.

And then she'd been climbing him like a monkey.

She'd never behaved so unprofessionally in her life. She lambasted herself, and ignored the screeching of every nerve-end that begged her to throw herself back into his arms.

Max looked every inch the disreputable playboy at that moment, with frustration stamped onto hard features as he observed his prey standing at several feet's distance. His cheeks were slashed with colour, his hair messy. *Oh, God.* She'd had her hands in his hair, clutching him to her like some kind of sex-starved groupie.

When she felt she could speak she said accusingly, '*That* should not have happened.'

Her hair was coming down from its chignon and she lifted her hands to do a repair job. The fact that Max's gaze dropped to her breasts made her feel even more humiliated. If they hadn't stopped when they had— She shut her mind down from contemplating where exactly she might be right now.

Allowing him to make love to her on his desk? Like some bad porn movie cliché: Darcy Does Her Boss.

She felt sick and took her hands down now her hair was secured.

Max looked at her and didn't seem to share half the turmoil she felt as he drawled, with irritating insouciance, '*That* did happen, and it was going to happen sooner or later.'

'Don't be ridiculous,' Darcy snapped on a panicked reflex at the thought that he had somehow seen something of her fascination with him. She was aghast to note that her legs were shaking slightly. 'You don't want me.'

Max folded his arms across his broad chest. 'I'm not in the habit of kissing women I don't want, Darcy.'

'Ha!' she commented acerbically as she started to hunt for her discarded shoes. She sent him a quick glare. 'You really expect me to believe you want *me*? That was nothing but a momentary glitch in our synapses, fuelled by fatigue and proximity.' She finally spotted her shoes and shoved her feet into them, saying curtly, 'This shouldn't have happened. It's completely inappropriate.'

'Fatigue and proximity?'

Max's scathing tone stopped Darcy in her tracks and she looked at him with the utmost reluctance. He was disgusted.

'That was chemistry—pure and simple. We wanted each other and, believe me, if we'd been wide awake and separated by a thick stone wall I'd still have wanted you.'

Darcy's heart pounded in the explosive silence left by his words. *He wanted her?* No way. She shook her head. Panic clutched her. 'I'll hand in my notice first thing—'

'You'll do no such thing!'

Darcy's heart was pounding out of control now. 'But we can't possibly work together after this.' She crossed her arms tightly. 'You have issues with PAs who don't know their place.'

He scowled. 'What just happened was entirely mutual. I have no issue with that—it was as much my responsibility as yours. More so, in fact, as I'm your boss.'

'Exactly,' Darcy pointed out, exasperated. 'All the

more reason why I can't keep working for you. We just crossed the line.'

Max knew on some rational level that everything Darcy was saying was true. He'd never lost control so spectacularly. He was no paragon of virtue, but he'd never mixed business with pleasure before, always keeping the two worlds very separate.

In all honesty he was still reeling a little from the fact that he'd so blithely allowed it to happen. And then his conscience mocked him. As if he'd had a choice. He'd been like a dog in heat—kissing Darcy had been a compulsion he'd been incapable of ignoring.

All day he'd been aware of her in a way that told him the feeling of desire that had sneaked up on him wasn't some mad aberration. As soon as she'd arrived for work he'd wanted to undo that glossy chignon and taste her lush mouth. All day he'd struggled with relegating her back to her appropriate position, telling himself he was being ridiculous.

Then they'd ordered takeout and she'd sat cross-legged on the floor, eating sushi out of a carton with chopsticks, and he'd found it more alluring than if they'd been in the glittering surroundings of a Michelin-starred restaurant. And when she'd taken her shoes off earlier and knelt down on the floor, to spread papers out and make it easier to sort them, he'd had to battle the urge to stride over and kneel down behind her, pulling her hips back—

Dio.

And now she was going to resign—because of *his* lack of control. Max's gut tightened.

'You're not walking away from this job, Darcy.'

She blinked, and a mutinous look came over her face. Her mouth was slightly swollen and Max was distracted by the memory of how soft it had felt under his. The sweet yet sharp stroke of her tongue against his… *Maledizione*. Just the thought of it was enough to fire him up all over again.

Darcy was cool. 'I don't think you have much choice in the matter.'

A familiar sense of ruthlessness coursed through Max and he reacted to her cool tone even when he felt nothing but heat. 'I do—if you care about your future job prospects.'

Darcy paled and a very unfamiliar stab of remorse caught at Max. He pushed it aside.

'I will not remain in a job where the lines of professionalism have been breached.'

Feeling slightly desperate, and not liking it, Max said again, 'It was just a kiss, Darcy.' He ran a hand impatiently through his hair. 'You're right, it shouldn't have happened, but it did.'

He thought of something else and realised with a jolt that he'd lost track of his priorities for a moment.

'I need you to help me close this deal with Montgomery. I can't afford the upheaval a new PA will bring at the moment.'

Max saw Darcy bite her lip, small white teeth sinking into soft pink flesh. For a wild second he almost changed his mind and blurted out that maybe she was right—they'd crossed a line and she should leave—but something stopped him. He told himself it was the importance of the deal.

She turned around and paced over to the window and looked out, her back to him. Max found his gaze travelling down over that tiny waist. Her shirt was untucked, dishevelled. *He'd* done that. He could remember how badly he'd wanted to touch her skin, see if it was as silky as he imagined it would be.

The knowledge hit him starkly: the most beautiful women in the world had treated him to personal erotic strip shows and yet Max was more turned on right now by an untucked piece of faux silk chainstore shirt.

And then Darcy turned around. Her voice was low. 'I know how important this deal is to you.'

The way she said it made Max feel exposed. She couldn't know the real extent of why it was so important—that it would bring him to a place of acceptance, both internally and externally, where he would finally be able to move on from the sense of exposure and humiliation that had dogged him his whole life. And, worse, the sense of being abandoned.

Yet he couldn't deny it. 'Yes. It's important to me.'

She fixed her wide blue gaze on him but he could see how pinched her face was. Reluctance oozed from her every pore.

'I'll stay on—but only until the deal is done and only if what happened tonight doesn't happen again.'

She looked at him, waiting for a response. The truth was that if Max wanted something he got it. And he wanted Darcy. But for the first time in his life he had to recognise that perhaps he couldn't always get what he wanted. That some things were more important than others. And this deal with Montgomery was more important than having Darcy in his bed, sating his clawing sense of frustration.

Also, he didn't want her to see that it was a struggle for him to back off. That would be far too exposing.

So he said, with an easiness that belied every bone in his body that wanted to throw her onto the nearest flat surface, 'It won't happen again, Darcy. Go home. We've got another long day and evening ahead of us tomorrow.

Don't forget to bring a change of clothes for dinner tomorrow night. We'll be going straight from the office.'

Darcy didn't say anything. She just turned and walked out of the room and the door closed with incongruous softness behind her.

Max walked over to the window. After a few minutes' delay he saw her emerge from the building in her coat, walking briskly away from the building, merging with Rome's late-night pedestrian traffic.

Something in his body eased slightly now that she was no longer in front of him, with those wide blue eyes looking so directly at him that he felt as if he were under a spotlight.

No woman was worth messing up this deal and certainly not little Darcy Lennox, with her provocative curves. Max finally turned around again and sighed deeply when he saw the slew of papers strewn across his desk and floor.

Instead of leaving himself, he went back to the bar, refilled his glass with whisky and then sat down and pulled the nearest sheaf of papers towards him. He put Darcy firmly out of his head.

Darcy tossed and turned in bed a little later, too wired to sleep. It was as if her body had been plugged into an electrical socket and she now had an excess of energy fizzing in her system.

She'd been plugged into Max.

Even though she was lying down, her limbs took on a jelly-like sensation when she recalled that moment of suspended tension just before he'd kissed her and everything had gone hazy and hot. She could still feel the imprint of his body against hers and between her legs she tingled. She clamped her thighs together.

They'd taken a quantum leap away from boss/PA, and it had happened so fast it still felt unreal. Had she really threatened to leave her job? And had he more or less threatened her future employment prospects if she did? She shivered slightly. She could well imagine Max doing just that—she'd witnessed his ruthlessness when it came to business associates first-hand.

The deal with Montgomery meant more to him than the potential awkwardness of having shared an intimate and highly inappropriate moment with his PA.

No matter what Max said, Darcy had no doubts that what had happened had been borne out of insanity brought on by fatigue and the moment of intimacy that had sprung up when he'd told her about his past.

She hadn't expected to hear him reveal that he'd been homeless. Any other student from Boissy wouldn't have lasted two days on the streets. But Max had lasted two years, and crawled his way out of it spectacularly.

He'd mentioned a brother, and his father. His parents' divorce. Questions resounded in Darcy's head as the enigmatic figure of Maximiliano Fonseca Roselli suddenly took on a much deeper aspect.

Unable to help herself, she leaned over and switched on the bedside light, picked up her tablet. She searched the internet for 'Max Fonseca Roselli family' and a clutch of pictures sprang up.

Darcy's breath was suspended as she scrolled through them. There was a picture of a very tall and darkly handsome man: Luca Fonseca, Brazilian industrialist and philanthropist. Max's brother. His name rang a bell. And then more pictures popped up of the same man with a stunningly beautiful blonde woman. They were wedding photos. Darcy recalled that she'd read about the wedding between Luca Fonseca and the infamous Italian socialite Serena DePiero recently.

Had Max gone to the wedding? Darcy was about to search for more information on his parents when she realised what she was doing and closed the cover of her tablet with force.

She flipped off the light and lay down, angry with herself for giving in to curiosity about a man with whom she'd shared a very brief and ill-advised moment of pure unprofessional madness. A man she should have no further interest in beyond helping him to get this deal so that she could get the hell out of his orbit and get on with her life.

CHAPTER THREE

DARCY LOOKED AT herself critically in the mirror of the ladies' toilet next to her office, but she didn't really see her own reflection. She was on edge after a long day in which Max had been overly polite and solicitous, with not so much as a sly look or hint that they'd almost made love on his desk the previous night.

At one stage she'd nearly snapped at him to please go back to normal and snarl at her the way he usually did.

The fact that she'd allowed a level of exposure and intimacy with Max she'd never allowed before was something she was resolutely ignoring. Her previous sexual experiences with men had come only after a lengthy dating period. And in each case once the final intimacy had been breached she'd backed off, because she'd realised she had no desire to deepen the commitment.

She snorted at herself now. As if she would have to worry about something like that with Max Fonseca Roselli. He was the kind of man who would leave so fast your head would be spinning for a week.

She forced her mind away from Max and took a deep breath. Her dress was black and had been bought for exactly this purpose—to go from work to a social event. And, as far as Darcy had been concerned when she'd bought it, it was modest.

Yet now it felt all wrong. It was a dress that suited her diminutive hourglass shape perfectly, but suddenly the scooped neckline was too low and the waist too cinched in. The clingy fabric was a little *too* clingy around her bottom and thighs, making her want to pluck it away from her body. The capped sleeves felt dressy, and when she moved the discreet slit up one side seemed to shout out, *I'm trying to be sexy!*

All at once she felt pressured and frazzled, aware of time ticking on. She'd already been in the bathroom for twenty minutes. She imagined Max pacing up and down outside, looking at his watch impatiently, waiting for her. Well, too late to change now. Darcy refreshed her make-up and spritzed on some perfume, and slid her feet into slightly higher heels than normal.

She'd left her hair down and at the last moment felt a lurch of panic when she looked at herself again. It looked way too undone. She twisted it up into a quick knot and secured it with a pin.

Her cheeks were hot and beads of sweat rolled down between her breasts. Cursing Max, and herself, she finally let herself out, her work clothes folded into a bag. It was with some relief that she noted that Max wasn't pacing up and down outside.

Stowing her bag in a cupboard, making a mental note to take it home after the weekend, Darcy took a deep breath and knocked once briefly on Max's office door before going in.

When she did, though, she nearly took a step back. Max was standing with a remote control in his hand, watching a financial news channel on the flat screen TV set into his wall. His hair was typically messy, but otherwise any resemblance to the Max she'd expected to see dissolved into a haze of heat.

His jaw was clean-shaven, drawing the eye to strong, masculine lines. He was wearing a classic three-piece suit in dark grey, with a snowy-white shirt and grey silk tie. Darcy swallowed as Max turned and his gaze fell on her. She couldn't breathe. Literally couldn't draw breath. She'd never seen anyone so arrestingly gorgeous in her life. And the memory of how that lean body had felt when it was pressed against hers, between her legs, was vivid enough to make her sway slightly.

There was a long, taut silence between them until Max clicked a button on the remote and the faint hum of chatter from the TV stopped.

He arched a brow. 'Ready?'

Darcy found her voice. 'Yes.'

He moved towards her and she backed out of his office, almost tripping over her own feet to pick up her evening bag and a light jacket matching the dress. As she struggled into it inelegantly she felt it being held out for her and muttered embarrassed thanks as Max settled it onto her shoulders.

She cursed the imagination that made her think his fingers had brushed suggestively against the back of her neck, and strode out of the office ahead of Max before she could start thinking anything else. Like how damn clingy her dress felt right then, and what rogue devil had prompted her not to wear stockings. The slide of her bare thighs against one another felt sensual in a way she'd never even noticed before. She'd never been given to erotic flights of fancy. Far too pragmatic.

Darcy didn't look at Max as they waited for his private lift, but once they were inside his scent dominated the small space.

He asked, 'You have the documents?'

'Yes.' Darcy lifted the slim attaché case she carried

alongside her bag. It held some documents they wanted to have on hand in case Montgomery asked for them.

The lift seemed to take an eternity to descend the ten or so floors to the bottom.

'You know, we *will* have to make eye contact at some point in the evening.' Max's voice was dry.

Reluctantly Darcy looked up at him, standing beside her, and it was as if a jolt of lightning zapped her right in the belly. She sucked in a breath and saw Max's eyes flare. The shift in energy was as immediate as an electric current springing up between them, as if it had been waiting until they got close enough to activate it.

No wonder they'd been skirting around each other all day. They'd both been avoiding *this*.

For the nano-second it took for this to sink in, and for Max to make an infinitesimally small move towards her—for her to realise how badly she wanted to touch him again—there was nothing outside of the small cocoon of the lift. Desire pulsated like a tangible thing.

But then a sharp *ping* sounded, the doors opened silently and they both stopped—centimetres from actually touching each other.

Max emitted a very rude Italian curse. He took her arm to guide her out of the lift, although it felt more as if he was marching her out of the building.

Once outside, walking to his chauffeur-driven car, he said tersely, 'I said eye contact, Darcy, not—'

'Not *what*, Max?' Darcy stopped and pulled her arm free, shaky from the rush of adrenalin and desire she'd just experienced, and self-conscious at the thought that she'd been all but drooling. 'I didn't do anything. *You're* the one who looked at me as if—'

He came close. 'As if *what*? As if I suddenly couldn't think of anything else except what happened last night?'

His mouth was a thin line. 'Well, I couldn't—and neither could you.'

Darcy had nothing to say. He was right. She'd been utterly naïve and clueless to think that she could experience a moment like that with Max Fonseca Roselli and put it down as a rash, crazy incident and never want him again. A hunger had been awoken inside her.

But she could deal with that.

What she couldn't deal with was the fact that Max—for some unfathomable reason—still wanted her too.

He glanced at his watch and said curtly, 'We'll be late. We can't talk about this now.'

And then he took her arm again and led her to the car, following her into the plush interior before she could protest or say another word.

The journey to the restaurant was made in a silence that crackled with electric tension. Darcy didn't look anywhere near Max, afraid of what she'd see if she did. She couldn't handle that blistering gaze right now.

One thing was clear, though. She would be handing in her notice *before* this deal was done. She couldn't continue to work for Max after this. But she didn't think he'd appreciate hearing her tender resignation right now.

The car came to a stop outside one of Rome's most exclusive restaurants. It took lesser mortals about six months to get a table, but Max had a table whenever he wanted.

He helped her out of the car, and even though Darcy wanted to avoid physical contact as much as possible she had to take his hand or risk sprawling in an ungainly heap at his feet.

She'd just stood up straight, and Max was still holding her hand, when a genial voice came from nearby.

'You didn't mention that you were bringing a date.'

Darcy tensed, and Max's hand tightened on hers reflexively. But almost in the same second she could tell he'd recovered and his hand moved smoothly to her arm as he brought her around to meet their nemesis.

Cecil Montgomery was considerably shorter than Max, and considerably older, with almost white hair. But he oozed charisma, and Darcy was surprised to find that on first impression she liked him.

His eyes were very blue, and twinkled benignly at her, but she could see the steeliness in their depths. A tall woman stood at his side, very elegant and graceful, with an open friendly face and dark grey eyes. Her hair was silver and swept up into a classic chignon.

'Please—let me introduce you to my wife, Jocasta Montgomery.'

'Pleasure…' Darcy let her hand be engulfed, first by Montgomery's and then by his wife's.

It was only when they were walking into the restaurant that Darcy realised Max hadn't actually introduced her as his PA—or had he and she just hadn't heard?

She hadn't had anything to do with Montgomery herself, as he and Max had a direct line of communication, so it was quite possible he still thought she was Max's date. The thought made Darcy feel annoyingly self-conscious.

They left their coats in the cloakroom and were escorted to their table, the ladies walking ahead of the men. The restaurant oozed timeless luxury and exclusivity. Darcy recognised Italian politicians and a movie star. The elaborate furnishings wouldn't have been out of place in Versailles, and even the low-pitched hum of conversation was elegant.

Jocasta Montgomery took Darcy's arm and said *sotto*

voce in a melodious Scottish accent, ‘I don’t know about you, my dear, but I always find that places like this give me an almost overwhelming urge to start flinging food around the place.’

It was so unexpected that Darcy let out a startled laugh and something inside her eased out of its tense grip. She replied, ‘I know what you mean—it’s an incitement to rebel.’

They arrived at a round table, the best in the room, and took their seats. To Darcy’s surprise the conversation started and flowed smoothly. Max and Montgomery dominated it, with talk of current business trends and recent scandals. At one point between starters and the main course Jocasta rolled her eyes at Darcy and led her into a conversation about living in Rome and what she liked about it.

They skirted around the edges of the fact that this dinner was really about whether or not Montgomery was going to hand his precious life’s blood to Max to manage until coffee had been served after dessert.

Darcy had almost forgotten why they were there, she’d enjoyed talking to Jocasta so much. But now there was a palpable buzz of tension in the air and Darcy saw the very evident steely gleam in Montgomery’s eyes as he looked at Max, who was unmistakably tense.

It was slightly disconcerting to recognise how keenly she felt Max’s tension as Montgomery looked at him over his coffee cup before putting it down slowly.

‘The fact is, Max, quite simply there is no one I can imagine handling this fund and making it grow into the future better than you. As you’re aware I’m very concerned about philanthropy, and your own brother’s work has been inspirational to me.’

Max inclined his head towards the older man, but his face was expressionless.

'My one reservation, however, is this…'

Darcy tensed and avoided looking at Max.

'You have been leading a committedly single lifestyle for a long time.' He glanced at Darcy and said half apologetically, 'Present company notwithstanding. My fund and my life's work has been built upon and developed with family in mind. *My* family, primarily, of course, but also for the benefit of many others. This would never have happened if I hadn't had a very strong sense of family values running through previous generations. That's why the Montgomery fund has lasted as long as it has, and grown so strong…'

Darcy was barely aware of Montgomery's continued misunderstanding about who she was. He was going on…

'And you, Max—you come from a broken home… For years you were estranged from your father, you didn't speak to your own twin brother, and you are not close to your mother.'

Darcy's mind boggled. Max's brother was a *twin*?

She looked at him now and could see his face was still expressionless, but a vein popped slightly over one temple, near his scar, which stood out against that dark olive skin. The scar he'd got because his own mother had forgotten about him. Left him defenceless on the streets.

'You've done your research,' Max said easily, but Darcy recognised the edge of something dangerous.

Montgomery shrugged. 'No more than you yourself have done, no doubt.'

'My relationship with my brother, my mother, has no bearing on my ability to manage your fund, Cecil.'

A lesser man would have quailed at the distinct threat in Max's voice. Not Montgomery.

'No,' said the other man, looking at Max assessingly. 'I think for the most part you are right. But my concern would be the risks you'd be prepared to take on behalf of my fund—risks that you might not consider taking if you had a different perspective on life. My fear is that, based on your experiences, you might actually be biased against the very values I've built this fund upon, and that it would influence your decision-making process because you have only yourself to worry about.'

Darcy's insides had turned to stone. Cecil Montgomery, with a ruthless precision she'd never even witnessed in Max, had just laid Max's life bare and dissected it with clinical and damning detachment.

She felt a very disturbing surge of something like protectiveness. A need to defend.

Even Jocasta Montgomery had put her hand on her husband's arm and was saying something indistinct to him.

Darcy looked at Max, who had carefully put his own coffee cup down. The restaurant was largely empty by now.

'You are right about almost everything, Cecil.' He smiled, but it was a thin, harsh line. 'I do come from a broken home, and my brother and I did suffer at the hands of two parents who really couldn't have cared less about our welfare.'

Jocasta broke in. 'Please, Max, don't feel you have to say—'

But Max held up a hand, not taking his gaze off Montgomery. 'I said that your husband is right about *almost* everything. There's one thing his research hasn't shown up, however.'

Montgomery raised a brow. 'I'm intrigued. What is it that I've missed?'

Max's jaw clenched, and to Darcy's shock he reached over and took her hand in his, holding it tight.

'Darcy.'

Darcy looked at Max, but he hadn't said her name to call her attention and speak to her.

He was still looking at Montgomery and gripping her hand tight as he said, 'You can be the first to congratulate my fiancée and I on our engagement.'

Darcy might have enjoyed Montgomery's almost bug-eyed response if she hadn't been so afraid that her own eyes were bugging out of her head at the same moment.

'But... But...' Jocasta Montgomery said, 'Darcy told me she's your PA...'

Max looked at Darcy briefly and through waves of shock she could see something implacable in his expression that forbade her from saying anything.

He looked back to the couple on the other side of the damask-covered table. 'She is. That's how we met... again.'

'Again?' asked Montgomery sharply.

Max nodded. 'Darcy and I went to the same school—Boissy le Chateau in Switzerland. That's where we first met. She came to work for me three months ago...' Max shrugged, 'And the rest, as they say, is history.'

'Oh, Cecil.' Jocasta Montgomery put her hand over her husband's and looked at him with suspiciously bright eyes. 'That's how *we* met.'

Darcy felt it like a punch to the gut. She remembered that small detail now. Jocasta had been his secretary in the seventies, in Edinburgh.

Cecil Montgomery was looking at Max through narrowed eyes. Obviously suspicious. And then he turned his gaze on Darcy and she could feel her cheeks grow hot.

'Well, then, my dear, it would seem that congratulations are in order. When did this happy event occur?'

Max's hand tightened on hers as he inserted smoothly, 'Some weeks ago… I knew after just a few weeks that Darcy was unlike any other woman I've ever known. We had a bond at school…and it was rekindled.'

Darcy was still too shocked even to consider saying anything, but she tried to pull her hand out from under Max's—to no avail.

'My dear, are you quite all right? You look a little ill.' Jocasta Montgomery was leaning forward with concern.

Darcy sensed Max's tension beside her, reaching out to envelop her, inhibit her. She knew that she should pull away, stand up, throw her napkin down and say that it was all untrue. This was her chance. She should walk away from Max right now and not look back.

And put a nail in the coffin of his chance to get this deal with Cecil Montgomery.

If she wanted revenge for what he'd just done that was what she'd do.

But she couldn't get out of her head the way Montgomery had so brutally assessed Max's background, casting doubts on his ability. And she couldn't get out of her head the way she'd felt that instinctive need to defend him. And right now the instinct was still there, in spite of the rage bubbling down low at having been put in this untenable position.

She forced a smile and looked at Jocasta. 'I'm fine—really. It's just a bit of a shock to hear it made official. Up till now it's been our secret.'

She risked a glance at Max and her gaze was caught and snared by his. It was expressionless, but something flickered in the depths of those extraordinary eyes. *Relief?* His hand loosened on hers fractionally.

Jocasta was making a *tsk*ing noise. 'And my husband provoked Max into letting it slip? Well, I think the least we can do is celebrate now that your secret is out.'

Before Darcy could say anything else a waiter was summoned and a bottle of vintage champagne was being delivered to the table and expertly poured into slim flutes. It seemed to Darcy that everything was moving at warp speed, and her heart was beating too fast.

They were all holding up their glasses and Jocasta was beaming at them. Her husband was still looking less than convinced though and Max's jaw was tight. Darcy felt an urge to giggle, and quickly took a sip of the sparkling drink to make it go down.

'When are you getting married?'

Darcy looked at Montgomery, just as Max said, with all the natural-born charm of a ruthless man intent on his prize, 'Two weeks.'

His hand tightened on Darcy's again and when she turned to him he looked at her so intently that her insides combusted.

'I want to make her mine before she realises what I'm really like and leaves me for ever.'

For the first time since Max had made his outrageous statement Darcy felt her wits return. She pulled her hand free and said with some acerbity, while holding up her hand, 'Well, seeing as you haven't even bought me a ring yet, *darling*, I'm thinking that perhaps there's a flaw in the arrangements.'

Jocasta chuckled. 'Yes, Max, a lady in possession of a marriage proposal generally deserves a beautiful ring.'

Max smiled, and it was dangerous. He took Darcy's hand again and lifted it to his mouth, pressing a kiss over her ring finger, making any of the wits that had come back to her melt again.

‘Which is why I’ve arranged to take my fiancée to Paris tomorrow, for a private appointment in Devilliers—it was meant to be a surprise.’

Darcy’s eyes opened wide. Devilliers was possibly the oldest and most exclusive jewellers in the world.

Jocasta made a noise. ‘And now we’ve ruined it. Cecil, stop goading Max. They’re engaged. Look at them—they can’t keep their eyes off each other.’

‘Well, then,’ said the older man. ‘It seems that perhaps your perspective is indeed changing, Max. However, I’ve decided that the announcement of my decision as to whom I’m entrusting my fund will take place at our fortieth wedding anniversary celebrations in Scotland, surrounded by my family.’

The Montgomerys shared a fond look and Max let Darcy’s hand go. Montgomery looked at him, and then to Darcy. ‘You will both, of course, be extended an invitation. It takes place in three weeks. Perhaps you could include the trip to Inverness as a detour on your honeymoon?’

Honeymoon?

The full enormity of what was occurring hit Darcy, and as if sensing her dawning horror Max put a firm hand on her leg, under the table, just above her knee.

‘We would like nothing more—would we, *cara*?’

Max was looking at her, his big hand heavy on her leg, and treacherous heat was spreading upwards to between her thighs. ‘No…’

Max knew exactly what Darcy’s very ineffectual ‘no’ meant. It didn’t mean that she agreed—it meant *Stop this now*. But he took ruthless advantage of the ambiguity and angled his body towards hers, slipping his other hand around the back of her bare neck, pulling her towards him so that he could cover her mouth with his and stop her from saying anything else.

By the time he let her go again she was hot, breathless, addled and completely out-manoeuvred by a master. The Montgomerys were preparing to leave, saying their goodbyes, clearly believing that they were playing gooseberry now.

Darcy didn't know if she wanted to stamp her foot, slap Max, or scream for them all to *stop* so she could put them right. But, like the treacherous heat that had licked up her thighs and into her belly during Max's kiss, something was holding her back—and she was too much of a coward to investigate what it was.

They stood to bid goodbye to the older couple and Darcy was vaguely aware that the restaurant had emptied. When they were alone again Max sat down, a look of supreme satisfaction on his face.

This time Darcy *did* throw down her napkin, and he looked at her. Anger at herself for being so weak made her blurt out, 'What the *hell* do you think you're playing at, Max?'

Max cast a quick look around and took Darcy's wrist, pulling her down. She landed heavily on the seat.

Something occurred to her then—an awful suspicion. 'Please tell me you didn't have that planned all along?'

Max's jaw firmed. He was unapologetic. 'No, but I saw an opportunity and took it.'

Darcy let out a slightly horrified laugh. 'An *opportunity*? That's what you call fabricating a fake engagement to your PA?'

He turned to face her, stretching an arm across the back of her chair, placing his other hand on the table. Boxing her in.

'It won't be a fake engagement, Darcy. We're going to get married.'

Darcy's mouth opened but nothing came out. On some level she had known what she was doing, going along with Max's crazy pronouncement, but she'd also expected that as soon as they were alone again he'd reassure her that of course it wouldn't happen. It had been just to placate Montgomery and there would be some method of undoing what had been done.

She shook her head, as if that might restore sanity and order. But he was still looking at her.

She found her voice. 'Maybe it's the fatigue, Max, or the stress, but I think it's quite possible that you've gone entirely mad. This conversation is over and this *relationship* is over. Find someone else to be your convenient bride/PA, because I'm not going to be it just because I'm under your nose and you've decided that it's appropriate to kiss me when you feel like it. We both know I'm not your type of woman. No one will ever believe you've chosen to marry someone like me—Montgomery patently didn't believe a word of it—so in the end it'll achieve nothing.'

Darcy was breathless after the tumult of words and stood up on shaky legs. Before Max could stop her she turned to walk quickly through the restaurant, reality slamming back into her with each step. And humiliation. Max had seen an opportunity, all right—a cheap one, at Darcy's expense. To think that he would *use* her like this, just to further his own aims, shouldn't have come as a shock. But it did.

Max watched Darcy walk away, rendered uncharacteristically dumb. He could appreciate her very apparent sense of shock because he was still reeling himself, trying to recall what exactly had prompted him to make such an outrageous statement to Montgomery.

And then he remembered. *'You come from a broken home…estranged from your mother…brother…different perspective…'* He remembered the hot rush of rage when Montgomery had so coolly laid his life bare for inspection. Questioning his motives and ability based upon his experiences.

He'd wanted to do something to take that knowing smirk off Montgomery's face. And in a moment of mad clarity he'd known what he had to do to push the man off his sanctimonious perch. Fake a marriage. To Darcy.

And she'd gone along with it—even if she *had* looked as if someone had just punched her in the belly.

Darcy. Max's usual clear-headed focus came back and he went cold inside at the thought of Darcy leaving. She wasn't going anywhere—not now. Not when everything was at stake.

'Get in the car, Darcy. Please.'

Darcy was valiantly ignoring Max and the open car door nearby. She was about to stretch her arm out to hail a passing taxi when he took her arm in a firm grip and all but manhandled her into the back of the car.

She sputtered, 'This is kidnap.'

Max was terse. 'Hardly. Take us to my apartment, please, Enzo.' And then he hit a button so that a partition went up, enclosing them in silence.

Darcy folded her arms and looked at the man on the other side of the car. In a louche sprawl of big long limbs, he'd never looked more like a rebel.

'You've gone too far this time, Max. I don't care what you have to do but we're *not* getting married—I've changed my mind, I'm not waiting until the deal is done. I'm on the first plane out of Rome as soon as you let me go.'

Max gave her a withering look. 'There's no need for dramatics. We are just going to talk.'

He leaned back and looked out of the window, clearly done with the conversation for now. Darcy fumed, hating the ever-present hum of awareness in her blood at being in such close proximity to him. He was such an arrogant…*bastard*. Saying the word, even silently, made her feel marginally better.

Within minutes they were pulling up outside a sleek modern building. Max was out of the car and holding out a hand for Darcy before she could think what to do. Knowing she couldn't escape now, she scowled and put her hand into his, let him help her out, jerking her hand away as soon as she was on her own two feet.

Max led her into a massive steel-and-chrome foyer, where huge works of modern art were hung on the walls. It was hushed and exclusive, and in spite of herself she found herself wondering what Max's apartment would be like.

With an acknowledgement to the concierge, Max led Darcy to an open lift and stabbed at the 'P' button. Of course, Darcy thought snarkily. Of *course* he'd be living in the penthouse.

Once in the lift she moved to the far corner. Max leaned back against the wall and looked at her from under hooded lids. 'No need to look like a startled rabbit, Darcy. I'm not going to eat you.'

'No,' she said sharply. 'Just turn my world upside down.'

CHAPTER FOUR

DARCY FOLLOWED MAX into his apartment warily. From what she could see, as he flicked on low lights, it was as sleek and modern as the building that housed it. Floor-to-ceiling windows offered astounding views of Rome glittering at night.

Her feet were sore in the high-heeled shoes, but she would let them bleed before taking them off. She was still recalling her bare feet in the office the previous night—the cocoon of intimacy and where that had led.

'Drink?'

Darcy looked over to where Max was pulling his tie out of its knot and undoing the top buttons of his shirt. He'd already taken off his jacket and he looked sinfully sexy in the waistcoat of the three-piece suit.

She shook her head. 'No. I don't want a drink, Max, and I don't want to talk. I'd like to go to some corner of the earth far away from you.'

He just shrugged, ignoring her pronouncement, and proceeded to pour himself a measure of something. He gestured to a seat. 'Please—sit down.'

Darcy clutched her bag tighter. 'I told you…I don't want to—'

'Well, tough, because we're talking.'

Darcy made a rude sound and stalked over to an uncomfortable-looking chair and sat down.

Max started to pace, then stopped and said, 'Look, I didn't plan to announce an engagement to you this evening.'

'I'm not so sure you didn't, Max. It certainly seemed to trip off your tongue very easily—along with that very inventive plan to treat me to a Devilliers ring. Tell me, are we taking your private jet?'

Max cursed before downing his drink in one and setting the glass down with a clatter.

He glared at her. 'I didn't plan it. He just... *Dio.* You heard him.'

Darcy's insides tightened as she recalled the sense of protectiveness that had arisen when Montgomery had baldly dissected Max's life. The truth was that no one goaded Max. He'd remained impervious in the face of much worse provocation. *But this had been personal. About his family.*

Darcy stood up, feeling vulnerable. 'I heard him, Max. The man clearly has strong feelings about the importance of family, but do you think he really cares if you're married or not?'

'You heard him. He believes my perspective will be skewed unless I have someone to worry about other than myself.' Max sounded bitter.

'So you fed me to him?'

He looked at her. 'Yes.'

'I'm just a means to an end—so you can get your hands on that fund.'

Max looked at Darcy. Her hair had begun to get dishevelled, falling down in tendrils around her face and neck. *'I'm just a means to an end.'* Why did those words strike at him somewhere? Of *course* she was a means to an end—everything in his life was a means to an end. And that end was in sight.

'Yes.'

Her jaw tightened and she stepped back. Max did not like the flash of something like panic in his gut.

'Yes, you *are* a means to an end—I won't pretty it up and lie to you. But, Darcy, if you do this you won't walk away empty-handed. You can name your price.'

She let out a short curt laugh and it made Max wince inwardly. It sounded so unlike her.

'Believe me, no price could buy me as your wife, Max. I don't think I even *like* you all that much.'

Max felt that like a blow to his gut, but he gritted out, 'I'm not asking you to like me, and I'm not *buying* a wife, Darcy. I'm asking you to do this as part of your job. Admittedly it's a little above and beyond the call of duty…but you will be well compensated.'

Darcy tossed her head. 'Nothing could induce me to do this.'

'Nothing…?' Max asked silkily as he moved a little closer, his vision suddenly overwhelmed with the tantalising way Darcy filled out her dress.

She put out a hand. 'Stop right there.'

Max stopped, but his blood was still leaping. He'd yet to meet a woman he couldn't seduce. *Was he prepared to seduce Darcy into agreement?* His mind screamed caution, but his body screamed *yes*!

He erred on the side of caution.

Darcy's hand was still held out. 'Don't even *think* about it, Max. That kiss…whatever happened between us…was a mistake and it won't be happening again.'

He kept his mouth closed even as he wanted to negate what she'd said. He needed her acquiescence now.

'Everyone has a price, Darcy. You can name yours. We only need to be married for as long as it takes the deal to be done, then we'll divorce and you can get on with your life. No harm done. It's just an extension of your job, and I'll make sure that you get a job wherever you want in the world after this.'

She snorted, telling him succintly what she thought of *that*. She moved away from him now, stalking over to one of the big windows.

Max felt disorientated for a moment. It wasn't usual for him to bring a woman back to his apartment. He preferred to keep women out of his private space. Especially women he seduced. Because he never wanted them to get any notions.

But Darcy was here, and it felt bizarrely as if she'd been here before. He was too consumed with bending her to his will right now to look at *that* little nugget. Too consumed with ignoring the inferno raging in his blood as he took in her curvy silhouette against the backdrop of Rome outside.

And then she turned around, her hands still clutching her bag. 'Why is this so important to you?'

Max immediately went still, as if drawing his energy back inwards. Darcy had a moment to collect herself, to try and remove her see-sawing emotions and hormones from this situation.

As she'd looked out of the window she'd had to ask herself why the prospect of marrying Max was such a red-hot button for her. Apart from the fact that it was a ludicrous thing to ask of anyone.

After all, she came from a *very* broken home, so if anyone had the necessary cynicsm to embark on a marriage of convenience it was her. And she was ambitious enough to appreciate the aspect that Max wasn't exaggerating—she *would* have the pick of any job she wanted if she did this. It would be the least he owed her.

But she was not stupid enough to think that the way she'd felt when Max had kissed her could be ignored. He'd tapped into something untouched deep inside her—something that went beyond the physical to a secret place she'd never explored herself, never mind with anyone else.

And there was his astounding arrogance in thinking she would just go along with this decree. Like some king who expected his minions to obey his every word.

'Well, Max? If I'm to even consider this crazy idea for one second I want to know why you want this so badly.'

He seemed to glower at her for a long moment, and then he stuck his hands in the pockets of his trousers and came closer. Darcy couldn't move back because the window was behind her. He came and stood near her, looking out at the view, face tight.

'Montgomery mentioned my brother. We're twins. We were six when our parents split up and split *us* up. I only ever saw Luca again when he came to Rome for brief holidays or on trips to see our mother. I see him a little more frequently since we've been adults.'

Max sighed.

'He grew up being groomed to be my father's heir. There was never any question of me getting a share. That was my punishment for choosing to go with my mother… not that our father really cared which son he got as long as he had an heir to pass his corrupt legacy on to. But that's just part of it. Luca did offer me my half of his inheritance after our father died, but I didn't want it.'

He looked at Darcy then, almost accusingly.

'I didn't want his charity and I still don't. By then I'd

already made my first million. I wanted to succeed on my own merit—surpass anything my father had ever done. Do it on my own. It's the one thing that's kept me going through it all. The need to know that I've done it without anyone handing me anything.'

He looked away again and Darcy was silent. Mesmerised by the passion blazing out of Max. And the unmistakable pride.

'For years I felt tainted. Tainted by my mother's lack of care and her sordid affairs. That's how she made her living—little better than women who call themselves what they really are: prostitutes.'

Darcy winced.

'I was on the streets one night, foraging for food in a bin at the back of an exclusive restaurant, when some guests came outside to smoke. Boys from my class at Boissy.'

She sucked in a breath, imagining the scene all too well.

As if he'd guessed her suspicion his mouth quirked and he said, 'There was no blood. I walked away—but not before they recognised me and told me that they'd never expected anything more of someone like me. I'd been born into one of the wealthiest families in South America, but thanks to my fickle parents my brother and I were used almost like an experiment to see who would flourish better. One of us was given everything. The other one had everything stripped away.'

He turned to look at her, his face stark in the dim lights.

'That's why I want this. Because if Montgomery hands me his fund I'll have proved that even when you have your birthright stripped away it's still possible to regain your dignity and get respect.'

He didn't have to elaborate for Darcy to imagine how his litany of humiliations had bred the proud man in front of her. Montgomery held an almost mythical place in the world's finances. Akin to financial royalty. Darcy knew that what Max said was true. His endorsement would make Max untouchable, revered. The boys who had bullied him at school and witnessed him at his lowest moment on the streets would be forced to respect him.

'And it's not just for me,' he said now, interrupting her thoughts. 'I'm a partner in a philanthropic organisation with my brother. We're finally putting our father's corrupt legacy to good use, and I'll be damned if I can't contribute my own share.'

Max turned to face her more fully.

'*That's* why I want this, Darcy. Everyone has a price. I've just told you mine. You can name yours.'

Why did that sound like the worst kind of deal with the devil?

Because it is, whispered a small voice.

When Darcy woke up the next day she felt strangely calm. As if a storm had passed and she'd been washed up on land—alive and breathing, if a little battered.

Max had made no further attempt to stop her from leaving once she'd said, 'I need a night to think it over.'

It was as if he'd recognised how precarious his chance was. He'd escorted her down to his car and bade her goodnight, saying, 'Just think of your price, Darcy.'

And so she had.

After hours of tossing and turning she'd got up and looked at her tablet, at the properties she'd marked on a website. It was her secret, most favourite thing to do. Earmark the properties she'd buy if she had the money.

Her heart had thumped hard when she'd seen that her current favourite was still available. The price, in her eyes, was extortionate; London property gone mad. But she knew to Max it would be a pittance. Was *this* her price? A place of her own? The base she wanted so badly? The base it would take her years to afford under normal working circumstances?

Darcy could empathise with Max's determination to do it all on his own. She could ask her parents for the money to buy a house and have it tomorrow. But when she'd seen her father almost lose everything it had forged in her a deep desire to ensure her own financial stability, to be dependent on no one else.

She'd been eight when her parents had split up and she'd been tossed back and forth like a rag doll, across time zones and countries, with nice airline ladies holding her hand through airports. It had been in those moments that Darcy had wished most fervently that she still had a home—somewhere she could go back to that would always be there. *Something that wasn't in a constant state of flux*. Security. Stability.

When Max had revealed that he'd been only six when his parents had split up her silly heart had constricted. And he had a twin brother. She couldn't imagine what it must have been like to have been ripped apart from a sibling. Never mind taken to the other side of the world, never to connect with one of your parents again.

She got up and showered and made herself coffee. She hated that knowing about Max's tumultuous past made it harder for her to keep seeing him as ruthless and cynical. But he *was*, she assured herself. Nothing had changed. He was out for himself—unashamedly. And yet who could blame him? He'd been abandoned by his own mother, forgotten by his father. Estranged from his brother.

The thing was, did he deserve for her to help him?

Darcy's mobile phone pinged with a text message. From Max.

Well?

She almost smiled. Something about his obvious impatience at the fact that she wouldn't come to heel easily comforted her. Things had morphed from relatively normal to seriously weird in a very short space of time.

She texted back.

Do you think you could use that word in a sentence?

She pictured him scowling. A couple of minutes passed and then…

Dear Darcy,
Please will you marry me so that I can secure Montgomery's fund and live happily ever after?
Yours truly, Max.

Darcy barked out a laugh. The man was truly a bastard. Her phone pinged again.

Well?

Now *she* scowled.

I'm thinking.

Think faster.

Darcy threw her phone down for a moment. Pressure was building in her chest. And then the picture of the property she loved so much caught her eye. If she did this, she would get that.

We all have a price.

She picked up the phone, almost daring it to ping again with some terse message—because if it did she would tell Max where to go. But it didn't, almost as if he knew how close she was to saying no.

She took a deep breath and texted.

If—and that's a big if—if I agree to do this I want £345,000.

She let out a breath, feeling like a mercenary bitch. But it was the price of the flat she loved. And if she was being a mercenary bitch she was nothing in comparison to Max. His soul was black.

She continued.

Also, this farcical marriage will last only for as long as it takes Montgomery to announce his decision, and then you will give me a stunning reference which will open the door to whatever job I want.

Her heart thumped hard as she looked over the text, and then her finger pressed the 'Send' button. 'Delivered' appeared almost straight away.

It took longer than she'd expected, but finally Max's response came back.

Done and done. Whatever you want. I told you. Now, what's it to be?

Darcy's finger traced over the picture of the flat. In a few months she could be living there, with a new job. A new start. A settled existence for the first time since she'd been a child. And no Max messing with her hormones and her ability to think clearly.

She texted quickly before she lost her nerve: Yes.

Almost immediately a message came back.

Good. My car will pick you up in an hour. We're going to Paris.

The ring. For a moment Darcy almost texted Max back, saying she'd changed her mind, but her fingers hovered ineffectually over her phone. And then she got distracted.

What the hell did someone wear on a whirlwind trip to Paris to buy an engagement ring for a fake wedding?

In the end Darcy decided to wear one of her smarter work outfits: a dark navy wrap dress with matching high heels. She felt self-conscious now, in the small plane, and resisted the urge to check and see if her dress was gaping a little too much. The way Max had looked at her when she'd walked out of her apartment building had almost made her turn around and change into jeans and a T-shirt.

He was dressed similarly, smart/casual in a dark blue suit and white shirt. When she'd walked over to the car earlier he'd smirked slightly and said, 'We're matching—isn't that cute?'

Darcy had scowled and dived into the car. When he'd joined her she'd said, 'Can you put up the partition, please?'

She'd been more discomfited than she'd liked to admit by this more unreadable and yet curiously accessible Max. The boundary lines had become so blurred now they were non-existent, and she'd needed to lay down some rules.

When the window had gone up she'd crossed her arms over her chest. Max's eyeline had dropped to her cleavage.

'We need to discuss some formalities.'

Max's eyes had snapped up. 'Formalities?'

'All this marriage is, as far as I'm concerned, is a serious amount of overtime. You're basically paying me to be an executive PA par excellence. It's still just *work*. And if I hadn't agreed to this I would still be tendering my notice because of what happened the other night.'

Max sat back, looking dangerous and sexy, jaw dark with stubble. 'What happened, Darcy?'

Darcy shot a look at the partition and back again, her cheeks growing hot. 'You know very well what happened. We crossed the line.'

'We almost made love on my desk.'

Darcy felt hotter. 'But we didn't.' *Thank God.* 'We came to our senses.' She waved a hand. 'What I'm trying to say is that even now we are embarking on this ridiculous charade—'

'That I'll be paying you handsomely for…' Max pointed out, immediately making Darcy's irritation levels rise.

'And for which you'll be earning your place among the financial giants of the world,' she lashed back.

Max's jaw clenched. 'Touché.'

Darcy had leaned forward in her agitation but she pulled back now, forcing herself to stay calm. 'What I'm saying is that this marriage is going to be fake in every sense of the word. If you want anything physical then I'm sure you can get it from the legion of women in your little black book.'

Max folded his arms and regarded her. 'There's something incredibly ironic about the fact that I always swore I'd never enter into the state of matrimony and yet now I find myself on the brink of such a situation—'

'Caused by *you*,' Darcy flung at him.

That made him dip his head in acknowledgement before he continued, 'I find myself with a wife who won't sleep with me. I would never have anticipated that as a problem to be surmounted.'

'No,' Darcy said waspishly. 'I don't imagine you would have. Like I said—call someone else to provide you with any extra-curricular services you might require. I'm sure you can be discreet.' She looked at him, wondering just why this conversation was making her so angry. 'I would just avoid a three-in-a-bed romp—that won't endear you to Montgomery if it gets out like the last one did.'

Max made an irritated sound. 'For what it's worth that was a PR stunt for charity that ended up being leaked before we could explain it, so it never got used. You can't seriously think I'd be so crass?'

Darcy looked at him and cursed him. He looked positively angelic. Wrapped up in a demon. And of *course* he wouldn't be so crass. Max oozed sophistication. She should have known better. And now she'd revealed that she'd been keeping an eye on his exploits. *Damn him.*

She looked away. 'Whatever, Max—just don't make me look like a fool.'

'The same goes for you, you know,' came the softly delivered response.

Darcy looked at him and for a moment all she could see was the way Max had looked at her the other night, when she'd pulled back from his embrace, cheeks flushed, eyes glittering dangerously. 'Don't worry,' she said, as frigidly as she could, 'I won't have a problem curbing *my* urges.'

Max had muttered something she couldn't catch—something like *We'll see about that*—just as the car had pulled up outside the small plane.

Darcy's attention came back to the plane. Max was staring out of his window. Not goading her or looking at her with those mesmerising eyes. She remembered what he'd told her last night and how she'd wanted to leave his apartment—get away before he might see something on her face or in her expression. Empathy. A treacherous desire to help him achieve what he wanted.

'I didn't know your brother was a twin.'

Max turned his head slowly and looked at her. 'It's not really common knowledge.'

'I saw pictures of him…the wedding. You're not identical?'

Max shook his head and smiled, but it was hard. 'I'm prettier than my brother.' His self-mocking expression was anything *but* pretty. It was utterly masculine, making a mockery of 'pretty'. Especially with that scar running from his temple to his jaw.

Darcy felt breathless. 'You said you're closer now?'

Max raised a brow. 'Did I?'

'Last night…you said you were working with him.'

Max's mouth tightened. 'For a cause—not because we sit up at night drinking cocoa and reminiscing about our childhood experiences.'

Darcy rolled her eyes at his sarcastic response just as the plane banked. She took the opportunity to escape Max's gaze and looked out to see Paris laid out in all its glory, the distinctive Eiffel Tower glinting in the distance. Fine. Obviously Max wasn't about to launch into any more confessionals. He'd probably already told her far more than he wanted to.

And she wasn't curious. Not at all.

Max watched as Darcy inspected the trays of rings laid out for their perusal. He almost smiled at her overwhelmed expression. She had been pretty slack-jawed since they'd walked into the opulent Rococo interior of one of the oldest jewellery establishments in the world. A byword in luxury, wealth and romance. These jewellers had supplied jewels for all the major royal houses, iconic movie stars and heads of state.

But he was still curbing the irritation he'd felt ever since Darcy's very stark insistence that they observe professional boundaries—marriage or no. Was the woman completely blind? All he had to do was come within two inches of her and the electricity was practically visible.

Even now he couldn't take his gaze off the way her breasts pressed lushly against the edge of the glass case they were sitting in front of. He'd noticed the sales assistant's eyes drop too, and had glared at the man so fiercely he'd almost dropped a tray of priceless rings.

Darcy's reminder that she would have been long gone if not for this wedding arrangement caused another ripple of irritation. Max wasn't used to things morphing out of his control. It was a sense of control hard won and fought for—literally.

But when Darcy looked at him with those huge blue eyes all he wanted to do was throw control out of the window and give in to pure basic instinct. And yet she had the wherewithal to sit there and draw a little prim circle around herself saying, *Not over the line.*

She looked at him now, and Max couldn't imagine a woman looking *less* enthusiastic to be here.

He frowned. 'What is it?'

She glanced at the assistant, who moved away for a moment, discreetly polishing a ring.

'I don't know what to choose—they're all so ridiculously expensive… I mean, you're going to insure the ring, right? I'd hate for anything to happen to it—especially when this isn't even for real.'

Max saw the clear turmoil on Darcy's face and it was

like a punch to his gut to realise just how different she was from any other woman he might have brought to a place like this. They would have had absolutely no qualms about choosing the biggest and most sparkly bauble in the shop. And he would have indulged them without even thinking. It gave him a sense of distaste now.

He took her hand in his. It felt unbearably small and soft. 'Darcy, you're overthinking this. Just choose a ring. We'll get it insured. Okay?'

After a moment she nodded, and then said, 'Sorry, I'm probably making this boring for you.'

She looked back at the rings and some hair slipped over her shoulder, obscuring her face. Without thinking Max reached for it and tucked it behind her ear again. She looked at him and he couldn't resist. He leaned forward and pressed a kiss next to the corner of that surprisingly lush mouth.

Immediately her eyes went darker, but then they flashed. 'I told you—'

His hand gripped hers and he smiled as he said, 'We're buying a ring for our whirlwind engagement, *cara mia*, people are watching.'

She looked around quickly and then ducked her head, whispering fiercely, 'Fine…just in public.'

Max said nothing, but vowed right then to make sure they were in public as much as possible.

Darcy looked at the ring on her finger from different angles as Max discreetly paid the bill. Someone had delivered her a glass of champagne and she sipped it now. Grateful for the slightly numbing sensation. Numbing her from thinking about how choosing the ring had impacted on her so much.

It had brought up all sorts of unwelcome and tangled

emotions. As a small girl she'd used to love going into her mother's jewellery box and looking at the glittering earrings and bracelets. But the engagement ring had been her favourite, made of nine baguette diamonds surrounded by sapphires and set in white gold.

Darcy had used to put it on, holding it in place and imagining herself in it, marrying a handsome prince.

And then one day it had disappeared. Darcy had asked her mother where it was, only to be told curtly that she'd sold it. That had been the beginning of the end of the fairytales in Darcy's imagination, as her parents' marriage had fractured and split apart over an agonising year of arguments and bitter recrimination.

Today the ring Darcy had chosen in the end had been far too close to something she might choose for real, but she hadn't been able to resist—some rogue devil had urged her on. A rectangular-shaped diamond, surrounded by smaller baguette diamonds, set in platinum. It was positively discreet when compared with some of the other choices, but right now it felt like an unbearably heavy weight on her hand.

'Ready?'

Darcy looked up to see Max waiting. She grew warm, thinking of him watching her as she'd been inspecting the ring, and almost sprang out of the chair.

'Ready.'

Max guided her solicitously out of the shop and Darcy couldn't help noticing a young couple as they passed, obviously head over heels in love. The pretty woman was crying as her boyfriend presented her with a ring.

Darcy caught Max's look and raised brows and scowled as he tutted, 'Now, *that's* not going to convince anyone.'

Just inside the clear revolving doors Max stopped her

and turned her towards him. 'What—?' was all she managed to get out before Max cupped her jaw in one big hand and angled her face up to his so that he could kiss her.

Immediately the hot insanity of the other night slammed back into Darcy with such force that she had to cling onto his shirt to stay standing. It was an explicit kiss, and Darcy was dimly aware that someone like Max probably couldn't deliver a chaste kiss if his life depended on it. He was like a marauding pirate, sweeping in and taking no prisoners. It was hot, decadent, and the slide of Max's tongue against hers made her want to press her breasts against his chest and ease their ache.

When he pulled back she went with him, as if loath to break the contact. She opened her eyes and Max said smugly, 'That's a bit better.'

Darcy's brain felt sluggish as Max pulled her out of the shop, but it snapped back to crystal clarity when they faced a veritable wall of flashing lights.

'Max! Over here! Max! Who is the lucky lady? What's her name?'

The barrage of questions was deafening and terrifying. Max had his arm around Darcy and her hand was still gripping his shirt. She could feel the tension in his body as he said, in a masterful voice that sliced through the cacaphony, 'We will be releasing a statement on Monday. Until then please afford my fiancée and I some privacy.'

'Show us the ring!'

But Max's car materialised then, as if out of nowhere, and he was guiding Darcy into the back of it, shutting the baying mob outside as it took off smoothly into the Paris traffic.

Darcy vaguely heard Max curse, and then a glass was

being pushed into her hands. She looked down, feeling a little blank and blinded.

'Take a sip, Darcy, you're in shock… *Maledizione*, I should have realised… You've never been papped before.'

When she didn't move he cursed again and lifted the glass to her lips, forcing liquid to trickle into her mouth and down her throat. She coughed as it smarted and burned and realised she was shaking from the adrenalin and shock of being in front of the paparazzi for the first time.

She looked at Max, who took the glass away and put it back in the car's mini-bar. 'How did they know?'

He had the grace to look slightly sheepish. 'I got my PR people to tip them off.'

Darcy thought of their kiss just inside the door, and all the lenses that must have been trained on them every moment, capturing her reaction. Not for one second did she want Max to know how angry it made her or how betrayed she felt. Stupid to think that a private moment had been invaded. It hadn't been a private moment—it had been manufactured.

'Well,' she said, as coolly as she could, 'I hope Montgomery sees it—or they'll have wasted an afternoon when they could have been chasing someone far more exciting.'

'I'm sorry. I should have warned you.'

Darcy feigned unconcern. 'Don't worry about it—at least it'll look authentic.'

'Good,' Max said briskly. 'Because we're going to a function in Rome this evening. It'll be our first official outing as a couple.'

Darcy looked at him and hated the way her voice squeaked as she said, 'Tonight?'

Max nodded. 'It's a charity gala.' His eyes flicked down over her chainstore dress and he glanced at his watch as he said, 'When we get back to Rome you'll be taken straight to meet with a stylist. She's going to put together a wardrobe for you. And a wedding dress.'

Darcy's hands curled into fists. She was barely aware that they were already on the outskirts of Paris again, heading back to the airport. 'I might have plans for tonight.'

Max looked at her, and there was something distinctly proprietorial in his gaze. 'Any plans you have from now on are *my* plans. And I've been thinking: it'll look better if you move in with me. You should pack a weekend bag for now—we can move the rest of your stuff next week…'

Darcy didn't even bother opening her mouth, knowing resistance was futile. That was it. In the space of twenty-four hours her life had been neatly pulled inside out, and the worst thing was she'd agreed to it all.

CHAPTER FIVE

MAX LOOKED AT his watch again. *Where was she?* He'd meant to go and meet her at the apartment, but he'd been delayed in the office by a conference call to New York, so he'd changed there.

He'd texted Darcy to explain and got back a terse, Fine. See you there.

Max almost smiled; he couldn't imagine many women he knew texting him back like that. His almost-smile faded, though, when he thought of that morning and choosing the ring in Paris, and afterwards when they'd run into that wall of paparazzi.

He could still recall Darcy's jerk of fright and the way she'd burrowed into him instinctively. He'd felt like a heel. He'd totally underestimated how frightening that might be for someone who hadn't experienced it before. He was used to women revelling in the attention, preening, lingering… Darcy had been pale and shaking in the aftermath—not that she'd let it show for too long.

Something in Max's chest tightened. And then she was there, in the doorway of the function room, looking for him. Hair pulled up. One shoulder bare in an assymetrical dress that clung to her breasts, torso, and hips, before falling to the ground in a swirl of black silk and chiffon.

The room fell away, and the ever-present thrum of awareness made his blood sizzle.

How had he ever thought she was unassuming? She was stunning.

He could see her engagement ring from here, the brilliant flash of ice-white, and he pushed down the tightness in his chest. That same sense of protectiveness and possessiveness he'd felt earlier outside the jewellers hit him again, and he pushed that down too. It was nothing. It was the thrill of anticipated triumph over the deal that would finally take him away from that moment on the streets in Rome, when his own peers had seen him shabby and feral. Reduced to nothing.

Her eyes met his and he went forward to meet her.

Darcy saw Max almost as soon as she stopped in the doorway. Of course she did. He stood head and shoulders above most of the crowd. He was wearing a classic black tuxedo and she felt as if someone had hit her right between the eyes.

He'd made some effort to tidy his hair and it was swept back from his face now, dark blond and luxurious, but still with that trademark unruly length. And she could see from here that his jaw was clean-shaven.

In truth, she'd been glad of a little space from Max for the rest of the day—especially now she knew she'd be heading back to his apartment with him that night. She wasn't ready for that at all.

He was cutting a swathe through the crowd, heading straight for her, and—damn it—her breath was short again.

When he got to her he just looked at her for a long moment before slipping a hand across her bare shoulder and around the back of her neck. Her skin sizzled as his head came closer and his mouth—that perfect sensual mouth that rarely smiled—closed over hers.

She wanted to protest—*Stop kissing me!*—even as she knew he was only doing it for the benefit of their audience. But the fact was that every time he kissed her another little piece of her defences around him fell away.

There was nothing but blinding white heat for a second, as the firm contours of Max's mouth moved enticingly over hers, and then a rush of heat swelled all the way up her body from the pulse between her legs.

When he took his mouth away and pulled back she was dizzy, hot. It had been mere seconds. A chaste kiss on the mouth.

Max still had a hand around her neck. He was so close she could smell him, feel his heat around her. It was as if he was cocooning her slightly from the crowd and Darcy was reminded of the shock and vulnerability she'd felt in front of those paparazzi.

She pulled away from him.

'You look…beautiful.'

'You don't have to say that.'

Darcy felt exceedingly self-conscious in the dress the stylist had picked out for her to wear tonight. She glanced up at him from her eyeline, which was roughly around the centre of his chest—she'd been avoiding his gaze till now and his jaw was tight.

'It's not a line, Darcy, I mean it. You look…stunning.'

'I…' She couldn't speak. No man had ever complimented her like this before. She'd never felt *beautiful* before. But for a second, now, she did.

Max took her hand and led her into the throng, stopping to take the glass of champagne offered by a waiter before handing it to Darcy. She took a gulp, glad of the sustenance, aware of the interested looks they were getting—or rather that *she* was getting.

She hated the prickling feeling of being under scrutiny. The crowd in the ballroom of the exclusive Rome hotel was seriously intimidating. This was A-list territory. Actually, this made the A-list look like the B-list. She'd just spotted a European royal and an ex-American president talking together in a corner.

In a bid not to appear nervous, Darcy asked, 'So, what charity is benefiting from this function?'

Max glanced down at her. 'Numerous charities—I've nominated one I run with my brother.'

Darcy looked at Max, wondering again about his relationship with his brother, but she found herself distracted by his clean-shaven jaw and the white line of his scar that gave her a small jolt every time she saw it.

Just then a gong sounded and the crowd started to move into another room.

Max explained, with a cynical tinge to his voice, 'They'll get the charity auction and the posturing out of the way now, so that they can get on with the *really* important stuff.'

Max let go of her hand so she could sit down, and Darcy smiled politely at the man next to her. When Max took the seat next to hers she said, 'You mean the wheeling and dealing? The real reason why people are here?'

He looked at her approvingly. 'I'll make a proper cynic of you yet.'

Darcy felt a little hollow. She didn't need Max to make her a cynic. Her parents' spectacular break-up had gone a long way to that end already. Not to mention this pseudo-engagement.

She thought of something then, and looked at Max.

'You said to Montgomery that we'd be getting married in two weeks?'

He looked at her. 'We will. I've arranged for a special licence.'

Darcy felt as if she was drowning a little. 'Is it really necessary to go that far?'

Max nodded. 'It's just a piece of paper, Darcy. Neither of us really believes in marriage, do we?'

For a moment Darcy wasn't sure *what* she believed. She'd always sworn she'd avoid such a commitment, but she knew deep inside that some small part of her still harboured a wish that it could be different. Buying the ring today had tapped into it. And she hated it that this weakness was becoming evident here, in front of Max, under that gold gaze.

She forced a brittle smile. 'No, of course not. With our histories we'd be mad to expect anything more.' And she needed to remember that—especially when Max's touch and kisses scrambled her brain.

To take her mind off that she looked around and took in the extreme opulence. Even though her parents had always been well off—apart from her father's recessionary blip—she'd never moved in circles like this. Except for her time at Boissy. She grimaced at that memory, wondering if any of her old Boissy classmates were here. It was quite likely. This was definitely their stomping ground. Some of the offspring of Europe's most prominent royal families had been at the school.

The auction started and it was mesmerising. The sheer amounts being bid escalated well into the millions.

After one bid she gasped. 'Did someone *really* just buy an island?' Max's mouth quirked and Darcy immediately felt gauche. 'Don't laugh at me. I haven't been to anything like this before.'

There was a lull after the last few bids and he reached for her hand and lifted it up, turning it so that he could press a kiss to her palm. Darcy's heart-rate accelerated and she tried to pull her hand back, but he wouldn't let go, those eyes unnervingly direct on hers.

Feeling more and more discomfited, she whispered tetchily, 'We need to set some rules for an acceptable amount of PDAs. I wouldn't have thought you were a fan.'

Inwardly, Max reacted to that. Normally he wasn't. *At all*. He hated it when lovers tried to stake some kind of a public claim on him. But every time he touched Darcy he felt her resistance even as she melted against him. It was a potent mix of push and pull, and right now he wanted to touch her.

'You're big on rules and boundaries, aren't you?' He kept her hand in his when she would have pulled away, fascinated by the way colour washed in and out of her face so easily.

Her mouth tightened. 'They're necessary—especially when one is trying to be professional.'

Max chuckled, surprised to find himself enjoying being here with her so much. It had been a long time since he'd seen anyone interested in a charity auction. 'I don't think I need to tell you our professional boundaries are well and truly breached.'

She hissed at him. 'As if I'm not aware of that. Do I need to remind *you* that if it wasn't for this crazy marriage farce I'd be long gone by now?'

Something inside Max went cold. She would be gone because of what had happened in his office that night. He didn't doubt it. But Max knew now that he would have felt compelled to try and persuade her to stay…or to seduce her properly. She'd set a fire alight that night, and a very unwelcome and insidious suspicion occurred to him. Had he on some level wanted to keep her at all costs? Precipitating his flashbulb idea of marrying her?

Panic washed through him and he handed her hand back. 'You're right. We don't want to overdo it—no one would believe it.'

The sudden hurt that lanced Darcy made her suck in a breath. Of course they wouldn't believe it. Because why on earth would someone like Max—a golden god—be with someone like *her*?

She got up jerkily and Max frowned.

'Darcy—wait. I didn't mean it like—'

But she cut him off with a tight smile and muttered something about the bathroom, making her escape.

Everyone was standing up now and moving, starting to go back out to the main ballroom, where a world-famous band were about to play a medley of their greatest hits. She found a blissfully empty bathroom off the main foyer and looked at herself in the mirror with horror.

In spite of Max's cruel words she was flushed, and her eyes looked wide and bright enough to be feverish. Just because he'd held her hand? *Pathetic.*

She ran the cold water and played it over her wrists, as if that could douse the fire in her blood. *Damn Max anyway.* He shouldn't have the power to hurt her.

Sounds came from outside—voices. She quickly dried her hands and left just as some women were coming in on a wave of expensive perfume. They were all chattering, and stopped abruptly as soon as they saw her.

Darcy pinned a smile on her face and tried not to let the fact that they'd obviously been discussing *her* intimidate her.

As she approached the ballroom again Darcy saw Max standing at the main door, hands in his pockets. He looked…magnificent. *Hateful*. Proud. But also apart. Like a lone wolf. *Good*. A man like him didn't deserve friends. And that just made Darcy feel horrible.

He turned around and saw her and she could almost feel the place where the cold water had run on her wrists sizzle.

He frowned as she came closer. 'Are you okay?'

Now she felt silly for rushing off. 'Fine. Needed to go to the bathroom.' She thought a little despondently that his usual lovers probably didn't suffer the mundane bodily functions of mortals—and certainly never mentioned them to him.

He took her arm. 'We're done now. Let's go.'

Suddenly the thought of going back to his apartment with him loomed like a spectre in the dark. Anger at him pierced her, and anger at herself—for letting him hurt her so easily.

A rogue voice made her dig her heels in and say, 'Actually, I'm not ready to go yet.'

He looked at her, not a little stunned. He was not used to people saying no to him.

She tipped up her chin and took a moment of inspiration from the music nearby. 'I like this band. I want to dance.'

Now Max looked horrified. 'Dance?' Clearly he never indulged in such pedestrian activities.

She arched a brow, enjoying needling Max a little. 'Dance, Max. You know—a recreational social activity designed to bring people together in a mutually satisfactory way.'

Clearly angry now, Max moved closer to Darcy and pulled her into his body. 'I can do a "mutually satisfactory" activity, *dolcezza*, if that's what you're looking for—but it's not called dancing.'

Darcy's breath hitched. She should have known better than to tease him. She was serious. 'A dance, Max. That's what I'm talking about.'

He lifted a hand and cupped her jaw, for all the world the besotted fiancé. She cursed. She was playing right into his hands.

'Fine, then. Let's dance.'

Max took her hand in a firm and slightly too tight grip that told her of his irritation and led her onto the dance floor just in time for a slow number. Darcy cursed herself again for opening her big mouth.

He turned and gathered her close and she had to put her arms around his neck. He looked down at her and said mockingly, 'Forgive me. I had no idea you were so eager to make our charade look even more authentic.'

Darcy snorted, and then went still when one of Max's hands moved lower, to just above her buttocks, pressing her even closer. She closed her eyes in frustration for a moment—as if she needed to be reminded that he resented this PDA as much as she did.

And then she felt his hand brush some hair back off her cheek and he said, in a different tone of voice that set off flutters in her belly, 'Darcy, look at me.'

Reluctantly she opened her eyes, far too aware of his lean, hard body pressed against hers.

'I think you misunderstood me before… I meant no one would believe it because I don't usually indulge in any kind of overt affection with lovers in public.'

Darcy hated it that he'd seen her hurt. She shrugged. 'It's cool, Max, you don't have to explain anything.'

Even so, the hurt dissipated like a traitorous little fog.

'The problem is,' he went on, as if she hadn't spoken, 'I can't seem to stop myself from touching you.'

She looked up at him, and they stopped moving on

the dance floor while everyone kept going around them. Max pressed against the small of her back, moving her closer to his body, where she could feel the distinctive thrust of his arousal.

Now he looked intense. 'This is not usual for me, Darcy.'

She was barely aware of where they were any more, and she whispered, 'You think it's usual for me?'

Max started to move again subtly, ratcheting up the tension between them. Panic flared at the thought of going back to his apartment. 'Max, this isn't… We can't do this. We need to keep this pro-professional.'

Great. She was stuttering now. All she knew was that if Max seduced her she wouldn't have anything left to hold him at bay with. He'd already swept through her life like a wrecking ball.

He arched a wicked brow. 'You know what I think of professionalism? It's overrated.'

And then he kissed her, deeply and explicitly, and Darcy knew she was right to fear him—*this*. Because she could feel her very cells dissolving, merging into his. She was losing herself.

She pulled back with effort. '*No*, Max.'

A faster, more upbeat song was playing now, and she and Max were motionless in the middle of the floor. He grabbed her hand and pulled her from the throng. Her legs were like jelly.

Once away from the dance floor Max stopped and turned to Darcy, running a hand through his hair, an intense look on his face.

'Look, Darcy—' He stopped suddenly as something caught his eye over Darcy's head. He cursed volubly and an infinitely hard expression came over his face.

Darcy frowned and looked behind her to see a stunningly beautiful woman in the far corner of the room.

Something pulled at a vague memory. She was wearing a skin-tight black dress that shimmered and clung to her spectacular figure. Dark hair was swept back and up from her high-cheekboned face, and jewels sparkled at her ears and throat.

Darcy's insides cramped a little as she wondered if it was an ex-lover of Max's she'd seen in a magazine.

He was propelling them across the room before she could say anything, and as they got closer she could see that the woman was older than she'd imagined—but incredibly well-preserved.

She was arguing with a tall, handsome man, holding a glass of champagne and gesticulating. The wine was slopping messily onto the ground.

The man looked at Max with visible relief and more than a little irritation. He said curtly, 'I've had enough—you're welcome to her, Roselli.'

The woman whirled around, and just as Darcy noticed with a jolt of shock that she had exactly the same colour eyes as Max he was saying, in a tone tinged with steel, 'Mamma.'

His mother issued a stream of vitriol. Her eyes were unfocused and there was a sheen of perspiration on her face. Her pupils were tiny pinpricks. It was shocking to come face-to-face with Max's mother like this, and it made Darcy's heart clench to think he'd probably only told her half of what she'd been like.

The other man had walked away. Max's mother made as if to go after him but Max let go of Darcy's arm to stop her, taking her glass away and handing it to Darcy. His mother screeched and Darcy could see people looking.

Max had his mother in a firm grip now, and he said to Darcy, 'I'll take her home. If you wait here I'll get my driver to come back for you.'

Darcy was about to agree, but then she said quickly, 'Shouldn't I go with you? It'll look a little odd if I don't.'

Max was clearly reluctant to have Darcy witness this scene—she had a keen sense that he wouldn't allow many, if *any* people to witness it—but he obviously realised she was right.

'Fine, let's go.'

Staff had ordered Max's car to come round and he got into the back with his mother, who was remonstrating volubly with Max now. Darcy got in the front, her nerves jumping. Max was apparently used to this, and was on his phone making a terse call.

When they pulled up outside an exclusive apartment block in a residential part of Rome a man in a suit was waiting. Max introduced him as Dr. Marconi and he came in with them. Once inside a palatial apartment Max and the doctor and his mother disappeared into one of the rooms, with the door firmly closed behind them.

Darcy waited in the foyer, feeling extremely out of place. Max's mother was shouting now, and crying. Darcy could hear Max's voice, low and firm.

The shouting stopped.

After a long while Max re-emerged and Darcy stood up from where she'd been sitting on a gilt-edged chair.

'How is she?'

Max's hair was dishevelled, as if he'd been running his hands through it, and his bow tie was undone. He looked grim. 'I'm sorry you had to witness that. I would have introduced you, but as you could probably tell her response was unlikely to be coherent.'

'You've dealt with this before…?'

Max smiled, but it didn't reach his eyes. 'You could say that. She's a drug addict. And an alcoholic. The man at the party was her latest enabler, but evidently he's had enough. So what'll happen now is she'll enter an exclusive rehab centre, that's got more in common with a five-star resort than a medical facility, and in about a month, when she's detoxed, she'll rise like a phoenix from the ashes and start all over again.'

The other man emerged now, and spoke in low tones to Max before taking his leave after bidding goodnight to Darcy. Max turned to her.

'You should go. My driver is outside. I'm going to wait for a nurse to come and then make sure my mother is settled before I go. I'll see you in the morning.'

Clearly he wanted her to go now. She backed away to the door.

'Goodnight, Max.' She turned back from the door to say impulsively, 'I'm sorry…about your mother. If there's anything I can do…' She trailed off, feeling helpless.

'Thank you,' Max said shortly. 'But it's not your problem. I'll deal with it.'

For a fleeting moment Darcy thought that if this was a real engagement then it would be her problem too. She wondered if a man like Max would ever lean on anyone but himself and felt an almost overwhelming urge to go to him and offer…what?

She left quickly, lest Max see anything of her emotions on her face.

In the car on the way home Darcy had a much keener and bleaker sense of what things must have been like for Max when he'd left Brazil with his mother. The fact that he'd ended up on the streets wasn't so hard to believe now, and the empathy she felt for him was like a heavy weight in her chest.

A few hours later Max sat back in the chair in his dark living room and relished the burn of the whisky as it slid down his throat. He finally felt the tension in his body easing. He'd left his mother sleeping, with a nurse watching over her.

When he'd seen Elisabetta Roselli across the function room earlier tension had gripped him, just as it always did. It was a reflex born of years of her inconsistant mothering. Never knowing what to expect. And even though he was an adult now, and she couldn't affect his life that way any more, his first reaction had been one of intense fear and anxiety. And he hated it.

Darcy… He could still see her face in his mind's eye when she'd turned back from the door, concerned. The fact that she'd handled seeing his mother in that state impacted on him in some deep place he had no wish to explore.

His brother had not had to suffer dealing with the full vagaries of their mother. Max was used to dealing with it on his own… But for a moment, with Darcy looking back at him, he'd actually wanted to reach out and pull her to him, feel her close, wrapping her arms around him…

A soft noise made Max's head jerk up. Darcy stood silhouetted in the doorway of the living room as if conjured right out of his imagination. She was wearing loose sleep pants and a singlet vest that did little to hide those lush heavy breasts, the tiny waist. Her hair was long and tumbled about her shoulders.

'Sorry, I heard a noise…you're back. Is she…your mother…is she okay?'

Max barely heard Darcy. He was so consumed with the sight of her breasts, recalling with a rush of blood to his groin how they'd felt pressed against him on that dance floor.

Damn it to hell. He didn't want to want her. Especially not when he felt so raw after the incident with his mother. But even from across the room her huge blue eyes seemed to see right through him—into him. Right down to the darkest part of him.

It made something twist inside him. A need to push her away, push her back. Avoid her scrutiny.

'Getting into character as my wife already, Darcy? Careful, now—I might believe you're starting to like me. I guess having an addict for a mother is bound to score *some* sympathy points...'

CHAPTER SIX

DARCY IMMEDIATELY PALED in the dim lighting, and Max didn't even have time to regret the words that had come out of his mouth before her eyes were flashing blue sparks.

'I know you're a ruthless bastard, Max, but I've never thought you were unnecessarily cruel. If that's the way this will play out then you can find yourself another convenient wife.'

She whirled around and was almost gone before Max acknowledged the bitter tang of instant remorse and shot up out of his chair, closed the distance between them and grabbed her arm in his hand, stopping her in her tracks.

He cursed and addressed the back of that glossy head. 'Darcy. I'm sorry.'

After a long moment she turned round. She was so tiny in her bare feet, and it reminded him of how she'd fitted against him earlier that day, making him aware of an alien need to protect, to cosset.

Her eyes were huge, wounded. He cursed himself silently. 'I'm sorry,' he said again, aware that he'd probably never uttered those words to anyone.

'You should be.'

Her voice was husky and it had an effect on every nerve-ending in Max's body.

'You didn't deserve that.'

'No, I didn't.'

And then, because it felt like the most natural thing in the world, as well as the most urgent, Max took her other arm and pulled her round to face him. The air crackled between them. He could see Darcy's breasts rise and fall faster with her breathing, and he was so hard he ached.

He dipped his head and pressed his mouth to Darcy's, drawing her up against him. She was as still as a statue for a long moment, as if determined to resist, and then on a small indrawn breath her mouth opened under Max's and the blood roared in his head.

His hands dropped and settled on her waist, over the flimsy fabric of her vest, relishing the contours of her tiny waist. She triggered something very primal in him in a way no other woman ever had.

His tongue stroked into her mouth, finding hers and tangling with it hotly. His erection jerked in his pants in response and he groaned softly.

Darcy tasted like the sweetest nectar on earth, but her small sharp tongue was a pointed reminder that she had an edge. That only fired up his blood even more. She was soft, sweet, malleable…and melting into him like his hottest fantasy.

Max took ruthless advantage, deepening the kiss, his hands gripping her waist, pulling her into him, feeling his aching hardness meet the soft resistance of her body. Her breasts were full, pressing against him, and his hand snaked under her vest, spreading out over her lower back. Her skin was silky and hot to the touch.

Lust such as he'd never experienced had him in a grip so strong he couldn't think beyond obeying this carnal need.

* * *

Darcy was dimly aware of a very distant voice in her head, screaming at her to stop and pull back. Moments ago she'd been blisteringly angry with Max. And hurt. But she didn't care any more. She was in his arms and her world was made up of heat and glorious pounding desire.

Every part of her exulted in his masculinity and his sheer size. Big hands were smoothing up her back, lifting her vest until it snagged under her breasts. He pulled away from her mouth and Darcy sucked in much needed oxygen—but it didn't go to her brain, it seemed only to fuel the hunger in her body.

Max's mouth feathered kisses along her jawbone and down to the sensitive part of her neck just under her ear.

The scent of sex was musky in the air and it was mixed with something very feminine. *Her desire.* Oh, God. She was so weak, but she didn't care any more.

When he pulled back to take her hand in his and lead her over to the sofa she went with him without hesitation. He sat down and guided her over him so that she ended up with her knees either side of his thighs, straddling his lap, his erection a hard ridge between her legs.

Some vital part of her brain had abdicated all responsibility for this situation. It felt dangerously liberating. He was looking at her with such dark intent that she felt dizzy even as her hands were already on his shirt, fumbling with the buttons, eager to explore the wide expanse of his chest.

He said thickly, '*Dio*, I want you so much.'

Darcy couldn't speak. So she bent her head and kissed him again. His hands gripped her waist for a moment before exploring upwards, pulling her vest up and over her breasts, baring them.

He broke the kiss and looked at her, eyes wide, feverish. *'Si bella...'*

He cupped one breast in his hand and squeezed the firm flesh. Darcy bit her lip at the exquisite sensation, and then cried out when he leaned forward and took the straining tip into his mouth, sucking it deep before letting it pop out and then ministering to her other breast with the same attention.

She wasn't even aware that her hips were making subtle circular motions on Max's lap, seeking to assuage the building tension at her core, where the slide of his erection between her legs was a wicked temptation. She only became aware when his hand moved down to her buttocks and held her there. His arousal was thrusting between them, touching her intimately through their clothes. She was pulsating, all over.

A wave of incredible tenderness moved over her as she saw his scar, gleaming white in the low lights. Without thinking Darcy reached out and traced it gently, running her finger down the raised and jagged length. Then she bent to kiss it.

And just as she did so the wave of tenderness finally triggered some faulty self-protection mechanism and she tensed all over, her mouth hovering just over Max's scar.

What the hell was she doing?

He'd just been a complete bastard and yet after a brief apology and a kiss hotter than Hades she was writhing in his lap, about to let emotion overwhelm her! A man who saw her as just a means to an end.

What was even worse was that she'd already seen some pictures online, of them in Paris, outside the jewellers. She looked like a rabbit caught in the headlights, small and chubby next to Max's tall, lean form, clutching at him. It was galling. Mortifying how ill-matched they were.

Darcy scrambled up and off Max's lap so fast she nearly fell backwards. She tugged her vest down over straining breasts.

Max sat forward, his shirt half open, deliciously dishevelled. 'Darcy…what the *hell*?'

Darcy's voice was shaky. 'This is a mistake.'

Every masculine bone in Max's body was crying out for completion, satisfaction. He could barely see straight. He'd been moments away from easing his erection free of confinement, ripping Darcy's clothes off and embedding himself so deeply inside her he'd see stars.

He hated it that she seemed to have more control than him—that she'd been the one to pull back. The rawness he'd felt earlier had returned. He felt exposed.

He stood up in a less than graceful movement, his body still clamouring for release, but he was damned if he was going to admit that to Darcy.

He bit out, 'I don't play games, Darcy, and I don't believe in mistakes. I believe in choices. And you need to be honest with yourself and make one.'

Darcy looked up at him for a long moment and the very thin edges of Max's control threatened to fray completely. But then she took a step back and said in a low voice, 'You're right. I'm sorry. It won't happen again.'

Frustration clawed at Max with talons of steel. That was *not* the answer he'd wanted to hear. As she moved to walk away he reached out and took her arm again, not liking the way she tensed.

'Damn it, Darcy. We both want this.'

She turned her head and looked at him. 'No, Max, we don't.'

She pulled free and walked quickly from the room.

Two weeks later

'I do hope that you haven't put me anywhere near your father. Honestly, if he turns up with his latest bimbo—'

'*Mother*. Please stop.' Darcy tried to keep the exasperation out of her voice. 'You're not near my father, you're at opposite ends of the reception lunch table *and* the registry office.'

Her mother, as petite as Darcy but über-slim sniffed. 'Well, that's good.'

Darcy sighed. She and Max had agreed that it would look better to have family there, and that they could serve as witnesses. Her parents were as bad as each other in different ways: her passionate Italian mother was on a constant quest to find security with ever younger and richer men, and her hopelessly romantic father got his heart broken on a regular basis by a stream of never-ending gold-diggers who saw Tom Lennox coming from a mile away.

She forced a smile at her mother in the mirror, not wanting to invite questions about anything beyond the superficial.

To say that the last two weeks had been a strain was an understatement. Luckily work had kept Darcy busy, preparing for the final reckoning with Montgomery. But the personal tension between Max and her had almost reached breaking point. Even though they'd barely seen each other in his apartment. He worked late most nights, so she was in bed when he returned, and he was gone before her in the morning. And Darcy, of course, had refrained from any more dangerous nocturnal wanderings.

Even now she burned with humiliation when she thought of the concern she'd felt when she'd seen him that night, staring broodingly into his drink. Alone…

Vulnerable... *Ha!* The man was about as vulnerable as reinforced steel.

Darcy was sure that he'd only been in London to meet with Montgomery for the last two days to get away from her, and she hated how that stung.

Since that night in his apartment he'd been cool to the point of icy. And she only had herself to blame. She'd been the weak one. Blowing hot and then cold. Running away because she couldn't handle the thought of Max breaching the final intimacy, afraid of what would happen to her if he did.

No doubt he was used to women who knew what they wanted and went after it—and him. No qualms. No questions. Maybe he'd been seeing one of those women in London, discreetly?

Her mother tugged at the back of her dress now, tutting. 'Honestly, Darcy, why couldn't you have bought a nice *long* dress? This one's more suitable for a cocktail party. This *is* quite likely to be your only wedding day, you know.'

Darcy welcomed the distraction and said fervently, 'I'm counting on it. And it's a registry office wedding, Mother. This dress is perfectly suitable.'

Her mother sniffed and tweaked Darcy's chignon, where a mother of pearl comb held the short veil back from her face. 'Well, I suppose it *is* a nice dress, for all that,' she admitted grudgingly.

Darcy ran a critical eye over herself, feeling slightly disembodied at the thought that she was getting married that day. To Max Fonseca Roselli. The dress was off-white satin, coming to just over her knee. It was a simple sheath design, overlaid with exquisitely delicate lace. It covered her arms and up to her throat.

It's fine, she told herself, hating that the little girl in her still yearned for something long and swirling…romantic.

Wanting to avoid any further scrutiny, she said to her mother, '*You* look gorgeous.'

Her mother preened—predictably. She was indeed stunning, in a dusky pink dress and matching jacket. An exotic fascinator was arranged in her luxurious dark hair, which was piled high.

As she zipped up her dress at the back Darcy referred to her mother's comment about her father. 'It's not as if you haven't brought your own arsenal, Mother.'

Viola Bianci glared at her daughter. 'Javier and I are very much in love.'

Darcy just arched a brow. From what she'd seen of the permatanned Spanish Lothario, he was very much in love with *himself*, but he was obviously enjoying parading the very well preserved and beautiful older woman on his arm. For whatever reason—whether it was love or something less—he was lavishing attention and money on her mother, so Darcy desisted from making any more comments.

Her mother came in front of her now, to pull the veil over her face, but she stopped and looked at Darcy.

'*Carina*…are you sure you're doing the right thing?' Her mother looked slightly discomfited for a moment. 'I mean, after your father and I… Well, our break-up… I always got the impression that you weren't really into marrying *anyone*.'

A familiar impulse to deflect any concern about her rose up, and even though Darcy recognised that it was totally misplaced she put a hand on her mother's arm and said reassuringly, 'Don't worry. I know what I'm doing.'

And she did, she told herself.

Her mother wasn't finished, though. 'But are you in

love with him, Darcy? You might think I don't notice much, but one thing I've always known about you is that you'd never settle for anything less than a lifetime commitment—whether it's through marriage or not.'

Darcy all but gaped at her mother. Since when did Viola Bianci display any perspicacity in looking into her daughter's psyche? It slammed into her gut and made her want to recoil and protect herself. *Lifetime commitment.* Was that really what she wanted? As a result of her experiences? More than a sense of security and a successful career?

Her mouth was opening and closing ineffectually. Finally she croaked, 'I… Well, I do… I mean, I am—'

Just then a knock came on the door and one of the wedding planner's team popped her head round the door. 'It's time to go.'

Saved by the bell—almost literally. As Darcy's mother began to flap, gathering up her personal belongings and Darcy's bouquet, she'd never been so glad for her gnat-like attention span. Clearly she wasn't that concerned about whether Darcy was marrying for true love or not—and frankly that one insight, no matter how erroneous Darcy assured herself it was, was discombobulating enough.

The registry office felt tiny and stifling to Max, but as he was about to ask for the window to be opened he saw that it was already open. He'd been talking to Darcy's father, who was a pleasant affable man, completely preoccupied with his much younger glamorous girlfriend, whom Max had categorised as a gold-digger in seconds. She was busy making eyes at Max whenever Tom Lennox's back was turned.

Max had to curb the urge to scowl at her. She was tall, slim, blonde and undeniably beautiful, but his head was still filled with the way Darcy had felt straddling his lap that night, the size of her tiny waist spanned by his hands. The feel of that hard nipple against his tongue. The scent of her.

Hell. It had been two weeks ago. He was usually hard-pressed to recall any liaison more than twenty-four hours after it had happened. Making love with women was a very pleasurable but transitory thing in his life.

He didn't wake up at night sweating, with the sheets tangled around his aching body like a vise. *He did now.* Which was why he'd been in London for the last two days, putting himself through more unsatisfactorily inconclusive meetings with Cecil Montgomery.

The man was still insisting that all would be revealed in a week's time. *Damn him.* The one thing easing his frustration was that Montgomery's attitude had definitely changed since Max had announced his marriage to Darcy. Gone was the slightly condescending and derisory tone. There was a new respect that Max couldn't deny.

So this would be worth it. The fact that Darcy was driving him slowly insane would all be worth it.

Max felt a prickling sensation across his skin and looked up just as the few people gathered in the room hushed.

She was here. And he couldn't breathe, seeing how beautiful she looked. It felt as if he hadn't seen her in weeks, not two paltry days.

She stood in the doorway with a woman he assumed to be her mother. But he only saw Darcy. The delicious curves of her body were outlined in a white lace dress. A short veil came to her chin, obscuring her face. But he could make out her huge blue eyes even through the gauzy material and he felt his belly tighten with something like…emotion?

She was doing this for him. A monumental favour. *You're paying her*, pointed out a pragmatic voice. But still… This went above and beyond payment.

It was gratitude he felt. Gratitude that she was doing this for him. That was all.

Her mother moved ahead of her, smiling winsomely at Max, who forced a smile back. But he couldn't take his eyes off Darcy as she came the short distance between the chairs towards him. She held a bouquet of flowers in front of her—not that Max could have said what they were.

And then she was beside him, and he was turning to the front, acutely aware of her body heat and her scent. He felt an urge to reassure her but pushed it down. Darcy knew what this was. She was doing it for her own reasons and because he was paying her handsomely.

He frowned minutely. Why had she asked for that specific amount of money?

'Signor Roselli?'

Max blinked. *Damn.* The registrar repeated the words for Max, which he duly recited, and then he was facing Darcy. He felt slightly dizzy. Rings were exchanged. Darcy's hands were tiny, her fingers cool as they slid the ring onto his finger. Her voice was low, clear. No hesitation.

And then he was lifting her veil back from her face and all he could see was an ocean of blue. And those soft lips, trembling ever so slightly.

'You may kiss your bride.'

He heard the smile in the registrar's voice but he was oblivious as he cupped Darcy's small face between his hands, tipping it up towards him, and bent to kiss her.

Darcy's mouth was still tingling and she had to stop herself from putting her fingers to it, to feel if it was swollen. Her hand was in Max's firm grip, her bouquet in the other hand, as he led her through the foyer of the exclusive Rome hotel and into the dining room where an intimate lunch was being held.

Along with her parents, who had been their witnesses, Max had invited his brother and new sister-in-law, and some business associates from Max's company.

Darcy felt like an absolute fraud, and was not looking forward to being under the inspection of people she didn't know well. Max made her feel so *raw*—and even more so now, after two weeks of minimal contact.

Max turned at the door to the dining room, where their guests were waiting, stopping her. His grip on her hand tightened and compelled her to look up at him. She'd been too wound up to really take him in before now, but his dark grey morning suit along with a silk cravat made him look even more handsome and masculine. He could have stepped out of the nineteenth century. A rake if ever there was one. Even though he was clean-shaven and his unruly hair was tamed. Well, as tamed as it would ever be.

Darcy felt a rogue urge to reach up and run her fingers through it, to muss it up.

'Okay?'

She looked deep into those golden eyes and felt her heart skip a beat. She nodded minutely. Max cupped her face with his hand and rubbed a thumb across her lower lip. Her body clamoured, telling her how much she'd missed his touch.

And then he tensed. Darcy looked to the side to see a tall dark man with possibly the most beautiful woman she'd ever seen in her life. White-blonde hair and piercing ice-blue eyes. But they were warm, and the woman was smiling at Darcy.

Max took his hand away from her jaw and stood straight. She could feel the tension in his form. 'Darcy,

I'd like you to meet Luca Fonseca, my brother, and his wife Serena.'

Max's twin was as tall, and as powerfully built as he was, but much darker, with black hair and dark blue eyes.

Darcy shook hands with both of them and Serena came closer to say, 'Your dress is beautiful.'

Darcy made a small face, feeling completely inadequate in the presence of this goddess. 'I felt less might be more, considering it was a registry office wedding.'

Serena made a sound of commiseration and said, 'My husband and I had a beach wedding, just us and close family, and I can't tell you how relieved I was not to be paraded down some aisle like a wind-up doll.'

Darcy let out a little laugh, surprised that she was so warm and friendly. She felt a pang to realise that she probably wouldn't ever meet her again after this.

A staff member interrupted them to let them know that everyone was ready for Max and Darcy to make their entrance as a married couple. Luca and Serena went inside and Darcy took a deep breath, glad that it was only a handful of guests. Max took her hand and she pasted a bright smile on her face as they walked into a welcome of clapping and cheers.

They were soon separated and caught up in a round of congratulations and chatter. Darcy felt even more like a fraud, aware of Max's tall form on the other side of the room as he spoke to his brother. She felt as if she had '*fake bride*' emblazoned on her forehead.

When there was a lull Serena surprised her by coming over and handing her a glass of champagne.

Darcy took a grateful sip. 'Thanks, I needed that.'

Serena frowned minutely. 'Are you okay? You look a little pale.'

Darcy smiled weakly. 'It's just been a bit of a whirlwind two weeks.'

Serena was about to say something when her husband Luca appeared at her side and wound his arm possessively around her waist. They shared a look so intimate that Darcy felt like a voyeur. And something worse: *envy.*

To Darcy's intense relief a gong sounded then, indicating that lunch would be served. She siezed on the excuse to break away and find her seat, and pushed down the gnawing sense of emptiness that had no place here, at a fake wedding.

The tension that gripped Max whenever he saw his brother had eased somewhat by the time they were sipping fragrant coffee after lunch. He looked around at the guests at the long table. He and Darcy were at the head and she was leaning towards the man on her left, one of Max's accountants.

This wedding was putting him in pole position to achieve everything he'd ever wanted: the ultimate respect among his peers. So why wasn't he feeling a sense of triumph? Why on earth was he preoccupied with his very fake wife and how delectable she looked in her wedding dress? How he'd like to peel it bit by bit from that luscious body?

At that moment he spied his brother and his wife, sitting halfway down the table. They were side by side and looking at one another with utter absorption. It made something dark twist inside him.

He shouldn't have invited them. All anyone would have to do would be to look at Luca and Serena and realise how flimsy the façade of his marriage to Darcy was.

Once again his brother was effortlessly proving Max's lack. And worse was the evidence that whatever blows

Luca had been dealt in his life they hadn't touched some deep part of him, tainting him for ever. For the first time, Max felt more than envy—he felt hollow.

'What is it? You look as if you're about to murder someone.'

The low voice came close to his ear and Max turned his head to see Darcy's face, a small frown between her eyes. He felt exposed—and frustrated. There was a futile sense of rage in his gullet that was old and dark, harking back to that one cataclysmic day in his childhood. Still to be bound by that day was galling.

He acted instinctively—seeking something he couldn't put a name to. Perhaps an antidote to the darkness inside him. An escape from the demons nipping at his heels. He uncurled his hand and put it around Darcy's waist, tugging her into him before claiming her mouth in a kiss that burned like wildfire through his veins.

It didn't bring escape, though. It brought carnal hunger, and a need that only she seemed able to tap into. Incensed that she could do this to him so easily—and here, in front of witnesses—made Max deepen the embrace. He felt rather than heard Darcy's moan as both hands moved around her back.

Eventually some sliver of sanity seemed to pierce the heat haze in his brain and he pulled back. Darcy took a second to open her eyes. Her mouth was pink and swollen, her breasts moving rapidly against him.

And then he saw her come to her senses. Those blue eyes went from hot to cold in seconds and she tried to pull free, but Max didn't let her go, keeping her attention on him.

Darcy couldn't seem to suck enough oxygen into her heaving lungs. When she could, she hissed at Max, 'What the *hell* was that little caveman move?'

She knew damn well that his urge to indulge in that very public display of affection hadn't been entirely inspired by the need to fool their guests, because the look on his face just before he'd kissed her had been dark and haunted. It struck a raw nerve.

She pushed herself free of Max's embrace and stood up.

He stood up too, frowning. 'Where are you going?'

Darcy whispered angrily, 'I'm taking ten minutes' break from this charade—if that's all right with you?'

She forced a poilte smile at their guests, who had now started moving around after lunch, but didn't stop, heading straight for a secluded balcony through an open set of French doors. She needed air. *Now.*

She went and stood at the stone wall and looked out over Rome, basking benignly in the midafternoon sun. It was idyllic, and a million miles from the turmoil in her belly and her head.

Damn Max and his effortless ability to push her buttons. The galling thing was she didn't even know what button he was pushing. She just knew she was angry with him, and she hated feeling like a puppet on a string. This was a mistake. No amount of money was worth this. She'd happily live as a nomad for the rest of her life if she could just be as far away from Max as possible.

Liar.

'Darcy?'

She closed her eyes. No escape.

Darcy turned from the view. It was the thread of concern in his voice that made her glance at him, but his face was unreadable.

She looked at him accusingly. 'Why did you kiss me like that? It wasn't just to put on a show for people.'

'No,' he admitted reluctantly, 'it wasn't just for that.'

A pain that Darcy knew she shouldn't be feeling gripped her when she thought of the anger and frustration she'd sensed in the kiss.

'It's one thing to be wilfully and knowingly used for another's benefit, and to agree to that, but I won't let you take the fact that I'm not the lover you want out on me.'

Max's eyes widened. And then he came in front of her and put his hands on the wall either side of her, caging her in. In a low, fierce voice he said, 'That statement is so far from the truth it's not even funny. The only woman I am remotely interested in is right in front of me.'

Darcy swallowed and tried not to let Max's proximity render her stupid. 'But you were angry…I could feel it.'

Max pushed himself off the wall and ran a hand around his jaw. He stood beside Darcy and looked out at the view. Then he sighed and without looking at her said, 'You're right. I was angry.'

Darcy rested her hip against the wall, her own anger diffusing treacherously. 'Why?'

Max's mouth twitched, but it wasn't a smile. More a reflex. 'My brother, primarily. I saw them—him and his wife…'

Without elaborating Darcy knew exactly what he meant. She'd seen it too. Their almost unbearable intimacy.

Max shrugged and looked down for a moment. 'He gets to me like no one else can. Pushes my buttons. I always feel like I'm just catching up to him, two steps behind.'

Darcy could see it then: the intense hunger Max had to feel he wasn't in competition with his brother any more. Whatever had happened when their parents had split up had marked these two men indelibly.

Feeling tight inside, she said, 'Well, I don't like being used to score a point. Next time find someone else.'

She went to move away, to go back inside, but Max caught her before she could leave with his hands around her waist, holding her fast. His eyes were blazing down into hers.

'I kissed you because I want you, Darcy. If there was anger there at my brother it was forgotten the moment my mouth touched yours. I do not want you to be under any illusions. When I kiss you I know exactly who I'm kissing and why.'

Darcy stared up at him, transfixed by the intensity of his expression.

'*Maledizione.* I can't think when you look at me like that.'

He pulled her closer and Darcy fell against him, unsteady in her shoes. She braced her hands against his chest. He was warm. Hard.

'Max…' Darcy protested weakly—*too* weakly. 'There's no one here to see.'

'Good,' he said silkily. 'Because this is not motivated by any reason other than the fact that I want you.'

One hand cupped the back of Darcy's head and the other was tight around her waist, almost lifting her off her feet. When Max's mouth met hers she was aghast to realise how badly she wanted it, and she met him with a fervour that should have embarrassed her. But it didn't. She wound her arms around his neck, her breasts swelling against his chest.

He backed Darcy into the wall, so it supported her, and their kiss was bruising and desperate. Two weeks of pent-up frustration and denial. Max's hands were on her hips and he gripped her so tightly she wondered dimly if the marks of his fingers would be on her flesh.

Darcy became aware of a noise after a few long seconds of letting Max suck her into a vortex of mindlessness and realised it was someone clearing his throat in a very obvious manner when she pulled back and was mortified to see a staff member—also mortified—waiting for them to come up for air.

Max released her hips from his grip and stood back. His hair was mussed, his tie awry. Darcy felt as if she might float away from the ground, she was so light-headed.

Max turned to face the red-faced staff member, who was obviously eager to pass on his message so he could escape.

'Sorry to disturb you, Signor Roselli, your car is ready when you are.'

The young man left and Darcy looked at Max, feeling stupid. 'Car? Where are we going?'

'The villa—Lake Como—for a long weekend.'

She must have looked as stupid as she felt.

'Our honeymoon?' he said.

Max had informed her a week before that they'd go away for a long weekend after the wedding, just so that everything looked as authentic as possible. She'd completely forgotten. Until now.

And suddenly the thought of a few days alone in a villa with Max was terrifying.

'Surely we can just stay here in Rome? There's so much to prepare for Scotland—' she gabbled.

Max was shaking his head and taking her hand to lead her back inside. 'We're going to Como, Darcy. Non-negotiable.'

He let go of her hand inside the door to the dining room and, as if sensing her growing desire to escape said firmly, 'Say goodbye to your parents, Darcy. I'll meet you in the foyer in an hour.'

She watched, still a little numb, as he strode over to some of the guests to start saying goodbye and felt a looming sense of futility wash over her. A weekend alone in a villa with Max Fonseca Roselli…after that kiss… She didn't stand a chance.

CHAPTER SEVEN

THE JOURNEY TO his private jet passed mainly in silence. Max had been waiting for Darcy in the lobby, as promised, and she'd been aware of every move he'd made in the car. Now, in the jet, he took a seat with graceful athleticism.

As much as she didn't want to attract his attention, it was hard to drag her eyes off him. He'd changed into dark trousers and a dark grey lightweight long-sleeved top that did little to disguise the sheer breadth and power of his chest. The grey of his top seemed to make his eyes burn more intensely, and Darcy looked away quickly, in case she was caught, as the small plane left the ground.

She'd changed too, into a 'going-away' outfit—a soft flowing knee-length sleeveless dress of dark cream with a matching jacket. Her hair was down and her scalp still prickled from the pins that had been holding it up, along with the veil.

She gently massaged her skull and thought of the poignant moment that had caught her unawares when she'd packed the dress and veil away in their boxes. She'd been thinking what a pity it was that she'd never have a daughter to hand it down to.

The stylist had seen her expression and said, 'Don't worry, Signora Roselli, we'll take good care of them for you.'

Hearing *Signora Roselli* had been enough to break her out of that momentary weakness and bring her back to reality. She was only Signora Roselli because Max craved world domination, and she—the fool—was helping him achieve it.

'For a new bride you're surprisingly quiet. Nervous about our wedding night, darling?'

Darcy cursed Max. If there was one mood in which he was pretty much irresisitible it was this more playful one that he so rarely displayed.

She glared at him and quirked a brow. 'I wouldn't know—not having much experience of being a new bride, and having even less inclination to be one ever again.'

Max tutted and smiled wolfishly. 'Don't worry, *dolcezza mia*, I'll be gentle with you.'

To Darcy's horror she felt herself getting hot, wondering what it would be like if this was *real* and Max was *really* promising to be gentle. She had an image of him with that intent look on his face as he thrust into her carefully, inch by inch… Between her legs she spasmed, her muscles reacting to her lurid imagination.

Horrified at her wayward body and, worse, at her desire to know what it would be like, she said curtly, 'Save it, Max. I'm not a virgin.'

She looked away when he said, 'So I don't need to be gentle, then? Good, because when we come together—'

Darcy snapped open her seatbelt and stood up, swaying a little as the plane hit some turbulence. She gripped the back of the seat to stay steady and said, 'I'm going to lie down. I'm tired.'

Max caught her wrist as she went past him and when she looked down he was frowning, all humour gone. 'What the hell, Darcy…? I'm just teasing you.'

She pulled her wrist free, already feeling like a prize

idiot to have risen to such easy bait. 'I'm fine. I told you—I'm just tired. It's been a long day.'

She made her way to the small bedroom and slammed the door shut behind her, pressing the backs of her hands to hot cheeks. She cursed herself roundly as she paced back and forth. Of all the stupid— Why had she let Max wind her up like that?

She sat down on the edge of the bed, suddenly weary. Because the truth was that this whole day had got to her much more than she'd ever imagined it would, and his teasing had just highlighted that.

When she'd agreed to this marriage with Max she'd somehow believed that she could do it and remain relatively intact. Unscathed by the man.

But that had all been shot to hell. It had been shot to hell after that night in his office, when the true depth of her attraction to him had become painfully apparent.

Why did he have to find her attractive? This wasn't how the world worked—men like Max did *not* find women like Darcy attractive. She had no doubt that it was an aberration—a freakish anomaly. A desire borne out of the fact that she was so different from his usual type of woman. Stress-induced. Something-induced. But not real.

Her circling thoughts brought her back to one question: why had she followed that crazy instinct to apply for a job working for the man in the first place?

With a heartfelt groan Darcy flopped back onto the bed and shut her eyes, willing sleep to come and make her mind blissfully blank.

A sleek car was waiting for them when they arrived at the small airport just outside Milan. When their bags had been stowed Max sat in the driver's seat and Darcy got into the passenger side. The car was luxurious, and obviously high-end. When Max drove out of the airport it felt as if it was barely skimming the road.

He must have seen something of her appreciation because he said, 'This is the new Falcone road car. I'm friends with Rafaele—he lends me cars to test-drive every now and then.'

Darcy's mouth quirked, even though she was still wary after her outburst earlier. But she couldn't let Max see that he could get to her so easily. 'The perks of being friends with one of the world's most famous car manufacturers?'

Max shrugged lightly, wearing his mantle of privilege easily. Darcy sighed. She couldn't even fault him for that, though. It wasn't as if he hadn't earned it.

'Darcy…' he said carefully. 'What happened earlier—'

She sat up and said quickly, 'It was nothing, really. It's just been a lot to take in.'

Max's hands clenched on the steering wheel and he said after a long moment, 'Do you know I've never really said thank you?'

She looked at him and his jaw was firm. He glanced at her, and then back to the road. 'Thank you, Darcy, for doing this. I don't underestimate how big a favour it is.'

Darcy felt herself weakening, any residual tendrils of anger fading. She knew Max well enough to know that he rarely said thank you unless it really meant something to him.

She was about to say something in response when an insidious suspicion occurred to her and her eyes narrowed on Max, taking in his oh, so benign expression in the half-light of the car. She folded her arms. 'I'm not sleeping with you, Max.'

He glanced at her again and that mocking look was back on his face. 'I wasn't aware I'd asked the question.'

'You don't have to. It's there between us… But I just can't.'

Because you'll hurt me.

Darcy sucked in a breath, the truth finally revealing itself to her. She was in way too deep with Max already. If they slept together his inevitable rejection would crush her. The thought was utterly galling, but it was a fact.

Max's jaw was firm again in the low light of the car. 'I said before that I don't play games, Darcy. It's your choice.' He slid her a darkly wicked look. 'But I won't promise not to try to change your mind.'

In a firm bid to ignore that disturbing promise, Darcy changed the subject. 'Who owns the villa we're going to?'

'A good friend of mine and his family—Dante D'Aquanni.'

'I've heard of him,' Darcy said. 'He's in construction?'

Max nodded, negotiating a hairpin turn by the lake with skill. 'He and his family are living temporarily in Spain while he works on a project.'

'How do you know him?'

Max's hands tightened momentarily on the wheel. 'We go back a long way… He was one of the first clients I had who trusted me to invest his money for him.'

Precluding any further conversation, Max turned into a clearing where huge ornate gates loomed in the dark, with stone walls on either side. When the gates swung open Max drove in and a stunningly beautiful villa was revealed, with stone steps leading up to an impressive porch and door.

Golden light spilled from the doorway when it opened and a housekeeper came bustling out. A younger man joined the old woman who met them and took their bags. Max greeted the housekeeper warmly and introduced Darcy to the woman, who was called Julieta.

The D'Aquannis' housekeeper led them inside, chatting to Max easily, and Darcy guessed he'd been there before. The interior was awe-inspiring, with high ceilings, an impressive staircase, and huge rooms visible off the stone-flagged reception area.

One room, when Darcy peeked into it, seemed to have a blue glass ceiling. Murano glass? she wondered.

Max turned to Darcy after Julieta had offered some refreshments and Darcy seized the opportunity to reply in front of a witness, saying in Italian that she was tired and would like to go to bed. She ignored Max's undoubtedly mocking look.

It was with a feeling of mounting dread, however, as they followed Julieta upstairs, that Darcy wondered if they were going to be shown to one bedroom…

To her abject relief Julieta opened a door, motioning to Max, and then led Darcy to the next door along the wide corridor, opening it to reveal a sumptuous bedroom with en suite bathroom and dressing room.

Julieta bustled off again, after pointing some things out to Darcy and telling her that breakfast would be ready at nine a.m.

Darcy's relief lasted precisely as long as it took for Max to appear in an adjoining doorway, with a wicked glint in his eye.

Arms folded across that broad chest, he leaned gracefully against the doorframe. 'I told Dante about the true nature of our marriage…needless to say I'm regretting that impulse now.'

Darcy put her hands on her hips. 'Well, I'm not. Goodnight, Max.'

Max said musingly, almost as if she hadn't spoken, 'You know, I've never really had to woo a woman before—I'm looking forward to it.'

Her belly exploded as if a hundred butterflies had been set free. Of *course* Max Fonseca Roselli Fonseca had never wooed a woman before, because they always fell into his lap like ripe plums.

She started walking towards the door, prepared to shut it in his face. 'I'll save you the trouble. I'm really not worth it.'

Max's gaze dropped down over her body with explicit directness. 'On the contrary…I think you'll be very worth it.' He stood away from the door then, and said, 'Goodnight, Darcy.'

And then the adjoining door closed in *her* face, before she could make a smart retort, and she looked at it feeling ridiculously deflated, curbing the urge to open it again and follow Max into his room.

What had she expected? That Max would ignore a challenge? She was very afraid that she'd handled this all wrong. Max would accept nothing less than total capitulation, and his tone of voice said that he didn't expect it to take all that long.

Darcy stomped around the thickly carpeted room, getting unpacked and ready for bed, and muttered to herself, 'Do your worst, Roselli. I'm stronger than you think.'

Apparently she wasn't as strong as she thought after all. When she emerged for breakfast the following morning and saw Max sitting at the table which had been set up on a terrace at the back of the villa she immediately felt weak.

She studiously ignored the spectacular view of the lake—she had a very old fear of any expanse of water, no matter how scenic it was.

Max was wearing worn jeans and a dark polo top, his hair dishevelled by the breeze. When he lifted his hand to take a sip from a small coffee cup his well-formed bicep bulged and Darcy went hot all over.

As if sensing her scrutiny, he looked up and smiled. 'Good morning…sleep well?'

She fixed a bright smile on her face and moved forward, avoiding direct eye contact. 'Yes, thank you—like a baby and all people with a clear conscience.'

Max made an *ouch* sound and said dryly, 'Then I hate to inform you that I must be on the side of the angels as I slept well too.'

Darcy snorted inelegantly, helping herself to some pastries and pungent coffee, closing her eyes for a moment to savour the smell. *Heaven.*

When she opened them again it was to find Max giving her a leisurely once-over. His gaze stopped at her breasts and Darcy looked down, aghast to see the hard points of her nipples pushing against the thin material of the light sundress she'd put on, in the absence of anything remotely businesslike.

She resisted the urge to fold her arms over her chest and took her time over eating the delicious pastries and some fruit, avoiding Max studiously. When she did glance at him he seemed fixated on the corner of her mouth, and then he leaned forward to reach out and touch it with his index finger.

When he sat back she saw some jam on it, and he proceeded to lick it off the top of his finger—which had a direct effect on the pulse between Darcy's legs and abruptly made her appetite fade to be replaced by a much earthier one.

Not willing to sit there like a mouse, while Max the predatory cat played with her, Darcy stood up and said briskly, 'I'll find out where the study is, shall I? And check e-mails and—'

Max stood up too and reached for Darcy easily, taking her hand. 'You're doing no such thing. I've got plans for today and they won't be taking place in a study.'

Darcy pulled free and stepped back, panic fluttering along her nerve-endings at the thought of Max devoting all his attention to her. 'I don't mind. We should really make sure that—'

Suddenly Max dipped out of sight and Darcy's world was upended. She found herself in his arms, clinging onto his neck in fright.

'What the hell—?' she got out in a choked voice.

But Max was saying something to Julieta over her head about being back later for dinner. The woman smiled at them benevolently, as if she saw this kind of thing all the time. It made Darcy wonder about the owners.

Max finally let her down once they were outside, in order to open the passenger door of the car. Darcy tried to make a dash for it, back to the villa, but he wound an arm around her waist, practically lifting her into the passenger seat.

Darcy fumed as she watched him come around the front of the car, his eyes on hers warning her not to defy him again. When he swung in and quickly locked the doors from the inside Darcy sputtered, 'This is tantamount to kidnap…and you're blatantly taking advantage of my size… You're a…a *sizeist*!'

Max was already driving smoothly out of the villa and he looked at her with dark amusement and said, 'I have to admit that your…portability makes you a little easier to control.'

Darcy made a strangled sound of outrage and crossed her arms over her chest, glaring out of the window as Max drove away from the villa. Damn him and his superior strength.

But while she hated the ease with which he was able to compel her to do his bidding all she could think about was how it had felt to be held so securely in his arms—how her instinct had been to burrow closer and seek a kind of refuge she'd never felt like seeking before. The fact that she could be as susceptible as the next woman to Max's caveman antics was not welcome.

Darcy only recognised where they were when she saw the signs for Milano. She turned to Max and said eagerly, 'You've come to your senses and we're going back to Rome to work?'

He quirked a half-smile. 'No. I'm taking you out.'

Out *where*, though? Darcy looked at him suspiciously but he gave nothing away.

And then he said, 'Apart from my very serious intention to get you into my bed, it'll be good for us to be seen together the weekend after our marriage. We *are* meant to be on honeymoon, after all.'

Darcy had no answer for that. He was right.

They parked in a private and exclusive car park with valet parking and emerged onto a busy Milan street that was bustling with weekend activity.

It was like a fashion parade, with beautiful women walking up and down—some with the requisite small dogs—and beautiful men… A little too metrosexual for Darcy, but then this was the fashion capital of Italy and arguably Europe. Predictably, Max stood out among these beautiful people and there were plenty of heads turning in recognition and appreciation.

After all, Darcy recalled, hadn't the Italians invented a word for walking around in order to be seen? *Passeggiata?*

Max took Darcy's hand in his and led her down the

street. She wanted to pull away, but as if reading her mind he held on tight. Veering off to a small side street, Max ducked into a boutique with a world-famous designer's name over the door.

He was greeted like a superstar—and as a regular, Darcy noted with a dart of something dark. But before she could emit so much as a squeak she was whisked away behind a curtain and Max was left out in the foyer. At one stage she caught a glimpse of him sipping coffee and reading a newspaper.

She was completely bemused as industrious assistants flitted around her like exotic butterflies. Finally fitted into a stunning bodycon cocktail dress—a bit *too* bodycon for Darcy's taste—she was all but pushed back out onto the main salon floor. She realised she was being paraded for Max's benefit when he lowered his paper and looked her over as if she were a brood mare.

Anger started down low and then rose through her body in a tidal wave of heat and humiliation. She hissed at him, 'What the *hell* is this?'

His eyes snapped to hers. 'I'm taking you shopping.'

'I don't need any more clothes.'

Max looked nonplussed for a moment, as if he literally could not compute Darcy's reaction. It would have been funny if she hadn't been so angry. And what was making her even angrier was the evidence that this was obviously a regular occurrence for him…bringing women shopping.

So angry that she couldn't see straight, and feeling seriously constricted in the dress, she went straight to the door and walked out, almost tripping in the ridiculous heels. She was halfway down the street, with steam coming out of her ears, before Max caught up with her, standing in front of her to block her way easily.

'What the hell was *that*?'

'Exactly. What the hell *was* that? I thought you said you weren't used to wooing women? Does taking them shopping not count as wooing? Because evidently you do it a lot, going by your familiarity with those assistants in that shop—and quite a few others, I'd imagine.'

Max threw his hands up in the air. 'What woman doesn't love shopping?'

Darcy pointed a finger at herself. 'This one.' Then she folded her arms, her eyes narrowed on him. 'Maybe you consider taking women shopping as foreplay?'

They glowered at each other for a long moment, and then Max sighed deeply and put his hands on his hips. Eventually he muttered something like, 'Should have known better…'

Darcy put a hand behind her ear. 'Sorry? What was that?'

Max looked at her and his mouth twitched ever so slightly. He said, with exaggerated precision, 'I'm sorry for assuming you would want to go shopping. I should have known better.'

Darcy's own mouth was tempted to twitch, but she curbed the urge. 'Yes, you should. And I can't breathe in this dress.'

Max's gold gaze dropped and took her in, and then he said roughly, 'I don't think *I* can breathe with you in that dress.'

Immediately Darcy's brain started to overheat and she was in danger of forgetting why she was angry.

Max put out his hand. 'Come on—let's take it back.'

With her hand in his, walking back down the street, Darcy felt a little foolish for storming out like a petulant child. That wasn't her. She winced. But it *was* her around Max. He just wound her up. After all, he'd only been doing what he'd thought would make her happy.

She squeezed his hand and he looked at her just before they got to the shop. 'I'm sorry. I just… I'm not that into shopping. It's not that I'm not grateful.'

Max gave her a wry grin. 'I didn't exactly go about it with any finesse. Come on.'

He pushed the door open and a very sheepish Darcy walked in behind him, mortified under the speculative gazes of the staff.

When she was dressed in her own clothes she breathed a sigh of relief, and when she was out in the main part of the shop again she spied a bright, colourful scarf and took it to the till.

Immediately Max was there to pay for it. Darcy glared at him, but he ignored her and she sighed. When they were outside she tucked the scarf into her bag and he looked at her expressively. Feeling defensive, she said, 'Well, I felt like I had to buy *something*!'

Max rolled his eyes and said dryly, 'Believe me, those saleswomen are like piranhas.'

Darcy sniffed. 'I just felt bad, that's all.'

Max took her hand and Darcy glanced up. He was looking at her with a funny expression on his face. 'You've got a good heart, Darcy Lennox.'

She snorted, but inwardly fluttered. 'Hardly.'

And then, just as they were passing another boutique—much smaller but no less exclusive—Darcy stopped in her tracks. The dress in the window was exquisite—off the shoulder, deep royal blue satin, with a scooped neck and a boned bodice that would accentuate an hourglass figure.

When Darcy realised what she was doing she grew hot with embarrassment and went to keep walking, but Max stopped her, an incredulous look on his face.

'And you call *me* mercurial?'

Darcy smiled weakly. 'I didn't say I *hate* shopping.

I'm like a heat-seeking missile—once I see what I want I go for it and then get out again.'

'*Do* you want it?' he asked.

Darcy squirmed. 'Well…I like it…' She looked at it wistfully.

Max pulled her into the shop and this time paced the small space while she tried the dress on, together with suitable underwear and shoes.

The assistant stood back and said appreciatively, '*Bella figura, signora.*'

Max appeared at the dressing room door, clearly a little bored. When his eyes widened Darcy's heart-rate zoomed skywards.

'Is it okay?' she asked shyly. And then she babbled, 'You know, I probably do need a dress for the Montgomerys' party, so…'

'We'll take it.' Max's voice sounded slightly constricted.

Once Max had arranged for the dress and sundries to be sent to his office in Rome they left again. Darcy had tried to pay for the dress but of course he hadn't let her.

Back out in the sunshine, he looked at her and said, almost warily, 'What now?'

Darcy looked around, enjoying seeing Max knocked slightly off his confident stride. 'Well, first I want some gelato…'

Max's eyes boggled. 'After you've just bought that dress?' And then he shook his head. '*Incredibile.*'

Smiling now, he took her hand and pressed a kiss to the palm. Darcy looked around surreptitiously for paparazzi, but couldn't see any obvious cameras pointed at them.

'And after the gelato?'

She screwed up her nose and thought. 'Well, I've never seen *The Last Supper* by Leonardo Da Vinci, so that'd be nice, and I'd like to walk on the roof of the Duomo and see if we can see the Alps.' Darcy looked at Max. 'What about you?'

Max blinked. What about *him*? No one had ever asked him before what *he'd* like to do. And the fact that he'd assumed for a second that he could just take Darcy shopping— He shook his head mentally now at his lack of forethought. But he hadn't been thinking—he'd just wanted to get them out of the villa before she could lock herself in the study.

Clearly, though, he'd underestimated her and would need to be far more inventive. For the first time in a long time Max felt the thrill of a challenge and something else—something almost…*light*.

'Do you know what I'd like?'

She shook her head.

'To go and see the AC Milan game.'

Darcy looked at her watch and then said impishly, 'Well, then, you're going to have your work cut out making sure we fit it all in, aren't you?'

'That last goal…' Darcy shook her head and trailed off.

Max glanced at her, sitting in the passenger seat. They were almost back at the villa and he couldn't remember a day he'd enjoyed as much.

They'd stood before one of the great artworks of the world and then climbed to the top of a magnificent cathedral to see the spectacular view. They hadn't seen the snowy Alps through the heat haze that hung over the city, much to Darcy's disappointment, and it had made Max feel an absurd urge to fix that for her. And they'd been to a football match. He *never* got to go to see his favourite team play. He was always too busy.

He teased Darcy. 'So you're a fan of AC Milan now?'

She looked at him and grinned. 'I could get used to it. I never realised football was so gladiatorial. My father's a rugby man, so I grew up being dragged to rugby matches. Whatever country we were in I found it was a way of orientating myself, because we moved around so much.'

Max found himself thinking of something that had nagged at him, and asked curiously, 'Does that have anything to do with the very specific amount of money you requested?'

Darcy went still, but then she wrinkled her nose and said lightly, 'Isn't it a little crass to talk about money with your fake wife?'

Max shook his head. 'You're not avoiding the question so easily. You should have asked for a different amount. Ever heard of rounding up?'

Darcy scowled, making Max even more determined to know what the money was for. He would have given it to her in bonuses anyway, but the fact that she'd asked for it…

She sighed, and then said, 'When my folks split up they sold the family home. They never really settled again. I went to boarding school, my dad was travelling all over the world, and my mother was wherever her newest lover was. When my father's business fell apart and I went back to the UK to a comprehensive school it was my most settled time—even if we were living out of a cheap hotel.'

She shrugged.

'I've just always wished that I had somewhere… somewhere that I knew would always be there.' She let some hair slip forward, covering her face, and muttered, 'It's silly, really. I mean, lots of people don't have a home at all—'

Max reached out and put his hand over hers. 'It's not silly.'

He couldn't say any more because he knew exactly what Darcy was talking about. He'd never had that safe centre either.

He took his hand away to change gears. 'So, the money—it's for a house?'

Darcy nodded and smiled, not looking at him. 'It's a small flat in London. I've been keeping my eye on it for a few months now.'

Max could see Darcy all too easily—stepping out of a cute little flat on a leafy street, getting on with her life, disappearing into the throng of people. And he wasn't sure he liked it at all. In fact, if he wasn't mistaken, the flare of dark heat in his gut felt suspiciously like jealousy.

When Darcy had freshened up and changed into comfortable loose trousers and a silk top she went downstairs to dinner. It was set up on the terrace, in the lingering twilight. Flickering candles lent everything a golden glow and the opulent rugs and furnishings made her wonder about the couple who were lucky enough to own this idyll. Did they have a happy marriage? Somehow, Darcy thought they must, because there was an air of quiet peace about the place.

And then she shook herself mentally. She wasn't usually prone to such flights of the imagination.

Max wasn't there yet and she breathed a sigh of relief, going to the stone wall and looking out over the dark expanse of the lake at the lights coming on on the other side.

Even here, far away from the water, she felt it like a malevolent presence and shuddered lightly.

'Cold?'

Darcy whirled around, her heart leaping into her throat, to see Max holding out a glass of wine. She took it quickly, ducking her head. 'No, I'm fine…just a ghost walking over my grave.'

She sneaked a look at him as he stood beside her. He'd changed too, into dark trousers and a white shirt which inevitably made his dark skin stand out even more. He oozed casual elegance, and yet with that undeniable masculine edge that made him all man.

The day they'd spent together had passed in an enjoyable blur of sights and sounds, but mostly Max had been a revelation. Darcy had never seen him so relaxed or easygoing. As if a weight had been lifted off his shoulders.

At the football match he'd been like a little boy—jumping up and down with the crowd, embracing her and the man next to him when his team scored. Also spouting language that had shocked her when things hadn't gone well.

Julieta and the young man who it had turned out was her grandson delivered their dinner: fragrant plates of pasta to start, and then a main course of tender pork in a traditional sundried tomato, prosciutto and sage sauce.

Darcy groaned appreciatively when she tasted the delicious pork and said wryly, 'I may have to be rolled out of here in a couple of days.'

Max looked at her, and his gaze running over her curves told her exactly what he thought of that. Unused to being appreciated for what she normally considered to be a drawback, she avoided his eye again. A part of her still couldn't really believe he wanted her, but all day he'd touched her with subtle intention, keeping her on a knife-edge of desire.

In a bid to try and pierce this bubble of intimacy that surrounded them on the terrace, with the sound of the lake lapping not far away, Darcy asked about the couple who owned the house. 'I just wondered what they're like. This seems to be a happy place.'

Max pushed his empty plate away and then stood up, saying, 'I'll show you a picture.'

He returned a couple of minutes later with a beaming Julieta, who was dusting a picture with her apron. She handed it to Darcy. It showed an insanely handsome dark man, smiling widely, with a very petite blonde woman whose hair was a mass of crazy curls. She was also grinning, and holding a young boy with dark hair by the hand, while the man held a toddler high in his arms—a little girl with dark curly hair, a thumb stuck firmly in her mouth, eyes huge.

Something lanced Darcy deep down. This was a picture of familial happiness that she only knew as a distant dream. And who was to say that they wouldn't split up, with those poor children destined to spend a lifetime torn between two parents?

Aghast that she was even thinking of this in the face of such evident joy, she handed the picture back quickly with a fixed smile. 'They're lovely.'

Julieta took the picture away, carefully cleaning it again. She obviously missed them. She must be more like a member of the family than a housekeeper to them, Darcy guessed.

Max said into the silence, 'Perhaps not everyone goes through what we experienced.'

Darcy looked at him, wondering why she was surprised he'd read her mind. It seemed to be a speciality of his. 'Do you really believe that?'

He smiled and shook his head. 'Personally? No. But I have to admit that Dante and Alicia seem very…happy.' And then he asked abruptly, 'Why did you step in that day? During the fight?'

Darcy knew immediately that Max was referring to what she'd witnessed at Boissy, when she'd intervened. The memory of how exposed she'd felt after doing it made her squirm now. 'I can't believe you remember that.'

Max's mouth tipped up at one corner. 'It was pretty memorable. You single-handedly scared off three guys who were all easily three times your size.'

Max took her hand in his and hers looked tiny. It made her too aware of their inherent differences.

She shrugged. 'I just…saw them…and I didn't really think, to be honest.' She bit her tongue to stop herself from revealing that she'd used to watch Max far too intently, far too aware of his presence. Aware of the insolence he'd worn like a shield.

Afraid that he might see it, she deflected the conversation back onto him.

'You and your brother…do you think you'll ever be close?'

Darcy thought he'd pull his hand away, but he left it there, holding hers.

Quietly, he said, 'We used to be close. Before we were separated. Closer than anyone.' He looked at Darcy and smiled. 'We had a special language. It used to drive our parents crazy.' And then the smile faded. 'Luca was stronger than me, though…older by a few minutes. When our parents told us they were taking one each he just stood there—not crying, not saying anything. I'll never forget it.' Max's mouth twisted. 'I was the one that fell apart.'

Darcy turned her hand in Max's and gripped it. A sense of rage at his parents filled her, shocking in its intensity. 'You were little more than a baby, Max…'

Just then Julieta appeared, with a coffee pot on a tray, and Darcy blinked up at her, broken out of the web of intimacy that had come down over her and Max without her even realising it. Suddenly she felt very raw, and absurdly emotional. The full impact of the day was hitting her. She was in danger of losing herself out here with Max.

Acting on impulse, she seized the opportunity like a coward, pulling her hand back from Max's, avoiding his eye. She stood up, smiled, and said, 'No coffee for me, thanks—it's been a long day.'

Unfortunately she couldn't quite manage to leave at the same time as Julieta because Max had caught her wrist. Darcy looked down and her heart skipped a beat. To her intense relief his expression indicated nothing of their recent conversation. He looked altogether far too sexy and dangerous. Far too reminiscent of that younger Max—cocky and confident, but still human underneath it all.

He smiled, and it was the smile of a shark. 'You're not willing to concede defeat yet?'

Darcy shook her head and struggled against the blood that pounded in her veins. 'No, Max, I still don't think it's a good idea.'

To her surprise he let her go and leaned forward to pour himself some coffee. '*Buonanotte*, then, Darcy...'

Feeling unsure, because she didn't trust Max an inch, Darcy sidled around him to get to the doorway.

And then she heard him say softly, 'It's better that you go to bed now because you'll need your sleep. I'll be waking you early in the morning. I've got more plans for tomorrow.'

She looked at him suspiciously. 'What are you talking about?'

He just smiled and said, 'You'll see.'

Darcy started to speak. 'Look, Max—'

He speared her a look that told her in no uncertain

terms that he was hanging on to his control by a thread and that if she stayed a moment longer he wouldn't be responsible for his actions.

'Goodnight, Darcy. Go to bed while you still can… or it won't be alone.'

She had the sense not to ask anything else and fled.

CHAPTER EIGHT

'LEMME ALONE. IT'S the middle of the night.' Darcy burrowed back into the bed as deep as she could, but big firm hands reached in determinedly and ripped the covers back.

She squealed, wide awake now, and looked at Max looming over her, in the *very* early morning gloom.

'Buongiorno, mia moglie.' My wife.

Darcy scowled, feeling thoroughly disgruntled and aware that she was in just skimpy pants and a vest top.

She scrabbled for a sheet but Max insisted on pulling it back again, saying briskly, 'Now, I can dress you, or you can dress yourself—it's up to you. I've laid some clothes out for you.'

There was enough light in the room for a squinting Darcy to see that Max was wide awake, dressed casually, and that those mesmerising eyes were making a very thorough and leisurely appraisal of her body.

Then he said throatily, '*If*, on the other hand, you'd prefer to stay in bed, I won't object.'

Her body jumped with anticipation but she ignored it and scrambled off the bed, reaching for a robe. 'I'm up.' She rounded on him, saying grumpily, 'And I can dress myself.'

Max made a considering noise. 'Not a morning person? I'll make a note to prepare myself for that in the future.'

'It'd be more accurate to say not a middle of the night person,' Darcy snapped.

Max was thankfully backing away, and he glanced at his watch, saying, 'Downstairs in fifteen minutes. We've time for a quick breakfast.'

Darcy grumbled about arrogant bossy men as she washed and got dressed in jeans and a pretty silk long-sleeved top, shoving her feet into flat shoes.

She didn't like to admit that her defences still felt a little battered after yesterday and their intimate supper last night. She'd had disturbing dreams of small boys clinging onto each other as unseen hands forced them apart, and of bright red blood on pristine snow.

When she went down she was surprised to see Julieta up and about, greeting her with a cheery hello. She showed her to a covered part of the terrace at the back of the villa, clearly in deference to the fact that only the faintest trails of dawn could be seen in the sky, like delicate pink ribbons.

Max was drinking coffee. He looked at her and stood to pull out a chair.

Darcy felt exposed, with her freshly scrubbed face and her hair tied back in a ponytail. She valiantly tried to ignore Max and picked at a croissant and some fruit, still feeling fuzzy from sleep.

'You're not going to tell me where we're going, are you?'

Max shook his head cheerfully. 'It's a surprise.'

Darcy was already reacting to the prospect of another day in close proximity to Max… Her body was humming with energy.

She pushed her plate back, having no appetite this

early, and said, 'I suppose now is as good a time as any to tell you I hate surprises?'

She did, too, having learnt long ago that they were usually of the very unwelcome variety—more often than not something promised by one or other of her parents to assuage their guilt or to compensate for their absence at some event or other.

Hence carving out a steady, dependable career for herself, where no surprises would jump out to get her.

Until she'd agreed to this ridiculous charade.

Max stood up and put down his napkin. 'You'll like it—I promise. Ready?'

Darcy looked up and sighed inwardly at the determination stamped on his face. 'I don't have much choice, do I?'

He shook his head. 'Not unless you want me to put you over my shoulder and carry you out.'

Darcy had no doubt that Max wouldn't hesitate to put her over his shoulder—after all, he'd picked her up as if she was a bag of flour yesterday.

She stood up with as much grace as she could muster and said witheringly, 'You don't have to demonstrate your he-man capabilities again. I can walk.'

They drove a relatively short distance to a big flat open field, with several low buildings inside the gates. Max parked the car alongside some other vehicles and got out.

When she met him in front of the car, thoroughly bemused, he handed her something. 'Here, you'll need this—it might be a bit chilly.'

She took the fleece and guessed it must belong to the lady of the villa, because it fitted her perfectly and she'd looked to be about as petite as Darcy—if not smaller. Darcy zipped it up, suddenly glad of the extra layer against Max's far too intense perusal.

He'd put on a fleece too, and now took a basket from the boot of the car. Determined not to give Max the satisfaction of knowing how curious she was, Darcy just followed him around one of the low hangar-like buildings—and then stopped in her tracks and gasped out loud.

As she took in the significance of the scene in front of her she could feel the last of her defences crumble to dust. And, absurdly, tears pricked her eyes.

Max had stopped and was looking at her, the picture of innocence. Darcy curled her hands into fists at her sides and glared at him, willing the emotion to stay down.

In a husky voice she said, 'Of all the low-down, dirty, manipulative things to do, Max Fonseca Roselli…this just proves how cold-hearted you are.'

It was a hot air balloon, on its side, being inflated by a crew.

And it was on her bucket list.

One night, while working late in the office in that first couple of months, Darcy had asked Max idly about what might be on *his* bucket list—because what could someone who had nearly everything possibly want?

He'd given her a typical non-answer, in true evasive Max style. And then he'd asked her what was on hers. She'd replied, with some measure of embarrassment, that she'd always wanted to take a hot air balloon ride.

And now he was giving it to her.

Emotion tightened her chest.

Max just looked amused. 'You don't want to go?'

She glared at him. 'Of *course* I want to go.'

She folded her arms across her chest, hating it that he could make her *feel* so much, wanting to extract some kind of payment.

'But I'm not going anywhere until you tell me what's on *your* bucket list. And I want a proper answer this time.'

Max's expression hardened. 'I don't have a bucket list. This is ridiculous, Darcy. We'll miss the best part of the sunrise if we don't move now.'

She could see the balloon, lifting into the air behind Max. She tapped her foot. Waiting…

He sighed deeply and ran a hand through his hair impatiently. 'Nothing with you comes easy, does it?'

'No.' She smiled sweetly, feeling some measure of satisfaction to be annoying him—especially when he'd hauled her out of bed so early.

'Okay, I'll tell you—but you're not to laugh.'

Darcy shook her head and said seriously, 'I promise I won't.'

Max looked up, as if committing his soul somewhere—or hers, more likely—and then down again, and said in a rush, 'I want to own a football club.'

He'd said it like a young boy, blurting something out before he could lose his nerve, and Darcy's chest squeezed even tighter.

She pushed the emotion down and nodded once. 'Thank you. Now we can go,' she said.

Once she felt on a more even keel with Max she was like a child, with the full excitement of what he'd organised for her—whatever his motive—finally hitting her.

They were helped into the basket alongside the pilot, and then suddenly they were lifting off the ground and into the clear dawn-streaked sky. Darcy wrapped her hands tight around the basket's edge, eyes wide at the way the ground dropped away beneath them.

It was pure terror and exhilaration. Max stood beside her as the pilot edged them higher and higher, but she couldn't look at him, too afraid of what he might see on her face.

Time and time again her father had promised to do

this with her and it had never happened. And now she was here with her husband. Except he wasn't really her husband.

Emotions twisted like a ball in her gut and she took a deep breath.

Max's hand covered hers. 'Okay?'

When she felt more in control she looked at him and smiled. 'Perfect.'

The balloon made lazy progress over the spectacular countryside, with the pilot pointing out Lake Como and the other lakes. Far in the distance they saw the snowy tips of the Alps. Milan was a dark blur in the distance as they passed over fields and agricultural lands.

Darcy was entranced. When the gas wasn't firing, to propel the balloon higher, she thought she'd never experienced such peace and solitude.

When she could, she tore her eyes from the view and looked at Max. 'Is this your first time in a balloon too?'

He nodded and smiled, leaning one elbow on the basket-edge. Darcy had the uncomfortable sensation that he'd been looking at her and not the view. And she hated it that she was relieved he hadn't done this with anyone else.

She teased him now. 'You're not twitching at being so far from communication and Montgomery?'

Max lifted his phone out of his pocket and held it up to show that it had no bars of service, then put it back. 'Nope.'

He sounded inordinately cheerful about the fact, and Darcy marvelled again at this far more relaxed Max.

The view filled her eyes so much that it almost hurt as the sky got lighter and lighter, exploding into shades of vivid pink and red as the sun came up over the Alps in the distance.

She didn't notice that Max had been doing anything until he produced a glass of sparkling wine for her and another for himself. He offered one to the pilot, who smiled but declined.

Max clinked his glass off hers and then the view was blotted out as his mouth came over hers and she fell deep into a spinning vortex that had only a little bit to do with the fact that they were suspended above the earth in a floating balloon.

Only their mouths were touching, but Darcy felt as if his hands were moving over her naked flesh. When Max pulled back she had to grip the edge of the basket tight, afraid she might just float off into the sky altogether. She was telling herself desperately that it had only been for the benefit of the pilot. To keep up appearances.

She took a sip of the wine and the bubbles exploded down her throat and into her belly. She couldn't be more intoxicated right now than if she'd drunk three bottles in quick succession.

They sipped their wine and gazed over the view in companionable silence. Every now and then the pilot pointed something out, or Max asked him a question about the balloon's mechanics.

Darcy hadn't even realised she was shivering lightly until Max came and took her empty glass and moved behind her, wrapping his arms around her, his hands over hers.

She settled into the hard cocoon of his body far too easily. Stripped bare by the experience. His fingers entwined with hers and his head bent and he feathered a hot kiss to her exposed neck. She shivered again, but this time it wasn't because of the cold.

They stood like that for a long time, and then the pilot said something low to Max and she felt him take in a breath behind her. Even though she knew what he was going to say, she didn't want it to end.

'We have to turn back… The air is starting to warm up…'

Darcy was glad he couldn't see her face. Tears stung her eyes but she said lightly, 'Okay.'

The ride back seemed to pass in a flash, and all too soon they were descending and the ground was rushing to meet them. They landed with a soft thud and a small bounce before the crew grabbed the basket and held it upright while they got out.

Max got out first and then lifted Darcy into his arms. For a moment he didn't put her down. Something in his eyes held her captive. And then she realised they had an audience and she blushed and scrambled down.

She went to the pilot and pressed an impetuous kiss to his cheek. 'I know you must be used to it—but, truly, that was magical. Thank you.'

The man looked pleased, but embarrassed, and said gruffly, 'You never get used to it. *Grazie*, Signora Roselli.'

Max took her by the hand, and as they walked to the car Darcy was aware that she'd made a decision. It was as if the balloon ride's unique perspective on the earth had shown her an eagle eye view of just how fragile life looked from above…how silly she was being not to reach out and grab precious moments, no matter how finite they might be.

The thought of continuing to deny herself after what she'd just experienced made her feel panicky—as if something incredibly precious might slip out of her grasp for ever. She didn't care about the consequences.

Max stopped at the car and faced her. He had a look of resolute determination on his face. 'Ready for the next part of the surprise?'

Darcy looked at him. She wouldn't put it past him to have organised something like a trip to Venice for the day… But she shook her head and said clearly, 'No more surprises.'

A range of expressions crossed Max's face: irritation, disappointment, renewed determination…

She took a breath. 'I don't mean what you think I mean. I'm wooed, Max. I don't even really care if that balloon ride was a purely cynical move on your part, I loved it too much and thank you for planning it. And I'm done fighting you. I want you. Take me back to the villa.'

Max wasn't sure how he drove in a straight line back to the villa. He kept Darcy's hand in his and the journey was made in silence, with the mounting anticipation coursing through his body saturating the air between them.

When he glanced at Darcy he could see a similar kind of tension on her small face and it only made his blood flow hotter. *Dio.* He wanted this woman so badly. More than he'd ever wanted anything.

Some kind of warning prickled over his skin at that assertion, but he ignored it.

She'd accused him of being cynical in his decision to organise the hot air balloon ride and he might have been…before. But he'd only thought of it the previous day, when they'd stood on the roof of the Duomo in Milan and she'd been disappointed not to see the Alps.

Max had remembered Dante talking about taking a hot air balloon ride with his family and seeing the Alps, and at the same time Max had recalled Darcy mentioning it some months ago.

In truth, the experience had moved him far more profoundly than he would ever have expected. He'd never seen the earth from above like that when not encased in a plane, with stacks of facts and figures in front of him, hurtling towards yet another meeting to shore up his funds, his reputation. That had all felt dangerously inconsequential when floating soundlessly through the sky.

Max was aware of the fact that this marriage to Darcy was not proceeding at all the way he might have expected when he'd first proposed the idea…the means to his end were veering way off the track. But right now he couldn't care less. All he cared about was Darcy and the fact that she would be *his*.

When they got back to the villa it was early afternoon. Darcy knew she should be feeling hungry because she hadn't had much breakfast, but she was only hungry for one thing: Max. Now that she'd decided to stop fighting him—and herself—the full extent of her desire was unleashed and it was fearsome.

He held her hand as they went into the villa and Julieta greeted them, clearly surprised to see them back early—evidently Max *had* had more plans for the day, but Darcy was too keyed up to care what they might have been.

She heard him say to Julieta that she could take the rest of the weekend off if there were some provisions in the kitchen. The housekeeper only lived in the gate lodge nearby, but still Darcy's face burned with embarrassment, as if it was glaringly obvious what they intended to do.

But the woman took her leave cheerfully, after extracting a promise that they'd ring if they needed anything. Evidently she was used to such instructions.

Once she was gone, and the villa had fallen silent around them, Darcy looked at Max. Within seconds she was in his arms, their mouths fused, desperation clawing up from somewhere…the deepest, hottest part of her.

After long, drugging kisses and shedding outer layers they broke apart, and Max said gutturally, 'I'm not taking you here in the hall.'

Before she could object he'd picked her up in his arms, taken the stairs two at a time and shouldered his way into his bedroom. Sunlight streamed in the window and bathed Max in a golden glow. Never more so than now had he looked so awe-inspiring, and Darcy had to push down the quiver of self-doubt that he really desired her at all.

He put her on her feet and reached behind him to pull his top over his head. His chest was bare and right in front of her face. Wide and muscled. Lean. Dark golden hair dusting the surface.

Darcy wasn't sure if she was breathing—but she was still upright, so she must be. She reached out a tentative hand and touched him, hearing his indrawn breath as her nail scraped a nipple.

He cupped her jaw and tipped her chin up. Dark colour slashed his cheekbones. She could see the question in his eyes and was surprised—she'd have expected him to take ruthless advantage of her acquiescence, giving her no time to change her mind.

To stop the rise of dangerous emotions, and before he could say anything, she put her hand over his mouth. 'I know who you are, I know who I am, and I know what I want—and that's you.'

She felt shaky. That was about as close as she could get to telling Max that she was perfectly aware that he'd move on once he'd had her but she was okay with that. If she didn't want him so badly right now she might hate herself for grinding her self-respect into the dust.

The question faded from Max's eyes and he put his hands to the bottom of her top, lifting it up. She raised her arms and it slipped up and over her head. Next Max pulled free the band holding her hair, so that it feathered down over her shoulders.

His gaze dropped to the swells of her breasts, encased in lace. *'Bella...'* His voice was thick.

Darcy reached around behind her and undid her bra, letting it slip to the floor. She groaned softly when Max reverently cupped her breasts, pushing the voluptuous mounds together, rough thumbs making her nipples spring to attention, tight with need. She'd never felt so grateful for her curves as she did right then.

Her hands were busy on his jeans, undoing the top button. Warm flesh and his hard lower belly contracted against her fingers. It was heady to know she could do this to him.

He'd lowered his head and was exploring her with his hot mouth, his wicked tongue flicking against her breasts, learning the shape of her and the way her flesh quivered and tightened at his touch.

Darcy's hands were clumsy as she ripped free buttons and felt the potent hard bulge of him against her knuckles. Eventually she was able to push down his jeans over lean hips, but then she had to stop because Max had one of her nipples between his teeth, teasing it gently before letting it go to suck the fleeting pain away.

Her legs wouldn't hold her up any more and she fell back onto the bed. Max stood tall, his chest moving rapidly with his breath. He pushed his jeans down the rest of the way, and then his briefs, and Darcy's eyes widened on his impressive erection.

Her mouth watered, and when Max bent over to undo her jeans and pull them down she lifted her hips to help him. She felt only mounting impatience as he looked her over with possessive heat, pulling her panties off to join her jeans on the floor. No teenage crush could have prepared her for this reality. She felt as if she was burning up from the inside out as her hungry gaze roved over Max's perfect form, every muscle hard and honed.

A broad chest tapered down to lean hips, where his masculinity was long and thick, cradled between his strong thighs, long legs. He truly was a warrior from another time.

The ache between her own legs intensified and she widened them in a tacit plea, not even really aware of what she was doing, knowing only that she craved this man deep in her core—*now*.

Max cursed softly and reached into his bedside console for something. Protection. He smoothed it onto his length and then came down over Darcy, an arm under her back, arching her up, mouths fused, tongues duelling. Her breasts were crushed against his chest and she was arching into him, begging…

Max pulled away for a second. 'I need you, Darcy… The first time I can't do slow.'

She felt as if she was caught in the grip of something elemental. 'I don't want slow. I need you too—*now*.'

For an infinitesimal moment everything seemed to be suspended, and then he thrust into her in one smooth move, so deep that Darcy gasped, and her back arched at this invasion of her flesh, ready as she was.

Max stopped. '*Dio*…have I hurt you? You're so small…'

'No,' said Darcy fiercely, wrapping her legs around him as far as they'd go. 'Don't stop…'

The initial sting of pain was fading. She'd never felt so stretched, so full. And as Max moved his big body in and out she felt a deep sense of peace bloom and grow within her even as intense excitement built and built, until all her muscles were shaking with the effort it took to hold on against the rising storm.

Max put a hand between them, unerringly finding her centre and touching her there. 'You first, Darcy... then I'll fall...'

Darcy looked deep into his eyes, locked onto them tight as she finally relinquished her control to this man and fell so hard and so fast that she blacked out for a moment. She only came back to her dulled senses when Max's heavy body slumped over hers, their breathing harsh and ragged in the quiet room.

When the sky was tinged with the dying rays of the sun outside they made love again. Slowly, taking the time to learn everything they hadn't had time to do the first time around. Hands slipped and glided, squeezed and gripped. Max's fingers explored, feeling the telltale slickness between Darcy's legs, needing no more encouragement. He wrapped his hand around the back of Darcy's thigh and lifted it so that he could deepen his thrust into her body. He groaned with sheer pleasure that she held him so snugly.

She smoothed back the hair from his forehead, her hands gripping his shoulders, urging him on. It was a long, slow dance, building and building to a crescendo that broke over them, taking Max by surprise with its intensity.

When he had the strength to move he scooped Darcy against his front, with her knees drawn up so her buttocks were cupped in his lap. Wrapping his arms tight around her, he felt his mind blank of anything but a delicious feeling of satisfaction, and slipped into oblivion.

When Darcy woke it was dark outside. She had no sense of time or space for a disorientating moment, not recognising the room she was in. And then she moved, and winced as muscles—intimate muscles—protested.

Max. His big body thrusting so deep that she'd been unable to hold back a hoarse cry of pleasure… It all rushed back. The desperation of that first coupling, followed by that lengthy, luxurious exploration. Her skin felt sensitive, tenderised.

She sat up now, looking around the moonlit room. No sounds from the bathroom. Moving to the side of the bed, Darcy stood up, wincing slightly again, and reached for the robe left on the end of the bed.

She opened the door and immediately a mouth-watering smell hit her nostrils. She followed it instinctively, realising just how hungry she was as she stumbled to a halt in the doorway of the kitchen.

Max was stirring something in a pot, humming tunelessly, wearing low slung sweat pants and a T-shirt.

'Hey…' Darcy hovered at the door, feeling ridiculously self-conscious.

Max turned around and looked her over, those dark eyes gleaming with something she couldn't read.

'Ciao.'

Darcy came further in. 'What time is it?'

'About three in the morning. You must be starving.'

There was a very wicked gleam in Max's eyes and Darcy fought back an urge to poke her tongue out at that and at his far too smug look. She was ravenous. Not that she'd admit it.

She shrugged a shoulder, feigning nonchalance. 'A little, I guess.'

'Liar,' Max said easily, and came around the kitchen island to scoop her up against him and kiss away any faux nonchalance for good.

He let her go and walked back around to the pot.

Darcy was dizzy. 'What are you cooking?' she managed to get out over her palpitating heart. That kiss had told her that they were nowhere near finished with this mutual…whatever it was…

'Pasta with *funghi porcini* in a creamy white wine sauce.'

Max had dished up the pasta now, into two bowls, and was bringing them over to a rustic table. He brought over some bread, and a bottle of wine and two glasses.

Darcy came over, mouth watering. When she took a bite the *al dente* pasta and its flavours exploded on her tongue. It all felt incredibly decadent—as if this were some kind of illicit midnight feast.

After finishing her pasta, Darcy took a long luxurious sip of wine and asked idly, 'So what was the other part of the surprise that we missed today?'

Max sat back, cradling his own glass of wine, and smirked at her. 'I don't think you deserve to know.'

Darcy dipped her fingers in her water glass and flicked some at him. 'That's *so* unfair.' She mock pouted. 'I put out before you even had to go through with it.'

Max gave her a considering look full of mischief. 'That's true. If I'd known how easy it would be—'

Now Darcy scooped up a much larger handful of water and threw it at him. An incredible lightness infused her as Max put down his glass and smiled devilishly at her. He still managed to look gorgeous, even as water dripped down his face and onto his chest.

He picked up his own glass of water and looked at her explicitly.

She gasped and got up from her chair, inching away from him. 'You wouldn't dare…'

But he would. Of course he would.

Max stood up and advanced on her as Darcy fled behind the kitchen island.

'Max, stop—we're adults, and this isn't our kitchen.'

She was attempting to sound reasonable, but the breathiness in her voice gave her away.

He raised a brow. 'It's only water, Darcy. Now, come here like a good girl. You can't tease me and expect to get away with it.'

Darcy crept around the island as Max followed her and eyed where the door was. When she made her move, feinting left before going towards the door, Max caught her with pathetic ease, grabbing her robe and pulling her into him.

He captured her hands with one of his and pulled her up against him. She caught fire. He was walking her backwards towards the huge table, and illicit excitement leapt in Darcy's blood. She didn't *play* like this. And she suspected Max didn't either. It was heady.

The back of the table hit her buttocks and Max nudged her until she was sitting on it. He still held the full glass of water over her and he said in a rough voice, 'Open your robe.'

A sliver of self-consciousness pricked her. 'Max…' she said weakly.

'Open it, Darcy, or I'll open it for you.'

With far less reluctance than she should have been feeling Darcy undid the tie on her robe and it fell open, exposing her upper body. Max smiled, and it was wicked. His eyes had turned dark and golden.

Darcy felt so hot she feared bursting into flames there and then. It was hard to breathe.

Very slowly and deliberately he tipped the glass over her, until a small stream of icy water trickled down over her chest and breasts. She gasped and tensed, and was almost surprised when the water didn't hiss on contact with her hot skin.

Her nipples pebbled into tight peaks under Max's torturously slow administration, and when she was thoroughly drenched, with water running down over her belly and between her legs to where she was hottest of all, he put down the glass and pushed her robe back further, baring her completely.

He braced himself with his hands either side of her body, holding the robe back, keeping her captive. His gaze devoured her and he bent and dipped his head, his hot tongue a startling contrast to the cold water on her skin as he teased and tormented her breasts, tasting them and sucking each hard tip into his mouth until Darcy cried out and begged him to stop.

He lifted his head and smiled the smile of a master sorceror. 'We haven't even started, *dolcezza*… Lie back on the table.'

Unable to stay upright anyway, Darcy sank back and felt Max's big body push her legs wide, coming between them, baring her to him utterly.

He pressed kisses down her body, over the soft swell of her belly, and his big hands kept her open to him as his mouth descended between her legs and he found the scorching centre of her being. He stroked and licked her with sinful precision, until her hands were clasped in his hair and she was bucking uncontrollably into his mouth…

Later, when they'd made it back to the bedroom, they made love again. And again.

Darcy lifted her head from Max's chest and asked sleepily, 'So, will you tell me now?'

Max huffed a small chuckle. 'I should have known you wouldn't forget.'

Darcy rested her chin on her hand and said, 'Well…?'

Max shifted then, and she could tell he was mildly uncomfortable. But he said, 'I had arranged to take you to Venice… We were going to do a gondola ride and stay the night in a hotel on the Grand Canal.'

He lifted his head then, and looked at her with an endearingly rueful expression—very *un*Max-like.

'It would have been the worst kind of cliché, wouldn't it?'

Darcy's heart twisted painfully. 'Yes,' she whispered, 'but it would have been lovely.'

And then she ducked her head and feigned falling asleep, because she was terrified to admit to herself just how completely Max had seduced her.

CHAPTER NINE

THE FOLLOWING MORNING Darcy woke to an insistent prodding that was becoming more and more intimate as a hand smoothed down over her bare backside and squeezed firmly. She smiled and wriggled, hoping to entice the hand into further exploration, but instead it delivered a short, sharp *thwack*.

She raised her head from the pillow, blinking in the daylight. *Max*. Looking thoroughly gorgeous and disreputable with a growth of stubble. And he was dressed.

'What was that for?'

His hand smoothed where he'd slapped her so playfully. 'That was to get you up and out of bed… I want to take you out on the lake.'

At the word *lake* Darcy went very still. That big body of water that she'd avoided looking at—probably the only person on the planet who didn't enjoy the splendour of Lake Como.

She flipped over and held the sheet to her breasts. Max was already leaning back, tugging it out of her hand, but she held on with a death grip and tried to say, as breezily as possible, 'I'm quite tired, actually… Why don't you go? You can tell me how it was when you get back.'

Max stopped and his gaze narrowed on her. *Damn*.

'Why don't you want to go on the lake, Darcy? I've noticed that you barely look at it.'

She avoided his eye and sat up, feeling at a disadvantage lying down, and plucked at the sheet. 'I have issues with water. I can't swim.'

Carefully, Max said, 'You know, some fishermen can't swim—because they believe that if the sea claims them it's meant to be. It doesn't stop them going out on the water.'

Sensing that Max had no intention of going anywhere until she explained herself, she sighed deeply and said, 'I nearly drowned as a child. We had a pool at our house and my father was teaching me how to swim. My mother appeared and they started having a row. He got out to argue with her, forgetting about me… I don't know what happened… One minute I was okay and the next I couldn't feel the bottom any more and I'd started to drop like a stone. I must have drifted from the shallow end. They were so busy arguing, and I couldn't get their attention. All I could see was their arms gesticulating and then everything went black, there was a pain in my chest—'

Darcy hadn't even realised that she was bordering on hyperventilation until Max put a hand over hers, his fingers twining around hers to make her loosen her grip on the sheet.

'Darcy, it's okay—just breathe…'

She took a deep breath and looked at Max. 'That's why I don't want to go on the lake.'

He looked as if he was considering something, and then he said, 'Do you trust me?'

'Of course not,' she said facetiously.

Max rolled his eyes. 'I mean, would you trust me not to let any harm come to you?'

Physically...yes. Emotionally...no.

Damn. Darcy realised it as the heavy weight of inevitability hit her. She was falling for him. She was a disgrace to womankind. One hot air balloon ride and even hotter sex and she was—

'Okay?'

She blinked at Max, not having heard a word he'd said over the revelation banging around in her head like a warning klaxon going off after the fire had started and the horse had bolted.

'What?'

He said, with extreme patience, 'I want to take you somewhere and I promise you won't have to do anything you don't want to—okay?'

Right now even a lake was preferable to sitting alone with this new knowledge. 'Okay…'

And that was how she found herself, a few hours later, in a swimsuit, shivering with fear by the side of a kiddies' pool at a local adventure centre that Max said was owned by Dante D'Aquanni. A child ran past her and cannonballed into the pool.

Max was standing waist-deep in the water and saying, 'Look, I promise you'll be able to touch the bottom. Come on.'

Not even his body was helping to distract her right now.

'Sit on the edge and come in bit by bit.'

More because she didn't want to look like a total fool in front of Max than anything else, she gingerly sat down on the edge and put her legs in the water. Immediately she started shaking, remembering how the water had sucked her down.

But Max had his hands on her waist and she gripped his arms.

Slowly, and with far more patience than she would have ever credited him with having, Max gently coaxed

Darcy until she was standing in the water. Once she knew she could touch the bottom, he persuaded her to let him pull her along while she kicked her legs.

At one point she saw Max send a glower in the direction of some sniggering kids, but she didn't care.

And then he turned her on her back, which she only agreed to because he kept his arms underneath her. He was talking to her, telling her something, instructing her to kick her feet, and she was just getting comfortable with the feeling of floating when he said, 'Darcy?'

'Hmm?' It was nice, floating like this.

'Look.'

She lifted her head and saw Max with his hands in the air. It took a second for the fact that she was floating unaided to compute, and when it did she started to sink. But just as her head was about to go under she was caught, standing with her feet firmly on the bottom and Max holding her.

She was breathing rapidly and he was making soothing noises.

'I can't…can't be—believe you just let me go.'

'You were totally fine—you'll be swimming in no time.'

Darcy looked up at Max and her heart turned over. The pool was empty now, and she moved closer to him until their bodies were touching.

'I know one way of taking my mind off things…'

She reached up and wrapped her arms around Max's neck, moaning her satisfaction when his mouth came down on hers. Then he was lifting her, and she was wrapping her legs around his waist as he sat her down on the side of the pool and proceeded to do very adult things—until the discreet coughing of a staff member forced them apart like guilty teenagers.

* * *

Much later that night, after Darcy had shown Max her gratitude for helping her to start overcoming her fear of water in a very imaginative way, using her mouth to drive him over the edge of his control, Max couldn't sleep.

His body was still humming with pleasure…but not yet with the full sense of satisfaction that he usually felt after he'd bedded a woman. The sense of satisfaction that led to a feeling of restlessness and usually preceded his moving on.

Okay, so he knew he couldn't move on because he and Darcy were married—whether for real or not, they'd gone way over the boundaries of pretence now. But was that it? *No.* He'd be feeling this way if he and Darcy had started an affair anyway…and that revelation was disturbing.

No woman kept a hold over Max beyond the initial conquest. If he continued a liaison it was usually because it served some purpose not remotely romantic.

But things had escalated with Darcy so fast that his head felt as if it was spinning. She'd made him work for it, but it hadn't really been game-playing. And the final capitulation… It hadn't been sweet—it had been fast and furious and intense.

Even now he knew that if she was to turn to him he'd be ready to take her again and again. And tomorrow all over again.

He cursed softly and got out of bed and went downstairs, raiding Dante's drinks cabinet for some of his fine whisky. He went out to the terrace, where the sound of the lake lapping against the shore should have been calming, but instead Max was remembering the look of stark terror on Darcy's face as he'd had to coax her into the pool.

Inferno. Since when did he mess about in paddling pools, teaching someone to swim? Yet he couldn't deny the sheer pleasure he'd taken from seeing her face lose its dread in the pool.

It had given him a kind of satisfaction that he usually reserved for each pinnacle he conquered on his way to the ultimate acceptance and respect in business. Which he still hadn't attained.

A shiver of something cold crawled up Max's spine—a memory…crying, feeling as though his guts were going to fall out of his body, his legs shaking…his mother gripping him. *'Stop snivelling. I'm taking you with me.'*

He'd told Darcy practically everything. More than he'd ever told anyone else.

He went even colder and realised that he wasn't even sure he recognised himself any more. Who *was* this person who made impromptu wedding proposals? Who chased a woman around a kitchen with a glass of water?

The memory made Max cringe now.

He'd let emotion get in the way once before and had paid the price.

Another more pertinent memory came back: the day he'd seen his old nemesis while he'd been foraging in that bin in Paris. It was one of those moments in life when the fates had literally laughed in his face just to torture him.

One of them had come back and handed Max a five-euro note. Max had taken it and ripped it up, before letting it drop to the ground and spitting on it.

He hadn't needed anyone then, and he didn't need anyone now. He knew better than anybody how life could be as fickle and as random as a pair of dice rolling to a stop, dictating the future.

But he'd changed that. The power to dictate everything lay with *him*.

He'd fought for this control over his destiny and he was damned if he was going to let it slip out of his grasp now just because he was forgetting where his priorities lay. Anger licked through his blood at the knowledge of just how far off course he was in danger of straying.

Darcy was distracting him.

And he was fogetting the most important thing: *She was just a means to an end.*

The following morning, on the plane ride home, Darcy didn't need to be psychic to know that something had changed during the night. Max was back in ruthless boss mode. Brusque. Abrupt.

He'd already been up when she'd woken, dressed and packed.

She'd felt flustered. 'You should have woken me.'

He'd been cool. 'I have some work to catch up on in Dante's study. We'll leave in half an hour.'

She couldn't fault Max for wanting to jump straight back into things—after all Montgomery's party was right around the corner, sealing the deal… But it was almost as if he had just carved out these few days to seduce Darcy and now it was mission accomplished and he was moving on.

She'd expected this. But she hadn't expected it to be quite so brutally obvious.

Was it a dream or had this man gripped her hips so hard last night that she still bore the marks of his fingers on her flesh? Had she imagined that he'd held her ruthlessly still so that he could thrust up into her body over and over again, until she'd been begging for mercy, and only then finally tipped them both over the edge?

No, because she'd seen the marks in the mirror in the bathroom and her muscles still ached pleasurably.

Darcy felt a little shattered—as if the pieces that Max

had rent asunder deep inside her would never come back together again.

Maybe he was regretting the weekend…realising that it had all been a huge mistake. Realising that she hadn't been worth all that effort…the shopping, the hot air balloon… But even if he was, she wasn't going to regret it. She'd made her choice.

'Darcy?'

She looked at Max, who was frowning impatiently. 'I need you to take some notes—we'll be going straight to the office from the airport.'

Ignoring the voices screaming at her to leave it alone, Darcy turned to him and said, 'So that's it, then? Honeymoon over. Back to work.'

Max looked at her and she shivered.

'What did you expect?'

'All that seduction…the hot air balloon…'

Max shrugged. 'You knew I wanted you in my bed—whatever it took.'

Incredible pain lanced her. 'I see.'

For a moment Darcy thought she might be sick, but she forced it down. She had to get away from Max. She hated it that she wasn't strong enough to weather the evidence of his ruthlessness in front of him.

She unbuckled her belt quickly and stood up, muttering something about the bathroom. Once locked inside the small space she saw her face in the mirror, leached of colour.

Stupid, stupid Darcy. How could she have forgotten that this man's two main traits were being ruthless and being more ruthless. He must have been laughing himself silly when Darcy had all but begged him to go to bed after his *piéce de résistance*: the balloon ride. It would be tainted in her head for ever now.

She thought of the pool then, of Max's patience and gentle coaxing, and this time she couldn't stop the contents of her stomach from lurching up.

When she'd composed herself she looked at herself in the mirror again. She had to get a grip. She'd lost herself for a moment and she'd done it willingly—her hands held tightly onto the sink—but it had only been for a moment. A weekend. She was okay. She could put this momentary weakness behind her and get on with things, and as soon as the ink was dry on the deal with Montgomery she'd be gone.

When they returned to Max's apartment after going into the office Max disappeared into his study to do some more work. Darcy took herself out for a long walk around the centre of Rome, coming back with no sense of peace in her head or her heart.

She was feeling increasingly angry with herself for giving in to his smooth seduction, having known what it was likely to do to her.

He was still working when she returned, so she ate alone and went to bed, telling herself that the ache she felt was just her pathetic imagination.

After midnight, just when she was hovering on the edge of sleep, Max came into her room.

'This isn't my room.'

Darcy came up on one elbow, anger rising. 'No, it's *my* room.'

'So why aren't you in my bed?'

'Because,' Darcy said tersely, well and truly awake now, 'I don't care for the hot and cold routine, and you've made it perfectly clear that now we've consummated the relationship you're done with any niceties.'

Max came close to the bed and Darcy hated the way her blood sizzled with anticipation.

'I never said I was *nice*, Darcy,' he pointed out. 'Are you going to come to my bed?'

'No,' Darcy said mutinously.

Max just shrugged and left, and Darcy let out a shaky sigh of...*disappointment*. She lambasted herself. She was pathetic. And then her mouth dropped open when Max walked back in with a bunch of clothes and some toiletries.

She watched, dumbfounded, as he proceeded to strip and get into the bed beside her. He leaned on one elbow, unselfconsciously naked in the way that only the most gorgeous people could be, and those tawny eyes glinted with pure devilment.

'The honeymoon is over, but this isn't.'

He reached for her and Darcy had a split second to realise that she could take the moral high ground and resist Max's arrogant pull or, as she asked herself belligerently, why shouldn't she use Max as he was using her? Take her own pleasure from him until *she* was sated?

That was the weak logic she used, anyway, as she hurled herself back into the fire.

When she woke in the morning and all those little voices were ready to rip her to shreds for her weakness she resolutely ignored them and told herself she could do this. Max didn't have the monopoly on being cold and ruthless.

As the days progressed, getting closer to the time they'd be leaving for Scotland, their working hours got longer. And in the nights...the passion between them seemed to burn brighter and fiercer with each coupling. Darcy's anger with herself and Max added something that seemed to hurl her over the edge further and further each time, until she was left spent and shaking.

Some nights Max seemed to forget what part he was playing, and he'd scoop her close and hold her to him with arms like vises around her. It was on those nights that Darcy knew she was fooling herself the most.

This game she was playing with Max *was* costing her. She knew that she wasn't strong enough emotionally to keep it up indefinitely, and that it would have to stop before she got burned in the fire completely.

But just not right now…

The Montgomery estate, north of Inverness

Darcy huffed out a breath and stopped to look at the view. It was spectacular, and it soothed some of the tension inside her. Hills and mountains stretched as far as the eye could see, and small lochs were dotted here and there like black pools. Clouds scudded across the blue sky.

In true Scottish fashion, even though it was summer, it had rained since they'd arrived, a couple of days ago. But now the sun was out and the countryside sparkled.

Darcy was relishing a rare chance to be alone. She'd had enough of Max's tense mood infecting her own.

Wily old Montgomery was playing hard to get right to the end. The party was tonight, and Max still wasn't sure where he stood. To make things even worse, there were several other high-profile financiers invited. Darcy almost felt sorry for Max—but then she thought of the sensual torture he'd put her through the previous night and promptly felt *un*sorry for him.

She sat down on a piece of soft springy ground and sighed, pushing her hair back off her hot cheeks. Here against this timeless and peaceful backdrop she couldn't keep running from her own conscience and her heart.

In spite of everything, she'd fallen for Max. Self-disgust that she should fall for someone so ruthless and single-minded took the edge off the awful tendency she felt to cry. And yet her bruised heart still pathetically wanted to believe that the Max she'd seen that weekend in Como was real…

One thing Darcy *did* know was that Max fooled himself as much as everyone around him. He had feelings, all right, but they were so buried after years of hiding them that it would be like mining for diamonds trying to extract them.

She knew why her instinct had always warned her off deeper commitment if this was the pain it brought.

But she couldn't continue with the status quo. It was a form of self-destruction that Darcy knew she had to stop now—he'd worn her down and broken her apart like the pro he was, and she couldn't let it continue.

Max wasn't going to like it, but he'd get over it. He'd have to, because nothing would compel her to change her mind. Not even his singular seduction.

That night Darcy felt jittery, and Max said beside her, 'Stop fidgeting.'

She sent him a dark look. She had her arm tucked into his, for all the world the happy newly married couple.

Mrs Montgomery had come up to Darcy earlier and said confidentially, 'Why, he's a new man, my dear. He was always so *brooding* before.'

Darcy had smiled weakly and looked to see Max throwing his head back and laughing at something his companion said. Her gut had twisted. *Was* he different?

And then she'd clamped down on that very dangerous line of thought.

She was wearing the royal blue satin dress she'd seen in the window of the boutique that day in Milan. When she'd spotted it hanging in her wardrobe in Max's apartment it had given her a jolt as she'd recalled a much more light-hearted Max.

She hadn't wanted to wear it, but he'd insisted. And the look in his eyes when she'd put it on had been nearly enough to make her skin sizzle.

He'd growled, 'If we weren't already late for dinner I'd lock the door to this room, make you take it off, make love to you and then make you put it on again… But I'd probably only want to take it off again…'

A voice had wheedled in Darcy's head—*What's one more night...?*—and she'd shut it out. She couldn't afford one more night with Max.

The crowd was making a toast now, to Cecil Montgomery, his smiling wife and their four children and assorted grandchildren. Darcy's heart constricted. Happiness was there for some people. The very few.

She felt Max tense beside her. Time for the announcement.

Montgomery started by going into a long-winded account of his career, clearly building up to the big moment. Darcy bit her lip and looked at Max, but his face was expressionless.

'As many of you will know, it's been my life's work to cultivate, protect and grow the famous private equity fund of this family that goes back generations. It's my legacy to my children and grandchildren—not to mention our very important philanthropic work…'

Montgomery cleared his throat and kept going.

'As we all know in these uncertain times, expert advice is necessary to ensure the growth and protection of anything of importance. And this fund is not just my life's work, but my ancestors'. It's been of the utmost importance that I choose someone who has those sensibilities in mind. Who understands the importance of family and legacy…for the benefit of not only my own family but also much larger concerns.'

He paused dramatically and then took a breath.

'There is only one person I would trust with this great responsibility, and I'm pleased to announce that that man is…Maximiliano Fonseca Roselli.'

Darcy could feel the surge of emotion in Max's body. He shook with it. She waited for him to turn and acknowledge her, as much for appearances' sake as anything else, but after a moment he just disengaged her arm from his and strode forward to accept Montgomery's handshake and congratulations.

Darcy could see people looking at her. It was as brutal a sign of where she really stood in his life as a slap in the face, and she realised then that all along she'd been harbouring some kind of pathetic hope that perhaps she was mistaken and he *did* feel *something* for her.

Seeing the crowd lining up to congratulate Max, Darcy took advantage of the moment to slip out of the room and walk blindly through the castle, eyes blurred but refusing to let the tears well and fall.

She would not cry over this man. She would *not*.

Max cursed silently. Where *was* she? He knew Darcy was petite, but he'd realised that somehow he had an uncanny knack of finding her glossy dark brown head in any crowd. He thought of her as she'd stood before him in the bedroom not long ago, the deep blue of the satin dress curving around her body in such a way that it had made him feel animalistic. He'd almost forgotten what the evening was about. *Almost.*

Lingering tendrils of relief and triumph had snaked through him as he'd forged his way through the throng, accepting congratulations and slaps on the back. Funny, he'd expected to bask in this moment for a lot longer, but he was distracted.

Darcy. Where was she?

She'd been standing beside him when Montgomery had called out his name and his first instinct had been to turn to her. She'd done this with him. He wouldn't have done it without her. *He'd wanted to share it with her.*

The surge of alien emotion that had gripped him had caught him right in his throat and at the back of his eyes, making them sting. Horrorstruck, in a nano-second he'd been aware that he was on the verge of tears and about to let Darcy see it. So at the last second he'd pulled away and strode forward. Not wanting her to see the rawness he was feeling. Not ready for the scrutiny of those huge blue eyes that saw too much.

He cursed again. She wasn't here. A quick tour of the surrounding rooms didn't reveal her either, and Max made his way to the bedroom with a growing sense of unease.

When he opened the door to the bedroom the sense of unease coalesced into a black mass in his gut. Darcy barely looked up when he walked in. She'd changed into black trousers and a stripy top. Her hair was pulled back into a ponytail. She looked about sixteen. She was packing her suitcase.

Max folded his arms, as if that might ease the constriction in his chest.

'What are you doing?'

She glanced at him, her face expressionless. 'I'm leaving.'

Seizing on his default mechanism of acerbity, Max drawled, 'I think I could have deduced that much.'

Darcy shrugged as she pulled the top of the suitcase down and started to zip it up. 'Well, then, if it's that obvious why ask?'

Anger started to flicker to life in Max's gut as the full impact of what he was looking at sank in. *She was leaving.* He didn't like the clutch of panic. Panic was not something he ever felt.

'What's going on, Darcy? They've only just made the announcement—dinner hasn't even been served yet.'

Darcy stopped zipping up the bag and looked at him. For a moment he saw something flicker in her eyes but then it was gone.

'I'm done, Max. I've more than paid my dues as your convenient wife. When you can't even acknowledge me in your moment of glory it's pretty obvious that I've become superfluous to your requirements.'

The panic gripped him tighter. He'd messed up. 'Look, Darcy, I know I couldn't have achieved this without you—'

She laughed, short and sharp. 'You had this all along. I think Montgomery just enjoyed watching you jump through hoops… It's not many deals or many men Maximiliano Fonseca Roselli will do that for.'

Darcy picked up the jacket that was laid over the back of a nearby chair and shrugged it on, turning those huge blue eyes on him.

'What did you expect to happen now, Max? Some kind of fake domestic idyll? The deal is done. This is over. There's no more need for the charade.'

Max felt tight all over, in the grip of something dark and hot. He bit out, 'You won't even stay one more night.'

He didn't pose it as a question, already hating himself for saying it.

Darcy shook her head and her glossy ponytail slid over one shoulder. 'No. I've given you enough of my time, Max. More than enough.'

Was it his imagination or had there been a catch in her voice? Max couldn't hear through the dull roaring in his head. He felt himself teetering on the edge of something… Asking her to stay? But, as she'd said, for what? What did he want from her now? And what was this terrifying swooping of emotion, threatening to push him over the edge, spurred on by the panic which made his insides feel as loose as they'd felt tight a moment ago…?

He'd only ever felt like this once before. When he'd stood before another woman—his mother—and let her see the full extent of his vulnerability and pain. He'd tipped over the edge then and his life had never been the same.

He was not going to tip over the edge for anyone else. He had just achieved the pinnacle of his success. What did he need Darcy for? He had everything that he'd ever wanted. He could go on from here and live his life and know that he was untouchable, that he had surpassed every one of his naysayers and doubters. Every one of the bullies.

He and Luca would finally be equals—on his terms.

The realisation that no great sense of satisfaction accompanied that knowledge was not something Max wanted to dwell on. Suddenly he was quite eager to get on with things. Without that incisive bluer than blue gaze tracking his every movement.

The fact that he looked at Darcy even now and felt nothing but hunger was irritating, but he told himself that once she was out of his orbit it would die down… fade away.

He would take a new lover. Start again.

He uncrossed his arms. 'Your bonus will be in your bank by Monday. My solicitor will work out the details of the divorce.'

'Thank you.' Darcy avoided his eye now, picking up her bag.

A knock came to the door and she looked up. 'That'll be the taxi. The housekeeper is sending someone up for my bags when it arrives.'

Max had pushed everything he was feeling down so deep that he was slightly light-headed. Like a robot, he moved over to the bed and took Darcy's suitcase easily in one hand. He took it to the door and opened it, handing it out to the young man on the other side. One of the estate staff.

And then Darcy was in the doorway, close enough for him to smell her scent. It had an immediate effect on him, making his body hard.

Damn her. Right now he was more than ready to see the back of her. That edge was beckoning again, panic flaring.

He stepped back, allowing her to leave the room. He forced himself to be solicitous even as he had a sudden urge to haul her back into the room and slam the door shut, locking them both inside.

And what then? asked a snide voice.

Another one answered: *Chaos.*

'Good luck, Darcy. If you need anything get in touch.'

'I won't.' Her voice was definitely husky now, and she wasn't looking at him. 'But thank you. Goodbye, Max.'

CHAPTER TEN

DARCY WASN'T SURE how she managed it, but she stayed in a state of calm numbness until she was on the train at Inverness Station and it was pulling out in the direction of Edinburgh, followed by London.

As the train picked up speed, though, it was as if its motion was peeling her skin back to expose where her heart lay in tatters, just under her breastbone. It had taken almost every ounce of her strength to stand before Max and maintain that icy, unconcerned front.

She just made it to the toilet in time, where she sat on the closed lid, shuddering and weeping and swaying as the train took her further and further away from the man who had taken all her vulnerabilities and laid them bare for his own ends.

And she couldn't even blame him. She'd handed herself over to his ruthless heartlessness lock, stock and barrel. *She'd* made that choice.

Three months later

Darcy climbed up the steps from the tube and emerged in a quiet road of a leafy suburb in north London. Well, not so leafy now that autumn was here in force, stripping everything bare.

After walking for a few minutes she hitched her bags to one hand as she dug out her key and put it in the front door of her apartment building. A familiar dart of pleasure rushed through her. *Her apartment building.* Which housed her bijou ground-floor two-bedroomed apartment that had French doors leading out to her own private back garden.

The bonus Max had provided had more than covered the cost of the apartment with cash—making the sale fast and efficient. She'd moved in three weeks ago.

Max. He was always on the periphery of her mind, but Darcy shied away from looking at him too directly—like avoiding the glare of the sun for fear of going blind.

For a month after she'd left him in Scotland she'd had to endure seeing him emblazoned over every paper and magazine: the wunderkind of the financial world, accepted into the highest echelons where heads of state and the most powerful people in the world hailed his genius.

The emotion she'd felt thinking that he finally must have found some peace had mocked her.

There'd been pictures of him in gossip columns too, attending glittering events with a different beautiful woman on his arm each time. The pain Darcy had felt had been like a hot dagger skewering her belly, so she'd stopped watching the news or reading the papers.

She put her shopping away with little enthusiasm and thought idly of inviting her neighbour from upstairs for something to eat. John was the first person to make her laugh since she'd left Max.

After a quick trip upstairs, and John's totally overjoyed acceptance of her invitation—*'Sweetie, you are the best! I was about to die of hunger...like literally die!'*—Darcy went back downstairs and prepared some dinner, feeling marginally better.

She could get through this and emerge intact. *She could*, she vowed as she skewered some chicken with a little more force than necessary.

'You know, if you ever want to tell Uncle John about the bastard who done you wrong, I'll get a few boxes of wine and we'll hunker down for the weekend. Make a pity party of it.'

Darcy smiled as she picked up the plates and said wryly, as she hid the dart of inevitable pain, 'Is it that obvious?'

John took a sip of wine, his eyes following Darcy as she went into the kitchen. 'Hate to say it, love, but *yes*. You've got that unmistakable Eeyore droop to your lovely mouth and eyes.'

Darcy laughed just as a knock came to her door. She looked at John and he shrugged. 'Must be another neighbour?'

She went over to open it and swung it wide to reveal a very tall, very beautifully disheveled man with dark blond hair, olive skin and tawny eyes. And a distinctive scar. Dressed all in black.

She could almost hear John's jaw drop behind her. And she was belatedly and bizarrely aware that she was still smiling after his comment.

The smile slid off her face as shock and disbelief set in. 'Max.'

'Darcy.'

Her name on his tongue curled through her like warm honey, oozing over the ice packed around her heart.

'Can I come in?'

It was shock that made her act like an automaton, standing back, opening the door wider so that Max could step in, bringing with him the cool tang of autumn.

Darcy saw him clock John and the way his face tightened and darkened. His jaw was shadowed with stubble, adding to his general air of effortless disrepute.

'I'm interrupting?' He sounded stiff. Not at all like his usual insouciant self. Fazed by nothing.

Darcy tore her eyes off Max, almost afraid that he might disappear, to see that John had somehow picked his jaw back up off the ground and was standing up.

'No, I was just leaving.'

She was glad he'd spoken, because she wasn't sure she could speak.

She felt a quick supportive squeeze of her hand and then her neighbour was gone, closing the door behind him.

Darcy realised how close she was standing to Max and how huge he seemed in her small flat. Had he always been so huge?

She moved away, towards the table that still held the dinner detritus.

'You've lost weight.' Max's tone was almost accusing.

Darcy turned around. Of all the things she'd expected to hear from him it hadn't been that. And for someone who'd spent much of her lifetime lamenting her fuller figure it was ironic that in the past few months she'd managed to drop the guts of a stone without even trying.

She crossed her arms, suddenly angry that Max was here. Invading her space. Invading her mind. Being angry with him was easier than analysing other, far more dangerous emotions.

'You've hardly come all this way to comment on my weight, Max.' Her insides tightened. 'Is it something to do with the divorce?' She hadn't received the papers yet, but had been expecting something soon.

Max shook his head and ran a hand through his hair, mussing it up. The gesture was so familiar that Darcy had to bite her lip for fear of emitting some sound.

'No, it's not about the divorce…it's something else.' Max started to prowl around the flat, as if inspecting it, looking into the kitchen. He turned to face her, frowning. 'Why didn't you buy a bigger place?'

Darcy felt defensive. 'I didn't want a mortgage and I like this—it suits me.'

'I would have given you more money for somewhere bigger.'

She dropped her arms, hands spread out. 'Max…why are you here?'

He looked at her so intently that she began to sweat, becoming self-conscious in her roll-neck top and jeans. It had been 'Casual Friday' at her new job that day. Working as PA to the CEO of a dynamic software company was sufficiently new and different to give her the illusion that she could avoid thinking about Max during the day. That illusion was now well and truly shattered.

'I wanted to make sure you had your place…that you were settled. I owe you that.'

Darcy's insides fluttered. 'I have it, Max. And I wouldn't have had it without you.'

He looked at her. 'You also wouldn't have had the media speculation and the intense scrutiny afforded to our marriage.'

Darcy almost winced. After she'd left him the papers had been consumed by what had happened to her. Luckily she'd been able to return to London and disappear into the crowds, unassuming enough that no one recognised her. They'd been married for such a short amount of time it had really only registered as a story in Italy.

'At least it didn't affect your deal with Montgomery.'

Max's mouth tightened. 'Your assessment of him was right. He'd always intended giving me the fund—he just enjoyed making me work for it.'

Darcy sat down heavily onto the chair behind her. 'So we never had to go through with the wedding?'

Max shook his head.

He came forward and touched the back of the chair next to hers and said, 'Do you mind if I sit?'

Darcy waved a hand vaguely, barely aware of Max's uncharacteristic reticence or solicitude. Or the starkness of his features.

'The man who was just here…he is your boyfriend?'

Darcy came back into the room from imagining what might have happened, or *not* happened, if they hadn't married. She didn't like to admit that she preferred the version where they'd married. In spite of the pain.

Not really thinking, she said, 'No, John's my neighbour. And he's gay.'

Max sucked in a breath and Darcy looked at him sharply. He looked gaunt. The flutters got stronger and she hated it.

Sharply, she said, 'Not that it's any business of yours. You've hardly been wasting any time proving that our marriage was a farce. I've seen those pictures of you with women.'

Max stood up then and shrugged off his jacket, revealing a long-sleeved top that clung almost indecently to his hard torso. For a second Darcy didn't hear what he was saying…she was too hot and distracted.

'…doing everything I could to try and pretend things can go back to normal.'

Darcy blinked. Max was pacing, talking as if to himself. She swivelled in the chair so she could watch him. He was like a glorious caged lion in the confines of her flat.

He turned to her. 'The evening Montgomery announced that he was giving me the fund to manage I was so overcome with emotion that I couldn't bear for you to see it.

In case you'd see that the front I'd put up after Como was just that: a stupid, pathetic front to hide behind.'

'Max, what are you talking about?'

But he wasn't listening to her. He was pacing again, becoming increasingly angry. At himself.

'When I went upstairs and saw you packing I felt panic. *Panic!* I've never panicked in my life—not even when I realised I had no option but to live on the streets.'

Darcy stood up, but Max continued.

'And then you were standing there, so cool and collected, asking me what else I wanted now that I had achieved my goal.'

Max stopped and turned to face her again.

'You were asking me to step out into an abyss and I was too much of a coward to do it. I told myself that I had everything I needed, that I didn't need you. I told myself that the hunger I felt every time I looked at you, which got worse if I wasn't near you, would fade in time. So I let you go, and I went back down to that function, and I told people you'd had to leave for a family emergency. I told myself I was *fine*. That I would be *fine*.'

He shook his head.

'But I wasn't. I'm not. The day my parents split my brother and I up I showed my emotions. I cried because I wanted to stay with my mother.'

His mouth twisted.

'I couldn't believe that she was going to leave me behind with my father… I had no thought for my brother, only myself. But he was the stoic one. I was the one falling apart. And so she took me, and I spent my life paying for it. When you were leaving me I wanted to slam the door shut and lock it to prevent you going. I didn't. Because I was afraid of what might happen if I just let all that emotion out. I was afraid my world would turn on its axis again and I'd lose it all just when I'd finally got it. I was afraid I'd lose myself again.'

Darcy's breathing was erratic. 'What are you saying, Max?'

'I wanted you to be settled, to find the home you wanted so badly. I wanted you to know that you have a choice.'

'A choice for what?'

Max took a deep breath. 'I want you to come back to me. I want you to stay being my wife. But if you don't want that I'll leave you alone.'

Darcy shook her head as if trying to clear it. 'You want me back…because it's convenient? Because—?'

Max held up a hand. *'No.'* And then he sliced into the heart of her with all the precision of a master surgeon. 'I want you to come back because you've broken me in two. I finally have everything I've always wanted—everything I've always *thought* I wanted. But it means nothing any more because you're not with me. I love you, Darcy.'

Darcy blinked. *I love you?* This was a Max she'd never seen before. Humbled. Broken. *Real.* For a second she couldn't believe it, but the depth of pain in his eyes scored at her own heart—because she knew what it felt like.

She whispered through the lump in her throat. 'There's never been a choice, Max. Not since the day we met again.' She waved a hand, indicating the flat. 'I finally have everything I thought I wanted too—a home of my own, a base—but it's meaningless because *you're* my centre.'

Max's face leached of colour. 'What are you saying?'

Darcy's vision blurred with tears and she could feel her heart knitting back together. 'I'm saying I love you too, you big idiot.'

She wasn't sure who moved, but suddenly she was in his arms with hers wrapped around him so tightly she could hardly breathe. They staggered back until Max fell onto the couch, taking Darcy with him so she was sitting on his lap.

She wasn't even aware she was crying until she felt Max's hand moving up and down her back rhythmically, heard him soothing her with words in Italian...*dolcezza mia...amore...*

Darcy finally lifted her head and looked up at Max, who smoothed some hair off her forehead. She manoeuvred herself so that she was straddling his lap and both her hands were on his shoulders. She saw the way his eyes flared and colour came back into his cheeks and moved experimentally, exulting when she could feel the evidence of his arousal.

She moved her hips against him subtly, but pulled back when he tried to kiss her. 'Who were the women?'

His eyes flashed with a hint of the old Max. 'They were my attempt to be *normal* again. And none of them was *you*. Which was *very* annoying.'

He attempted to kiss her again but Darcy arched away, making Max scowl.

'Did you kiss any of them?'

Max's scowl deepened. 'I tried.'

Darcy went still as a hot skewer of jealousy ripped through her.

'But I couldn't do it. For one thing they were too tall, too skinny, too chatty about stupid things. *Not you.*'

Darcy smiled. 'Good.'

'What about Jack, are you sure he's gay?'

Now Max looked as if he wanted to skewer someone with a hot poker.

Darcy rolled her eyes. 'It's *John.* And yes, he's gay, Max. I can practically hear him drooling from here.'

Max looked smug. 'Good.'

Darcy brought her hands up to Max's face, cupping it. And then she bent her head to kiss her husband, showing him with everything in her just how much she loved him. The emotion was almost painful. Max's hands moved all over her, undoing her hair, lifting her top up and off so that she was just in her bra.

She rested her forehead against his, wondering if this was a dream. 'I thought I'd never see you again.'

Max's hands closed tight around her hips. He shook his head. 'I would have come sooner, but I was a coward, and then when I heard you'd bought a place already I thought you were moving on.'

Darcy's heart clenched. She looked into Max's eyes. 'You're not a coward, Max…anything but.'

She ran a finger lightly down over his scar and he caught her hand and pressed a kiss to the centre of her palm. He looked at her. 'The night we met Montgomery for dinner…?'

Darcy nodded.

'I think that on some subconscious level I knew I wanted you badly enough to tie you to me by any means necessary. The thing is, I wouldn't have made that impetuous decision if you had been anyone else… It's because it was *you*, and I had to have you no matter what.'

Max's confession eased some tiny last piece of doubt inside Darcy. She smiled and shifted against him again, putting her hands on the couch behind him, pushing her breasts wantonly towards Max's mouth.

'I think we've said all that needs to be said for now.'

Max smiled at her, long and slow and with a cocksure *Maxness* that told Darcy it wouldn't be long before he was back to his arrogant self again.

'I love you, Signora Fonseca Roselli. These last three

months have been a torture I wouldn't wish on my worst enemy. You're never leaving my side again.'

She brought her hand around to the back of his head, gripping his hair, tugging at it. 'I love *you*, Signor Fonseca Roselli, and I have no intention of ever leaving your side again.'

And then she bent her head and pressed a kiss to the corner of his mouth.

Max growled his frustration, cupping her jaw and angling her head so that within seconds they were kissing so deeply that there was no need for any more words for quite a while.

EPILOGUE

FOR TWO AND a half years Darcy and Max lived an idyllic existence, locked happily in a bubble of love and sensuality. She continued to work for him—but only when he travelled abroad and they didn't want to be separated.

Meanwhile, Darcy set up a business as a freelance business interpreter and frequently travelled all over Europe for different assignments—which Max invariably grumbled about. Darcy ignored him. He liked to use them as an excuse to surprise her, anyway—like the time he'd appeared in Paris when she'd walked out of a meeting and whisked her off on his private jet to the romantic and windswept west coast of Ireland. They'd ended up staying in Dromoland Castle for a week…

They bought a house in Rome's leafy exclusive Monteverde district and together made it a true home, keeping on her place in London as a pied-à-terre. Max still hadn't taken the plunge and bought a football club, but he spent lots of time at matches, investigating various teams.

One of the things Darcy was happiest about, though, was the rebuilding of Max's relationship with his brother Luca. It had been slow at first, but with the help of Luca's wife Serena, whom Darcy now counted as a firm friend, the two men were now in regular contact and needed no encouragement to spend time together. Which suited Darcy and Serena fine, especially when *they* wanted to catch up, without their husbands doing that annoying attention-seeking thing they did.

Max's relationship with his mother stayed strained, but he'd finally come to terms with the way she was and, together with Darcy, had managed to learn how to support her without taking on her addictions as his responsibility.

As for Darcy with her parents, she had learnt to tolerate their various love catastrophes with much more humour and less of a feeling of impending doom.

And then, two and a half years into their marriage, Darcy had walked white-faced into their bedroom one morning, holding a small plastic stick.

Max had looked at her and immediately frowned, concerned. *'Ché cosa?'*

She'd felt a very ominous tightening of her chest at the thought of his reaction and what it might to do them. This was the one thing they'd never really talked about, and when Serena had fallen pregnant Darcy had seen how Max had reacted in private—by shutting it out. So she knew this was a potential minefield for him—for the young boy who had been so hurt by his own parents.

Silently she'd handed him the plastic and watched as comprehension dawned.

He'd gone a little green and looked at her. 'But…*how*?'

She'd shrugged, feeling slightly sick herself at his reaction. 'I don't know. I've never missed a pill… But I had that flu a while back…'

They'd never spoken about Darcy coming off the pill. She'd hoped with time that they would discuss it…but now it was beyond discussion. She was pregnant.

She'd watched Max absorb the news, much in the same way she was, but whereas *she* felt a tiny burgeoning excitement starting to grow, she feared Max might feel the opposite.

After a long moment he'd looked at her resolutely and had come to sit on the end of the bed, the sheets tangled around his naked body. He'd reached for her and pulled her down onto his lap.

Her heart had clenched to see the clear battle going on in the golden depths of those amazing eyes but she'd waited for him to speak, and eventually he'd said gruffly, 'You know that this was never going to be easy for me... but I love you...and I can't imagine not loving any baby of ours even if I am scared to death of hurting it as Luca and I were hurt...'

Overcome with emotion at the extent of his willingness not to run scared from this, which he might have done before, Darcy had felt tears prickle behind her eyes as she'd cupped Max's jaw and pressed her mouth to his, kissing him gently.

'I trust in you, Max. You who overcame adversity time and again and who survived your own parents' woeful lack of care. You aren't capable of giving anything less than one hundred per cent commitment and love to any baby of ours. They'll be the luckiest child in the world to have you as a father.'

He'd looked at her, his eyes suspiciously bright. 'And you as their mother. I wouldn't want to do this with anyone else.'

And now, eight months later the reality that they'd come to terms with was manifest *times two*!

Darcy opened tired but happy eyes to take in the scene in the corner of her private hospital room.

And she would have laughed if she hadn't been afraid of bursting her Caesarean stitches.

Max was sprawled in a chair, shirt open at the neck

haphazardly, jeans low on his hips. His hair was even more mussed than usual, his jaw stubbled. If it hadn't been for the two small bundles carefully balanced, one in the crook of each arm, he might have looked like the reprobate playboy he'd used to be, coming home after a debauched night out.

But he was no playboy. He was a lover and a husband. And now a father. Of twins.

They'd realised that Darcy must have had twins somewhere in her family line too when they'd been informed of the news by their consultant early on in the pregnancy. Much to their stunned shock.

Max was looking at his son and daughter as if they were the most prized jewels in the world. Awed. Domino and Daisy—named after Max's Italian grandfather and Darcy's English grandmother. They'd asked the Montgomerys—who had become good friends—to be godparents to a baby each, and already the older couple had proved to be far more dedicated than *real* grandparents.

Max said now to his son, whose eyes were shut tight, 'Dom, just because you came first it doesn't mean anything. In fact…' He looked at his daughter, whose eyes were open wide, and said, *sotto voce*, 'We'll pretend *you* came first, Daisy, hmm? That way he won't be able to get too big for his boots…and your *mamma* has had a lot of drugs, so maybe we can convince her of this too…?'

He looked up at Darcy then, and smiled goofily at being caught out. Love made her chest swell so much she had to take a breath. She smiled back and love stretched between them, binding them all together for ever.

* * * * *

THE BILLIONAIRE OF CORAL BAY

NIKKI LOGAN

For Pete
Who came when I needed him most.

CHAPTER ONE

THE LUXURY CATAMARAN had first appeared two days ago, bobbing in the sea off Nancy's Point.

Lurking.

Except Mila Nakano couldn't, in all fairness, call it lurking since it stood out like a flashing white beacon against the otherwise empty blue expanse of ocean. Whatever its crew were doing out there, they weren't trying to be secretive about it, which probably meant they had permission to be moored on the outer fringes of the reef. And a vessel with all the appropriate authorisation was no business of a Wildlife Officer with somewhere else to be.

Vessels came and went daily on the edge of the Marine Park off Coral Bay—mostly research boats, often charters and occasionally private yachts there to enjoy the World Heritage reefs. This one had 'private' written all over it. If she had the kind of money that bought luxury catamarans she'd probably spend it visiting places of wonder too.

Mila peeled her wetsuit down to its waist and let her eyes flutter shut as the coastal air against her sweat-damp skin tinkled like tiny, bouncing ball bearings. Most days, she liked to snorkel in just a bikini to revel in the symphony of water against her bare flesh. Some days, though, she just needed to get things done and a wetsuit was as good as noise-cancelling headphones to someone with synaesthesia—or 'superpower' as her brothers had always referred to her cross-sensed condition—because she couldn't *hear* the physical sensation of swimming over the reef when it was muted by thick neoprene. Not that her condition was conveniently limited to just the single jumbled sensation; no, that would be too pedestrian for Mila Nakano. She *felt* colours. She *tasted* emotion. And she attributed random personality traits to things. It might make no sense to anyone else but it made total sense to her.

Of course it did; she'd been born that way.

But today she could do without the distraction. Her tour-for-one was due any minute and she still needed to cross the rest of the bay and clamber up to Nancy's Point to meet him, because she'd drifted further than she meant while snorkelling the reef. A tour-for-one was the perfect number. *One* made it possible for her to do her job without ending up with a thumping headache—complete with harmonic foghorns. With larger groups, she couldn't control how shouty their body spray was, what mood the colours they wore would leave her in, or how exhausting they were just to be around. They would have a fantastic time out on the reef, but the cost to her was sometimes too great. It could take her three days to rebalance after a big group.

But one… That was doable.

Her *one* was a Mr Richard Grundy. Up from Perth, the solitary, sprawling metropolis on Australia's west coast, tucked away in the bottom corner of the state, two days' drive—or a two-hour jet flight—from here. From *anything*, some visitors thought because they couldn't see what was right in front of them. The vast expanses of outback scrub you had to pass through to get here.

The nothing that was always full of something.

Grundy was a businessman, probably, since *ones* tended to arrive in suits with grand plans for the reef and what they could make it into. Anything from clusters of glamping facilities to elite floating casinos. Luxury theme parks. They never got off the ground, of course; between the public protests, the strict land use conditions and the flat-out *no* that the local leaseholder gave on development access through their property, her tour-for-one usually ended up being a tour-*of*-one. She never saw them, their business suit or their fancy development ideas again.

Which was fine; she was happy to play her part in keeping everything around here exactly as it was.

Mila shed the rest of her wetsuit unselfconsciously, stretched to the heavens for a moment as the ball bearings tinkled around her bikini-clad skin and slipped into the khaki shorts and shirt that identified her as official staff of the World Heritage Area. The backpack sitting on the sand bulged first with the folded wetsuit and then with bundled snorkelling gear, and she pulled her dripping hair back into a ponytail. She dropped the backpack into her work-supplied four-wheel drive then jogged past it and up towards the point overlooking the long, brilliant bay.

She didn't rush. *Ones* were almost always late; they underestimated the time it took to drive up from the city or down from the nearest airport, or they let some smartphone app decide how long it would take them when a bit of software could have no idea how much further a kilometre was in Western Australia's north. Besides, she'd parked on the only road into the meeting point and so her *one* would have had to drive past her to get to Nancy's Point. So far, hers was the only vehicle as far as the eye could see.

If you didn't count the bobbing catamaran beyond the reef.

Strong legs pushed her up over the lip of the massive limestone spur named after Nancy Dawson—the matriarch of the family that had grazed livestock on these lands for generations. Coral Bay's first family.

'Long way to come for a strip-show,' a deep voice rumbled as she straightened.

Mila stumbled to a halt, her stomach sinking on a defensive whiff of old shoe that was more back-of-her-throat *taste* than nose-scrunching *smell*. The man standing there was younger than his name suggested and he wasn't in a suit, like most *ones*, but he wore cargo pants and a faded red T-shirt as if they were one. Something about the way he moved towards her… He still screamed 'corporate' even without a tie.

Richard Grundy.

She spun around, hunting for the vehicle that she'd inexplicably missed. Nothing. It only confounded her more. The muted red of his T-shirt was pumping off all kinds of favourite drunk uncle kind of associations, but she fought the instinctive softening that brought. Nothing about his sarcastic greeting deserved congeniality. Besides, this man was anything but uncle-esque. His dark blond hair was windblown but well-cut and his eyes, as he slid his impenetrable sunglasses up onto his head to reveal them, were a rich blue. Rather like the lagoon behind him, in fact.

That got him a reluctant bonus point.

'You were early,' she puffed.

'I was on time,' he said again, apparently amused at her discomfort. 'And I was dropped off. Just in time for the show.'

She retracted that bonus point. This was *her* bay, not his. If she wanted to swim in it before her shift started, what business was it of his?

'I could have greeted you in my wetsuit,' she muttered, 'but I figured my uniform would be more appropriate.'

'You're the guide, I assume?' he said, approaching with an out-thrust hand.

'I'm *a* guide,' she said, still bristling, then extended hers on a deep breath. Taking someone's hand was never straightforward; she never knew quite what she'd get out of it. 'Mila Nakano. Parks Department.'

'Richard Grundy,' he replied, marching straight into her grasp with no further greeting. Or interest. 'What's the plan for today?'

The muscles around her belly button twittered at his warm grip on her water-cool fingers and her ears filled with the gentle brush of a harp. That was new; she usually got anything from a solo trumpet to a whole brass section when she touched people, especially strangers.

A harp thrum was incongruously pleasant.

'Today?' she parroted, her synapses temporarily disconnected.

'Our tour.' His lagoon-coloured eyes narrowed in on hers. '*Are* you my guide?'

She quickly recovered. 'Yes, I am. But no one gave me any information on the purpose of your visit—' except to impress upon her his VIP status '—so we'll be playing it a bit by ear today. It would help me to know what you're here for,' she went on. 'Or what things interest you.'

'It all interests me,' he said, glancing away. 'I'd like to get a better appreciation for the…ecological value of the area.'

Uh-huh. Didn't they all…? Then they went back to the city to work on ways to exploit it.

'Is your interest commercial?'

The twin lagoons narrowed. 'Why so much interest in my interest?'

His censure made her flush. 'I'm just wondering what

filter to put on the tour. Are you a journalist? A scientist? You don't seem like a tourist. So that only leaves Corporate.'

He glanced out at the horizon again, taking some of the intensity from their conversation. 'Let's just say I have a keen interest in the land. And the fringing reef.'

That wasn't much to go on. But those ramrod shoulders told her it was all she was going to get.

'Well, then, I guess we should start at the southernmost tip of the Marine Park,' she said, 'and work our way north. Can you swim?'

One of his eyebrows lifted. Just the one, as if her question wasn't worth the effort of a second. 'Captain of the swim team.'

Of course he had been.

Ordinarily she would have pushed her sunglasses up onto her head too, to meet a client's gaze, to start the arduous climb from *stranger* to *acquaintance*. But there was a sardonic heat coming off Richard Grundy's otherwise cool eyes and it shimmered such a curious tone—like five sounds all at once, harmonising with each other, being five different things at once. It wiggled in under her synaesthesia and tingled there, but she wasn't about to expose herself too fully to his music until she had a better handle on the man. And so her own sunglasses stayed put.

'If you want to hear the reef you'll need to get out onto it.'

'Hear it?' The eyebrow lift was back. 'Is it particularly noisy?'

She smiled. She'd yet to meet anyone else who could perceive the coral's voice but she had to assume that however normal people experienced it, it was as rich and beautiful as the way she did.

'You'll understand when you get there. Your vehicle or mine?'

But he didn't laugh—he didn't even smile—and her flimsy joke fell as flat as she inexplicably felt robbed of the opportunity to see his lips crack the straight line they'd maintained since she got up here.

'Yours, I think,' he said.

'Let's go, then.' She fell into professional mode, making up for a lot of lost time. 'I'll tell you about Nancy's Point as we walk. It's named for Nancy Dawson…'

Rich was pretty sure he knew all there was to know about Nancy Dawson—after all, stories of his great-grandmother had been part of his upbringing. But the tales as they were told to him didn't focus on Nancy's great love for the land and visionary sustainability measures, as the guide's did, they were designed to showcase her endurance and fortitude against adversity. *Those* were the values his father had wanted to foster in his son and heir. The land—except for the profit it might make for WestCorp—was secondary. Barely even that.

But there was no way to head off the lithe young woman's spiel without confessing who his family was. And he wasn't about to discuss his private business with a stranger on two minutes' acquaintance.

'For one hundred and fifty years the Dawsons have been the leaseholders of all the land as far as you can see to the horizon,' she said, turning to put the ocean behind her and looking east. 'You could drive two hours inland and still be on Wardoo Station.'

'Big,' he grunted. Because anyone else would say that. Truth was, he knew exactly how big Wardoo was—to the square kilometre—and he knew how much each of those ten thousand square kilometres yielded. And how much each one cost to operate.

That was kind of his thing.

Rich cast his eyes out to the reef break. Mila apparently knew enough history to speak about his family, but not enough to recognise his surname for what it was. Great-Grandma Dawson had married Wardoo's leading hand, Jack Grundy, but kept the family name since it was such an established and respected name in the region. The world might have known Jack and Nancy's offspring as Dawsons, but the law knew them as Grundys.

'Nancy's descendants still run it today. Well, their minions do…'

That drew his gaze back. 'Minions?'

'The family is based in the city now. We don't see them.'

Wow. There was a whole world of judgement in that simple sentence.

'Running a business remotely is pretty standard procedure these days,' he pointed out.

In his world everything was run at a distance. In a state this big it was both an operational necessity and a survival imperative. If you got attached to any business—or any of the people in it—you couldn't do what he sometimes had to do. Restructure them. Sell them. Close them.

She surveyed all around them and murmured, 'If this was my land I would never ever leave it.'

It was tempting to take offence at her casual judgement of his family—was this how she spoke of the Dawsons to any passing stranger?—but he'd managed too many teams and too many board meetings with voices far more objectionable than hers to let himself be that reactive. Besides, given that his 'family' consisted of exactly one—if you didn't count a bunch of headstones and some distant cousins in Europe—he really had little cause for complaint.

'You were born here?' he asked instead.

'And raised.'

'How long have your family lived in the area?'

'All my life—'

That had to be…what…? All of two decades?

'And thirty thousand years before that.'

He adjusted his assessment of her killer tan. That bronze-brown hue wasn't only about working outdoors. 'You're Bayungu?'

She shot him a look and he realised that he risked outing himself with his too familiar knowledge of Coral Bay's first people. That could reasonably lead to questions about why he'd taken the time to educate himself about the traditional uses of this area. Same reason he was here finding out about the environmental aspects of the region.

He wanted to know exactly what he was up against. Where the speed humps were going to arise.

'My mother's family,' she corrected softly.

Either she didn't understand how genetics worked or Mila didn't identify as indigenous despite her roots.

'But not only Bayungu? Nakano, I think you said?'

'My grandfather was Japanese. On Dad's side.'

He remembered reading that in the feasibility study on this whole coast: how it was a cultural melting pot thanks to the exploding pearling trade.

'That explains the bone structure,' he said, tracing his gaze across her face.

She flushed and seemed to say the first thing that came to her. 'His wife's family was from Dublin, just to complicate things.'

Curious that she saw her diversity as a *complication*. In business, it was a strength. Pretty much the first thing he'd done following his father's death was broaden WestCorp's portfolio base so that their eggs were spread across more baskets. Thirty-eight baskets, to be specific.

'What did Irish Grandma give you?' Rich glanced at her dark locks. 'Not red hair…'

'One of my brothers got that,' she acknowledged, stopping to consider him before sliding her sunglasses up onto her head. 'But I got Nan's eyes.'

Whoa...

A decade ago, he'd abseiled face-first down a cliff for sport—fast. The suck of his unprepared guts had been the same that day as the moment Mila's thick dark lashes lifted just now to reveal what they hid. Classic Celtic green. Not notable on their own, perhaps, but bloody amazing against the richness of her unblemished brown skin. Her respective grandparents had certainly left her a magnetising genetic legacy.

He used the last of his air replying. 'You're a walking billboard for cultural diversity.'

She glanced away, her mocha skin darkening, and he could breathe again. But it wasn't some coy affectation on her part. She looked genuinely distressed—though she was skilled at hiding it.

Fortunately, he was more skilled at reading people.

'The riches of the land and sea up here have always drawn people from around the world,' she murmured. 'I'm the end result.'

They reached her modest four-wheel drive, emblazoned with government logos, halfway down the beach she'd first emerged from, all golden and glittery.

'Is that why you stay?' he asked. 'Because of the riches?'

She looked genuinely horrified at the thought as she unlocked the vehicle and swung her long sandy legs in. 'Not in the sense you mean. My work is here. My family is here. My heart is here.'

And clearly she wore that heart on the sleeve of her Parks Department uniform.

Rich climbed in after her and gave a little inward sigh. Sailing north on the *Portus* had been seven kinds of awesome. All the space and quiet and air he needed wrapped up in black leather and oiled deck timber. He'd even unwound a little. But there was something about driving… Four wheels firm on asphalt. Owning the road.

Literally, in this case.

At least for the next few months. Longer, if he got his way.

'Is that why you're here?' she asked him, though it looked as if she had to summon up a fair bit of courage to do it. 'Drawn by the riches?'

If he was going to spend the day with her he wasn't going to be able to avoid the question for long. Might as well get in front of it.

'I'm here to find out everything I can about the area. I have…business interests up here. I'd like to go in fully informed.'

Her penetrating gaze left him and turned back to the road, leaving only thinned lips in its wake.

He'd disappointed her.

'The others wanted to know a bit about the history of Coral Bay.' She almost sighed. 'Do you?'

It was hard not to smile at her not so subtle angling. He was probably supposed to say *What others?* and she was going to tell him how many people had tried and failed to get developments up in this region. Maybe he was even supposed to be deterred by that.

Despite Mila's amateurish subterfuge, he played along. A few friendly overtures wouldn't go amiss. Even if she didn't look all that disposed to overtures of any kind—friendly or otherwise. Her job meant she kind of had to.

He settled into the well-worn fabric. 'Sure. Take me right back.'

She couldn't possibly maintain her coolness once she got stuck into her favourite topic. As long as Mila was talking, he had every excuse to just watch her lips move and her eyes flash with engagement. If nothing else, he could enjoy that.

She started with the ancient history of the land that they drove through, how this flat coast had been seafloor in the humid time before mammals. Then, a hundred million years later when the oceans were all locked up in a mini ice age and sea levels had retreated lower than they'd ever been, how her mother's ancestors had walked the shores on the edge of the massive continental drop-off that was now five kilometres out to sea. Many of the fantastical creatures of the Saltwater People's creation stories might well have been perfectly literal, hauled out of the deep sea trenches even with primitive tools.

The whole time she talked, Rich watched, entranced. Hiring Mila to be an ambassador for this place was an inspired move on someone's part. She was passionate and vivid. Totally engaged in what was obviously her favourite topic. She sold it in a way history books couldn't possibly.

But the closer she brought him to contemporary times, the more quirks he noticed in her storytelling. At first, he thought it was just the magical language of the tribal stories—evocative, memorable…almost poetic—but then he realised some of the references were too modern to be part of traditional tales.

'Did you just call the inner reef "smug"?' he interrupted.

She glanced at him, mid-sentence. Swallowing. 'Did I?'

'That's what I heard.'

Her knuckles whitened on the steering wheel. 'Are you sure I didn't say warm? That's what I meant. Because it's shallower inside the reef. The sand refracts sunlight and leads to—' she paused for half a heartbeat '—warmer conditions that the coral really thrives in.'

Her gaze darted around for a moment before she continued and he got the distinct feeling he'd just been lied to.

Again, though, amateurish.

This woman could tell one hell of a tale but she would be a sitting duck in one of his boardrooms.

'Ten thousand years from now,' she was continuing, and he forced himself to attend, 'those reef areas out there will emerge from the water and form atolls and, eventually, the certainty of earth.'

He frowned at her augmented storytelling. It didn't diminish her words particularly but the longer it went on the more overshadowing it became until he stopped listening to *what* she was saying and found himself only listening to *how* she said it.

'There are vast gorges at the top of the cape that tourists assume are made purely of cynical rock, but they're not. They were once reef too, tens of millions of years ago, until they got thrust up above the land by tectonic plate action. The enduring limestone is full of marine fossils.'

Cynical rock. *Certain* earth. *Enduring* limestone. The land seemed alive for Mila Nakano—almost a person, with its own traits—but it didn't irritate him because it wasn't an affectation and it didn't diminish the quality of her information at all. When she called the reef *smug* he got the sense that she believed it and, because she believed it, it just sounded...possible. If he got to lie about in warm water all day being nibbled free of parasites by a harem of stunning fish he'd be pretty smug too.

'I'd be interested to see those gorges,' he said, more to spur her on to continue her hyper-descriptive storytelling than anything else. Besides, something like that was just another string in his bow when it came to creating a solid business case for his resort.

She glanced at him. 'No time. We would have had to

set off much earlier. The four-wheel drive access has been under three metres of curi—'

She caught herself and he couldn't help wondering what she'd been about to say.

'Of sea water for weeks. We'd have to go up the eastern side of the cape and come in from the north. It's a long detour.'

His disappointment was entirely disproportionate to her refusal—sixty seconds ago he'd had zero interest in fossils or gorges—but he found himself eager to make it happen.

'What if we had a boat?'

'Well, that would be faster, obviously.' She set her eyes back on the road ahead and then, at this silent expectation, returned them to him. '*Do* you have one?'

He'd never been prouder to have the *Portus* lingering offshore. But he wasn't ready to reveal her just yet. 'I might be able to get access…'

Her green gaze narrowed just slightly. 'Then this afternoon,' she said. 'Right now we have other obligations.'

'We do?'

She hit the indicator even though there were no other road-users for miles around, and turned off the asphalt onto a graded limestone track. Dozens of tyre-tracks marked its dusty white surface.

'About time you got wet, Mr Grundy.'

CHAPTER TWO

BELOW THE SLIGHTLY elevated parking clearing at Five Fingers Bay, the limestone reef stretched out like the splayed digits in the beach's name. They formed a kind of catwalk, pointing out in five directions to the outer reef beyond the lagoon. Mila led her *one* down to it and stood on what might have been the Fingers' exposed rocky wrist.

'I was expecting more *Finding Nemo*,' he said, circling to look all around him and sounding as disappointed as the sag of his shoulders, 'and less *Flintstones*. Where's all the sea life?'

'What you want is just out there, Mr Grundy.'

He followed her finger out beyond the stretch of turquoise lagoon to the place the water darkened off, marking the start of the back reef that kept most predators—and most boats—out, all the way up to those gorges that he wanted to visit.

'Call me Richard,' he volunteered. 'Rich.'

Uh, no. 'Rich' was a bit too like friends and—given what he was up here for—even calling them acquaintances was a stretch. Besides, she wasn't convinced by his sudden attempt at graciousness.

'Richard…' Mila allowed, conscious that she represented her department. She rummaged in the rucksack she'd dragged from the back seat of the SUV. 'I have a spare mask and snorkel for you.'

He stared at them as if they were entirely foreign, but then reached out with a firm hand and took them from her. She took care not to let her fingers brush against his.

It was always awkward, taking your clothes off in front of a stranger; it was particularly uncomfortable in front of a young, handsome stranger, but Mila turned partly away, shrugged out of her work shorts and shirt and stood in her bikini, fiddling with the adjustment straps on her mask while Richard shed his designer T-shirt and cargo pants.

She kept her eyes carefully averted, not out of any prudishness but because she always approached new experiences with a moment's care. She could never tell how something new was going to impact on her and, while she'd hung out with enough divers and surfers to give her some kind of certainty about what senses a half-naked person would trigger—apples for some random guy peeling off his wetsuit, watermelon for a woman pulling hers on—this was a *new* half-naked man. And a client.

She watched his benign shadow on the sand until she was sure he'd removed everything he was going to.

Only then did she turn around.

Instantly, she was back at the only carnival she'd ever visited, tucking into her first—and last—candyfloss. The light, sticky cloud dissolving into pure sugar on her tongue. The smell of it, the taste of it. That sweet, sweet rush. She craved it instantly. It was so much more intense—and so much more humiliating—than a plain old apples association. But apparently that was what her synaesthesia had decided to associate with a half-naked Richard Grundy.

The harmless innocence of that scent was totally incompatible with a man she feared was here to exploit the reef.

But that was how it went; her associations rarely had any logical connection with their trigger.

Richard had come prepared with navy board shorts beneath his expensive but casual clothes. They were laced low and loose on his hips yet still managed to fit snugly all the way down his muscular thighs.

And they weren't even wet yet.

Mila filled her lungs slowly and mastered her gaze. He might not be able to read her dazed thoughts but he might well be able to read her face and so she turned back to her rummaging. Had her snorkelling mask always been this fiddly to adjust?

'I only have one set of fins, sorry,' she said in a rush. 'Five Fingers is good for drift snorkelling, though, so you can let the water do the work.'

She set off up the beach a way so that they could let the current carry them back near to their piled up things by the end of the swim. Her slog through sun-soaked sand was accompanied by the high-pitched single note that came with a warmth so everyday that she barely noticed it anymore. When they reached the old reef, she turned seaward and walked into the water without a backward glance—she didn't need the sugary distraction and she felt certain Richard would follow her in without invitation. They were snorkelling on his dollar, after all.

'So coral's not a plant?' Richard asked once they were waist-deep in the electric-blue water of the lagoon.

She paused and risked another look at him. Prepared this time. 'It's an animal. Thousands of tiny animals, actually, living together in the form of elk horns, branches, plates, cabbages—'

He interrupted her shopping list ramble with the understated impatience of someone whose time really was money. Only the cool water prevented her from blushing. Did she always babble this much with clients? Or did it only feel like babbling in Richard Grundy's presence?

'So how does a little squishy thing end up becoming rock-hard reef?' he asked.

Good. Yes. Focusing on the science kept the candyfloss at bay. Although as soon as he'd said 'rock-hard' she'd become disturbingly fixated on the remembered angles of his chest and had to severely discipline her unruly gaze not to follow suit.

'The calcium carbonate in their skeletons. In life, it provides resilience against the sea currents, and in death—'

She braced on her left leg as she slipped her right into her mono-fin. Then she straightened and tucked her left foot in with it and balanced there on the soft white seafloor. The gentle waves rocked her a little in her rooted spot, just like one of the corals she was describing.

'In death they pile up to form limestone reef,' he guessed.

'Millions upon millions of them forming reef first, then limestone that weathers into sand, and finally scrubland grows on top of it. We owe a lot to coral, really.'

Mila took a breath and turned to face him, steadfastly ignoring the smell of carnival. 'Ready to meet the reef?'

He glanced out towards the reef break and swallowed hard. It was the first time she'd seen him anything other than supremely confident, verging on arrogant.

'How far out are we going?'

'Not very. That's the beauty of Coral Bay; the inside reef is right there, the moment you step offshore. The lagoon is narrow but long. We'll be travelling parallel to the beach, mostly.'

His body lost some of its rigidity and he took a moment to fit his mask and snorkel before stepping off the sandy ridge after her.

* * *

It took no time to get out where the seafloor dropped away enough that they could glide in the cool water two metres above the reef. The moment Mila submerged, the synaesthetic symphony began. It was a mix of the high notes caused by the water rushing over her bare skin and the vast array of sounds and sensations caused by looking down at the natural metropolis below in all its diversity. Far from the flat, gently sloping, sandy sea bottom that people imagined, coral reef towered in places, dropped away in others, just like any urban centre. There were valleys and ridges and little caves from where brightly coloured fish surveyed their personal square metre of territory. Long orange antenna poked out from under a shelf and acted as the early warning system of a perky, pincers-at-the-ready crayfish. Anemones danced smooth and slow on the current, their base firmly tethered to the reef, stinging anything that came close but giving the little fish happily living inside it a free pass in return for its nibbly housekeeping.

Swimming over the top of it all, peering down through the glassy water, it felt like cruising above an alien metropolis in some kind of silent-running airship—just the sound of her own breathing inside the snorkel, and her myriad synaesthetic associations in her mind's ear. The occasional colourful little fellow came up to have a closer look at them but mostly the fish just went about their business, adhering to the strict social rules of reef communities, focusing on their eternal search for food, shelter or a mate.

Life was pretty straightforward under the surface.

And it was insanely abundant.

She glanced at Richard, who didn't seem to know where to look first. His mask darted from left to right, taking in the coral city ahead of them, looking below them at some particular point. He'd tucked his hands into balls by his hips and she wondered if that was to stop him reaching out and touching the strictly forbidden living fossil.

She took a breath and flipped gently in the water, barely flexing her mono-fin to effect the move, swimming backwards ahead of him so that she could see if he was doing okay. His mask came up square onto hers and, even in the electric-blue underworld, his eyes still managed to stand out as they locked on hers.

And he smiled.

The candyfloss returned with a vengeance. It was almost overpowering in the cloistered underwater confines of her mask. Part of her brain knew it wasn't real but as far as the other part was concerned she was sucking her air directly from some carnival tent. That was the first smile she'd seen from Richard and it was a doozy, even working around a mouthful of snorkel. It transformed his already handsome face into something really breath-stealing and, right now, she needed all the air she could get!

She signalled upwards, flicked her fin and was back above the glassy surface within a couple of heartbeats.

'I've spent so much time on the water and I had no idea there was so much going on below!' he said the moment his mouth was free of rubbery snorkel. 'I mean you know but you don't...*know*. You know?'

This level of inarticulateness wasn't uncommon for someone seeing the busy reef for the first time—their minds were almost always blown—but it made her feel just a little bit better about how much of a babbler she'd been with him.

His finless legs had to work much harder than hers to keep him perpendicular to the water and his breath started to grow choppy. 'It's so...structured. Almost city-like.'

Mila smiled. It was so much easier to relate to someone over the reef.

'Coral polyps organise into a stag horn just like a thousand humans organise into a high-rise building. It's a futuristic city…with hovercraft. Ready for more?'

His answer was to bite back down onto his snorkel's mouthpiece and tip himself forward, back under the surface.

They drifted on for another half-hour and she let Richard take the lead, going where interest took him. He got more skilled at the suspension of breath needed to deep snorkel, letting him get closer to the detail of the reef, and the two of them were like mini whales every time they surfaced, except they blew water instead of air from their clumsy plastic blowholes.

There was something intimate in the way they managed to expel the water at the same time on surfacing—relaxed, not urgent—then take another breath and go back for more. Over and over again. It was vaguely like…

Kissing.

Mila's powerful kick pushed her back up to the surface. That was not a thought she was about to entertain. He was a *one*, for a start, and he was here to exploit the very reef he was currently going crazy over. Though if she did her job then maybe he'd change his mind about that after today.

'Seen enough?' she asked when he caught up with her.

His mask couldn't hide the disappointment behind it. 'Is it time to go in?'

'I just want to show you the drop-off, then we'll head back to the beach.'

Just was probably an understatement, and they'd have to swim out of the shallow waters towards the place the continental shelf took its first plunge, but for Richard to understand the reef and how it connected to the oceanic ecosystem he needed to see it for himself.

Seeing was believing.

Unless you were her, in which case, seeing came with a whole bunch of other sensations that no one else experienced. Or necessarily believed.

She'd lost enough friends in the past to recognise that.

Mila slid the mouthpiece back into her snorkel and tooted out of the top.

'Let's go.'

Richard prided himself on being a man of composure. In the boardroom, in the bedroom, in front of a media pack. In fact, it was something he was known for—courage under fire—and it came from always knowing your strengths, and your opponents'. From always doing your homework. From controlling all the variables before they even had time to vary.

This had to be the least composed he'd been in a long, long time.

Mila had swum alongside him, her vigilant eyes sweeping around them so that he could just enjoy the wonders of the reef, monitoring their position to make sure they didn't get caught up in the current. He'd felt the change in the water as the outer reef had started to rise up to meet them, almost shore-like. But it wasn't land; it was the break line one kilometre out from the actual shore where the reef grew most abundant and closest to the surface of anywhere they'd swum yet. So close, the waves from the deeper water on the other side crashed against it relentlessly and things got a little choppier than their earlier efforts. Mila had led him to a channel that allowed them to propel themselves down between the high-rise coral—just like any of the reef's permanent residents—and get some relief from the surging waves as they'd swum out towards a deeper, darker, more distant kind of blue. The water temperature had dropped and the corals started to change—less of the soft, flowy variety interspersed with dancing life and more of the slow-growing, rock-hard variety. Coral mean streets. The ones that could withstand the water pressure coming at them from the open ocean twenty-four-seven.

Rich lifted his eyes and tried to make something out in the deep blue visible beyond the coral valley he presently lurked in. He couldn't—just a graduated, ill-defined shift from blue to deep blue to dark blue looking out and down. No scale. No end point. Impossible to get a grip on how far this drop-off actually went.

It even had the word 'drop' in it.

His pulse kicked up a notch.

Mila swam on ahead, rising briefly to refill her lungs and sinking again to swim out through the opening of the coral valley straight into all that vast blue…nothing.

And that was where his courage flat ran out.

He'd played hard contact sports, he'd battled patronising boardroom jerks, he'd wrangled packs of media wolves hell-bent on getting a story, and he'd climbed steep rock faces for fun. None of those things were for the weak-willed. But could he bring himself to swim past the break and out into the place the reef—and the entire country—dropped off to open, bottomless ocean?

Nope.

He tried—not least because of Mila, back-swimming so easily out into the unknown, her dark hair floating all around her, mermaid tail waving gently at him like a beckoning finger—but even that was not enough to seduce him out there. The vast blue was so impossible to position himself in, he found himself constantly glancing up to the bright surface where the sunlight was, just to keep himself oriented. Or back at the reef edge to have the certainty of it behind him.

Swimming out over the drop-off was as inconceivable

to him as stepping off a mountain. His body simply would not comply.

As if it had some information he didn't.

And Richard Grundy made it his priority always to have the information he needed.

'It's okay,' Mila sputtered gently, surfacing next to him once they'd moved back to the side of the reef protected from the churn of the crest. 'The drop-off's not easy the first time.'

No. What wasn't easy was coming face to face with a limitation you never knew you had, and doing it in front of a slip of a thing who clearly didn't suffer the same disability. Who looked as if she'd been born beneath the surface.

'The current…' he hedged.

As if that had anything to do with it. He knew Mila wouldn't have taken him somewhere unsafe. Not that he knew her at all, and yet somehow…he did. She just didn't seem the type to be intentionally unkind. And her job relied on her getting her customers back to shore in one piece.

'Let's head in,' she said.

There was a thread of charity in her voice that he was not comfortable hearing. He didn't need anyone else's help recognising his deficiencies or to be patronised, no matter how well-meant. This would always be the first thing she thought of when she thought of him, no matter what else he achieved.

The guy that couldn't swim the drop-off.

It only took ten minutes to swim back in when he wasn't distracted by the teeming life beneath them. Thriving, living coral turned to rocky old reef, reef turned to sand and then his feet were finding the seafloor and pushing him upwards. He'd never felt such a weighty slave to gravity—it was as indisputable as the instinct that had stopped him swimming out into all that blue.

Survival.

Mila struggled a little to get her feet out of her single rubber fin and he stepped closer so she could use him as a brace. She glanced at him sideways for a moment with something that looked a lot like discomfort before politely resting her hand on his forearm and using him for balance while she prised first one and then the other foot free. As she did it she even held her breath.

Really? Had he diminished himself that much? She didn't even want to *touch* him?

'That was the start of the edge of Australia's continental shelf,' she said when she was back on two legs. 'The small drop-off slopes down to the much bigger one five kilometres out—'

Small?

'And then some of the most immense deep-sea trenches on the planet.'

'Are you trying to make me feel better?' he said tightly.

And had failing always been this excruciating?

Her pretty face twisted a little. 'No. But your body might have been responding instinctively to that unknown danger.'

'I deal with unknowns every day.'

Dealt with them and redressed them. WestCorp thrived on *knowns*.

'Do you, really?' she asked, tipping her glance towards him, apparently intent on placating him with conversation. 'When was the last time you did something truly new to you?'

Part of the reason he dominated in business was because nothing fazed him. Like a good game of chess, there was a finite number of plays to address any challenge and once you'd perfected them the only contest was knowing which one to apply. The momentary flare of satisfaction as the challenge tumbled was about all he had, these days. The rest was business as usual.

And outside of business…

Well, how long had it been since there was anything outside of business?

'I went snorkelling today,' he said, pulling off his mask.

'That was your first time? You did well, then.'

She probably meant to be kind, but all her condescension did was remind him why he never did anything before learning everything there was to know about it. Controlling his environment.

Open ocean was not a controlled environment.

'How about you?' he deflected as the drag of the water dropped away and they stepped onto toasty warm sand. 'You don't get bored of the same view every day? The same reef?'

She turned back out to the turquoise lagoon and the deeper blue sea beyond it—that same blue that he loved from the comfort and safety of his boat.

'Nope.' She sighed. 'I like a lot of familiarity in my environment because of—' she caught herself, turned back and changed tack '—because I'm at my best when it's just me and the ocean.'

He snorted. 'What's the point of being your best when no one's around to see it?'

He didn't mean to be dismissive, but he saw her reaction in the flash behind her eyes.

'I'm around.' She shrugged, almost embarrassed. 'I'll know.'

'And you reserve the best of yourself *for* yourself?' he asked, knowing any hope of a congenial day with her was probably already sunk.

Her curious gaze suggested he was more alien to her

than some of the creatures they'd just been studying. 'Why would I give it to someone else?'

She crossed to their piled-up belongings and began to shove her snorkelling equipment into the canvas bag.

Rich pressed the beach towel she'd supplied to his chest as he watched her go, and disguised the full-body shiver that followed. But he couldn't blame it on the chilly water alone—there was something else at play here, something more…disquieting.

He patted his face dry with the sun-warmed fabric to buy himself a moment to identify the uncomfortable sensation.

For all his success—for all his professional renown—Rich suddenly had the most unsettling suspicion that he might have missed something fundamental about life.

Why *would* anyone give the best of themselves to someone else?

CHAPTER THREE

MILA NEVER LIKED to see any creature suffer—even one as cocky as Richard Grundy—but, somehow, suffering brought him closer to her level than he'd yet been. More likeable and relatable Clark Kent, less fortress of solitude Superman. He'd taken the drop-off experience hard, and he'd been finding any feasible excuse not to make eye contact with her ever since.

Most people got no phone reception out of town but Richard somehow did and he'd busied himself with a few business calls, including arranging for the boat he knew of to meet them at Bill's Bay marina. It was indisputably the quickest way to get to the gorges he wanted to see. All they had to do was putter out of the State and Federal-protected marine park, then turn north in open, deregulated waters and power up the coast at full speed, before heading back into the marine park again. They could be there in an hour instead of the three it would take by road. And the three back again.

It looked as if Richard would use every moment of that hour to focus on business.

Still, his distraction gave her time to study him. His hair had only needed a few strategic arrangements to get it back to a perfectly barbered shape, whereas hers was a tangled, salt-crusted mess. Side on, she could see behind his expensive sunglasses and knew just how blue those eyes were. The glasses sat comfortably on high cheekbones, which was where the designer stubble also happened to begin. It ran down his defined jaw and met its mirror image at a slightly cleft chin. As nice as all of that was—and it was; just the thought of how that stubble might feel under her fingers was causing a flurry of kettledrums, of all things—clearly its primary role in life was to frame what had to be his best asset. A killer pair of lips. Not too thin, not too full, perfectly symmetrical. Not at their best right now while he was still so tense, but earlier, when they'd broken out that smile…

Ugh…murder.

The car filled with the scent of spun sugar again.

'Something you need?'

He spoke without turning his eyes off the road ahead or prising the phone from his ear, but the twist of the mouth she'd just been admiring told her he was talking to her.

She'd meant to be subtle, glancing sideways, studying him in her periphery, yet apparently those lips were more magnetic than she realised because she was turned almost fully towards him. She snapped her gaze forward.

'No. Just…um…'

Just obsessing on your body parts, Mr Grundy...

Just wondering how I could get you to smile again, sir...

'We're nearly at the boat launch,' she fabricated. 'Just wanted you to know.'

If he believed her, she couldn't tell. He simply nodded, returned to his call and then took his sweet time finishing it.

Mila forced her mind back on the job.

'This is the main road in and out of Coral Bay,' she said as soon as he disconnected his call, turning her four-wheel drive at a cluster of towering solar panels that powered streetlights at the only intersection in the district. 'It's base camp for everyone wanting access to the southern part of the World Heritage area.'

To her, Coral Bay was a sweet, green little oasis existing in the middle of almost nowhere. No other town for two hundred kilometres in any direction. Just boundless, rust-coloured outback on one side and a quarter of a planet of ocean on the other.

Next stop, Africa.

Richard's eyes narrowed as they entered town and he saw all the caravans, RVs, four-by-fours and tour buses parked all along the main street. 'It's thriving.'

His interest reminded her of a cartoon she'd seen once where a rumpled-suited businessman's eyes had spun and rolled and turned into dollar signs. It was as if he was counting the potential.

'It's whale shark season. Come back in forty-degree February and it will be a ghost town. Summer is brutal up here.'

If he wanted to build some ritzy development, he might as well know it wasn't going to be a year-round goldmine.

'I guess that's what air-conditioning is for,' he murmured.

'Until the power station goes down in a cyclone, then you're on your own.'

His lips twisted, just slightly. 'You're not really selling the virtues of the region, you know.'

No. This wasn't her job. This was personal. She forced herself back on a professional footing.

'Did you want to stop in town? For something to eat, maybe? Snorkelling always makes me hungry.'

Plus, Coral Bay had the best bakery in the district, regardless of the fact it also had the only bakery in the district.

'We'll have lunch on the *Portus*,' he said absently.

The *Portus*? Not one of the boats that frequented Coral Bay. She knew them all by sight. It hadn't occurred to her that he might have access to a vessel from outside the region. Especially given he'd only called to make arrangements half an hour ago.

'Okay—' she shrugged, resigning herself to a long wait '—straight to Bill's Bay, then.'

They parked up on arrival at the newly appointed mini-marina and wandered down to where three others launched boats for a midday run. Compared to the elaborate 'tinnies' of the locals, getting their hulls wet on the ramp, the white Zodiac idling at the end of the single pier immediately caught her attention.

'There's Damo.' Rich raised a hand and the Zodiac's skipper acknowledged it as they approached. 'You look disappointed, Mila.'

Her gaze flew to his, not least because it was the first time he'd called her by her name. It eased off his lips like a perfectly cooked salmon folding off a knife.

'I underestimated how long it was going to take us to get north,' she said, flustered. 'It's okay; I'll adjust the schedule.'

'Were you expecting something with a bit more grunt?'

'No.' *Yes.*

'I really didn't know what to expect,' she went on. 'A boat is a boat, right? As long as it floats.'

He almost smiled then, but it was too twisted to truly earn the name. She cursed the missed moment. A tall man in the white version of her own shorts and shirt stood as they approached the end of the pier. He acknowledged Richard with a courteous nod, then offered her his arm aboard.

'Miss?'

She declined his proffered hand—not just because she needed little help managing embarkation onto such a modest vessel, but also because she could do without the associated sounds that generally came with a stranger's skin against hers.

The skipper was too professional to react. Richard, on the other hand, frowned at her dismissal of a man clearly doing him a favour.

Mila sighed. Okay, so he thought her rude. It wouldn't be the first time someone had assumed the worst. And she wouldn't be seeing him again after today, so what did it really matter?

The skipper wasted no time firing up the surprisingly throaty Zodiac and reversing them out of the marina and in between the markers that led bigger boats safely through the reef-riddled sanctuary zone towards more open waters. They ambled along at five knots and only opened up a little once they hit the recreation zone, where boating was less regulated. It took just a few minutes to navigate the passage that put them in open water, but the skipper didn't throttle right up like she expected; instead he kept his speed down as they approached a much larger and infinitely more expensive catamaran idling just beyond the outer reef. The vessel she'd seen earlier, at Nancy's Point. Slowing as they passed such a massive vessel seemed a back-to-front kind of courtesy, given the giant cat would barely feel their wake if they passed it at full speed. It was only as their little Zodiac swung around to reverse up to the catamaran that she saw the letters emblazoned on the big cat's side.

Portus.

'Did you think we were going all the way north in the tender?' a soft voice came to her over the thrum of the slowly reversing motor.

'Is this yours?' she asked, gaping.

'If she's not, we're getting an awfully accommodating reception for a couple of trespassers.'

'So when you said you were "dropped off" at Nancy's Point…?'

'I didn't mean in a car.'

With those simple words, his capacity to get his mystery development proposal through where others had failed increased by half in Mila's mind. A man with the keys to a vessel like this in his pocket had to have at least a couple of politicians there too, right?

The tender's skipper expertly reversed them backwards, right up to the stern of the *Portus,* where a set of steps came down each of the cat's two hulls to the waterline. A dive platform at the bottom of each served as a disembarkation point and she could see where the tender would nest in snugly under its mother vessel when it wasn't in use. Stepping off the back of the tender and onto the *Portus* was as easy as entering her house. Where the upward steps delivered them—to an outdoor area that would comfortably seat twelve—the vessel was trimmed out with timber and black leather against the boat's white fibreglass. Not vinyl… Not hardy canvas like most of the boats she'd been on. This was *leather*—soft and smooth under her fingers as she placed a light hand on the top of one padded seat-back. The sensation was accompanied by a percussion of wind chimes, low and sonorous.

Who knew she found leather so soothing!

The colour scheme was conflicting, emotionally, even as it was perfect visually. The tranquillity of white, the sensuality of black. Brown usually made her feel sad, but this particularly rich, oiled tone struck her more specifically as…isolated.

But it was impossible not to also acknowledge the truth.

'This is so beautiful, Richard.'

To her left, timber stairs spiralled up and out of view to the deck above.

'It does the job,' he said modestly, then pulled open two

glass doors into the vessel's gorgeous interior, revealing an expansive dining area and a galley twice as big as her own kitchen.

She just stared at him until he noticed her silence.

'What?'

'Surely, even in your world this vessel is something special,' she said, standing firm on the threshold, as though she needed to get this resolved before entering. False humility was worse than an absence of it, and she had a blazing desire to have the truth from this man just once.

On principle.

'What do you know about my world?' he cast back easily over his shoulder, seemingly uncaring whether she followed him or not.

She clung to *not* and hugged the doorway.

'You wouldn't have bought the boat if you didn't think it was special.'

He turned to face her. 'It wouldn't be seemly to boast about my own boat, Mila.'

'It would be honest.' And really, what was this whole vessel but big, mobile bragging rights? 'Or is it just saying the words aloud that bothers you?'

He turned to face her, but she barrelled on without really knowing why it affected her so much. Maybe it had something to do with growing up on two small rural incomes. Or maybe it had something to do with starting to think they might be closer to equals, only to be faced with the leather and timber evidence very much to the contrary.

'I'll say it for you,' she said from the doorway. 'The *Portus* is amazing. You must be incredibly relaxed when you're out on her.' She glanced at the massive dining table. 'And you must have some very happy friends.'

'I don't really bring friends out,' he murmured, regarding her across the space between them.

'Colleagues, then. Clients.'

He leaned back on the kitchen island and crossed his ankles. 'Nope. I like silence when I'm out on the water.'

She snorted. 'Good luck with that.' He just stared at her. 'I mean it's never truly silent, is it?'

He frowned at her. 'Isn't it?'

No. Not in her experience.

She glanced around as the *Portus*' massive engines thrummed into life and they began to move, killing any hope of silence for the time being. Although they weren't nearly as loud as she'd expected. How much did a boat have to cost to get muted engines like that?

Richard didn't invite her in again. Or insist. Or cajole. Instead, he leaned there, patience personified until she felt that her refusal to step inside was more than just ridiculous.

It was as unfriendly as people had always thought her to be.

But entering while he waited felt like too much of a concession in this mini battle of wills. She didn't want to see the flare of triumph in his eyes. Her own shifted to the double fridge at the heart of the galley.

'I guess lunch won't be cheese sandwiches out of an Esky, then?'

The moment his regard left her to follow her glance, she stepped inside, crossing more than just a threshold. She stepped wholly into Richard's fancy world.

He pulled the fridge doors wide. 'It's a platter. Crayfish. Tallegio. Salt and pepper squid. Salad Niçoise. Sourdough bread.'

She laughed. 'I guess I was wrong, then. Cheese sandwich it is.' Just fancier.

He turned his curiosity to her. 'You don't eat seafood?'

'I can eat prawns if I have to. And molluscs. They don't have a strong personality.'

That frown just seemed to be permanently fixed on his face. 'But cray and squid do?'

Her heart warmed just thinking about them and it helped to loosen her bones just a little. 'Very much so. Particularly crayfish. They're quite…optimistic.'

He stared—for several bemused moments—clearly deciding between *quirky* and *nuts*. Both of which she'd had before with a lot less subtlety than he was demonstrating.

'Is it going to bother you if I eat them?'

'No. Something tells me I won't be going hungry.' She smiled and it was easier than she expected. 'I have no strong feelings about cheese, either way.'

'Unlucky for the Tallegio then,' he murmured.

He pulled open a cabinet and revealed it as a small climate-controlled wine cellar. Room temperature on the left, frosty on the right. 'Red or white?' he asked.

'Neither,' she said regretfully. Just looking at the beading on the whites made her long for a dose of ocean spray. 'I'm on the clock.'

'Not right now you're not,' he pointed out. 'For the next ninety minutes, we're both in the capable hands of Captain Max Farrow, whose jurisdiction, under international maritime law, overrules your own.'

He lifted out one of the dewy bottles and waved it gently in her direction.

It was tempting to play at all this luxury just for a little while. To take a glass and curl up on one of those leather sofas, enjoy the associated wind chimes and act as if they weren't basically complete strangers. To talk like normal people. To pretend. At all of it.

'One glass, then,' she said. 'Thank you.'

He poured and handed her a glass of white. The silent moments afterwards sang with discomfort.

'Come on, I'll give you a tour,' he eventually offered.

He smiled but it didn't ring true and it certainly didn't set off the five-note harmony or the scent of candyfloss that the flash of perfect teeth previously had. He couldn't be as nervous as she was, surely. Was he also conscious of how make-believe this all was?

Even if, for him, it wasn't.

She stood. 'Thank you, Richard.'

'Rich,' he insisted. 'Please. Only my colleagues call me Richard.'

They were a good deal less than colleagues, but it would be impossible now to call him anything else without causing offence. *More* offence.

'Please, Mila. I think you'll like the *Portus*.' Then, when she still didn't move, he added, 'As much as I do.'

That one admission… That one small truth wiggled right in under her ribs. Disarming her completely.

'I would love to see more, Rich, thank you.'

The name felt awkward on her lips and yet somehow right at the same time. Clunky but…okay, as if it could wear in comfortably with use.

The tour didn't take long, not because there wasn't a lot to look at in every sumptuous space but because, despite its size, the *Portus* was, as it happened, mostly boat. As Rich showed her around she noted a jet ski securely stashed at the back, a sea kayak, water skis—everything a man could need to enjoy some time *on* the water. But she saw nothing to indicate that he enjoyed time *in* it.

'No diving gear?' she commented. 'On a boat with not one but two dive decks?'

His pause was momentary. 'Plenty to keep me busy above the surface,' he said.

Something about that niggled in this new environment of truce between them. That little glimpse of vulnerability coming so close on the heels of some humble truth. But she didn't need super-senses to know not to push it. She carried on the tour in comparative silence.

The *Portus* primarily comprised of three living areas: the aft deck lounge that she'd already seen, the indoor galley and the most incredibly functional bedroom space ever. It took up the whole bow, filling the front of the *Portus* with panoramic, all-seeing windows, below which wrapped fitted black cupboards. She trailed a finger along the spotless black surface, over the part that was set up as a workspace, complete with expensive camouflaged laptop, hip-height bookshelves, a disguised mini-bar and a perfectly made up king-sized bed positioned centrally in the space, complete with black pillow and quilt covers. The whole space screamed sensuality and not just because of all the black.

A steamy kind of heat billowed up from under Mila's work shirt. It was way too easy to imagine Rich in here.

'Where's the widescreen TV?' she asked, hunting for the final touch to the space that she knew had to be here somewhere.

Rich leaned next to the workspace. 'I had it removed. When I'm in here it's not to watch TV.'

She turned to face him. 'Is that because this is an office first, or a bedroom first?'

The moments the words left her lips she tried to recapture them, horrified at her own boldness. It had to be the result of this all-consuming black making her skin tingle, but talking about a client's bedroom habits *with* said client was not just inappropriate, it was utterly mortifying.

'I'm so sorry…' she said hurriedly.

Rich held up a hand and the smile finally returned, lighting up the luxurious space.

'My own fault for having such a rock star bedroom,' he joked. 'I didn't buy the *Portus* for this space, but I have to admit it's pretty functional. Everything I need is close by.

But who needs a TV when you have a wraparound view like this, right?'

She followed his easy wave out of the expansive windows. There was something just too…perfect about the image he created. And she just couldn't see him sitting still long enough to enjoy a view.

'You work when you're on board, don't you?'

Those coral-coloured lips twisted. 'Maybe.'

Mila hunted around for a topic of discussion that would soak up some of the cotton candy suddenly swilling around the room. 'Where do your crew sleep?'

The business of climbing down into one of the hulls, where a small bed space and washing facility were, gave her the time she needed to get her rogue senses back in order.

'…comfortable enough for short trips,' Rich was saying as she tuned back in.

'What about long ones?'

He glanced out of the window. 'WestCorp keeps me pretty much tethered to the city. This is shaping up to be the longest trip I've taken since I got her. Three days.'

Wow. Last of the big spenders.

'Come on.' He straightened, maybe seeing the judgement in that thought on her face. 'Let's finish the tour.'

The rest of the *Portus* consisted of a marble-clad *en suite* bathroom, appointed with the same kind of luxury as everywhere else, and then a trip back out to the aft deck and up a spiral staircase to the helm. Like everything else on the vessel, it was a wonder of compact efficiency. Buttons and LED panels and two screens with high-tech navigation and seafloor mapping and a bunch of other equipment she didn't recognise. The *Portus*' captain introduced himself but Mila stood back just far enough that a handshake would be awkward to ask for. She'd rather not insult a second man today. Maybe a third.

'Two crew?' she murmured. The vessel was large enough for it, but for just one passenger…?

'It's more efficient to run overnight. Tag-teaming the skippering. Get up from the city faster. I left the office at seven two nights ago and woke up here the next morning. Same deal tonight. I'll leave before sunset and be back in Perth just in time for my personal trainer.'

Imagine having a boat like this and then rushing every moment you were on her. This gorgeous vessel suddenly became relegated to a water taxi. Despite the wealth and comfort around her, she found herself feeling particularly sorry for Richard Grundy.

Captain Farrow pressed a finger to his headset and spoke quietly, then he turned to Rich.

'Lunch is served, sir.'

'Thanks, Max.'

They backtracked and found the sumptuous spread and the remainder of the wine set out on the aft deck. The deck-hand known as Damo lowered his head respectfully then jogged on tanned legs up the spiral stairs to the helm and was gone.

Rich indicated for her to sit.

The first thing she noticed was the absence of the promised crayfish. In its place were some pieces of chicken. The little kindness touched her even as she wondered exactly how and when he'd communicated the instruction. Clearly, his crew had a talent for operating invisibly.

'This is amazing,' she said, curling her bare legs under her on the soft leather. The deep strains of wind chimes flew out of the back of the boat and were overwhelmed in the wash, but they endured. Mila loaded her small plate with delicious morsels.

'So how long have you worked for the Department?'

Rich asked, loading a piece of sourdough with pâté and goat's cheese.

It wasn't unusual for one of her tour clients to strike up a personal conversation; what was unusual was the ease with which she approached her answer.

She normally didn't *do* chatty.

'Six years. Until I was eighteen, I instructed snorkelers during the busy season and volunteered on conservation projects in the off-season.'

'While most other teens were bagging groceries or flipping burgers after school?'

'It's different up here. Station work, hospitality or conservation. Those are our options. Or leaving, of course,' she acknowledged. Plenty of young people chose that.

'Waiting on people not your thing?'

She studied her food for a moment. 'People aren't really my thing, to be honest. I much prefer the solitude of the reef system.'

It was the perfect *in* if he wanted to call her on her interpersonal skills. Or lack of.

But he didn't. 'What about working on the Station? Not too many people out there, I wouldn't have thought.'

'I would have worked on Wardoo in a heartbeat,' she admitted. 'But jobs there are very competitive and the size of their crew gets smaller every year as the owners cut back and back.' She looked out towards the vast rust-coloured land on their port side. 'And back.'

He shifted on the comfortable cushions as though he was perched on open reef flat.

'Vast is an understatement,' he murmured, following the direction of her eyes. And her thoughts.

That was not awe in his voice.

'Remote living is not for everyone,' she admitted, refocusing on him. 'But it has its perks.'

He settled back against the plush cushions but his gaze didn't relax with him. If anything, it grew more focused. More intense. 'Like what?'

'You can breathe up here,' she started, remembering how cloistered she'd felt on her one and only visit to the capital when she was a teen. 'The land sets the pace, not someone else's schedule. It's…predictable. Ordered.'

She forked up a piece of chicken and dipped it in a tangy sauce before biting into it and chewing thoughtfully.

'Some people would call that dull…' he started, carefully.

Meaning he would? 'Not me. Life has enough variability in it without giving every day a different purpose.'

'And that's important…why, exactly?'

His gaze grew keen. Too keen, as if he was poking around in a reef cave for something.

Oh...

She should have known he would notice. A man didn't get a boat like this—or the company that paid for it—without being pretty switched on. A deep breath lifted her shoulders before dropping them again. For a moment, Mila was disappointed that he couldn't just…let it lie. She understood the curiosity about her crossed senses, but all her life she'd just wanted someone to *not* be interested in her synaesthesia. So that she could feel normal for a moment.

Apparently, Richard Grundy wasn't going to be that someone.

She sighed. 'You're asking about…'

Funny how she always struggled to broach the subject. He helped her out.

'About crayfish with optimism and the smug reef.' She held her tongue, forcing him to go on. 'You seem very connected to the environment around you. I wondered if it was a cultural thing. Some affinity with your ancestors…?'

Was that what he thought? That it was *cultural*? Of all the things she'd ever thought were going on with her, it had truly never occurred to her that it had anything to do with being raised Bayungu. Probably because no one else on that side of the family had it—or any of the community.

It was just one more way that she was different.

'It's not affinity,' she said simply.

It was *her*.

'If anything, it probably comes from my Irish side. My grandmother ended up marrying a Japanese pearler because other people apparently found her—'

Unrelatable. Uncomfortable. Any of a bunch of other 'un's that Mila lived with too.

'Eccentric.'

But not Grandfather Hiro, with his enormous heart. A Japanese man in outback Australia during the post-war years would have known more than a little something about not fitting in. Pity he wasn't still around to talk to…

Rich laid his fork down and just waited.

'I have synaesthesia,' she blurted. 'So I hear some sensations. I taste and smell some emotions. Certain things have personalities.'

He kept right on staring.

'My synapses are all crossed,' she said in an attempt to clarify. Although even that didn't quite describe it.

'So…' Rich looked utterly confounded. '…the crayfish has an *actual* personality for you?'

'Yes. Kind of…perky.'

'All of them?'

'No. Just the dead one in your fridge.'

It was impossible not to ruin her straight face with a chuckle. Force of habit; she'd been minimising her condition with laughter for years. Trying to lessen the discomfort of others. Even if that meant taking it on herself. 'Yes, all of them, thank goodness. Things are busy enough without giving them *individual* traits.'

He sat forward. 'And the reef is actually—'

'Smug,' she finished for him. 'But not unpleasantly so. Sky, on the other hand, is quite conceited. Clouds are ambitious.' She glanced around at things she could see for inspiration. 'Your stainless steel fridge is pleasantly mysterious.'

He blinked. 'You don't like sky?'

'I don't like conceit. But I don't pick the associations. They just…are.'

He stared, then, so long and so hard she grew physically uncomfortable. In a way that had nothing to do with her synaesthesia and everything to do with the piercing intelligence behind those blue eyes.

Eventually his bottom lip pushed out and he conceded, 'I guess sky is kind of pleased with itself. All that overconfident blue…'

The candyfloss surged back for a half-moment and then dissipated on the air rushing past the boat. She was no less a spectacle but at least he was taking it in his stride, which wasn't always the case when she confessed her unique perception to people.

'What about the boat?' he asked after a moment. 'Or is it just natural features?'

Her lips tightened and she glanced down at the rapidly emptying platter. 'I'm not an amusement ride, Rich.'

'No. Sorry, I'm just trying to get my head around it. I've never met a…'

'Synaesthete.'

He tested the word silently on his lips and frowned. 'Sounds very sci-fi.'

'My brothers did call it my *superpower,* growing up.'

Except that it wasn't terribly super and it didn't make her feel powerful. Quite the opposite, some days. 'I didn't even know that other people didn't experience the world like I did until I was about eleven.'

Before that, she'd just assumed she was flat-out unlikeable.

Rich dropped his eyes away for a moment and he busied himself topping up their glasses. 'So you mentioned sensation? Is that why you tensed up when you shook my hand?'

Heat rushed up Mila's cheeks. He'd noticed that? Had he also noticed every other reaction she'd had to being near him?

That could get awkward fast.

'Someone new might feel okay or they might…not.' She wasn't about to apologise for something that just…was… for her.

Rich studied her. 'Must be lonely.'

Her spine ratcheted straight. The only thing she wanted more than to be treated normally was *not* to be treated with pity. She took her time taking a long sip of wine.

'Are my questions upsetting you?'

'I don't… It's not something I usually talk about with strangers. Until I know someone well. People generally react somewhere on a spectrum from obsessive curiosity to outright incredulity. No one's ever just shrugged and said, *All right, then. More sandwiches?*'

Oh, how she longed for that.

'Thank you for making an exception, then.' His eyes stayed locked on hers and he slid the platter slightly towards her. 'More sandwiches?'

It was so close, it stole her breath.

'Why are you really up here, Rich?' she asked, before thinking better of it. It shouldn't matter why; she was paid to show him the area, end of story. His business was as much his own as hers was. But something pushed her on. And not just the desire to change the subject. 'I'm going to look you up online anyway. Might as well tell me. Are you a developer?'

He shifted in his seat, took his time answering. 'You don't like developers, I take it?'

'I guide a lot of them. They spend the day banging on about their grand plans for the area and then I never see them again. I'm just wondering if you'll be the same.'

Not that she was particularly hoping to see him again. *Was she?*

His body language was easy but there was an intensity in his gaze that she couldn't quite define.

'None of them ever come back?'

'Some underestimate how remote it is. Or how much red tape there will be. Most have no idea of the access restrictions that are in place.'

He tipped his head as he sipped his wine. 'Restrictions? Sounds difficult.'

'Technically,' she went on, 'the land all the way up to the National Park is under the control of three local pastoralists. Lifetime leaseholds. In Coral Bay, if anyone wants to get a serious foothold in this part of the Marine Park, they have to get past the Dawsons. No one ever has.' She shifted forward. 'Honestly, Rich? If you do have development plans, you might as well give up now.'

Why was she giving him a heads-up? Just because he'd been nice to her and given her lunch? And looked good in board shorts?

Blue eyes considered her closely. 'The Dawsons sound like a problem.'

The boiled eggs of loyalty materialised determinedly at the back of her throat. 'They're the reason the land around Coral Bay isn't littered with luxury resorts trying to position themselves on World Heritage coast. They're like a final rampart. Yet to be breached. That makes them heroes in my book.'

Rich studied her for a long time before lifting his glass in salute. And in thanks. 'To the Dawsons, then.'

Had she said too much? Nothing he probably didn't already know, or wouldn't find out soon enough. But still…

She ran her hands up and down arms suddenly bristling with goose pimples.

'Cold?' Rich asked, even though the sun was high.

Mila shook her head. 'Ball bearings.'

CHAPTER FOUR

RICH WANTED TO believe that 'ball bearings' referred to the breeze presently stirring wisps of long, dark hair around Mila's face, but what if she sensed ball bearings when she was feeling foreboding? Or deception. Or distrust.

What if she had more 'extra-sensory' in her 'super-sensory' than she knew? He *was* keeping secrets and she *should* feel foreboding. But that wasn't how Mila's condition worked. Not that he had much of an idea how it *did* work, and he didn't want to pummel her with curious questions just for his own satisfaction. He'd just have to use the brain his parents had spent a fortune improving to figure Mila out the old-fashioned way—through conversation.

A big part of him wished that the heroic Dawsons *were* an impediment to his plans—a good fight always got his blood up. But Mila would be dismayed to discover just how easy it was going to be for him to build his hotel overlooking the reef. The handful of small businesses running here might have had mixed feelings about the percentage that WestCorp took from their take—the motel, the café, the fuel station, even the hard-working glass-bottom boat tours—but they couldn't honestly expect not to pay for the privilege of running a business on Wardoo's land, just as Wardoo had to pay the government for the privilege of running cattle on leasehold land.

Money flowed like an ebbing tide towards the government. It was all part of the food chain.

Except now that same government was shifting the goalposts, looking to excise the coastal strip from the leasehold boundaries. The only part that made any decent profit. And his analysts agreed with him that the only way to get them to leave the lucrative coastal strip in the lease was to make a reasonable capital investment in the region himself—put something back in.

Governments liked to see potential leveraged and demand met.

And—frankly—he liked to do it.

WestCorp needed the lucrative coastal strip to supplement the Station's meagre profits. Without it, there was nothing holding Wardoo in any half-competent finance holdings and, thanks to his father's move to the big smoke forty years ago, there was nothing holding *him* to Wardoo. His heritage.

That was why he'd hauled himself out of the office—out of the city—and come north, to see for himself the place that had been earmarked for development. Just so he could be as persuasive as possible when he pitched it to the responsible bureaucrat. He'd lucked out with a guide who could also give him a glimpse of community attitudes towards his business—forewarned absolutely was forearmed.

It didn't hurt that Mila was such a puzzle—he'd always liked a challenge. Or that she was so easy on the eye. He'd always liked beautiful things. Now she was just plain intriguing too, courtesy of her synaesthesia. Though he'd have to temper his curiosity, given how touchy she was about it. Had someone made her feel like a freak in the past?

The *Portus'* motor cut out and they slowed to a drift. Mila twisted and stared at the ancient rocky range that stretched up and down the coast, red as far as they could see. She knew where they were immediately.

'We'll have to take the tender in; there's only a slim channel in the reef.'

It was narrow and a little bit turbulent where the contents of the reef lagoon rushed out into open water but they paused long enough to watch a couple of manta rays rolling and scooping just there, clearly taking advantage of the fishy freeway as they puttered over the top of it. Damo dropped them close enough to wade comfortably in, their shoes in one hand and sharing the load of the single kayak they'd towed in behind the tender in the other. They hauled it up to the sandbar that stretched across the mouth of Yardi Creek. Or once had.

'This is why we couldn't just drive up here,' she said, indicating the mostly submerged ridge. 'Thanks to a ferocious cyclone season earlier in the year, the sandbar blew out, taking the four-wheel drive access with it. It's only just now reforming. It'll be good to go again at the end of the year but for now it makes for a convenient launch point for us.'

And launch they did. His sea kayak was wider and flatter than a regular canoe, which made it possible for two of them to fit on a vessel technically designed for half that number. He slid down into the moulded seat well and scooted back to make room for Mila, spreading his legs along the kayak's lip so she could sit comfortably between them at the front of the seat well, with her own bent legs dangling over each side. Once she was in, he bent his knees up on either side of her to serve as some kind of amusement park ride safety barrier and unlocked his double paddle into a single half for each of them.

They soon fell into an easy rhythm that didn't fight the other, though Mila's body stayed as rigid and unyielding as the hard plastic of the kayak against his legs. Given what he now knew about her, this kind of physical contact had to be difficult for her. Not that she was snuggled up to him exactly, but the unconventional position wasn't easy for either of them. Though maybe for different reasons. *He* was supposed to be paying attention to everything around him yet he kept finding his gaze returning to the slim, tanned back and neck of the young woman seated between his knees, her now-dry ponytail hanging not quite neatly down her notched spine. She'd shrugged out of her uniform shirt and folded it neatly into her backpack but somehow—in this marine environment—the bikini top was as much of a uniform as anything.

She was in her mid-twenties—nearly a decade younger than he was—but there was something about her… As if she'd been here a whole lot longer. Born of the land, or even the sea. She just…belonged.

'Looks like we have the creek to ourselves.' Mila's soft words came easily back to him. courtesy of the gorge's natural acoustics.

Sure enough, there was not another human being visible anywhere—on the glassy water, up on the top of the massive canyon cliffs, in the car park gouged out of the limestone and dunes. Though it was easy to imagine a solitary figure, dark and mysterious, silhouetted against the sun, spear casually at hand, watching their approach far below.

It was just that kind of place.

Mila stopped paddling and he copied her, the drag of his paddle embedded in the water slowing them to almost nothing. Ahead, a pair of nostrils and a snub-nosed little face emerged from the water, blinking, checking them out. The kayak drifted silently past him on inertia. Only at the last moment did he dip back underwater and vanish to the depths of the deep canyon creek.

'Hawksbill turtle,' Mila murmured back to him once they were clear. 'Curious little guy.'

'You get curiosity for turtles?'

She turned half back, smiled. 'No. I mean he was *actually* curious. About us. I get bossy for turtles.'

They paddled on in silence. Rich battled with a burning question.

'Does it affect how you feel about some things?' he finally asked, as casually as he could. 'If your perception is negative?'

'It can.'

She didn't elaborate and he wondered if that question—or any question—held some hidden offence, but her voice when she finally continued wasn't tight.

'I'm not a huge fan of yellow fish, for instance, through no fault of their own. I read yellow as derisive and so…' She shrugged. 'But, similarly, people and things can strike me positively because of their associations too.'

'Like what?' he asked.

She paused again, took an age to answer. 'Oak moss. I used to get that when I was curled in my mother's arms as a child. I get it now when I'm wrapped up in my softest, woolliest sweater on a cold night, or snuggled under a quilt. It's impossible not to feel positive about oak moss.'

Her love came through loud and clear in her low voice and he was a bit sorry that he was neither naturally oaky nor mossy. It threw him back to a time, long ago, when he'd done the same with his own mother. Before he'd lost her at the end of primary school. Before he'd been dumped into boarding school by his not-coping father.

There'd been no loving arms at all after that.

She cleared her throat and kept her back firmly to him. 'Once, I met someone who registered as cotton candy. Hard not to respond positively to such a fun and evocative scent memory. I was probably more predisposed to like and trust him than, say, someone who I read as diesel smoke.'

Lucky cotton candy guy. Something told him that being liked and trusted by Mila Nakano was rarer than the mysteries in this gorge.

'What's the worst association you've ever made?' Curious was as close to 'accepting' as she was going to let him get.

'Earwax,' she said softly.

'Was that a person or a thing?'

The kayak sent out ripples ahead of them but it was easy to imagine they were soundwaves from her laughter. It was rich and throaty and it got right in between his ribs.

'A person, unfortunately.' She sighed. 'The one kid at primary school that gave me a chance. Whenever they were around I got a strong hit of earwax in the back of my throat and nose. Now, whenever my heart is sad for any reason at all, I get a delightful reminder…'

Imagine trying to forge a friendship—or, worse, a relationship—with someone who struck you so negatively whenever they were around. How impossible it would be. How that would put you off experimenting with pretty much anyone.

Suddenly, he got a sense of how her superpower worked. He was going to find it difficult to go out on this kayak ever again without an image of Mila's lean, long back popping into his head. Or to watch ripples radiate on still water anywhere without hearing her soft voice. The only difference was that her associations didn't need to have a foundation in real life.

Mila dug the paddle hard into the water again and turned her face up and to the right as the kayak slowed. 'Black-flanked rock wallaby.'

Rich followed her gaze up the towering cliffs that lined

both sides of the deep creek and hunted the vertical, rust-coloured rock face. 'All I see are some shadowy overhangs. What am I missing?'

'That's where the wallabies like to lurk. It's why they have evolved black markings.'

He scanned the sheer cliffs for camouflaged little faces. 'What are they, half mountain goat? Don't they fall off?'

'They're born up there, spend their lives leaping from claw-hold to claw-hold, nibbling on the plants that grow there, sleeping under the overhangs, raising their own young away from most predators. They're adapted to it. It's totally normal to them. They would be so surprised to know how impossible we find it.'

He fell back into rhythm with her gentle paddling. Was she talking about wallabies now or was she talking about her synaesthesia?

The more he looked, the more he saw, and the further he paddled, the more Mila showed him. She talked about the prehistoric-looking fish species that liked the cold, dark depths of the creek's uppermost reaches, the osprey and egrets that nested in its heights, the people who had once lived here and the ancient sites that were being rediscovered every year.

It was impossible not to imagine the tourist potential of building something substantial down the coast from a natural resource like this. An eco-resort in eco-central. Above them, small openings now occupied by wallabies hinted at so much more.

'The cavers must love it here,' he guessed. He knew enough about rocks to know these ones were probably riddled with holes.

'One year there was a massive speleologist convention and cavers from all over the world came specifically to explore the uncharted parts of the Range. They discovered nearly twelve new caves in two days. Imagine what they might have found if they could have stayed up here for a week. Or two!'

'Why couldn't they?'

'There just aren't any facilities up here to house groups of that size. Or labs to accommodate scientists or…really anything. Still, the caves have waited this long, I guess.' Her shoulders slumped. 'As long as the sea doesn't rise any faster.'

In which case the coastal range where the rock wallabies clung would go back to being islands and the exposed rock they were exploring would eventually be blanketed in corals again.

The circle of life.

They took their time paddling the crumbled-in end of the gorge, looking closely at the make-up of the towering walls, the same shapes he'd seen out on the reef here, just fossilised, the synchronised slosh of their oars the only sounds between them.

The silence in this beautiful place was otherwise complete. It soaked into him in a way he'd never really felt before and he finally understood why Mila might have thought that open ocean wasn't really that quiet at all.

Because she had *this* to compare it to.

'So, I'm thinking of coming back on the weekend,' he said when they were nearly done, before realising he'd even decided. 'For a couple more days. I've obviously underestimated what brings people here.'

They bumped back up against the re-establishing sand bar and Mila clambered out then turned to him with something close to suspicion on her pretty face. After the connection he thought they'd just made it was a disappointing setback.

'I'm only booked for today,' she said bluntly. 'You'll have to find someone else to guide you.'

Denial surged through him.

'You have other clients?' He could get that changed with one phone call. But pulling rank on her like that would be about as popular as…earwax.

'No, but I've got things on.'

'What kind of things?'

'An aerial survey of seagrasses and some whale shark pattern work. A tagging job. And the neap tide is this weekend so I'll be part of the annual spawn collection team. It's a big deal up here.'

Rich felt his chance at continuing to get quality insider information—and his opportunity to get to know Mila a bit better—slipping rapidly away.

'Can I come along? Two birds, one stone.' Then, when she hesitated awkwardly, he added, 'Paid, of course.'

She winced. 'It's not about money. I'm just not sure whether that's okay. Most of our work isn't really a spectator sport.'

It was a practical enough excuse. But every instinct told him it was only half the truth. Was she truly so used to only ever seeing developers the one time? Well, he liked to be memorable.

'Put me to work, then. I can count seagrass or study the…spawn.'

Ten minutes ago that would have earned him another throaty laugh. Now, she just frowned.

'Come on, Mila, wasn't it you who asked when I'd last done something completely new to me? This is an opportunity. A bunch of new experiences.' He found the small tussle of wills disproportionately exhilarating. 'I'll be low-maintenance. Scout's honour.'

She shrugged as she bent to hike her side of the kayak

up, but the lines either side of her flat lips told him she wasn't feeling that casual at all.

'It's your time to waste, I guess.'

He only realised he'd been holding his breath when he was able to let it out on a slow, satisfied smile. More time to get a feel for this district and more time to get his head around Mila Nakano.

The return trip felt as if it took half the time, as return trips often did. But it was long enough for Mila to carefully pick her way out to the front of the *Portus* and slide down behind the safety barrier on one of the catamaran hulls. Rich did the same on the other and—together but apart—they lost themselves in the deep blue ocean until they reached the open waters off Coral Bay again. Over on her side, the water whooshing past sang triumphantly.

Regardless, she shifted on the deck and let her shoulders slump.

She'd been rude. Even she could see that. Properly, officially rude.

But the moment Rich had decided to return to Coral Bay for a more in-depth look she'd felt a clawing kind of tension start to climb her spine. Coming back meant he wasn't a *one* any more. Coming back meant that none of the remoteness or the politics or the environmental considerations had deterred him particularly.

Coming back meant he was serious.

She'd guided Rich today because that was her job. But she'd let herself be disarmed by his handsome face and fancy boat and his apparently genuine interest in the reef and cape. Her only comfort was that he still had to get past the Dawsons—and no one had ever managed that—but she still didn't want him to think that she somehow endorsed his plans to develop the bay.

Whatever they were.

Regardless of the cautious camaraderie that had grown between them, Richard Grundy was still her adversary. Because he was the reef's adversary.

She cast her eyes across the deep green ocean flashing by below the twin hulls. Rich sat much as she did, legs dangling, spray in his face, but his gaze was turned away from her, his focus firmly fixed on the coast as they raced south parallel to it. No doubt visualising how his hotel was going to look looming over the water. Or his resort.

Or—perish the thought—his casino.

Knowing wouldn't change anything, yet she had to work hard at not being obsessed by which it would be.

They met on the aft deck as the catamaran drew to an idling halt off Bill's Bay an hour later. Behind them, the sun was making fairly rapid progress towards the horizon.

'It was good to meet you,' she murmured politely, already backing away.

Rich frowned. 'You say that like I won't be seeing you again…'

The weekend was four days away. Anything could happen in that time, including him losing his enthusiasm for returning. Just because he was eager for it now didn't mean he'd still be hot for it after the long journey back to the city and his overflowing inbox. Or maybe she'd have arranged someone else to show him around on Saturday. That would be the smart thing to do. This could quite easily be the last she ever saw of Richard Grundy.

At the back of her throat the slightest tang began to climb over the smell of the ocean.

Earwax.

Which was ridiculous. Rich was virtually a stranger; why would her heart squeeze even a little bit at the thought of parting? But her senses never lied, even when she was lying to herself. That was unmistakably earwax she could taste.

Which made Saturday a really bad idea.

She hurried down to the dive platform on one of the *Portus*' hulls when Rich might have kissed her cheek in farewell, and she busied herself climbing aboard the tender when he might have offered her a helpful outstretched hand. But once she was aboard and the skipper began to throttle the tender out from under the *Portus* she had no real excuse—other than rudeness—not to look back at Rich, his hands shoved deeply into his pockets, still standing on the small dive platform. It changed the shape of his arms and shoulders below the T-shirt he'd put on when they'd got back aboard, showing off the sculpted muscles she'd tried so hard not to appreciate when they were snorkelling. Or when they brushed her briefly while they were paddling the kayak.

'Seven a.m. Saturday, then?' he called over the tender's thrum and nodded towards the marina. It would have sounded like an order if not for the three little forks between his blue eyes.

Doubt.

In a man who probably never second-guessed himself.

'Don't look for me,' she called back to him. 'Look for the uniform.' Just in case. Any one of her colleagues could show him the area.

She should have scrunched her nose as the tender reversed through a light fog of its own diesel exhaust, but all she could taste and smell in the back of her throat was candyfloss. The flavour she was rapidly coming to associate with Rich.

The flavour she was rapidly coming to crave like a sugary drug.

She was almost ashore before she realised that the presence of candyfloss in her mind's nose meant she'd already decided to be the one who met him on Saturday.

The first thing Mila did when she got back to her desk was jump online and check out the etymology of the word *portus*. She'd guessed Greek—some water god or something—but it turned out it was Latin…for port. *Duh!* But it also meant sanctuary, and the imposing vessel certainly was that—even up here, where everything around them was already nine parts tranquil. She'd felt it the moment she'd stepped aboard Rich's luxurious boat. She could only imagine what it was like for him to climb aboard and motor away from the busy city and his corporate responsibilities for a day or two.

No…only ever one. Hadn't he told her as much?

What were those corporate responsibilities, exactly?

It took only moments to search up WestCorp and discover how many pies the corporation had its fingers in. And a couple of media stories that came back high in the search results told her that Richard Grundy was the CEO of WestCorp and had been since the massive and unexpected heart attack that had taken his father. Rich had been carrying the entire corporation since then. No wonder he'd been on the phone a lot that morning. No wonder he didn't have time to use his boat. The Internet celebrated the growth of WestCorp in his few short years. There were pages of resource holdings and she lost interest after only the first few.

Suffice to say that Mr Richard Grundy was as corporate as they came.

Despite that, somewhere between getting off the *Portus* and setting foot back on land she'd decided to definitely be the one to meet him on Saturday. Not just because of the candyfloss, which she reluctantly understood—biology was biology and even hers, tangled as it was with other input, was working just fine when it came to someone so high up on the Mila Nakano Secret Hotness Scale—but because of the earwax.

Her earwax couldn't be for Rich—she just didn't know him well enough—it had to be for the reef. For what a company like WestCorp could do to it. If she left him in the hands of anyone else, could she guarantee that they'd make it as abundantly clear as she would how badly this area did not need development? How it was ticking along just fine as it was?

Or should she only trust something that important to herself?

She reached for her phone.

'Hey, Craig, it's Mila…'

A few minutes later she disconnected her call, reassured that the pilot of Saturday's aerial survey could accommodate an extra body without compromising the duration of the flight. So that was Rich sorted; he would get to see a little more of the region he wanted to know about, and she…

She, what?

She'd bought herself another day or two to work on him and convince him exactly why this region didn't need his fancy-pants development. It happened to also be another day or two for Rich to discover how complicated she and her synaesthesia were to be around but, at the end of the day, the breathy anticipation of her lonely heart had to mean less than the sanctity and security of her beloved reef.

It just had to.

CHAPTER FIVE

'WE'RE MAPPING WHAT?' Rich asked into the microphone of the headset they each wore on Saturday morning as the little Cessna lifted higher and higher. Coasting at fifteen hundred feet was the only way to truly appreciate the size and beauty of the whole area.

Dugongs, Mila mouthed back, turning her face out towards a nook in the distant coast where the landforms arranged themselves into the kind of seagrass habitat that the lumbering animals preferred. 'Manatees. Sea cows.'

When he just blinked, she delved into her pocket, swiped through an overcrowded photo roll and then passed the phone back to him.

'Dugong,' she repeated. 'They feed on the seagrasses. They all but disappeared at the start of the century after a cyclone smothered the seagrasses with silt. The department has been monitoring their return ever since.'

She patted the sizeable camera that was fixed to the open window of the aircraft by two heavy-duty braces. 'Their main feeding grounds are a little south of here but more and more are migrating into these sensitive secondary zones. We're tracking their range to measure the viability of recovery from another incident like it.'

The more she impressed upon him the complexity of the environmental situation, the less likely he would be to go ahead with his plans, right? The more words like 'sensitive' and 'fragile' and 'rare' that she used, the harder development would seem up here. Either he would recognise the total lack of sense of developing such delicate coast or—at the very least—he would foresee how much red tape lay in his future.

It couldn't hurt, anyway.

Rich shifted over to sit closer to her window, as if her view was any more revealing than his. This close, she could smell him over the residual whiff of aviation fuel. Cotton candy, as always, but there was something else… Something she couldn't identify. It didn't ring any alarm bells; on the contrary, it made her feel kind of settled. In a way she hadn't stopped feeling since picking him up at the marina after four days apart.

Right.

It felt right.

'Craig comes up twice a day to spot for the whale shark cruises,' she said to distract herself from such a worrying association. To keep her focus firmly on work. She nodded down at the four white boats waiting just offshore. 'If he isn't scheduled to take tourists on a scenic flight then I hitch a lift and gather what data I can while we're up here.'

'Opportunistic,' Rich observed.

'Like the wildlife.' She smiled.

Okay, so he hadn't technically earned the smile, but she was struggling not to hand them out like sweets. What was going on with her today? She hadn't gushed over Craig when she saw him again after a week.

They flew in a wide arc out over the ocean and Rich shifted back to his own window and peered out. Below, areas of darkness on the water might have been the shadow of clouds, reef or expansive seagrass beds.

'We're looking for pale streaks in the dark beds,' Mila

said. 'That's likely to be a dugong snuffling its way along the seafloor, vacuuming up everything it finds. Where there's one, hopefully there'll be more.'

Until you saw it, it was difficult to explain—something between a snail's trail and a jet stream—but, as soon as you saw it, it was unmistakable in the bay's kaleidoscopic waters.

They flew lower, back and forth over the grasses, eyes peeled. When she did this, she usually kept her focus tightly fixed on the sea below, not only to spot an elusive dugong but also to limit the distracting sensory input she was receiving from everything else she could see in her periphery. Today, though, she was failing at both.

She'd never been as aware of someone else as she was with Rich up here. If he shuffled, she noticed. If he smiled, she felt it. If he spoke, she attended.

It was infuriating.

'Is that one?' Rich asked, pointing to a murky streak not far from shore.

'Sure is!' Mila signalled to Craig, who adjusted course and took them closer. She tossed a pair of binoculars at Rich and locked onto his eyes. 'Go you.'

Given the animal she was supposed to be fascinated by, it took her a worryingly long time to tear her eyes away from Rich's and focus on the task at hand.

Through the zoom lens of her camera it was possible to not only get some detail on the ever-increasing forage trail of a feeding dugong but to also spot three more rolling around at the surface enjoying the warmest top layer of the sea and the rising sun. Her finger just about cramped on the camera's shutter release and she filled an entire memory card with images. Maybe a dozen or so would be useful to the dugong research team but until she got back to her office she couldn't know which. So she just kept shooting.

Rich shook his head as they finished up the aerial survey. 'Can't believe you get paid to do this.'

'Technically, I don't,' Mila admitted. 'I'm on my own time today.'

He turned a frown towards her and spoke straight into her ear, courtesy of the headsets. 'That doesn't seem right.'

She looked up at him. 'Why? What else would I do with the time?'

'Uh… Socialise? Sleep in? Watch a movie?'

'This is plenty social for my liking.' She chuckled, looking between Craig and Rich. 'And why watch a movie when I can be watching dugongs feeding?'

'So you never relax? You're always doing something wildlifey?'

His judgement stung a little. And not only because it was true. 'Says the man who has an office set up on his boat so he doesn't miss an email.'

'I run a *Fortune 100* company.' He tsked. 'You're just—'

'Dude…!' Craig choked out a warning before getting really busy flying the plane. All those switches that needed urgent flipping…

'Just?' Mila bristled, as the cabin filled with the unmissable scent of fried chicken. 'Is that right?'

But he was fearless.

'Mila, one of the few advantages to being an employ*ee* and not an employ*er* is that you get to just…switch off. Go home and not think about work until Monday.'

Wow. How out of touch with ordinary people was he?

'My job title may not be comprised of initials, Rich, but what I do is every bit as important and *as occupying* as what you do. The only difference is that I do it for the good of the reef and not for financial gain.'

Craig shook his head without looking back at either of them.

'I'm out,' she thought she heard him mutter in the headset.

Rich ignored him. 'Oh, you're some kind of philanthropist? Is that it?'

'How many voluntary hours did *you* complete last month?'

His voice crept up, even though the microphone at his throat meant it didn't need to. 'Personally? None; I don't have the time. But WestCorp has six new staff working for us in entry level roles who were homeless before we got to them and that's an initiative *I* started.'

Mila's outrage snapped shut.

'Oh.' She puffed out a breath. 'Well… That's not on your website.'

'You think that's something I should be splashing around? Exposing those people to public scrutiny and comment?'

No, that would be horrible. But would a corporation generally care about that when there was good press to be had?

The Cessna's engines spluttered on.

'So you made good on your threat to check up on me, I see,' he eventually queried, his voice softening.

Sour milk mingled in with the bitter embarrassment of Brussels sprouts for a truly distasteful mix. Though she was hardly the only uncomfortable one in the plane. Rich looked wary and Craig looked as if he wanted to leap out without wasting time with a parachute.

'I was just curious about what you did,' she confessed.

'Find anything interesting?'

'Not really.' But then she remembered. 'I'm sorry about your father.'

The twitch high in his clenched jaw got earwax flowing again and this time it came with a significant, tangible and all too actual squeeze behind her breast. Had she hurt him with her clumsy sympathy?

But he didn't bite; he just murmured, 'Thank you.'

The silence then was cola-flavoured and she sank into the awkwardness and chewed her lip as she studied the ocean below. Craig swung the plane around and headed back towards Coral Bay.

'Okay, we're on the clock,' he said, resettling in his seat, clearly relieved to have something constructive to say. 'Whale sharks, here we come.'

Rich knew enough about this region to know what it was most famous for—the seasonal influx of gentle giants of the sea. Whale sharks. More whale than shark, the massive fish were filter feeders and, thus, far safer for humans than the other big sharks also out there. Swimming out in the open waters with any of them was a tightly regulated industry and a massive money-spinner.

But, frankly, anyone doing it for fun had to be nuts.

The water was more than beautiful enough from up here without needing to be immersed in it and all its mysteries.

'What do you need with whale sharks?' he asked, keen to undo his offence of earlier with some easier conversation.

Mila couldn't know how secretly he yearned to be relieved of the pressure of running things, just for a while. A week. A weekend even. He hadn't had a weekend off since taking over WestCorp six years before. Even now, here, he was technically on the job. Constantly thinking, constantly assessing. While other people dreamed of fancy cars and penthouse views, his fantasies were a little more…*suburban.* A sofa, a warm body to curl around and whatever the latest hit series was on TV.

Downtime.

Imagine that.

He couldn't really name the last time he'd done something just for leisure. Sport was about competitiveness, rock-climbing was about discipline and willpower. If he read a book it was likely to be the autobiography of someone wildly successful. It was almost as if he didn't *want* to be alone. Or quiet. Or thoughtful.

So when he'd commented on Mila's downtime, he hadn't meant it as a criticism. Of everything he'd seen in Coral Bay so far, the thing that had made the biggest impression on him was the way Mila spent her days.

Spectacularly simple. While also being very full.

She patted her trusty camera.

'Whale sharks can be identified by their patterning rather than by invasive tagging. The science employs the same algorithms NASA uses to chart star systems.'

A pretty apt analogy. The whale sharks he'd seen in photos were blanketed in constellations of pale spots on a Russian blue skin.

Mila turned more fully to him and her engagement lit up her face just like one of those distant suns he saw as a star. It almost blinded him with optimism. 'Generally, the research team uses crowd-sourced images submitted by the tourists that swim with them but I try and contribute when I can.'

'You can photograph them from up here?'

'Oh, we'll be going lower, mate,' Craig said, over the rattle of the Cessna's engine. 'We're looking for grey tadpoles at the surface. Shout out if you see any.'

Tadpoles? From up here? He looked at Mila.

Her grin was infectious. 'You'll see.'

He liked to do well at things—that came from results-based schooling, an all-honours university career, and a career where he was judged by his successes—so he was super-motivated to replicate his outstanding dugong-spotting performance. But this time Mila was the first to spot a cluster of whale sharks far below.

'On your left, Craig.'

They banked and the sharks came into view.

'Tadpoles,' Rich murmured. Sure enough: square-nosed, slow-swimming tadpoles far, far below. 'How big are they?'

'Maybe forty feet,' Mila said. 'A nice little posse of three.'

'That'll keep the punters happy,' Craig said and switched channels while he radioed the location of the sharks in to the boats waiting patiently but blindly below.

'We'll stay with this pod until the boats get here,' Mila murmured. 'Circle lower and get our shots while we wait.'

Craig trod a careful line between getting Mila the proximity she needed and not scaring the whale sharks away into deeper waters. He descended in a lazy circle, keeping a forty-five-degree angle to the animals at all times. While Mila photographed their markings, Rich peered down through the binoculars to give him the same zoomed-in views she was getting. Far below, the three mammoth fish drifted in interlocking arcs, their big blunt heads narrowing down into long, gently waving tail fins. As if the tadpoles were moving in slow motion. There was an enviable kind of ease in their movements, as if they had nowhere better to be right now. No pressing engagements. No board meeting at nine. No media pack at eleven.

Hard not to envy them their easy life.

'The plankton goes down deep during the day so the whale sharks take long rests up here before going down to feed again at dusk,' Mila said. 'That's why they're so mellow with tourists, because they have a full belly and are half asleep.'

'How many are there on the whole reef?'

'Right now there's at least two dozen and more arriving

every day because they're gathering for the coral spawn this weekend.'

'They eat the spawn?'

'Everyone eats the spawn. It's why the entire reef erupts all on the same night—to increase the chances of survival.' She glanced back at him. 'What?'

'You're pretty impressed with nature, aren't you?'

'I appreciate order,' she admitted. 'And nothing is quite as streamlined as evolution. No energy wasted.'

If his world was as cluttered as hers—with all her extrasensory input—he might have a thing for order too. His days tended to roll out in much the same way day in, day out.

Same monkeys, different circus.

'If it was just about systems you'd be happy working in a bank. Why out here? Why wildlife?'

She gave the whale sharks her focus but he knew he had her attention and he could see her thinking hard about her answer—or whether or not to give it to him, maybe. Finally, she slipped the headset off her head, glanced at an otherwise occupied Craig and leaned towards him. He met her in the middle and turned his ear towards her low voice.

'People never got me,' she said, low. And painfully simple. He got the sense that maybe this wasn't a discussion she had very often. Or very easily. 'Growing up. Other kids, their parents. They didn't hate me but they didn't accept me either, because I saw or heard or smelled things that they couldn't. Or they thought I was lying. Or making fun of them. Or defective. One boy called me "Mental Mila" and it kind of…stuck.'

Huh. He'd never wanted to punch a kid so much in his life.

'I already didn't fit anywhere culturally, then I discovered I didn't fit socially.' She looked down at the reef. 'Out there every species is as unique and specialised as the one next to it yet it doesn't make them exclusive. If anything, it makes them inclusive; they learn to work their specialties in together. Nature cooperates; it doesn't judge.'

Mankind sure did.

She slid the headset back on, returned to her final photos and the moment—and Mila's confidence—passed. He could so imagine her as a pretty, lonely young girl who turned her soft heart towards the non-judgemental wildlife and made them her friends.

The sorrowful image sucked all the joy out of his day.

The Cessna kept on circling the three-strong pod of whale sharks, keeping track of them until the boats of tourists began to converge, then Craig left them to their fun and scoured up the coast for a back-up group in case those ones decided to dive deep. As soon as they found more and radioed the alternate location, their job was done and Craig turned for Coral Bay's airfield, charting a direct line down the landward side of the coast.

As they crossed back over terra firma, Rich peered through the dusty window of his door at the red earth below. He knew that land more for its features on a map than anything else. The distinctive hexagonal dam that looked like a silver coin from here, but was one of the biggest in the region from the ground. The wagon wheel of stock tracks leading to it. The particular pattern of eroded ridges in Wardoo's northwest quadrant. The green oasis of the waterhole closer to the homestead. When he was a boy he'd accompanied his father on a charter flight over the top of the whole Station and been arrested by its geometry. For a little while he'd had an eight-year-old's fantasies of the family life he might have had there, as a kid on the land with a dozen brothers and sisters, parents who sat around a table at night, laughing, after a long day mustering stock…

'That's the Station I told you about,' Mila murmured, misreading his expression as interest. 'Wardoo isn't just beautiful coastline; its lands are spectacular too. All those fierce arid ripples.'

Fierce. He forced his mind back onto the present. 'Is that what you feel when you look at the Station?'

It went some way to explaining her great faith in Wardoo as a protector of the realm if looking at it gave her such strong associations.

'Isolation,' she said. 'There's an undertone in Wardoo's red… I get the same association with jarrah. Like the timber deck on your boat. It's lonely, to me.'

He stared down at all that red geometry. Fantasy Rich and his enormous fantasy family were pretty much all that had got him through losing his mother and then being cast off in boarding school. But by the time he was old enough to consider visiting by himself, he had no reason and even less time to indulge the old crutch. He'd created a stable, rational world for himself at school and thrown himself into getting the grades he needed to get into a top university. Once at uni he'd been all about killing it in exams so that he could excel in the company he'd been raised to inherit. He'd barely achieved that when his father's heart had suddenly stopped beating and, since then, he'd been all about taking WestCorp to new and strictly governable heights. There'd been very little time for anything else. And even less inclination.

Thus, maps and the occasional financial summary were his only reminder that Wardoo even existed.

Until now.

'Actually, I can see that one.'

Her eyes flicked up to his and kind of…crashed there. As if she hadn't expected him to be looking at her. But she didn't look away.

'Really?' she breathed.

There was an expectation in her gaze that stuck in his gut like a blade. As if she was hunting around for someone to understand her. To connect with.

As if she was ravenous for it.

'For what it's worth, Mila,' Rich murmured into the headset, 'your synaesthesia is the least exceptional thing about you.'

Up front, Craig's mouth dropped fully open, but Mila's face lit up like a firework and her smile grew so wide it almost broke her face.

'That's so lovely of you to say,' she breathed. 'Thank you.'

No one could accuse him of not knowing people. And people the world over all wanted the same thing. To belong. To fit. The more atypical that people found Mila, the less comfortable she was bound to be with them. And, even though it was a bad idea, he really wanted her to be comfortable with him for the few short hours they would have together. He turned and found her eyes—despite the fact that his voice was feeding directly to her ears courtesy of the headphones—and pumped all the understanding he could into his gaze.

'You're welcome.'

The most charged of silences fell and Craig was the only one detached enough to break it.

'Buckle up,' he told them both. 'Airstrip's ahead.'

Mila shifted towards the open door of the Cessna, where Rich had just slid out under its wing. As long as his back was to her she was fine, but the moment he turned to face her she knew she was in trouble. Normally she would have guarded against the inevitable barrage of crossed sensations that being swung down bodily by someone would bring. But, in his case, she had to steel herself against the pleasure—all that hard muscle and breadth against her own little body.

Tangled sensations had never felt so good.

Twenty-four hours ago she would have found some excuse to crawl through to the other door and exit far away from Rich, or accepted his hand—*maybe*—and limit the physical skin-on-skin to just their fingers, but now… She rested her hands lightly on his shoulders and held her breath. He eased her forward, over the edge of the door, and supported her as she slid his full length until her toes touched earth. Even then he didn't hurry to release her and the hot press of his body sent her into a harpy, sugary overdrive.

Your synaesthesia is the least exceptional thing about you.

To have it not be the first thing someone thought about when they thought about her… The novelty of that was mind-blowing. And it begged the question—what *did* he associate first with her? Not something she could ever ask for shame; ridiculous to be curious about and dangerous to want, given what he did for a living.

But there it was. As uncontrollable and illogical as her superpower. And she'd learned a long time ago to accept the inevitability of those.

Her nostrils twitched as her feet found purchase on the runway; alongside the usual carnival associations there was something else. Some indefinable…closeness. She felt inexplicably drawn to Richard Grundy. She'd been feeling it all morning.

It took a moment for her to realise.

She spun on him, eyes wide. 'What are you wearing?'

He didn't bother disguising his grin. He reached up with one arm and hooked it over the strut holding the Cessna's wing and fuselage to each other. The casual pose did uncomfortable things to her pulse.

'Do you have any idea how hard it is to find a cologne with oak moss undertones on short notice?' he said.

Mila stared even as her chest tightened. 'You wore it intentionally?'

'Totally. Unashamedly,' he added, as the gravity of her expression hit him. 'I wasn't sure it was working. You seemed unaffected at first.'

That was because she was fighting the sensation to crawl into his lap in the plane and fall asleep there.

Oak moss.

'Why would you do that?' she half whispered, thinking about that murmured discussion without their headsets. The things she'd confessed. The access she'd given him into her usually protected world.

He shrugged the shoulder that wasn't stretched up towards the plane's wing. 'Because you associate it with security.'

She fought back the rush of adrenaline and citrus that he'd cared at all how she felt around him and gave her anger free rein. 'And you thought manipulating the freak would somehow make me feel safe with you?'

He lowered his arm and straightened, his comfortable expression suddenly growing serious. 'Whoa, no, Mila. That's not what—'

'Then what? Why do I need to feel safe with you?'

She'd not seen Rich look anything but supremely confident since he'd first come striding towards her with his hand outstretched at Nancy's Point. Now he looked positively bewildered. And a little bit sick. It helped ease the whiff of nail varnish that came with the devastation.

This whole conversation stank more than an industrial precinct.

'Because you're so wary and I…' He greyed just a little bit more as his actions dawned on him. 'Oh, God, Mila—'

'Way to go, bro!' Craig called as he breezed past them with a hand raised in farewell and marched towards the little shed that served as the airfield's office.

Rich was way too fixated on her face to acknowledge his departure, but it bought them both a moment to take a breath and think. Mila fought her natural inclination to distrust.

Richard Grundy was not a serial killer. He hadn't just spiked her drink in a nightclub. He wasn't keeping strangers locked up in a basement somewhere.

He'd worn something he thought would make her comfortable around him.

That was all.

Mila could practically see his mind whirring away in that handsome head. He dropped his gaze to the crushed limestone runway and when it came back up his eyes were bleak. But firm. And she registered the truth in them.

'I wanted to ask you to dinner,' he admitted, low. 'And I wanted you to feel comfortable enough around me to say yes.'

'Do I look comfortable?'

He sagged. 'Not even a little bit.'

But every shade paler Rich went helped with that. He saw his mistake now and something told her that he very rarely made them. Old habits died hard, yet something in his demeanour caused a new and unfamiliar sensation to shimmer through her tense body.

Trust.

She wanted to believe in him.

'Why would you care whether I come to dinner or not?' Which was coward-speak for, *Why do you want to have dinner at all?*

With me.

'You intrigue me,' he began. 'And not because of the synaesthesia. Or not *just* because of it,' he added when she lifted a sceptical brow. 'I just wanted to get to know you better. And I wanted you to get to know *me* better.'

'I'm not sure you improve on repeat exposure, to be honest.'

Conflict shone live in his intense gaze. He battled it for moments. Then he decided.

'You know what? This was a mistake. *My* mistake,' he hurried to clarify.

'Big call from a man who never makes mistakes.'

His laugh was half-snort. And barely even that.

'Apparently, I save them up to perpetrate in one stunning atrocity.' His chest broadened with one breath. 'I succeed in business because of my foresight. My planning. Because I anticipate obstacles and plan for them. But I'm completely out of my depth with you, Mila. I have no idea where the boundaries are, never mind how I can control them. But that's a poor excuse for trying to game you.' He stepped out from under the shade of the Cessna's wing. 'Thank you for everything you've shown me and I wish you all the best for the future.'

He didn't try and shake her hand, or to touch her in any way. He just delivered an awkward half-bow like some lord of a long-ago realm and started to back away. But at the last moment he stopped and turned back.

'I meant what I said, Mila, about you being exceptional for a whole bunch of reasons that have nothing to do with your synaesthesia. There's something about how you are on that reef, in this place… I think you and your super-connectedness to the world might just hold the secret to life. I don't understand it, but I'm envious as hell and I think I was just hoping that some of it might rub off on me.'

He nodded one last time and strode away.

A slam of freshly made toast hit her. *Sorrow.* Rich was saying goodbye just as she'd finally got to meet the real him. Just as he'd dropped his slick veneer and let her in through those aquamarine eyes—the colour that always energised her. She would never again know the harp strains of his touch, or the coffee of his easy company or the sugar-rush of his sexy smile. He would be just like every other suited stranger she'd ever guided up here.

A *one.*

She wasn't ready to assign him to those dreaded depths just yet. And not just because of the rapidly diminishing oak moss that made her feel so bereft. She'd spent her life being distanced by people and here was a man trying to close that up a little and she'd gone straight for the jugular.

Maybe she needed to be party to the distance-closing herself.

Maybe change started at home.

'Wait!'

She had to call it a second time because Rich had made such long-legged progress away from her. He stopped and turned almost as he stepped off the airfield onto the carefully reticulated grass that lined it. Some little voice deep down inside urged her that once he'd stepped onto that surface it would have been too late, that he'd have been lost to her.

That she'd caught something—barely—before it was gone for ever. 'What about the coral spawn?'

He frowned and called back. 'What about it?'

'You can't leave before you've seen it, surely? Having come all this way.'

His face grew guarded and she got toast again as she realised that she'd made him feel as bad about himself as others had always made her feel.

'Is it that spectacular?' he called back warily.

'It's a miracle,' she said, catching up. Puffing slightly. More aware of someone than ever before in her life. 'And it should start tonight.'

He battled silently with himself again, and she searched his eyes for signs of an angle she just couldn't find.

'It would be my first miracle…' he conceded.

'And the moon has to be high to trigger it so, you know, we could grab something to eat beforehand.' She huffed out a breath. 'If you want.'

His smile, when it came, was like a Coral Bay sunrise. Slow to start but eye-watering when it came up over the ridge. It was heralded by a tsunami of candyfloss.

'That won't be weird? After…' He nodded towards the plane.

Cessna-gate?

'No,' she was quick to confirm. 'It wasn't the brightest thing you've done but I believe that you meant no harm.'

His handsome face softened with gratitude. But there was something else in there too, a shadow…

'Okay then,' he said, pushing it away. 'I'll meet you at the marina at six?'

Her breath bunched up in her throat like onlookers crowding around some spectacle. It made it hard to say much more than, 'Okay.'

It was only at the last moment that she remembered to call out.

'Bring your fins!'

CHAPTER SIX

RICH BRACED HIS feet in the bottom of the tender as it puttered up to the busy pier, then leapt easily off onto the unweathered timbers without Damo needing to tie up amongst the dozen boaters also coming ashore for the evening.

Mila had been on his mind since he'd left her earlier in the day, until the raft of documents waiting for him had forced her out so that he could focus on the plans.

I believe that you meant no harm, she'd said.

Purposefully wearing one of her synaesthesia scents was only a small part of the hurt he feared he might be gearing up to perpetrate on this gentle creature. A decent man would have accepted another guide, or gone back to the city and stayed there. Made the necessary decisions from afar. A decent man wouldn't be finding reasons to stay close to Mila even as he did the paperwork that would change her world for ever. A driven man would. A focused man would.

He would.

Was there no way to succeed up here *and* get the girl?

Deep down, he knew that there probably wasn't.

Mila wouldn't be quite so quick to declare her confident belief in him if she knew that he had the draft plans for a reef-front resort sitting on his desk on board the *Portus*.

Or why he was so unconcerned about any eleventh-hour development barriers from the local leaseholders.

Because he *was* that final barrier.

He *was* Wardoo.

And Wardoo's lease was up for renewal right now. There was no time to come up with another strategy, or for long-winded feasibility testing. *Someone* was going to develop this coast—him, the government, some offshore third party—and if he didn't act, then he would lose the coastal strip or the lease on Wardoo. Possibly both.

Then where would Mila and her reef be?

Better the devil and all that.

He waved Damo off and watched him putter past incoming boats, back out towards the *Portus*' holding site beyond the reef. As the sun sank closer to the western horizon, it cast an orange-yellow glow over everything, reflected perfectly in the still, mirrored surface of the windless lagoon. Did Mila dislike golden sunsets the way she distrusted yellow fish? He couldn't imagine her disliking anything about this unique place.

'Beautiful, isn't it,' a soft voice said behind him. 'I could look at that every day.'

Rich turned to face Mila, standing on the marina. He wanted to comment that she *did* look at it every day but the air he needed to accomplish it escaped from his lungs as soon as he set eyes on her.

She wasn't wet, or bedraggled, or crunchy-haired. She wasn't in uniform. Or in a bikini. Or any of the ways he'd seen her up until now. She stood, weight on one leg, hands twisted in front of her, her long dark hair hanging smooth and combed around her perfectly made-up face. All natural tones, almost impossible to see except that he'd been remembering that face without its make-up every hour of the day since he'd left on Tuesday and comparing it subconsciously to every other artfully made-up female face he'd seen since then. That meant he could spot the earthy, natural colours, so perfect on her tanned skin. A clasp of shells tightly circled her long throat while a longer strand hung down across the vee of smooth skin revealed by her simple knitted dress, almost the same light brown as her skin. The whole thing was held up by the flimsiest of straps, lying over the bikini she wore underneath. She looked casual enough to walk straight out into the glassy water, or boho enough to dine in any restaurant in the city. Even the best ones.

'Mila. Good to see you again.' *Ugh, that was formal.* He held up the snorkelling gear he'd purchased on his way back to the *Portus* that morning. 'Fins.'

Her smile seemed all the brighter in the golden light of evening and some of the twist in her fingers loosened up. 'I thought you might have left them on the boat by-accident-on-purpose. To get out of tonight.'

'Are you kidding? Miss out on such a unique event?'

She chewed her lip and it was adorable. 'I should confess that not everyone finds mass spawning as beautiful as I do.'

'Seriously? A sea full of floating sex cells. What's not to love?'

She stood grinning at him long enough for him to realise that he was standing just grinning at her too.

Ridiculous.

'Want me to drive?' he finally managed to say. 'It's such a long way.'

His words seemed to break Mila's trance and her laugh tinkled. 'I think I can handle it.'

He rolled around in that laugh, luxuriating, and his mind went again to the stack of plans on his desk.

Jerk.

It only took three minutes to drive around into the heart of Coral Bay. On the way, she asked him about his day at large in town and he asked her about hers. They filled the three minutes effortlessly.

And then they ran flat out of easy conversation.

As soon as they stepped out of her four-wheel drive in front of the restaurant, Mila's body seemed to tighten up. Was she anticipating the sensory impact of sharing a meal with dozens of others, or the awkwardness of sharing a meal with him? Whichever, her back grew rigid as her hand lifted to push the door open.

'Would it be crazy to suggest eating on the beach instead?' he asked before the noise from the restaurant reached more fully out to them. 'The lagoon is too beautiful not to look at tonight.'

As was Mila.

And he didn't really feel like sharing her with a restaurant full of people.

He watched her eagerness to seek the solace of the beach wrestle with her reluctance to be so alone with him. After what he'd pulled earlier, who could blame her? Sharing a meal in a crowded restaurant was one thing; sharing it on a moonlit beach made it much harder to pretend this was all just...business.

'I'm scent-free tonight,' he assured her, holding his hands out to his sides. Trying to keep it light.

'If only,' he thought he heard her mutter.

But then she spoke louder. 'Yes, that would be great; let's order to go.'

And go they did, all of one hundred metres down to the aptly named Paradise Beach, which stretched out expansively from the parking area. The tide was returning but, still, the beach was wide and white and virtually empty. A lone man ran back and forth with a scrappy terrier, white and flying against the golden sunset. The dog barked with exuberant joy.

'This looks good,' Rich said, unfolding the battered fish and potato scallops.

'Wait until you taste it,' she promised as the man and dog disappeared up a sandy track away from the beach. 'That fish was still swimming a couple of hours ago. They source locally and daily.'

Talking about food was only one step removed from talking about the weather and it almost pained him to make such inane small talk when his time with Mila was so limited.

He wanted to see the passion in her eyes again.

'Speaking of swimming, why exactly are we heading out into spawn-infested waters?' he encouraged. 'More volunteering?'

'This one's work-related. My whole department heads out at different points of the Northwest Cape on the first nights of the eruption to collect spawn. So we have diverse genetic stock.'

'For what?'

'The spawn bank.'

He just blinked. 'There's a spawn *bank*?'

'There is. Or…there will be, one day. Right now it's a locked chest freezer in Steve Donahue's fish shed, but some day the fertilised spawn will help to repopulate this reef if it's destroyed. Or we can intentionally repopulate individual patches that die off.' She turned to him, her eyes glowing as golden as the sunset. 'Tonight we collect and freeze, and in the future they'll culture and release the resulting embryos to wiggle their way back onto the reef and fix there.'

'That sounds—' *Desperate? A lost cause?* '—ambitious.'

'We have to do something.' She shrugged. 'One outbreak

of disease or a feral competitor, rising global temperatures or a really brutal cyclone… All of that would be gone.'

His eyes followed hers out to the darkening lagoon and the reef no longer visible anywhere above it. The water line was nearly twice as far up the beach as it had been when the *Portus* set him ashore. He didn't realise there were so many threats to the reef's survival.

Threats that didn't include him, anyway.

'And how do you know it will be tonight?'

'It's usually triggered by March's full moon.'

He glanced up at the crescent moon peeking over the eastern horizon. 'Shouldn't you have done this last week, then?'

'By the time they've grown for ten days, the moonlight is dim enough to help hide the spawn bundles from every other creature on the reef waiting to eat them.' She glanced out to the horizon. 'It will probably be more spectacular tomorrow night but I like to be in the water for the first eruptions. Not quite so soupy.'

'Sounds delicious,' he drawled.

But it didn't deter his enjoyment of his seafood as he finished it up.

'How far out are we going this time?'

He hated exposing himself with that question but he also liked to be as prepared as possible for challenges, including death-defying ones. Preparedness was how you stayed alive—in the boardroom and on the beach. There was nothing sensible about swimming out onto a reef after dark.

He'd seen the documentaries.

'The species we're after are all comfortably inside the break.'

Comfortably. Nothing about this was comfortable. It was testament to how badly he wanted to be with Mila that he was entertaining the idea at all.

They fell to silence and talked about nothing for a bit, Mila glancing now and again out to the lagoon to check that the spawning hadn't commenced while they were making small talk.

'Can I ask you something?' she eventually said, bringing her eyes back to him. 'How come the captain of the swim team doesn't like water? And don't mention your jet ski,' she interrupted as he opened his mouth. 'I'm talking about being *in* water.'

Given how she'd opened herself up to him about her synaesthesia, not returning the favour felt wrong. Yet going down this path scarcely felt any better, because of where he knew it led. And how she might judge him for that.

'I'm hurt that you've forgotten our first snorkel already…'

Her green eyes narrowed at his evasion.

He leaned forward and rested his elbows on his knees. 'I like to be the only species in the water. Swimming pools are awesome for that.'

'Spoken like a true axial predator. You don't like to share?'

'Only child,' he grunted. But Mila still wasn't satisfied. That keen gaze stayed locked firmly on his until he felt obliged to offer up more. 'I like to know what I'm sharing with.'

'You know there's more chance of being killed by lightning than a shark, right?'

'I'd like to see those odds recalculated in the middle of an electrical storm.' Which was effectively what swimming out into their domain was like. Doubly so at night. On a reef.

He could stop there. Leave Mila thinking that he was concerned about sharks. Or whales. Or Jules Verne–type squid. She looked as if she was right on the verge of believing him.

But he didn't want to leave her with that impression. Sharks and whales and squid mattered to Mila. And it mattered to *him* what she thought.

He sighed. 'Open ocean is not somewhere that mankind reigns particularly supreme.'

'Ah...' Awareness glowed as bright as the quarter-moonlight in Mila's expression. 'You can't control it.'

'I don't expect to,' he pointed out. 'It's not mine to control. I'm just happier not knowing what's down there.'

'Even if it's amazing?'

Especially if it was amazing. He was better off not knowing what he was missing. Wasn't that true of all areas of life? It certainly helped keep him on track at WestCorp—the only times he wobbled from the course he'd always charted for himself was when he paused to consider what else might be out there for him.

'As far as I'm concerned, human eyes can't see through ocean for a reason. Believing that it's all vast, empty nothing fits much better with my understanding of the world.'

Though that wasn't the world that Mila enjoyed, and it had nothing to do with her superpower.

'It is vast,' she acknowledged carefully. 'And you've probably become accustomed to having things within your power.'

'Is that what you think being CEO is about? Controlling things?'

'Isn't it?'

'It's more like a skipper. Steering things. And I've worked my whole life towards it.'

'You say that like you were greying at the temples when you stepped up. What are you now, mid-thirties? You must have been young when it happened.'

He remembered the day he'd got the call from the hospital, telling him about his father. Telling him to come. The sick feeling of hitting peak-hour traffic. The laws he'd broken trying to get there in time. Wishing for lights or sirens or *something* to help him change what was so obviously happening.

His father was dying and he wasn't there for it.

It was his mother all over again. Except, this time, he couldn't disappear into a child's fantasy world to cope.

'Adult enough that people counted on me to keep things running afterwards.'

'Was it unexpected?' she murmured.

'It shouldn't have been, the way he hammered the liquor and the cigarettes. The double espressos so sweet his spoon practically stood up in the little cup. But none of us were ready for it, him least of all. He still had lots to accomplish in life.'

'Like what?'

He hoped the low light would disguise the tightness of his smile. 'World domination.'

'He got halfway there, at least,' she murmured.

'WestCorp and all its holdings are just an average-sized fish on our particular reef.'

'I've seen some of those holdings; they're nothing to sneeze at.'

Rich tensed. That's right; she'd done her homework on him. He searched her gaze for a clue but found only interest. And compassion.

So Mila hadn't dug so deep that she'd found Wardoo. She wasn't skilled enough at subterfuge to have that knowledge in her head and be able to hide it. Of course it wouldn't have occurred to her to look. Why would it? And Wardoo—big as it was—was still only a small pastoral holding compared to some of WestCorp's mining and resource interests. She'd probably tired of her search long before getting to the smaller holdings at the end of the list.

'For a woman who hangs out with sea stars and coral for a living you seem to know a lot about the Western Australian corporate scene. I wouldn't have thought it would interest you.'

He saw her flush more in the sweep of her lashes on her cheeks in the moonlight than in her colour. 'Normally, no—'

Out on the water, a few gulls appeared, dipping and soaring, only to dip again at the glittering surface. The moon might not be large but it was high now.

'Oh! We're on!' Mila said, excitement bubbling in her voice.

Compared to the last time she'd stripped off in front of him, this time she did it with far less modesty. It only took a few seconds to slide the strings holding up her slip of a dress off her shoulders and step out of the pooled fabric, leaving only bare feet and white bikini. Her shell necklace followed and she piled both on the table with the same casual concern that she'd balled up the paper from their fish and chips. She gathered her snorkelling gear as Rich shed a few layers down to his board shorts and he followed her tensely to the high tide mark. Their gear on, she handed him a headlamp to match her own and a calico net.

There was something about doing this together—as partners. He trusted Mila not to put him in any kind of danger, and trusting her felt like an empowered decision. And empowerment felt a little like control.

And that was all he needed to step into the dark shallows.

'What do I do with this?' he asked, waving the net around his head, as if it was meant for butterflies.

'Just hold it a foot above any coral that's erupting. Ten seconds maximum. Then find a coral that looks totally different to the first and repeat the process.'

'This is high stakes.'

He meant that glibly but he knew by the pause as she studied him that, for her, it absolutely was.

'You can't get it wrong. Come on.'

She waded in ahead of him and his headlamp slashed across her firm, slim body as she went. Given they were on departmental business, it felt wrong to be checking out a fellow scientist. It would have helped if she'd worn a white lab coat instead of a white bikini.

Focus.

The inky water swallowed them up, and its vastness demanded his full attention even as his mind knew it wasn't particularly deep. He fought to keep a map of the lagoon in his head so that his subconscious had something to reference when it was deciding how much adrenaline to pump through his system.

They were on the shallow side of the drop-off, where everything was warm and golden and filled with happy little sea creatures during the day. There was no reason that should change just because it was dark. Robbed of one of his key senses, his others heightened along with his imagination. In that moment he almost understood how Mila saw the reef. The water was silky-smooth and soft where it brushed his bare skin. Welcoming.

Decidedly un-soupy.

He kept Mila's fins—two of them this time—just inside the funnel of light coming from his headlamp. Beyond the cone of both their lights it was the inkiest of blacks. But Mila swam confidently on and the sandy lagoon floor fell away from them until the first corals started to appear a dozen metres offshore.

'They need a good couple of metres of water above them to do this,' she puffed, raising her head for a moment and pushing out her snorkel mouthpiece. Her long hair glued to her neck and shoulders and her golden skin glittered wet in his lamplight. 'So that the receding tide will carry their spawn bundles away to a new site while the embryos mature. Get ready…'

He mirrored her deep breath and then submerged, kicking down to the reef's surface. At first, there was nothing. Just the odd little bit of detritus floating across his field of light, but between one fin-kick and the next he swam straight into a plume of spawning coral. Instantly, he was inside a snow dome. Hundreds of tiny bundles wafted around him on the water's current, making their way to the surface. Pink. White. Glowing in the lamplight against the endless black background of night ocean. As each one met his skin, it was like rain—or tiny reverse hailstones—plinking onto him from below then rolling off and carrying on its determined journey to the surface. As soft as a breath. Utterly surreal. All around them, tiny bait fish darted, unconcerned by their presence, and picked off single, unlucky bundles. The bigger fish kept their distance and gorged themselves just out of view and, though he knew that *even bigger* fish with much sharper teeth probably watched them from the darkness, he found it difficult to care in light of this once-in-a-lifetime moment.

Mila was right.

It was spectacular.

And he might have missed it if not for her.

He surfaced for air again, glanced at the lights of the beach car park to stay oriented and then plugged his snorkel and returned to a few metres below. Just on the edge of his lamp, Mila back-swam over a particularly active plate coral and held her net aloft, letting the little bundles just float right into its mesh embrace. He turned to the nearby staghorn and did the same. On his, the spawn came off in smoky plumes and it was hard to know which was coral and which was some local fish timing its own reproductive activity within the smokescreen of much more obvious targets. He scooped it all up regardless. For every spawn bundle he caught, thousands more were being released.

Besides, the little fish were picking off many more than he was.

Ten seconds...

A sea jelly floated across the shaft of his lamp, glowing, but it was only when a cuttlefish did the same that he stopped to wonder. He'd only ever seen them dead on the seashore—as a kid he'd used them to dig out moats on sandcastles—like small surfboards. Live and lamplit, the cuttlefish glowed with translucent beauty and busied itself chasing down a particular spawn bundle, with a dozen crazily swimming legs.

But, as he raised his eyes, the shaft of his light filled with Mila, her limbs gently waving in a way the cuttlefish could only dream of, pink-white spawn snowing in reverse all around her, her eyes behind her mask glinting and angled. He didn't need to see her smile to feel its effect on him.

She was born to be here.

And he was honoured to be allowed to visit.

The reef at night reminded him of an eighties movie he'd seen. A dying metropolis, three hundred years from now, saturated with acid rain and blazing with neon, the skies crowded with grungy air transport, the streets far below pocked with dens and cavities of danger and the underbelly that thrived there.

This reef was every bit as busy and systematic as that futuristic world. Just far more beautiful.

She surfaced for a breath near to him.

'Ready to go in?' she asked.

'Nope.' Not nearly.

She smiled. 'It's been an hour, Rich.'

He kicked his legs below the surface and realised how

much thicker the water had become in that time. 'You're kidding?'

'Time flies…'

Yeah. It really did. He couldn't remember the last time he'd felt this relaxed. Yet energised at the same time.

'I'm happy with that haul,' she said. 'I missed the *Porites* coral last year so they'll be awesome for the spawn bank.'

'Is that what I can smell?' he said, nostrils twitching at the pungent odour.

'It's probably better not to think about exactly what we're swimming in,' she puffed, staying afloat. 'But trust me when I say it's much better being out here in freshly erupted spawn than tomorrow in day-old spawn. Or the day after.'

She deftly twisted her catch net and then his so that the contents could not escape and then they turned for shore. They had drifted out further than he'd thought but still well within the confines of the lagoon. He could only imagine what a feeding frenzy this night would be beyond the flats where the outer reef spread. In the shallow water, she passed him the nets and then kicked free of her fins to jog ashore and collect the big plastic tub waiting there. She half filled it with clear seawater and then used her snorkelling mask to pour more over the top of her reversed net, swilling out the captured spawn into their watery new home. Maskful after maskful finally got all of his in too. They wrestled the heavy container up to their table together.

After the weightlessness of an hour in the dystopian underworld his legs felt like clumsy, useless trunks and he longed for the ease and effectiveness and freedom of his fins.

Freedom...

'So what did you think?' Mila asked, straightening.

Because they'd carried the tub together, she was standing much closer to him than she ever had before and her head came to just below his shoulder, forcing her to peer up at him with clear green eyes. Even bedraggled and wet, and with red pressure marks from her mask around her face, he wasn't sure he'd ever seen anything quite as beautiful. Except maybe the electric snowfield of spawning coral rising all around her as she did her best mermaid impersonation.

He'd never wanted to kiss someone so much in his life.

'Speechless,' he murmured instead. 'It was everything you said it would be.'

'Now do you get it?'

Somehow he knew what she was really asking.

Now do you get me*?*

He raised a hand and brushed her cheek with his knuckles, tucking a strand of soggy hair behind her ear. She sucked in a breath and leaned, almost easily, into his touch. It was the first time she hadn't flinched away from him.

His chest tightened even as it felt as if it had expanded two-fold with the pride of that.

'Yeah,' he breathed. 'I think I do. What is it like for you?'

'A symphony. So many sounds all working together.' Her eyes glittered at the memory. 'Not necessarily in harmony—just a wash of sound. The coral bundles are like tiny percussions and they build and they build as the sea fills with them and the ones that touch my skin are like—' she searched around her as if the word she needed was hovering nearby '—a mini firework. Hundreds of tiny explosions. The coral itself is so vibrant under light it just sings to me. Seduces. Breathtaking, except that I'm already holding my breath.' She dropped her head and her wet locks swayed. 'I can't explain it.'

He brought her gaze back up with a finger beneath her chin. His other hand came up to frame her cheek. 'I think I envy you your superpower right now.'

Lips the same gentle pink as the coral spawn parted slightly and mesmerised his gaze just as the little bundles had.

'It has its moments,' she breathed.

Mila was as much a product of this reef as anything he saw out there. Half-mermaid and easily as at home in the water as she was on land. Born of the Saltwater People and she would die in it, living it, loving it.

Protecting it.

This land was technically his heritage too, yet he had no such connection with it and no such protective instincts. He'd been raised to work it and maximise its yield. To exploit it.

For the first time ever he doubted the philosophy he'd been raised with. And he doubted himself.

Was he exploiting Mila too? Mining her for her knowledge and expertise? Wouldn't kissing her when she didn't know the truth about him just be another kind of exploitation? As badly as he wanted to lower his mouth onto hers, until he rectified *that*, any kiss he stole would be just that…

Stolen.

'You have spawn in your hair,' he murmured as she peered up at him.

It said something about how used to the distance of others Mila was that she was so unsurprised when he stepped back.

'I'm sure that's the least of it,' she said. 'Let's get this all back to my place and we can both clean up.'

He retreated a step, then another, and he lifted the heavy spawn-rich container to save Mila the chore. Her dress snagged on her damp skin as she wriggled back into it but then she gathered up the rest of their gear and followed him up to her truck.

CHAPTER SEVEN

IT ONLY OCCURRED to Mila as she pulled up out the front that Rich was the first person she'd ever brought into this place. When she needed to liaise with work people she usually drove the long road north to the department's branch office or met them at some beach site somewhere. She never came with them here, to the little stack of converted transport modules that served as both home and office.

Safe, private spaces.

Rich stood by her four-wheel drive, looking at the two-storey collection of steel.

'Are those…shipping containers?'

The back of her mouth filled with something between fried chicken and old leather. She looked at the corrugated steel walls in their mismatched, faded primary colours as he might see them and definitely found them wanting.

'Up here the regular accommodation is saved for the tourists,' she said. 'Behind the scenes, everyone lives in pretty functional dwellings. But we make them homey inside. Come on in.'

She led him around the back of the efficient dwelling where a weathered timber deck stretched out between the 'U' of sea containers on three sides—double-storey in the centre and single-storey adjoining on the left and right. He stumbled to a halt at the sight of her daybed—an old timber dinghy, tipped on an angle and filled with fat, inviting cushions. A curl of old canvas hung above it between the containers like a crashing wave. He stood, speechless, and stared at her handiwork.

'You're going to see a bit of upcycling in the next quarter-hour…' she warned, past the sour milk of self-consciousness.

Mila pushed open the double doors on the sea container to her left and stepped into her office. Despite the unpromising exterior, inside, it looked much like any other workspace except that her furniture was a bit more eclectic than the big city corporate office Rich was probably used to. A weathered old beach shack door for a desk, with a pair of deep filing cabinets for legs. An old paint-streaked ladder mounted lengthways on the wall served as bookshelves for her biology textbooks and her work files. The plain walls were decorated with a panoramic photograph she had taken of her favourite lagoon, enlarged and mounted in three parts behind mismatched window frames salvaged from old fishing shacks from down the coast.

Rich stared at the artwork.

'My view when I'm working,' she puffed, fighting the heat of a blush. 'Could you put that by the door?'

He positioned the opaque tub by the glass doors so that the moonlight could continue to work its magic on the coral spawn within until she could freeze them in the morning. Those first few hours of moonlight seemed critical to a good fertilisation result; why else had nature designed them to bob immediately to the surface instead of sink to the seafloor?

She killed the light and turned to cross the deck. 'I inherited this stack from someone else when I first moved out of home, but it was pretty functional then. I like to think I've improved it.'

She opened French windows immediately opposite her office and led Rich inside. His eyes had barely managed to stop bulging at her makeshift office before they were goggling again.

'You did all this?' he asked, looking around.

Her furniture mostly consisted of another timber sailing boat cut into parts and sanded within an inch of its life before being waxed until it was glossy. The stern half stood on its fat end at the end of the room and acted as a bookshelf and display cabinet, thanks to some handiwork flipping the boat's seats into shelves; its round little middle sat upturned at the centre of the space and held the glass that made it a coffee table, and its pointed bow was wall-mounted and served as a side table.

'I had some help from one of Coral Bay's old sea dogs, but otherwise, yes, I made most of this. I hate to see anything wasted. Feel free to look around.'

She jogged up polished timber steps to the bedroom that sat on top of the centremost sea container—the one that acted as kitchen, bathroom and laundry. She rustled up some dry clothes and an armful of towels and then padded back down to take a quick shower. Rich hadn't moved his feet but he'd twisted a little, presumably to peer around him. Was it in disbelief? In surprise?

In horror?

To her, it was personalised expression—her little haven filled with things that brought her pleasure. But what did Rich see? Did he view it as the junkyard pickings of some kind of hoarder?

His eyes were fixed overhead, on the lighting centrepiece of the room. A string of bud lights twisted and wove back on itself but each tiny bulb was carefully mounted inside a sea urchin she'd found on the shore outside of the sanctuary zone. Some big. Some small. All glowing their own delicate shades of pinks and orange. The whole thing tangled around an artful piece of driftwood she'd just loved.

The room filled with sour milk again and it killed her that she could feel so self-conscious about something that had brought her so much joy to create. And still did. She refused to defend it even though she burned to.

'I'll be just five minutes,' she announced, tossing the towel over her shoulder. 'Then you can clean up too.'

She scurried through the kitchen to the bathroom at the back of the sea container. If you didn't know what you were standing in you might think you were in some kind of up-market beach shack, albeit eclectically furnished. Rich had five minutes to look his fill at all her weird stuff and then he'd be in here—her eyes drifted up to the white, round lightshade to which she'd attached streaming lengths of plaited fishing net until the whole thing resembled a cheerful bathroom jellyfish—for better or worse.

When she emerged, rinsed and clean-haired, Rich was studying up close the engineering on a tiered wall unit made of pale driftwood. She moved up next to him and lit the tea lights happily sitting on its shelves. They cast a gentle glow over that side of the room.

'Will I find an ordinary light fitting anywhere in your house?' he murmured down at her.

She had to think about it. 'The lamp in the office is pretty regular.' If you didn't count the tiny sea stars glued to its stand. 'This is one of my favourites.'

She lit another tea light sitting all alone on the boat bow side table except for a tiny piece of beach detritus that sat with it. It looked like nothing more than a minuscule bit of twisted seaweed. But, as the flame caught behind it, a shadow cast on the nearby wall and Rich was drawn by the flickering shape that grew as the flame did.

'I found the poor, dried seahorse on the marina shore

when it was first built,' she said. 'Took me ages to think how I could celebrate it.'

He turned and just stared, something rather like confusion in his blue gaze.

Mila handed him a small stack of guest towels and pointed him in the direction of the bathroom. 'Take your time.'

As soon as he was safely out of view, she sagged against the kitchen bench. Nothing should have upstaged the fact that there was a naked man showering just ten feet away in her compact little bathroom, but Rich had given her spectacular fodder for distraction.

That kiss...

Not an actual kiss, but nearly. Cheek-brushing and chest-heaving and lingering looks. Enough that she'd been throbbing candyfloss while her pulse had tumbled over itself like a crashing wave. Lucky she'd built up such excellent lung capacity because she'd flat-out forgotten to breathe during the whole experience. Anyone else might have passed out.

'An almost-kiss isn't an actual kiss,' she lectured herself under her breath.

Even if it was the closest she'd come in a long, long time. Rich had been overwhelmed by his experience on the reef and had reached out instinctively, but—really—who wanted to kiss a woman soaked in spawn?

'No one.'

She rustled up a second mug and put the kettle on to boil. It took about the same time to bubble as the ninety seconds Rich did to shower and change back into his black sweater and jeans. When he emerged from the door next to her, all pink and freshly groomed, the bathroom's steam mingled with the kettle's.

'I made you tea,' she murmured.

He smiled as he took the mug. 'It's been a long time since I've had tea.'

Her eyes immediately hunted for coffee. 'You don't like it?'

'It's just that coffee's more a thing in the corporate world. I've fallen out of practice. It was a standard at boarding school until eleventh form, when we were allowed to up-grade to a harder core breakfast beverage.'

She started rummaging in the kitchen. 'I have some somewhere…'

He met her eyes and held them. 'I would like to drink tea with you, Mila.'

She couldn't look away; she could barely breathe a reply. 'Okay.'

He looked around her humble home again. 'I really like your place.'

'It's different to the *Portus*.'

He laughed. 'It's not a boat, for one thing. But it suits you. It's unique.'

Unique. Yep, that was one word for her.

'I hate to see anything wasted,' she said again. Her eyes went to her sea urchin extravaganza. 'And I hate to see beautiful things die. This is a way I can keep them alive and bring the reef inside at the same time.'

He studied her light art as if it was by a Renaissance sculptor, his brows drawn, deep in thought.

'What is your home like?' she went on when he didn't reply.

The direct question brought his gaze back to her. 'It's not a *home*, for a start. I don't feel like I've had one of those since… A long time.' He peered around again. 'But it's nothing like this.'

No. She couldn't imagine him surrounded by anything other than quality. She sank ahead of him onto one of two sofas made out of old travelling chests. The sort that might have washed up after a shipwreck. The sort that was perfect to have upholstered into insanely comfortable seats.

Rich frowned a little as he examined the seat's engineering.

'Home is something you come back to, isn't it?' he went on. 'About the only thing I have that meets that definition is the *Portus*. I feel different when I step aboard. Changed. Maybe she's my home.'

Mila sipped at her tea in the silence that followed and watched Rich grow less and less comfortable in her company.

'Is everything all right, Rich?' she finally braved.

He glanced up at her and then sighed. Long and deep.

'Mila, there's something I haven't told you.'

The cloves made a brief reappearance but she pushed through the discomfort. Trust came more easily with every minute she spent in Rich's company.

'Keeping secrets, Mr Grundy?' she quipped.

'That's just it,' he went on, ignoring her attempt at humour. 'I'm not Mr Grundy. At least… I am, and I'm not.'

She pressed back into the soft upholstery and gave him her full attention.

He lifted bleak eyes. 'Nancy Dawson married a Grundy.'

Awareness flooded in on a wave of nostalgia. 'Oh, that's right. Jack. I forgot because everyone up here knows them as Dawson. Wait…are you a relative of Jack Grundy? Ten times removed?'

'No times removed, actually.' Rich took a long sip of his tea. As if it were his last. 'Jack was my great-grandfather.'

Mila just stared. 'But that means…'

Nancy's Point. She'd stood there and lectured him about his own great-grandmother. The more immediate ramification took a little longer to sink in. She sat upright and placed her still steaming mug onto the little midships coffee table. The only way to disguise the sudden tremble of her fingers was to lay them flat on the thighs of her yoga pants. Unconsciously bracing herself.

'Are you a Dawson? Of the Wardoo Dawsons?'

Rich took a deep breath. 'I'm *the* Dawson. The only son of an only son. I hold the pastoral rights on Wardoo Station and the ten thousand square kilometres around it.'

Mila's hands dug deeper into her thighs. 'But that means…'

'It means I hold the lease on the land that Coral Bay sits on.'

The back of her throat stung with the taste of nail varnish and it was all she could do to whisper, 'You own my town?'

Rich straightened. 'The only thing I *own* is the Station infrastructure. But the lease is what has the value. And I hold that, presently.'

Her brain finally caught up and the nail varnish dissipated. 'Wardoo is yours.'

Because there was no Wardoo without the Dawsons. Just as there was no Coral Bay without them either.

Rich took a deep breath before answering. 'It is.'

Her eyes came up. 'Then you've been stopping the developers in their tracks! I thought you were one!'

His skin greyed off just a bit. Maybe he wasn't comfortable with overt gushing, but the strong mango of gratitude made it impossible for her to stop.

'WestCorp has been denying access for third-party development, yes—'

Whatever that little bit of careful corporate speak meant. All she heard was that *Rich* was the reason there were no towering hotels on her reef. *Rich* had kept everyone but the state government out of the lands bordering the World Heritage Marine Park. *Rich* was her corporate guardian angel.

Despite herself, despite everything she knew about people and every screaming sense she knew she'd be triggering, Mila tipped herself forward and threw her arms wide around his broad shoulders.

'Thank you,' she gushed, pressing herself into the hug. 'Thank you for my reef.'

CHAPTER EIGHT

RICH COULDN'T REMEMBER a time that he'd been more comfortable in someone's arms yet so excruciatingly uncomfortable as well.

Mila had only grasped half the truth.

Because he had only told half of it.

He let his own hands slide up and contribute to Mila's fervent embrace, but it was brief and it took little physical effort to curl his fingers and ease her slightly back from him. The emotional effort was much higher; she was warm and soft under his hands and she felt incredibly right there—speaking of going *home*—yet he felt more of a louse than when he'd nearly kissed her earlier.

Telling her had been the right thing to do but, in his head, this moment was going to go very differently. He'd steeled himself for her shock, her disappointment. Maybe for an escaped tear or two that he'd been keeping the truth from her. Instead, he got…this.

Gratitude.

He'd confessed his identity now but Mila only saw half the picture… The half that made him a hero, looking out for the underdog and the underdog's reef. She had no sense for the politics and game playing behind every access refusal. The prioritising.

It wasn't noble… It was corporate strategy.

'Don't be too quick to canonise me, Mila,' he murmured as she withdrew from the spontaneous hug, blushing. The gentle flush matched the colour she'd been when she came out of the bathroom. 'It's business. It's not personal. I hadn't even seen the reef until you showed me.'

Even now he was avoiding putting the puzzle fully together for her. It would only take a few words to confess that—yeah, he was still a developer and he was planning on developing her reef. But he wasn't strong enough to do that while he was still warm from her embrace.

'How could you go to Wardoo and not visit such a famous coast?' she asked.

'Actually, I've never been to Wardoo either,' he confessed further. 'I flew over it once, years ago.'

The quizzical smile turned into a gape. 'What? Why?'

'Because there's no need. I get reports and updates from the caretaking team. To me, it's just a remote business holding at the end of one of my spreadsheets.'

The words on his lips made him tense. As though the truth wasn't actually the truth.

Her gape was now a stare. 'No. Really?'

'Really.' He shrugged.

'But… It's *Wardoo.* It's your home.'

'I never grew up there, Mila. It holds no meaning for me.'

A momentary flash of his eight-year-old self tumbled beneath his determination for it to *be* the truth.

She scrabbled upright again and perched on her seat, leaning towards him. 'You need to go, Rich.'

No. He really didn't.

'You need to go and see it in its context, not in some photograph. Smell it and taste it and…'

'Taste it?'

'Okay, maybe that's just me, but won't you at least visit

the people who run it for you? Let them show you their work?'

It was his turn to frown. Her previous jibe about *minions* hit home again.

'I'm sure they'd be delighted with a short-notice visit from their CEO,' he drawled.

She considered him. 'You won't know if you don't ask.'

He narrowed his eyes. 'You're very keen for me to visit, Mila. What am I missing?'

Her expression grew suspiciously innocent. 'I *might* be thinking about the fact that you don't have a car. And that I do—'

'And you're offering to lend it to me?' he shot back, his face just as impassive. 'Thanks, that's kind of you.'

Which made it sound as if he was considering going. When had that happened?

'Actually, it's kind of hinky to drive. I'd better take you. Road safety and all.'

'You don't know the roads. You've never been out there.'

Hoisted by her own petard.

'Okay, fine. Then take me in return for the coral spawn.' She shuffled forward. 'I would give anything to see Wardoo.'

Glad one of them was so keen. 'You know there's no reef out there, right? Just scrub and dirt.'

'Come on, Rich, it's a win-win—I get to see Wardoo and you get to have a reason to go there.'

'I don't need a reason to go there.'

And he didn't particularly *want* to. Though he did, very much, want to see the excited colour in Mila's cheeks a little bit longer. It reminded him of the flush as he'd stroked her cheek. And it did make a kind of sense to check it out since he was up here on an official fact-finding mission. After all, how convincing was he going to be if that government bureaucrat discovered he'd never actually been to the property? Photos and monthly reports could only do so much.

'What time?' he sighed.

Mila's eyes glittered like the emeralds they were, triumphant. 'I have a quickish task to do at low tide, but it's on the way to Wardoo so… Eight?'

'Does this *task* involve anything else slimy, soupy or slippery?' he worried.

'Maybe.' She laughed. 'It involves the reef.'

Of course it did.

'How wet will I be getting?'

'You? Not at all. I might, depending on the tide.'

'Okay then.' He could happily endure one last opportunity to see Mila in her natural habitat. Before he told her the full truth. And he could give her the gift of Wardoo, before pulling the happy dream they were both living out from under her too.

The least he could do, maybe.

'Eight it is, then.'

Her gaze glowed her pleasure and Rich just let himself swim there for a few moments. Below it all, he knew he was only delaying the inevitable, but there really was nothing to gain by telling her now instead of tomorrow.

'I should get back to the *Portus*,' he announced, reaching into his pocket for his phone. 'Need my beauty sleep if I'm going to wow the minions tomorrow.'

Her perfect skin flushed again as she remembered her own words and who she'd been talking about all along. But she handled the embarrassment as she handled everything—graciously. She crossed the small room to get her keys off their little hook.

'I'll drive you to the marina.'

* * *

Not surprisingly, given the marina was only a few minutes away, there was no sign of Damo when they climbed out of the four-wheel drive at the deserted ramp, although Mila could clearly see the *Portus* waiting out beyond the reef. Had it done laps out there the whole night, like a pacing attendant waiting for its master?

'He won't be long,' Rich murmured as a floodlight made its way steadily across the darkness that was the sea beyond the reef. The speed limits still applied even though no one else was using the channel. They weren't there to protect the boats.

'Did you enjoy dinner?' Rich asked after a longish, silence-filled pause. He turned closer to her in the darkness.

She'd totally forgotten the eating part of the evening. All she'd been fixating on was the looking part, the touching part. The just-out-of-the-shower part.

'Very much,' she said, looking up to him. 'Always happy not to go into a crowded building.'

'Thank you for letting me tag along on the spawn; it really was very beautiful.'

It was impossible not to chuckle but—this close and in this much darkness—it came out sounding way throatier than she meant it. 'I'm pretty sure I bullied you into coming.'

Just like she'd talked her way into Wardoo tomorrow.

'Happy to have been bullied then. I never could have imagined…'

No. It really was *un*imaginable until you'd seen it. She liked knowing that they had that experience in common now. Every shared experience they had brought them that little bit closer. And now that she knew he was a Dawson… every experience would help to secure the borders against developers even more.

A stiff breeze kicked up off the water and reminded Mila that she was still in the light T-shirt and yoga pants she'd shrugged into in her steamy little bathroom inside her warm little house. Gooseflesh prickled, accompanied by imaginary wings fluttering as the bumps raced up her skin.

'You should head home,' Rich immediately said as she rubbed her arms. 'It's cold.'

'No—'

She didn't want to leave. She didn't want to wait until eight a.m. to see him again. She wasn't ready to leave this man who turned out to have had the back of everything she cared about for all these years. If he asked her back to his boat to spend the night she was ready to say yes.

'I'm good.'

Large hands found her upper arms in the light from the silvered moon and added their warmth to her cold skin. Harps immediately joined the fluttering wings.

'Here…'

Rich moved around close behind her and then rubbed his hands up and down her arms, bringing her back against his hard, warm, sweater-clad chest. He'd shifted from a client to an acquaintance somewhere around the visit to Yardi Creek, and from acquaintance to a friend when she'd agreed to have dinner. But exactly when did they become *arm-rubbing* kinds of friends? Was it when they'd stood so close by the shore this evening? When they'd shared the majesty of the spawn event? The not-quite kiss?

Did it even matter? The multiple sensations of his hands on hers, his body against hers was a kind of heaven she'd secretly believed she would never experience.

It was only when she saw the slash of the tender's arriving floodlight on the back of her eyelids that she realised they'd fluttered shut.

Rich stepped away and the harps faded to nothing at the loss of his skin on hers.

'I'll see you here at eight,' he said, far more composed than she felt. But then his big frame blocked the moonlight as he bent to kiss her cheek. His words were a hot caress against her ear and the gooseflesh worsened.

'Sleep well.'

Pfff... As if.

Before she could reply, he had stepped away and she mourned not only the warmth of his hands but now the gentle brush of his lips too. Too, too brief. He stepped down onto the varnished pier out to the tender and left her. Standing here, watching him walk away from her, those narrow jeans-clad hips swinging even in the dim moonlight, was a little too much like self-harm and so she turned to face her truck and took the few steps she needed to cross back to it.

At the last moment she heard a crunch that wasn't her own feet on the crushed gravel marina substrate.

'Mila...'

She pivoted into Rich's return and he didn't even pause as he walked hard up against her and bent again, to her lips this time. His kiss was soft but it lingered. It explored. It blew her little mind. And it came with a sensation overload. He took her too much by surprise to invoke the citrus of anticipation but it kicked in now and mingled with the strong, candy surge of attraction as a tiny corner of her mind wondered breathlessly how long his kiss could last. Waves crashed and she knew it wasn't on the nearby shore; it was what kissing gave her, though not always like this... Not always accompanied by skin harps and the crackle of fireplace that was the heat of Rich's mouth on her own. And all that oak moss...

Her head spun with want as much as the breathless surprise of Rich's stealthy return.

'I should have done that hours ago,' he murmured at last, breathing fast. 'I wanted to right after the coral.'

'Why didn't you?' Belatedly, she realised she was probably supposed to protest his presumption, or say something witty, or be grown up and blasé about it. But really, all she wanted to know was why they hadn't been kissing all evening.

'I wanted you to know about me. Who I was. So you had the choice.'

Oh, kissing him was a *choice*? That was a laugh, and not because he'd sneaked up on her and made the first move. She'd been thinking about his mouth for days now.

There was no choice.

But she was grateful for the consideration.

'I like who you are,' she murmured. 'Thank you for telling me.'

Besides, she was the last person who could judge anyone else for keeping themselves private.

He dipped his head again and sent the harps a-harping and the fire a-crackling for more precious moments. Then he straightened and stepped back.

'Tomorrow then,' he said and he and his conflicted gaze were gone, jogging down the pier towards the *Portus'* waiting tender.

Mila sagged against her open car door and watched until he was out of sight. Even then, she stared at the inky ocean and imagined the small boat making its way until it reappeared as a shadow against the well-lit *Portus*. Impossible to see Rich climb aboard at this distance but she imagined that too; in her mind's eye she saw him slumping down on that expansive sofa amid the polished chrome and glass. She tried to imagine him checking his phone or picking up a book or even stretching out on that king-sized bed and watching the night sky through the wraparound windows, but it was easier to imagine him settling in behind his laptop at the workstation and getting a few more hours of corporate in before his head hit any kind of pillow.

That was just who he was. And it was where he came from.

A whale shark couldn't change its spots.

Except this one—just maybe—could.

CHAPTER NINE

MILA TOOK A careful knife to the reef and carved out a single oyster from a crowded corner, working carefully not to injure or loosen the rest. Then she did it again at another stack. And again. And again. On the way out to this remote bay, she'd told Rich that her department's licence called for five test oysters every month and a couple of simple observational tests to monitor oyster condition and keep them free of the disease that was ravaging populations down the east coast of the country.

Rich held the little bag for her as she dropped them in one by one.

She smiled shy thanks, though not quite at him. 'For a CEO you make an excellent apprentice ranger.'

So far this morning the two of them had been doing a terrific job of ignoring exactly what it was that had gone down between them last night. The kissing part, not the sharing of secrets part. One was planned, the other… Not so much. He hadn't even known he was going to do it until he'd felt his feet twisting on the pier and striding back towards her.

'Now I understand your fashion choice,' he murmured, nodding at her high-vis vest emblazoned with the department logo. It wasn't the most flattering thing he'd seen her in since they'd met yet she still managed to make it seem… intriguing.

'Don't want anyone thinking they can just help themselves to oysters here,' she said. 'This is inside the sanctuary zone.'

Not that there was a soul around yet. The tide was way too low to be of interest to snorkelers and the fishermen had too much respect for their equipment to try tossing a line in at this razor-ridden place.

They waded ashore and Mila laid the five knotted shells out on the tailgate of her four-wheel drive. She placed a dog-eared laminated number above each, photographed it and then set about her testing. All that busyness was a fantastic way of not needing to make eye contact with him.

Was she embarrassed? Did she regret participating quite so enthusiastically in last night's experimental kiss? Or was she just as focused on her work as he could be when he was in the zone? Given how distracted he'd been last night, going over and over the proposal, it was hard to imagine ever being in the zone again.

Mila picked one oyster up and gently knocked its semi-open shell. It closed immediately but with no great urgency.

'That's a four,' she told him, and he dutifully wrote it down on the form she'd given him.

The others were all fours too, and one super-speedy five. That made her happy. She'd clearly opened an oyster or three in her time and she made quick work of separating each one from its top shell by a swift knife move to its hinge. She wafted the inner scent of each towards her nostrils before dipping her finger in and then placing it in her mouth to taste its juices. He wrote down her observations as she voiced them.

'If these five exemplars are responsive, fresh and the

flesh is opaque then it's a good sign of the health of the whole oyster community,' she said.

'What do you do with them, then—toss them back?'

'These five are ambassadors for their kind. I usually wedge the shells back in to become part of the stack, but I don't waste the meat.'

'And by that you mean…?'

'I eat them,' she said with a grin. 'Want to help?'

Rich frowned. 'Depends on whether you have any red wine vinegar on hand.'

She used the little knife to shuck the first of them and flip it to study its underside. Then she held up the oyster sample in front of her lips like a salute. *'Au naturel.'*

Down it went. She repeated the neat move and handed the finished shuck to him.

His eyebrows raised as soon as he bit down on the ultra-fresh mollusc. 'Melon!'

'Yeah, kind of. Salty melon.'

'Even to you?'

She smiled. 'Even to me. With a bonus hit of *astute*.'

Rich couldn't really see how a hibernating lump of muscle could have any personality at all but he was prepared to go with 'astute'. He'd never managed to taste the 'ambition' in vintage wine either, but he was prepared to believe that connoisseurs at the fancy restaurants he frequented could.

Maybe Mila was just a nature connoisseur.

Oyster number three and four went the same way and then there was only the one left. He offered it to Mila. 'You know what they say about oysters…'

She blinked at him. 'Excellent for your immune system and bone strength?'

He stared at her, trying to gauge whether she was serious. He loved not being able to read her. How long had it been since someone surprised him?

'Yeah, that's what they say.'

It was only when she smiled, slow and sexy, that he knew *she* knew. But obviously she wasn't about to mention it in light of last night's illicit kiss.

She gasped, scribbling in her log what she'd found on the oyster's underside. 'A pearl.'

Rich peered at the small cream mass. It wasn't much of one but it undoubtedly *was* a pearl. 'Is that a good sign?'

'Not really.' Mila poked at it carefully. 'It could have formed in response to a parasite. Too much of that would be a bad sign for these stacks.'

'Pearls are a defect?' he asked.

'"Out of a flaw comes beauty",' Mila quoted.

She might as well have been describing herself.

She lifted it out with her blade and rinsed it in the seawater, then swallowed the last of the oyster flesh.

'Here,' she said, handing it to him. 'A souvenir.'

'Because you have so many littering your house?'

Just how many had she found in her time?

'It's reasonably rare to find a wild one,' she said, still smiling. 'This is only my second in all the time I've been working here. But I don't feel right about keeping them; I'm lucky enough just to do this for a living without profiting from it further. I gave the last one away to a woman with three noisy kids.'

Rich stared. She was like a whole different species to him. 'Do you know what they're worth?'

'Not so much when they're this small and malformed, I don't think.' She laid it out on her hand and let the little lump flip over on her wet palm. 'But I prefer them like this. Rough and nature-formed. Though it's weird, I don't get any kind of personality off them. I wonder why.'

She studied it a moment longer, as if *willing* it to perform for her.

'Here…' She finally thrust her hand out. 'Something to remember Coral Bay by. Sorry it's not bigger.'

Something deep in his chest protested. Did she imagine he cared about that? When he looked at the small, imperfect pearl he would remember the small, imperfect woman who had given it to him.

And how perfect her imperfections made her.

He closed his hand around the lumpy gem. 'Thank you.'

She took the empty shell parts and jogged back into the water to wedge them back into the stacks as foundation for future generations, then she returned and packed up. Rich took the opportunity to watch her move, and work, without making her self-conscious.

He found he quite liked to just watch her.

'Okay,' she finally puffed. 'All done for the month. Shall we get going? Did you tell Wardoo you were coming?'

'Panic duly instigated, yes.'

She smiled at him and he wondered when he'd started counting the minutes between them. She'd smiled more at him in the last hour than she had in the entire time he'd known her. It was uncomfortably hard not to connect it to her misapprehension that he was some kind of crusading, conservation good guy.

'I think you'll like it. This country really is very beautiful in its own unique way.'

As he followed her up the path to her car all he could think about was an old phrase…

Takes one to know one.

Their arrival at Wardoo was decidedly low-key. If not for the furtive glance of a man crossing between one corrugated outbuilding and the next she'd have thought no one was all that interested in Rich's arrival. But that sideways look spoke volumes. It was more the kind of surreptitious play-down-the-moment peek reserved for politicians or rock stars.

Or royalty.

Some of the men who had worked Wardoo their whole adult lives might never have seen a Dawson in person. *Grundy*, she reminded herself.

A wide grin in a weathered, masculine face met them, introduced himself as the Station foreman and offered to show them, first, through the homestead.

'Jared Kipling,' he said, shaking Rich's hand. 'Kip.'

She wasn't offended that Kip had forgotten to shake her hand in the fluster of meeting his long-absent boss. It saved her the anxiety of another first-time touch.

It was only when she watched Rich's body language as he stepped up onto the veranda running the full perimeter of the homestead that she realised he'd slipped back into business mode. She recognised it from that first day at Nancy's Point. Exactly when he'd stopped being quite so…corporate she wasn't as sure.

'It's vacant?' Mila asked as she stepped into the dust-free hall of Wardoo homestead ahead of the men. Despite being furnished, there was something empty about it, and not just because the polished floorboards exuded isolation the way jarrah always did for her.

Wardoo was…hollow. And somehow lifeless.

How incredibly sad. Not what she had imagined at all.

'Most of our crew live in transportables on site or in town. We keep the house for the Dawsons,' Kip said. 'Just in case.'

The Dawsons who had never visited? The hollowness only increased and she glanced at Rich. He kept his gaze firmly averted.

She left the men to their discussions and explored the homestead. Every room was just as clean and just as empty as the one before it. She ran her fingertips along the rich old surfaces and enjoyed the myriad sensations that came with them. When she made her way back to the living room, Rich and the foreman were deep in discussion on the unused sofas. She heard the word 'lease' before Rich shot to his feet and brought the conversation to a rapid halt.

'If you've seen enough—' Kip floundered at the sudden end to their conversation '—I can show you the operations yards and then the chopper's standing by for an aerial tour.'

Rich looked decidedly awkward too. What a novelty—to be the least socially clumsy person in a room.

'You have your own chopper?' Mila asked him, to ease the tension.

It did the trick. He gifted her a small smile that only served to remind her how many minutes it had been since the last one.

Because apparently she counted, now.

He turned for the door as if she'd been the one keeping him waiting. 'It seems I do.'

'It's a stock mustering chopper,' Kip went on, tailing them. 'There's only room for two. But it's the only way to get out to the perimeter of Wardoo and back in a day.'

'The perimeter can wait,' Rich declared. 'Just show us the highlights within striking distance by road.'

Us. As if she were some kind of permanent part of the Richard Grundy show.

She trotted along behind Rich as he toured the equipment and sheds closest to the Homestead. Of course, on a property of this scale 'close' was relative. Then they piled into a late model Land Cruiser and set off in a plume of red-brown dust to the north. Mila lost herself in the Australian scrub and let time flow over her like water as Rich and Kip discussed the operations of the cattle station. She was yet to actually see a cow.

'The herds like to range inland this time of year,' Kip said when she asked. 'While the eastern dams are full. We'll see some soon.'

She lost track of time again until the brush of knuckles on her cheek tingled her out of a light doze.

'Lunchtime,' Rich murmured.

'How long have…?' Lord, how embarrassing.

'Sorry, there was a lot of shop-talk.'

And she'd only slept fitfully last night. Something to do with being kissed half to death at the marina had left her tossing and turning and, clearly, in need of some decent sleep. Mila scurried to climb out of the comfortable vehicle ahead of him.

'The missus made you this,' Kip said, passing Rich a hamper. 'She wasn't expecting two of you but she's probably over-catered so you should be right. Follow the track down that way and you'll come to Jack's Vent. A nice spot to eat,' he told them and then raised Rich's eyebrows by adding, 'No crocs.'

'No crocs…' Rich murmured as they set off. 'Good to know.'

His twisted smile did the same to her insides, and she'd grown to relish the pineapple smell when he gave her that particular wry grin. Pineapple—just when she thought she'd had every fruit known to man.

They walked in silence as the track descended and the land around them transformed in a way that spoke of regular water. Less scrub, more trees. Less brown, more colours peppering the green vegetation. Even the surface of the dark water was freckled with oversized lily pads, some flowering with vibrant colour. Out of cracks in the rock, tall reeds grew.

They reached the edge of Jack's Vent and peered down from the rocky ledge.

Mila glanced around. 'A waterhole seems out of place here where it's so dry.'

Though it certainly was a tranquil and beautiful surprise.

'I've seen this on a map,' Rich murmured. 'It's a sinkhole, not a waterhole. A groundwater vent.'

Golden granite ringed the hole except for a narrow stock trail on the far side where Wardoo's cattle came to drink their fill of the icy, fresh, presumably artesian water, and a flatter patch of rock to their right. It looked like a natural diving platform.

'Wish I'd brought my snorkelling gear,' she murmured. 'I would love to have a look deeper in the vent.'

'You're off the clock, remember?'

'I could do that while you and Kip talk business.'

He gave her his hand to step down onto the rocky platform, which sloped right down to the water's edge. She moved right down to it and kicked off her shoes.

'It's freezing!' she squealed, dipping a toe in. 'Gorgeous.'

Rich lowered the hamper and toed off his own boots, then rolled his jeans up to his knees and followed her down to a sitting position. He gingerly sank his feet.

'There must be twenty sandwiches in here,' Mila said, looking through the hamper's contents and passing him a chilled bottle of water to match her own. 'All different.'

'I guess they were covering all bases.'

'Eager to impress, I suppose. This is a big moment for them.'

Rich snorted then turned his gaze out to the water. They ate in companionable silence but Mila felt Rich's focus drift further and further from her like the lily pads floating on the sinkhole's surface.

'For someone sitting in such a beautiful spot, you look pretty unhappy to be here,' she said when his frown grew too great. Guilt swilled around her like the water at her feet; she had nagged him to bring her. To come at all.

'Sorry,' he said, snapping his focus back to the present. 'Memories.'

She kept her frown light. 'But you haven't been here before.'

'No.' And that was all he gave her. His next words tipped the conversation back her way. 'You were the one panting to come today. How's it living up to your expectations?'

She looked around them. 'It's hard to sit somewhere like this and find fault. Wardoo offers the best of both worlds—the richness of the land and the beauty of the coast. I feel very—'

What? What was the quality she felt?

'*Comfortable* here,' she said at last. 'Maybe it's some kind of genetic memory doing its thing. Oh!'

He glanced around to see what had caught her eye.

'I just realised that both our ancestors could have sat right on this spot, separated by centuries. And now here we are again. Maybe that's why I feel so connected to you.'

Those words slipped out before she thought of the wisdom of them.

Eyes the colour of the sky blazed into her. 'Do you? Feel connected?'

Sour milk wafted around them but Rich's nostrils didn't twitch the way hers wanted to. 'You don't?'

He considered her, long and hard. 'It's futile but… I do, yes.'

Her breath tightened in a way that made her wonder whether her sandwich was refusing to go down.

'Futile?' she half breathed.

'We have such different goals.' His eyes dropped away. 'You're Saltwater People and I'm…glass-and-chrome people.'

She'd never been more grateful to not fit any particular label. That way anything felt possible.

'That's just geography, though. It doesn't change who we are at heart.'

'Doesn't it? I don't know anyone like you back home. So connected to the land…earth spirit and mermaid all at once. That's nurture, not nature. You're as much a product of this environment as those waterlilies. You wouldn't last five minutes in the city, synaesthesia or not.'

Did he have so little faith in her? 'You think I wouldn't adapt?'

'I think you'd *wither*, Mila. I think being away from this place would strip the best of you away. Just like staying here would kill me.'

'You don't like the Bay?'

Why did that thought hurt so very much?

'I like it very much but my world isn't here. I don't know how long I would be entertained by all the pretty. Not when there's work to be done.'

Did he count her in with that flippant description? She had no right to expect otherwise, yet she was undeniably tasting the leather of disappointment in the back of her throat.

'Is that what I've been doing? Entertaining you?'

The obvious answer was yes, because she was paid to show him the best of the Marine Park, but they both knew what she was really asking.

'Mila, that was—' He glanced away and back so quickly she couldn't begin to guess what he was thinking. 'No. That wasn't entertainment. I kissed you because…'

Because why, Rich?

'It was an impulse. A moment. I couldn't walk off that marina without knowing whether the attraction was mutual.'

Given she'd clung to him like a remora, he'd certainly

got his answer. Heat billowed up under the collar of her Parks uniform.

'It was,' she murmured. Then she sighed. 'It *is*. I'm awash in candyfloss twenty-four-seven. I'd be sick of it if it didn't smell—' *and feel* '—so good.'

'I'm candyfloss guy?' he breathed. 'I was sure I was earwax.'

He'd eased back on one strong arm so he could turn his body fully to her for this delicate conversation. It would be so easy to lean forward and find his lips, repeat the experiment, but…to what end? She would eventually run out of things to show him in Coral Bay and then he'd be gone, back to the city, probably for good, and the kissing would be over. And he was right. She wouldn't cope in the city. Not long-term.

'Candyfloss is what I get for…' *attraction* '…for you.'

If Rich was flattered to get a scent all to himself, he didn't show it. He studied her and seemed to glance over her shoulder, his head shaking.

'The timing of this sucks.'

'Would six months from now make a difference?'

'Not a good one,' she thought she heard him mutter.

But he leaned closer, bringing his face within breathing distance, and Mila thought that even though these random kisses confused the heck out of her she could certainly get used to the sensation. Pineapple went quite well with candyfloss, after all. But his lips didn't meet hers; his right shoulder brushed her left one as he leaned beyond her for a moment. When he straightened, he had a flower in his hand, plucked with some of its stem still attached. The delicate pink blossom fanned out around a thatch of golden-pink stamens. On its underside it was paler and waxier, to help it survive the harsh outback conditions.

'One of my favourites,' she said, studying it but not taking it. If she took it he might lean back. 'Desert rose.'

'It matches your lips,' he murmured. 'The same soft pink.'

She couldn't help wetting them; it was instinctive. Rich brushed her cheek with the delicate flower, then followed it with his bare knuckles. Somewhere, harps sang out.

'Pollen,' he explained before folding her fingers around the blossom's thick-leaved stem.

But he didn't move back; he just stayed there, bent close.

'I need you to know something—' he began, a shadow in his gaze.

But no, she wasn't ready to have this amazing day intruded upon by more truths. If it was bad news it could wait. If it wasn't…it could wait too.

'Will you still be here tomorrow?'

He took her interruption in his stride. 'I'm heading back overnight. I have an important meeting at ten a.m.'

Panic welled up like the water in this vent.

Tonight… That was just hours away. A few short hours and he would be gone back to his in-tray, twelve hundred kilometres south of here. After which there were no more reasons for him to return to Coral Bay, unless it was to visit Wardoo, which seemed unlikely given he'd never had the interest before.

And they both knew it.

Mila silenced any more bad news with her fingers on his lips. 'Tell me later. Let's just enjoy today.' Then, when the gathering blue shadows looked as if they weren't going to be silenced, she added, 'Please.'

There wasn't much else to do then than close up the short distance between them again. Mila sucked up some courage and took care of that herself, leaning into the warmth of Rich's cheek, brushing hers along it, seeking out his mouth.

Their kiss was soft and exploratory, Rich brushing his lips back and forth across hers, relearning their shape. She inhaled his heated scent, clung to the subtle smell of *him* through the almost overpowering candyfloss and pineapple that made her head light. He tasted like the chutney in Kip's wife's sandwiches but she didn't care. She could eat pickle for the rest of her days and remember this place. This kiss.

This man.

Long after he'd gone.

'Have dinner with me,' he breathed. 'On the *Portus*. Tonight before I leave.'

Dinner… Was that really what he was asking? Or was he hoping to cap off his northern experience with something more…satisfying? Did she even care? She should… She'd only just begun to get used to the sensations that came with kissing; how could she go from that to something so much more irrevocable in just one evening?

Rich watched her between kisses, his blue eyes peering deeply into hers. He withdrew a little. 'Your mind is very busy…'

This moment would probably be overwhelming for anyone—even those without a superpower. She'd never felt more…normal.

'I'm going out on the water this afternoon,' she said. 'Come with me. One last visit onto the reef. Then I'll have dinner with you.'

Because going straight from this to dinner to goodbye just wasn't an option.

'Okay,' he murmured, kissing her softly one last time.

She clung to it, to him, then let him go. In the distance, the Land Cruiser honked politely.

'Back to work,' Rich groaned.

Probably just as well. Sitting here on the edge of an ancient sinkhole, older than anything either of them had ever known, it was too easy to pretend that none of it mattered. That real life didn't matter.

She nodded and watched as he pushed to his feet. When he lowered a strong hand towards her she didn't hesitate to slide her smaller fingers into his. The first time ever she didn't give a moment's thought before touching someone.

Pineapple wafted past her nostrils again.

CHAPTER TEN

'ARE YOU KIDDING ME?' Rich gaped at her. 'How dangerous is this?'

'It's got to be done,' Mila pointed out.

Right. Something about baselines for studying dugong numbers. He understood baselines; he worked with them all the time. But not like this.

'Why does it have to be done by *you*?' he pointed out, pretty reasonably he thought, as he did his part in the equipment chain, loading the small boat.

'It's not just me,' she said, laughing. 'There's a whole team of us.'

Yeah, there was. Four big, strong men, experienced in traditional hunting methods. It was the only bit of comfort he got for this whole crazy idea.

'You hate teams,' he pointed out in a low voice. She loved working solo. Just Mila and the reef life. A mermaid and her undersea world.

'I wouldn't do it every day,' she conceded. 'But I'm way too distracted to think about it until it's over. You don't have to come...'

Right. If a gentle thing like Mila could get out there and tackle wild creatures he wasn't about to wuss out. Besides, if anything went wrong he wanted to be there to help make sure she came out of it okay. Finally, those captain-of-the-swim-team skills coming in useful. Though it wasn't likely she'd be doing this in the comfortable confines of Coral Bay's shallows.

The team loaded up the fast little inflatable and all five of them got in—Mila and her ranger quarterbacks—then the documentary crew that were capturing the dugong tagging exercise for some local news channel loaded into their own boat and Rich got in with them. Not close enough, maybe, but as close as he was going to get out on the open water. And the documentary crew would make sure they had a good view of the activities—which meant he would have a good view of Mila's part in it.

I'm just the tagger, she'd said and he'd thought that was a good thing. Until he realised she'd be in the open ocean down the thrashing end of a wild, defensive dugong fitting that tag.

Rich held on as they headed out. The inflatable wasted no time getting well ahead and the film crew did their thing as Rich watched.

'They've spotted a herd,' the documentary producer called to her crew. 'Twenty animals.'

Twenty? Rich swore under the engine noise and his gut fisted. Anything could happen in a herd that size.

As soon as they reached the herd, the little inflatable veered left to cut an animal off the periphery and chase it away rather than drive it into the herd and risk scattering them. Or, worse, hurting them. They ran it in a wide arc for ten minutes, wearing it down, preventing it from reentering the herd and then he watched as three of the four wetsuit-clad Rangers got to their feet and balanced there precariously as the fourth veered the inflatable across the big dugong's wake. Mila held on for her life in the back of the little boat.

'Get ready!' the producer called to her two camera operators.

Rich tensed too.

When it happened, it all happened in a blinding flash. The puffed animal came up for a breath, then another, then a third. As soon as they were sure it had a good lungful of air, the first dugong-wrangler leapt over the edge of the inflatable and right onto the dugong's back. The two others followed suit and, though he couldn't quite see what was happening in the thrashing water, he did see Mila toss them a couple of foam tubes, which seemed to help keep the hundred-kilogram dugong incredulously afloat while the men kept its nose, flippers and powerful tail somewhat contained.

Then Mila jumped. Right in there, into that surging white-water of death, with the tracking gear in her tiny hands. Rich's heart hammered almost loud enough to hear over the engine of the documentary boat and he leapt to his feet in protest. Her bright red one-piece flashed now and again above the churning water and kept him oriented on her. The video crew were busy capturing the rest of what was happening, but he had eyes for only one part of that animal—its wildly thrashing back end and Mila where she clung to it, fitting the strap-on tracker to the narrowest point of its thick tail. How that could possibly be the lesser of jobs out there…

She and the dugong both buffeted against the small boat and he realised why they used an inflatable and not a hard shell like the one he was in. Its cushioned impact protected the animal and bounced Mila—equally harm-free—back onto the dugong's tail and helped keep her where she needed to be to finally affix the tracker.

While he watched, they measured the animal in a few key spots and shouted the results to the inflatable's skipper, who managed to scrawl it in a notebook while also keeping the boat nice and close.

Then…all of a sudden, it was over. The whole thing took less than three minutes once the first body hit the water. The aggravated dugong dived deep the moment it was released and the churning stopped, the water stilled and the five bodies tumbling around in its turbulence righted themselves and then swam back to the inflatable. The men hauled Mila in after them and they all fell back against the rubber, their chests heaving. One of the neoprene-suited quarterbacks threw up the stomachful of water he'd swallowed in the melee.

Rich's own heart was beating set to erupt from his chest. He couldn't imagine what theirs were like.

Of all the stupid things that she could volunteer to help with…

Mila fell back against the boat's fat rim and stared up into the blue sky. Then she turned and sought out his boat. His eyes. And as soon as he found them she laughed.

Laughed!

Who was this woman leaping into open ocean with a creature related more closely to an elephant than anything else? What had she done with gentle, mermaid Mila? The woman who took such exquisite care of the creatures on the reef, who didn't even tread on an ant if she could avoid it. Where was all this strength coming from?

He sank back down onto his seat and resigned himself to a really unhappy afternoon. This activity crossed all the boxes: dangerous, deep and—worst of all—totally uncontrollable. Beyond a bit of experience and skill, their success was ninety per cent luck.

It occurred to him for a nanosecond that experience, skill and luck were pretty much everything he'd built his business on.

All in all, they tagged six animals before the team's collective exhaustion called a halt to the effort. Science would glean a bunch of something from this endeavour but Rich didn't care; all he cared about was the woman laid out in the back of the inflatable, her long hair dangling in the sea as the inflatable turned for shore and passed the film crew's boat.

Rich was the first one off when it slid up onto the beach, but Mila was the last one off the inflatable, rolling bodily over its fat edge, her fatigued legs barely holding her up. In between, he stood, fists clenched, bursting with tension and the blazing need to wrap his arms around Mila and never let her go.

Ever.

'Rich!' she protested as he slammed bodily into her, his arms going around to hold her up. 'I'm drenched.'

'I don't care.' He pressed against her cold ear. 'I *so* don't care.'

What was a wet shirt when she'd just risked her life six times over? Mila stood stiffly for a moment but the longer he held onto her, the more she relaxed into his grip and the more grateful she seemed for the strength he was lending her. Her little hands slid up his back and she returned his firm embrace.

Around them, the beach got busy with the packing up of gear and the previewing out of video and the relocation of vessels but Rich just stood there, hugging her as if his life depended on it.

In that moment it felt like absolute, impossible truth.

'Ugh, my legs are like rubber,' Mila finally said, easing back. She kept one hand on his arm to steady herself as her fatigued muscles took back reluctant responsibility for her standing. She glanced up at him where a Mila-shaped patch clung wetly to his chest.

'Your shirt—'

'Will dry.' He saw the sudden goose pimples rising on her skin. 'Which is what you need to be. Come on.'

'I'm not cold,' she said, low, but moved with him up the beach compliantly.

'You're trembling, Mila.'

'But not with cold,' she said again, and stared at him until her meaning sank in. 'I'm having a carnival moment.'

Oh. Candyfloss.

The idea that his wet skin on hers had set her shivers racing twisted deep down in his guts. He wanted to be at least as attractive to her as she was to him. Though that was a big ask given how keyed-up he was whenever she was around. Yet still his overriding interest was to get her somewhere warm…and safe. Like back into his arms.

That was disturbingly new.

And insanely problematic given he was leaving tonight. And given that he'd vowed to finish the conversation he'd wanted to have out at the sinkhole.

He stopped at their piled-up belongings on the remote beach and plucked the biggest towel out of the pile, wrapping it around her almost twice. He would much rather be her human towel but right now the heat soaked through it was probably more useful to her. She stood for minutes, just letting the lactic acid ease off in her system and walking off the fatigue. Then she passed him the towel and pulled on her shorts and shirt with what looked a lot like pain. She glanced at her team, still packing up all their gear.

'I should help,' she murmured.

Rich stopped her with a hand to her shoulder. 'You're exhausted.'

'So are they.'

'I'm not. I'll help in your place.'

'I'm not an invalid, Rich.'

'No, but it's something I can do to feel useful. I'd like to do this for you, Mila.' When was the last time he'd felt as…impotent…as he had today? Out on that boat, on all that water, witness to Mila risking her life repeatedly while he just…watched. And there was nothing he could do to help her.

It was like sitting in traffic while his father's heart was rupturing.

His glare hit its target and Mila acquiesced, nodding over mumbled thanks.

Rich turned and crossed to help with the mounded pile of equipment from his boat.

He didn't want her gratitude; a heavy hauling exercise was exactly what he needed to get his emotions back in check. The more gear he carried back and forth across the sand, the saner he began to feel—more the composed CEO and less the breathless novice.

Though maybe in this he *was* a novice. It certainly was worryingly new territory.

He was attracted to everything that was soft about Mila—her kindness, her gentleness; even her quirky superpower was a kind of fragile curiosity. Attraction he could handle. Spin out the anticipation and even enjoy. But this…this was something different. This was leaning towards *admiration*.

Hell, today was downright *awe*.

Gentle, soft Mila turned out to be the strongest person he knew, and not just because she'd spent the day wrestling live dugongs. How much fortitude did it take to engage with a world where everyone else experienced things completely differently to you? Where you were an alien within your own community? Every damned day.

So, *attraction* he could handle. *Admiration* he could troubleshoot his way through. *Awe* he would be able to smile and enjoy as soon as the adrenaline spike of today wore off. But there was something else… Something that tipped the scales of his comfort zone.

Envy.

He was coveting the hell out of Mila and her simple, happy, *vivid* life. Amid all the complexity that her remote lifestyle and synaesthesia brought, Mila just stuck to her basic philosophy—protect the reef. Everything else fell into place behind that. Her goals and her strengths were perfectly aligned. No wonder she could curl up in that quirky little stack-house surrounded by all her treasures and sleep deep, long and easy.

When had he ever slept the night through?

When he'd come to Coral Bay on a fact-finding mission, his direction had been clear. Get a feel for the issues that might hamper his hotel development application. The hotel he needed to build to keep the lucrative coastal strip in Wardoo's lease.

Simple, right?

But now nothing was simple. Mila had more than demonstrated the tourism potential of the place but she'd also shown him how inextricably her well-being was tangled up with the reef. They were like a symbiotic pair. Without Mila, the reef would suffer. Without the reef, Mila would suffer.

They were one.

And he was going to put a hotel on her back.

His eyes came up to her as she joined in on the equipment hauling, finding strength from whatever bottomless supply she had. He could yearn like a kid for Mila's simple, focused life and he could yearn like a grown man for her body—but this *need* for her, this *fear* for her… Those weren't feelings that he could master.

And he didn't do powerless. Not any more.

Mila Nakano never was for him. And he was certainly no good for her. If anything, he was the exact opposite of what was good for her.

And he wasn't going to leave tonight without letting her know how much that was true.

CHAPTER ELEVEN

THE *PORTUS* WAS closer by a half-hour than Mila's little stack-house in Coral Bay town centre and, given she was coming to him for dinner anyway, Rich had called his crew up the coast and had the tender pick them both up at the nearest authorised channel in the reef. The last time she'd been aboard she had done everything she could not to touch either of the men wanting to help her board safely; it was probably wrong to feel so much satisfaction at the fact that she didn't even hesitate to put her hand into his now.

Or that she'd looked at him with such trust as he'd helped her aboard.

It warmed him even as it hurt him.

He'd led her into the *Portus*' expansive bow bedroom, piled her up with big fluffy towels, pointed her in the direction of his bathroom and given her a gentle shove. Then he'd folded back the thick, warm quilt on his bed in readiness so that she could just fall into it when she was clean, warm and dry.

That was two hours ago and he'd been killing time ever since, vacillating between wanting to wake her and spend what little time he could with her, and putting off the inevitable by letting her sleep. In the end, he chose sleep and told himself it wasn't because he was a coward. She'd been almost wobbling on her feet as he'd closed the dark bedroom doors behind him; she needed as much rest as he could give her.

Now, though, it was time for Sleeping Beauty to wake. He'd made sure to bang around on boat business just outside the bedroom door in the hope that the sounds would rouse her naturally, but it looked as if she could sleep through a cyclone—*had he ever slept that well in his life?*—so he had to take the more direct approach now.

'Mila?' He followed up with a quiet knock on the door. Nothing.

He repeated her name a little louder and opened the door a crack to help her hear him. Still not so much as a rustle of bedclothes on the other side. He stepped onto the bedroom's thick carpet and took care to leave the door wide open behind him. If she woke to find him standing over her he didn't want it to be with no escape route. He also didn't want it to be *over* her.

'Mila?' he said again, this time crouched down to bed level.

She twitched but little else, and he took a moment to study her. She looked like a child in his massive bed, curled up small, right on the left edge, as though she knew it wasn't her bed to enjoy. As though she was trying to minimise her impact. Or maybe as though she was trying to minimise its impact *on her*. He studied the expensive bedding critically—who knew what association was triggered by the feel of silk against her skin?

Yet she slept practically curled around his pillow. Embracing it. Would she do that if she wasn't at least a little comfortable in this space? She'd been exhausted, yes, but not so shattered that she couldn't have refused if curling up in a bed other than her own had been in any way disturbing to her. There was no shortage of sofas she could have taken instead.

Rich reached out and tucked a loose lock of hair back in with its still-damp cousins. Mila twitched again but not away from him. She seemed to curl her face towards him before burrowing down deeper into his pillow. Actually, his was on the other side of the bed but he would struggle, after he'd left this place, not to swap it for the one Mila practically embraced. Just to keep her close a little longer. Until her scent faded with Coral Bay on the horizon behind him.

He placed a gentle hand on her exposed shoulder. 'Mila. Time to wake up.'

She roused, shifted. Then her beautiful eyes flickered open and shone at him, full of confused warmth as she tried to remember where she was. It only took a heartbeat before she mastered them, though, and looked around the space.

'How did you sleep?' he asked, just to give her an excuse to look back at him.

She pushed herself up, and brought his quilt with her.

'This bed…' she murmured, all sleepy and sexy.

His chest actually hurt.

'Best money could buy,' he squeezed out.

'How do you even get out of it?' Her voice grew stronger, less dreamy with every sentence she uttered. 'I'm not sure I'm going to be able to.'

That was what he wanted; the kind of sleep the bed promised when you looked at it, lay on it. The kind of sleep that Mila's groggy face said she'd just had. And now that he'd seen his bed with her in it, that was what he wanted too.

But *wanting* didn't always mean *having.*

'Damo will have dinner ready in a half hour,' he said. 'Do you want to freshen up? Maybe come out on deck for some air?'

It was only then that the darkness outside seemed to dawn on her. She pushed up yet straighter.

'Yes, I'm sorry. It was only supposed to be a nap—'

'Don't apologise. After the day you've had, you clearly needed it.' He pushed to his feet. 'I'll see you on deck when you're ready.'

He left her there, blinking a daze in his big bed, and retreated up the steps to the galley, where he busied himself redoing half the tasks his deckhand had already done. Just to keep busy. Just to give Mila the space he figured she would appreciate. He lifted the clear lid on the chowder risotto steaming away beneath it and then, at Damo's frustrated cluck, abandoned the galley, went out on the aft deck and busied himself decanting a bottle of red.

'Gosh, it's even more beautiful at night,' a small voice eventually said from the galley doorway.

His gaze tracked hers across the *Portus'* outer deck. He took it for granted now, but the moody uplights built into discreet places along the gunnel did cast interesting and dramatic shapes along the cat's white surfaces.

'I forget to appreciate it sometimes.'

'Human nature,' she murmured.

But was it? Mila appreciated what she had every single day. Then again, he wasn't at all sure she was strictly human. Maybe all mermaids had synaesthesia.

'What smells so good?'

'No crayfish on the menu tonight,' he assured her. 'I believe we're having some kind of chowder-meets-risotto. What are your feelings about rice?'

Her dark eyes considered that. 'Ambivalent.'

'And clams?'

'Clams are picky,' she said immediately. 'I'm sure they would protest any use you made of them, chowder or otherwise.'

The allusion brought a smile to his lips. 'But you eat them?'

'Honestly? After today, I would happily eat the cushions on your lovely sofa.'

She laughed and he just let himself enjoy the sound. Because it was the last time he ever would.

He led her to the sofa and poured two glasses of Merlot. ‘This isn’t going to help much with the sleepiness, I’m afraid.’

Mila wafted the glass under her nose and her eyes closed momentarily. ‘Don’t care.’

He followed her down onto the luxurious sofa that circled the low table on three sides. Her expression made him circle his glass with liquid a few extra times and sip just a little slower. Craving just a hint of whatever it was that connected Mila so deeply with life.

Pathetically trying to replicate it.

They talked about the dugong tagging—about what the results would be used for and what that meant for populations along this coast. They talked about the coral spawn they’d collected and how little it would take to destroy all that she’d ever collected. One good storm to take out the power for days, one fuel shortage to kill Steve Donahue’s generator and the chest freezer they were using would slowly return to room temperature and five years’ worth of spawn would all perish. They talked about the two big game fishermen who’d gone out to sea on an ill-prepared boat during the week, and spent a scary and frigid few nights being carried further and further away from Australia on the fast-moving Leeuwin Current before being rescued and how much difference an immediate ocean response unit would have made.

Really he was just raising anything to keep Mila talking.

She listened as well as she contributed and her stories were always so engaging. These were not conversations he got to have back in the city.

He thought that he was letting her talk herself almost out of breath because he knew this might well be the last opportunity he had to do it. But the longer into the night they talked, the more he had to admit that he was letting her dominate their conversation because it meant he didn't have to take such an active part. And if he took a more active part then he knew he would have to begin the discussion he was quietly dreading.

'I'm sorry,' Mila said as she forked the last of the double cream from her dish with the last of her tropical fruit. A gorgeous shade of pink stained her cheeks. 'I've been talking your ear off since the entree.'

'I like listening to you,' he admitted, though *like* wasn't nearly strong enough. But he didn't have the words to describe how tranquil he felt in her presence. As if she were infecting him with her very nature.

That, itself, was warning enough.

'Besides,' he said, beginning what had to be done, 'this might be my last chance.'

Mila frowned. 'Last chance for what?'

'To hear your stories. To learn from you.' Then, as she just stared, he added, 'I have what I need now. There's no reason for me to come back to Coral Bay.'

Yeah, there was. Of course there was. There was Wardoo and there was his proposed development and there was Mila. She was probably enough all by herself to lure him back to this beautiful place. What he meant, though, was that he *wouldn't* be coming back, despite those things.

She just blinked at him as his words sank into her exhausted brain. What kind of a jerk would do this to someone so unprepared?

'No reason? At all?'

He shrugged, but the nonchalance cost him dear. 'I have what I came for.'

It was hard to define the expression that suffused her face

then: part-confusion, part-sorrow, part-disappointment. 'What about Wardoo?'

It was impossible not to mark the perfect segue into the revelation he wanted so badly not to make. To hurt this gentle creature in a way that was as wrong as taking a spear gun to some brightly coloured fish just going about its own business on the reef.

But he'd already missed several opportunities to be strong—to be honest—and do the right thing by Mila.

He wasn't about to leave her thinking the best of him.

Not when it was the last thing he deserved.

'Mila, listen—' Rich began.

'I wasn't making any assumptions,' she said in a rush. 'I know I don't have any claims on you. That I'm necessarily anything more than just…'

Entertainment.

Though the all too familiar and awkward taste of cola forming at the back of her throat suggested otherwise.

*Mila, listen…*was as classic an entrée into the *it's-not-you-it's-me* speech as she'd ever heard. Except she well knew the truth behind that now.

It was *always* her.

Just because she'd found someone that she could be comfortable around—with—didn't necessarily mean Rich felt the same way. Or, even if he did, that it was particularly unique for him. There were probably a lot of women back in the city that he felt comfortable around. More business-like women with whom he could discuss current affairs. More suitable women that he could take to important functions. More cognitively conventional women that he could just be normal with.

The cola started to transition into the nose-scrunching earwax that she hated so much.

'We've spent days together,' he began. 'We've eaten together and we've kissed a couple of times. It's not unreasonable for you to wonder what we are to each other, Mila.'

He spoke as if he were letting an employee go. Impersonal. Functional. Controlled. It was hard not to admire the leader in him, but it was just as impossible not to resent the heck out of that. He'd clearly had time to prepare for this moment whereas she'd walked into it all sleepy-eyed and Merlot-filled.

Yet, somehow, this felt as prepared as she was ever going to get.

'And what is that, exactly?' she asked.

'There's a connection here,' he said, leaning in. 'I think it would be foolish to try and pretend otherwise. But good chemistry doesn't necessarily make us a good fit.'

She blinked at him. *They* didn't fit? He would fit in anywhere. He was just that kind of a man. Which meant…

'You mean *I'm* not.'

'That's not what I was saying, but you have to admit that you would fit about as well in my world as I've fit in yours.'

'You fit in mine just fine.' Or so she'd thought.

His laugh wasn't for her. 'The man who can't go in open water? That novelty wouldn't last long.'

She refused to let him minimise this moment. 'Do you not like it here?'

'I didn't say I haven't enjoyed it. I said I don't *fit* here.'

Why? Because he was new to it? 'You haven't really given it much of a chance.'

It was so much easier to defend the place she loved than the heart that was hurting.

Rich sighed. 'I didn't come here looking for anything but information, Mila…'

'Why *did* you come, Rich?' she asked. He'd avoided the

question twice before but asking that bought her a few moments to get her thoughts in order. To chart some safe passage out of these choppy emotional waters.

He took a deep, slow breath and studied her, tiny forks appearing between his eyes. Then he leaned forward with the most purpose she'd seen in him and she immediately regretted asking.

'The government is proposing a re-draft of the boundaries of the leaseholdings on the Northwest Cape,' he began. 'They want to remove the coastal strip from Wardoo's lease.'

His words were so unlike the extreme gravity in his face it took her a moment to orient. That was not the terrible blow she'd steeled herself for.

'Why?'

'They want to see the potential of the area fulfilled and remove the impediments to tourism coming in.'

Impediments like the Dawsons protecting the region by controlling the access.

'It's a big deal that this is a World Heritage Marine Park,' he went on. 'They want the world to be able to come see it. But until now they haven't been able to act.'

There was a point in all this corporate speak, somewhere. Mila grappled for it. 'What's changed now?'

'Wardoo's fifty-year lease is up. They're free to renegotiate the boundaries as they wish.'

Ironic that the very listing that was supposed to recognise and protect the reef only made it more attractive for tourists. And all those people needed somewhere to stay.

'And redrawn boundaries are bad?'

'The new leasehold terms will make it nearly impossible to turn a reasonable profit from this land. Without the coastal strip.'

Was she still feeling the effects of her not-so-power nap?

Somehow, she was failing to connect the dots that Rich was laying out. 'What has the coastal strip got to do with Wardoo's profitability?'

Rich's broad shoulders lifted high and then dropped slowly as he measured his words.

'Every business that operates in Coral Bay pays a percentage to WestCorp for the opportunity to do so. Tourism has been keeping Wardoo afloat for years.'

The stink of realisation hit her like black tar. She sagged against the sofa back. *That* was why the Dawsons were so staunchly against external developers in Coral Bay.

'So…you weren't protecting the reef,' she whispered. 'You were protecting your profits?'

'WestCorp is a business, Mila. Wardoo is just one holding amongst three dozen.'

She pushed her empty dish away. 'Is that why you were up here? To check up on your tenants?' It hit her then. 'Oh, God! A percentage of my rent probably goes to you too. You should have said it was a rental inspection, I would have tidied up—'

'Mila—'

She pushed to her feet as her stomach protested the mix of yeast and cherry that came with all the anger and confusion—on top of the clam chowder, red wine and utter stupidity, it threatened a really humiliating resurgence.

'Excuse me, I need a moment.'

She didn't wait for permission. Before Rich could even rise to his own feet, she'd crossed the room and started negotiating the steps down to his bedroom. Once in the spacious en suite bathroom, she braced her hands either side of the sink until she was sure that her churning stomach was not going to actually broil over. Then she pressed a damp cloth to her face and neck until the queasiness eased off.

This was not the first time she'd had synaesthesia-prompted nausea. Her body really couldn't discriminate between actual tastes and imagined, so some combinations, usually reserved for really complicated moments, ended up in long sojourns to a quiet, cool place.

She sagged down onto her elbows on the marble vanity and pressed the cloth to her closed eyes.

If she'd given it any real thought she wouldn't have been surprised to discover Wardoo was getting kickbacks from the local businesses. If they were in the city they'd definitely have been paying rent to someone.

No, the churning cherry was all about how stupid she had been to just assume that Rich would find the *reef* the most valuable part of the Bay. If he liked the reef at all, it was secondary to the income that the tenants could bring him. He was still here for the money.

He was all about the money.

WestCorp is a business, Mila...

He'd even hinted at as much, several times. But she hadn't listened. She and Rich saw the world completely differently. She had no more right to judge him for the way he perceived the world than he had to judge her synaesthesia.

They just came at life from very different places.

Too different.

Leveraging a bunch of cafés and caravan parks and glass-bottom boat operators for a percentage did not make him a bad person.

It just meant he was no white knight to her reef after all.

She'd have to carry on doing her own white knighting.

She patted her face dry, pinched her cheeks to encourage a little colour into them and switched off the fancy lights as she stepped back into the bedroom. Such a short time ago she'd curled up in that bed—in amongst Rich's lingering scent—and thought drowsily how nice it would be to stay there for ever. Now, that moment felt as dream-like as the past few days.

When viewed with the cold, hard light of reality.

She'd stumbled against Rich's office chair as she'd staggered into the bedroom a few minutes earlier and she took a moment now to right it, sliding it back into the cavity under the workstation and setting to rights the documents she'd splayed across the desktop with her falter. As she did, her eyes slashed across a bound wad of pages that had slipped out from under a plain file.

The word 'Coral Bay' immediately leapt out at her.

She glanced at the empty doorway and then lifted the corner on the cover page like a criminal.

Words. Lots and lots of words. Some kind of summary introduction. She flipped to the next page and saw a map of the coast—as familiar to her as the shape of her own hand. A large area was shaded virtually across the coast road from Nancy's Point.

That was where she stopped being covert.

Mila pulled out the chair, let her wobbly legs sink her into it and unclipped the binder so she could turn the pages more fully. Another plan showing massive trenching down from Coral Bay township—water, power, sewer. Over the page another, showing side elevations of a mass-scale construction—single, two and three storeys high in different places. Swathes of parking. Irrigation. Gardens.

A helipad, for crying out loud.

Her fingers trembled more with every page she turned. Urgent eyes scanned the top of every plan and found the WestCorp logo. Waves of nausea rolled in again and Mila concentrated on slowing her patchy breathing. She bought herself more time by tidying the pages and fixing the binding. Just before she stood, she glanced again at the summary introduction and her eyes fell to the page bottom. An elaborate signature in ink. Rich's signature.

And that was yesterday's date beside it.

The *Portus* seemed to lurch beneath her as if it had been hit by some undersea quake.

Rich was developing the reef—a luxury resort on the coast of Wardoo's land. No wonder he protested the government's plans to excise the coastal strip.

He had *this* under development.

And he'd signed off on it after he'd seen the coral spawn. After he'd first kissed her.

She wobbled to her feet and pressed the incriminating evidence to her chest as she returned to the aft deck. Rich rose politely as she came back out but if he noticed what she was clinging to he showed no sign.

Mila dropped the report on the table between them and let it lie there like some dead thing.

Rich's eyes fell shut briefly, but then found hers again—one hundred per cent CEO. 'WestCorp isn't a charity, Mila. I have shareholders and other ventures to protect.'

No. That wasn't what he was supposed to protect.

'You're forsaking the reef?' she cut in. 'And the Bay.'

And me, a tiny, hurt voice whimpered.

'I admit it is beautiful, Mila. And diverse. UNESCO obviously agreed to give it World Heritage status. But without the revenue from tourism activity, without the coastal strip, I can't see how I can justify maintaining Wardoo.' His chest rose high and then fell.

Couldn't justify it? Did every part of his world have to pay for itself? Did life itself come with a profit margin?

Her voice fell to a hoarse whisper. 'It's your heritage, Rich. Your roots are here. You're a Dawson. Does that not matter?'

'That's like me saying that your roots are in Tokyo because your surname is Nakano. Do you *feel* Japanese, Mila?'

She'd never fully identified with any one culture in her crazy patchwork quilt family. That had always been part of her general disconnection with the world until the day she'd woken up and realised that where she belonged was *here*. The reef was her roots. Regardless of the many where-elses she had come from.

She identified as *Mila.* Wildlife was her people.

And she would defend them against whoever came.

'You're Saltwater People too, Rich. You just don't know it. Look at who you become on the *Portus*. Look at where you go to find peace.'

'Peace doesn't put food on the table.'

'Does everything have to revolve around the almighty dollar?'

'We can't all live in shipping containers and spend our days frolicking with sea life, Mila. Money matters. Choosing it isn't a bad choice; it's just not your choice.'

Her beautiful little home had never sounded so tawdry—nor her job so unimportant—and when those two things formed at least half of your world believing in them mattered.

A lot.

She pushed to her feet. Words tumbled up past the ear-wax taste of heartbreak and she had to force them over her tight lips so they could be heard up on the fly bridge. Though there was no chance on earth that the crew hadn't heard their most recent discussion.

'Damo? I would like to go to shore, please.'

Rich rose too. 'Mila, we're not done…'

'Oh, yes. We are.' *Completely*. 'As soon as you're free, Damo.'

There was enough anxiety in her voice to get anyone's attention.

'Mila,' Rich urged, 'you don't understand. If it's not me, it will be someone else...'

'I understand better than you think,' she hissed. 'You used me and you lied to me. About why you were here. About who you are. I squired you around the district like some royal bloody tour and showed you all its secrets, and I thought I was making a difference. I thought you saw the Bay the way I do. And maybe you actually did, yet you're *still* happy to toss it all away with your trenches and your pipes and your helipads.'

Her arms crept around her middle. 'That was my mistake for letting my guard down for you; I won't be so foolish again.'

She stepped up to him as he also rose to his feet.

'But if you think for one minute that I am going to let anyone hurt the place and people that I love, then you—' she pushed a finger into his chest '—don't understand me. I will whip up a PR nightmare for WestCorp. I'll get every single tourist who visits this place to sign my petition and every scientist I know to go on record with the damage that commercialisation does to reefs. You go ahead and throw the Bay to the wolves. You go make your money and spend it on making more money and don't worry about any of us. But I want you to think on something as you sit on your big stockpile of cash, tossing it over your head and letting it rain down on you...'

She flicked her chin up.

'What are you keeping the money for, exactly, if not to allow you to have ten thousand square kilometres of gorgeous, red, barely productive land in your life? Or an ocean. Or a reef. Or a luxury catamaran. Things that might not make any money but are completely priceless because of what they bring you. Money is a means to an end; it's not the end itself. Surely wealth is meaningless unless it buys you freedom or love or—'

She stumbled on the word as soon as it fell across her lips because she hadn't meant to say it. And she hadn't meant to feel it. But the subtlest undertones of pineapple told her that she did.

Richard Grundy, of all people…

She took a steadying breath.

'Or sanctuary! It won't keep you warm at night and it won't fill the great void inside you that you try so hard to disguise.'

'I don't have a void—'

'Of course you do. You pack your money down into it like a tooth cavity.' She frowned and stepped closer. 'What if wealth is the thing that people like you are raised to believe matters in lieu of the things that actually matter?'

'People like me?' he gritted.

'Disconnected people. Empty people. Lonely people.'

Rich's strong jaw twitched and he paled a little. 'Really, Mila? The poster-child for dysfunction wants to counsel me on being disconnected?'

His hard words hit home, but she could not deny the essential truth in them.

'Has it not occurred to you yet that I am far richer than you could ever be? *Will* ever be? Because I have all of this.' She held her hands out to the moonlight and the ocean and the reef they couldn't see and the wonders they both knew to be on it. 'And I have my *place* within it. The certainty and fulfilment of that. All of this is more wealth than anyone could ever need in a dozen lifetimes.'

Damo appeared at the bottom of the steps down from the bridge, looking about as uncomfortable as she suddenly felt. Here, in this place that she'd already started to think of as a second home.

Mila turned immediately to follow him down to the tender.

'If WestCorp opts not to renew the lease then who knows who would come in or what they might do with it? The only thing that will keep the government from excising the coastal strip is significant capital investment in the area,' he called after her. 'I need to build something.'

She called back over her shoulder. 'Why don't you build an undersea hotel? That would be awesome.'

She refused to think of what she'd seen on his desk as a reasonable compromise. And she refused to let herself believe that the project was still open to amendment, any more than she could believe that *she* made the slightest difference to his secret plans.

He'd *signed* it. In ink.

'Or, better yet, don't build anything. Just let Wardoo stand or fall on its own merits.'

'It will fall.'

'Then give up the lease, if that's what it takes.'

'I don't *want* to give it up. I'm trying to save it.'

She stared at him, her chest heaving. Even he looked confused by that.

'If I surrender the lease,' he went on after the momentary fumble, 'then anyone could take it up. You could end up with a million goats destroying the land. If I keep the lease and don't develop then the government will excise the strip and someone else will come in and do it. Someone who doesn't care about the reef at all.'

'Funny,' she spat. 'I thought that was you.'

For a moment she thought that Rich was going to let her go with the last word still tasting like nail varnish on her lips. But he was a CEO, and people with acronyms for titles probably never surrendered the final word. On principle.

'Mila, don't go. Not like this.'

But final words could sometimes be silent. And she was determined that hers should be. Besides which, her lungs were too full of the scent of earwax for adequate speech and the last thing she wanted was for Richard Grundy to hear her croak. So she kept moving. Her feet reached the timber dive platform. The jarrah deck's isolation practically pulsed through her feet. Resonating with a kindred spirit, perhaps. She accepted Damo's hand without thought and stepped into the tender, sinking down with her back firmly to the man she'd accepted so readily into her life.

Nothing.

No solo trumpet at Damo's touch. No plinking ball bearings at the breeze rushing under the *Portus*. No fluttering of wings as her skin erupted in gooseflesh.

It was as if every part of her was as deadened as her heart.

Had he not taken enough from her this night? Now he'd muted her superpower.

Behind her, Rich stood silent and still. Had she expected an eleventh-hour apology? Some final sense of regret? An attitudinal about-face?

Just how naive was she, really?

Richard Grundy was making decisions based on the needs and wants of his shareholders. She couldn't reasonably expect him to put anyone else's needs ahead of his own. And certainly not hers. She was his tour guide, nothing more. A curiosity and an entertainment. A woman he'd known only days in the greater scheme of things. It was pure folly to imagine that she would—or even could—affect any change in his deep-seated attitudes.

Then again, folly seemed to be all Rich thought she was

capable of here. In her quaint little shack with her funny little job…

Damo had the good sense to stay completely silent as he ran her back to the marina and dropped her onto the pier. She gave him the weakest of smiles in farewell and didn't wait to watch him leave, climbing down onto the beach and turning towards town. The tide was far enough out that she could wade around the rocks to get back to town and, somehow, it felt critical that she put her feet back in the water, that she prove to herself that Rich had not muted her senses for good.

That he had not broken her.

But there was no symphony as the water swilled around her bare feet. And as she turned to look out to the reef, imagining what was down there, there was no sound or sensation at all.

Everything was as deadened as her heart.

It was impossible to imagine a world without her superpower to help her interpret it. Or without her reef to help her breathe. And, though she hated to admit it after such a spectacularly short time, she was struggling to even imagine a world without Rich in it.

To help her live.

How had he done that? So quickly. So deeply. And—knowing what he'd done—how could she ever trust any of her senses ever again?

CHAPTER TWELVE

'I'VE GOT NEWS,' her supervisor said down the telephone, his voice grave. 'But you're not going to like some of it.'

Mila took a deep breath. There had been much about the past nine weeks that she didn't like, least of all her inability to get the treacherous Richard Grundy completely from her mind. Whether she was angry at herself for failing to heed her own instincts or angry at him for turning out to be such a mercenary, she couldn't tell.

All she knew was that time had not healed that particular wound, no matter what the adage promised. And no matter how many worthy distractions she'd thrown at it.

It was her own stupid fault that many of her favourite places were now tainted with memories of Rich in them. She had to go showing them off…

'Go ahead, Lyle.'

'First up… Wardoo's lease has been renewed.'

Her stomach clenched. *Renewed*, Lyle had said. Not *refilled.*

Part of the emotional swell she'd been surfing these past months—up, down, up, down—was due to the conflict between wanting Rich to keep his heritage and wanting him to surrender his resort plans. If Rich kept Wardoo it meant he must have kept the coastal strip, which meant going ahead with the resort. But if he dropped the resort, it meant he must have given up Wardoo. And giving up Wardoo meant there was no conceivable reason for Rich to ever be in Coral Bay again.

So, secretly craving an opportunity to see Rich again meant secretly accepting commercialisation of her beloved coast.

'By the Dawsons?'

How her stomach could leap quite that high while still fisted from nerves she didn't know but it seemed to lurch almost into her throat, accompanied by the delicious hot chocolate of hope behind her tongue.

'Looks like they're staying.'

He's staying. Impossible to think of Wardoo as West-Corp's. Not when she'd eaten sandwiches with and stood in the living room with—and *kissed*—the the man who owned it.

'I'm looking at a copy of an agreement that I'm probably not supposed to have,' Lyle admitted. 'Friends in high places. It's not the whole thing, just highlights.'

'And the coastal strip?'

Please… There was still a chance that Rich had negotiated a different outcome. That he'd dropped the resort plans. Or that he'd found a way to keep Wardoo profitable without the coastal strip.

Not the perfect outcome, but one she only realised in this moment that she would accept. As long as it wasn't *Rich* trashing her reef…

'It's staying in the leasehold,' Lyle admitted and her heart sank. 'Not without conditions, though. That's what I want to talk to you about.'

She'd been the one to tell her boss about the government's plans for the coastal strip, but she never told him about Rich's development. Or that she was on a first name basis with the Dawsons.

The hopeful hot chocolate wavered into a cigarettey kind of mocha.

'What kind of conditions?' she asked suspiciously. Though, really, she knew.

The helicopters were probably circling Coral Bay right now, waiting for that helipad.

'Government has approved a development for the Bay,' he said.

Courtesy of a two-month head start, that news didn't send her to water, but it still hurt hearing it. Had she really imagined he would change his multi-million-dollar plans…?

For her?

The hot chocolate completely dissipated and Mila wrapped the arm not holding the phone around her middle and closed her eyes. She asked purely because she was not supposed to already know.

'What kind of development, Lyle?'

'Like I said, I've only got select pages,' he started. 'But it's big, some kind of resort or hotel. Dozens of bathrooms or kitchens; it's hard to tell. No idea why they'd need quite that many, so far from the accommodation,' Lyle flicked through pages on his end of the phone, 'but there's lots of that too. Looks like a theatre of some kind, and a massive wine cellar, maybe? Underground, anyway, temperature-controlled. And a helipad of all things. It's hard to say what it is. But it's not small, Mila. And it can't be a coincidence that it's coming up just as Wardoo's lease is resolved.'

No. It was no coincidence.

'Do you know where it's approved for?' she breathed.

This was her last hope. Maybe he'd shifted its site further south, out of the Marine Park. Though really, wouldn't that defeat the purpose?

'There is a sketch map. Looks like it's about a half-hour south of you. Nancy's Point, maybe?'

Ice began to crystallise the very cells in her flesh.

So it was done. And at his great-grandmother's favourite point, of all places.

'Lyle, look through the documents. Is there any reference to a company called WestCorp anywhere in them?'

Lyle shuffled while Mila died inside.

'Yeah, Mila. There is a WestCorp stamp on one of the floor plans. Who are they?'

Mila stared at the blank space on the wall opposite her.

'WestCorp is the Dawsons,' she breathed down the line.

Lyle seemed as speechless as she was. 'Dawsons? You're kidding. They're the last ones I would have thought—'

'We don't know them,' Mila cut in. 'Or what they're capable of. They're just a family who loved this land once. They haven't lived here for decades.'

'But still—'

'They're not for the reef any more, Lyle.' She realised she was punishing him for Rich's decisions. 'I'm sorry, I have to go. Can you send me those documents?'

This time his hesitation was brief. 'I can't, Mila. I'm not even supposed to have seen them. This was just a heads-up.'

Right. Like a five-minute warning siren that a tsunami was coming. What was she supposed to do with that?

'I understand,' she murmured. 'And I appreciate it. Thank you, Lyle.'

It took no time to lock up her little office and get into her four-wheel drive. Then about a half-hour more to get down to Nancy's Point, half expecting to see site works underway—survey pegs, vehicle tracks, a subterranean wine cellar. But there was nothing, just the same rocky outlook she'd visited a hundred times. The place Rich had first come striding towards her, his big hand outstretched.

Impotence burned as bourbon in her throat. She tried to imagine the site filled with tourists, staff, power stations and treatment plants and found she couldn't. It was simply inconceivable.

And in that moment she decided to tell Rich so.

If she didn't fight for her reef, who would?

There had been no communication between them since he'd left all those weeks ago but this was worth the precedent—now that it was a reality. But she wasn't brave enough to talk to him face to face or even voice to voice. A big part of her feared what it would do to her heart to hear his voice right inside her ear, and what it would do to her soul to have to endure his justification for this monstrosity. She had a smartphone and she had working fingers, and she could tap him one heck of a scathing email telling him exactly what she thought of his plans to put a resort at Nancy's Point. And she could do it right now while she was still angry enough to be honest and brave.

Brave in a way she hadn't been when she'd fled the *Portus* that night.

She climbed back into her car and reached into her dashboard for her phone, then swiped her way through to her email app. She gave a half-moment's consideration to a subject line that he couldn't ignore and then began tapping on letters.

Subject: Nancy will turn in her grave!

'All right, folks, time to get wet!'

Mila sat back and let the excited tourists leap in ahead of her. If they'd been nervous earlier, about snorkelling in open ocean, the anxiety dissipated completely when they spotted their first whale shark, the immense shape looming as a shadow in the water ahead. There were two out here, but the boat chose this one to centre on while another vessel chugged their passengers closer to the other one. But not too close…there were rules. It was up to the tourists to swim the distance and close up the gap between them.

Not everyone was a natural swimmer and so every spare member of crew got in the water with them and shepherded a small number of snorkelers each. Each leader took an underwater whiteboard so they could communicate with their group without having to get alongside them or surface constantly. Easier when you were navigating an animal as big as a whale shark to be able to keep your eyes on its every move.

The last cluster slipped off the back of the boat and into the open water in an excited, splashy frenzy.

That left Mila to go it alone—just how she liked it. She'd eased herself right out onto the front of the big tourist boat where none of them thought to go and so she hadn't had to sit amongst them with the smells and sounds of unfamiliar people. Now, she gave the captain a wave so he knew she was in, and slid down quietly and gently into the silken water.

It was normally completely clear out here, barring the odd cluster of weed floating along or balls of fish picking at the surface, but the churning engines of two boats and the splashing of the associated snorkelling tourists made the water foggy with a champagne of bubbles in all directions. Easy to forget what was out here with them when she couldn't see it, but Mila swam a wide arc to break out of the white-water. As the boats backed away from the site, the water cleared, darkened and then settled a little. The surface turbulence still rocked her but, with her head under, it was much calmer. Calm enough to get on with the job. She looked around her at the light streaming down into the deep blue, converging on some distant point far below, her eyes hunting for the creature so big it seemed impossible that it could hide out here.

The first clue that it was with them was the frenzied flipper action of the nearby tourists, then a great looming shape materialised in slow motion out of the blue below them straight towards her. The whale shark's camouflage—the very thing she'd come to photograph—made it hard for Mila to define its distinctive shape until it was nearly upon her, but it did nothing more dramatic than cruise silently by, its massive tail fanning just once to propel it the entire distance between the other tourists and her group. Everyone else started swimming to keep up with it while Mila back-pedalled madly to get herself out of its way.

She dived under as it passed her, and she got a good view of the half-dozen remoras either catching a ride on the shark's underside or using its draught to swim against its pale underbelly. She swung her underwater camera up and took a couple of images of the patterning around its gills—the ones that the star-mapping software needed—and then watched it disappear once again into the deep blue. But she knew it wouldn't be gone long. Whale sharks seemed to enjoy the interaction with people and this one circled around and emerged out of nothing again to swim between them once more. Mila photographed it on the way back through in case it wasn't the same one at all, then set off after its relaxed tail, swimming back towards the main group of tourists. Two boatloads were combined now, all eager to see the same animal.

As she approached, a staff member in dive gear held up a whiteboard with four letters on it.

R U OK?

Mila gave him an easy thumbs-up and he turned and focused on the less certain swimmers. It was more exhausting than many expected, being out here in the open current and trying to swim clear of a forty-foot-long prehistoric creature.

Mila let herself enjoy the shark, the gorgeous light filtering down through the surface and the sensations both brought with them. She attributed whale sharks with regal qualities—maybe her most literal association yet—and this one was quite the prince. Comparatively unscarred, spectacular markings, big square head, massive gaping mouth that swallowed hundreds of litres of seawater at a time. When it wasn't gulping, it pressed its lips together hard to squeeze the headful of water out through its gills and then swallow what solids were left behind in its massive mouth. To Mila, the lips looked like a vaguely wry smirk.

Her chest squeezed and not because of exertion.

She'd seen that smirk before. But not for months.

She back-swam again, to maintain the required safety distance, and watched the swimmers on the far side of the animal move forward as it swam away from them. Another carried a whiteboard, but he wasn't a diver and he wasn't in one of the company wetsuits. Mila tipped her head and looked closer.

The snorkeler wrote something on his board with waterproof marker then held it aloft in the streaming light.

NOT...

She had to wait for the long tail of the whale shark to pass between them before she could read it properly.

NOT EN SUITES... LABS.

What? What did that mean? She straightened to read it again, certain she'd misread some diving instruction.

The man wiped it off with his bare arm and wrote again. Something about the way he moved made her spine ratchet straighter than even the circling whale shark did. But she could not take her eyes off his board. He held it up again and the words were longer and so the letters were smaller. Mila had to swim a little closer to read them.

ROOMS NOT 4 TOURISTS.
4 RESEARCHERS.

Her heart began to pound. In earnest. She tried to be alert to what the shark was doing but found it impossible to do anything other than stare at that whiteboard and the man holding it.

'Rich?'

She couldn't help saying it aloud and the little word must have puffed out of the top of her snorkel into the air above the surface to be lost on the stiff ocean breeze.

He held the board up again, the words newly written.

NOT U/GROUND WINE CELLAR...

The whale shark swam back through between them, doing its best to drag her eyes off the man wiping the board clean again and back onto the *true* ocean spectacle, but Mila paid it no heed, other than to be frustrated by the spectacular length of the shark as it blocked her view of Rich. As soon as it passed, she read the two words he'd replaced on the board. Her already tight breath caught altogether.

SPAWN BANK.

She pushed her feet and gasped for air above the surface. Water splashed and surged against her body, buffeting her on two sides. Using the clustered snorkelers for reference, she stroked her way towards them with already weary muscles. Just out of voice range, another snorkeler rose above the splash. The only head other than hers poking out of the water while the massive shark dominated attention below.

Rich.

They swam directly towards each other, oblivious to any monsters of the deep still doing graceful laps below them. But when they got close, Mila pulled up short and slid her mask up onto her head.

'What are you doing here?' Her arms and legs worked in opposition to keep her stable in the undulating water.

'I got your email,' Rich answered, raising his mask too. His thick hair spiked up in all directions.

'You could have just replied,' she gasped as the gently rolling seas pitched her in two directions at once.

Rich swam a little closer and Mila turned to keep some distance between them. As life-preserving as the four metres' clearance she was supposed to give the whale shark. They ended up swimming in a synchronised arc in the heaving swell, circling each other.

'Yeah, I could have. But I wanted to see you.'

Hard enough to speak as all her muscles focused on keeping her afloat without the added complication of a suddenly collapsing chest cavity.

She didn't waste time with coyness. 'Why? To break the news in person?'

His voice was thick as he answered. 'It's not a resort, Mila. It's a technology centre. The Wardoo Northern Studies Centre.'

Labs. Accommodation for researchers.

Incongruous to smell hot chocolate over the smell of fresh seawater and marine diesel, but that was hope for you…

'It has a helipad, Rich.'

He ignored her sarcasm and answered her straight. 'For a sea rescue chopper.'

She just blinked. Hadn't they talked about that the night on the *Portus*? The difference it would make to lives up here?

Her voice was as weak as her breath, suddenly. 'And the spawn bank?'

'Subterranean. Temperature-controlled. Solar-powered. You can't keep that stuff in a fish freezer, Mila. It's too important.'

She circled him warily in the water.

'Why?'

There it was again. Such a simple little word but it loomed as large as the whale shark now swimming away in the distance.

A wave splashed Rich full in the face. 'Is this really where you want to have this discussion?'

'You picked it,' she pointed out.

Mila could see all the tourists making their way back to their respective boats, ready to go and find another shark at another location. But, in the distance between them, she saw something else. The flashing white double hull of the *Portus*. Poised to whisk Rich away from her once again.

He puffed, as the swell bobbed them both up and down.

'A state-of-the-art research and conference facility appealed to the government's interest in improving the region.' He swam around her as he spoke but kept his eyes firmly locked on hers. Effort made every word choppy. 'It satisfies the need for facilities for all the programmes running up here.'

The scientists, the researchers. Even the cavers. They would all have somewhere local to work now.

She wanted to reply but didn't. Breathing was hard

enough without wasting air on pointless words. Besides which, she didn't trust herself to speak just yet.

His eyes darted to the *Portus*, to his sanctuary, but it was too far away to provide him with any respite now. 'They didn't have the funding for something like that; it had to be private investment.'

And who else was going to invest in a region like this for something like that, if not a local?

Mila lifted her mouth above the waterline. 'I can't imagine Wardoo will ever make enough to pay for a science centre. Even with kickbacks from your tenants.'

'The centre should pay for itself eventually. With grants. And conference business. The emergency response bit, WestCorp will be covering.'

His breath-stealing revelation was interrupted by the burbling arrival of Mila's charter boat alongside them; it towered above and dozens of strangers' eyes peered over the edge at them. Rich passed the little whiteboard back to whoever he had borrowed it from and waited until she was able to scrabble aboard the dive platform. Gravity immediately made its presence felt in muscles that had been working so hard to keep her afloat and away from the whale sharks. Rich had a quick word with the crew and the charter chugged happily over to the *Portus* and waited as they transferred from one dive deck to the other.

Moments later, the twenty curious tourists were happily heading off after another whale shark sighting signalled by Craig in his Cessna high above them.

A science centre. Rich was planning on building an entire facility so that all the work being done on the reef could be done locally, properly and comfortably. No more long-haul journeys. No more working out of rust-flecked transportables or four-wheel drives. No more vulnerable, fish-filled freezers for her spawn. The researchers of Coral

Bay would have facilities at least as good as the visitors who flocked here in the high season.

It was a godsend in so many ways.

But Rich has used it to buy his way to holding onto the revenue-rich coastal strip, a flat inner voice reminded her.

He could have just freed himself of Wardoo and run, a perkier voice said. *He didn't have to come back.*

Is he even 'back'? the cynical voice said. *He's owned and run it for years without ever setting foot on the property. You still might never see him again.*

I'm seeing him now, aren't I...?

Yes. She was. Fulfilling her most secret hopes. The ones she'd pushed down and down until the only place they could be expressed was in her dreams. Mila stripped off her mask and snorkel and dropped them on the dive deck but left her flippered feet dangling in the deep.

Ready for a fast getaway.

'Do you even want Wardoo?' she challenged without looking at him.

'I thought I didn't,' he admitted, casting the words to the sea like she had. 'Not if I couldn't make it profitable. I thought it was just a business like any other to me. A means to an end. A millstone even.'

'But it's not?'

'Turns out I'm more northern than I thought,' he quipped. 'I didn't know how much until that night on the *Portus*. After we'd been there and I was able to conceptualise what I'd be losing.'

Mila studied her waving fins in the undulating water below the *Portus*.

'Wardoo was an emotional sanctuary when my mother died, and I'd forgotten how much. I let myself forget. I painted a picture of what it could be—full of children, full of love—and all of that came rushing back when I faced the reality of losing it. That's why I was reluctant to go out there; I feared it wouldn't make my decision any easier.'

She remembered his quietness at Jack's Vent. Were those the thoughts he'd been struggling with?

'And what about the reef?' she pressed. 'How was discovering that going to help you make your decision?'

'I needed to know what I was up against with the development. See it as the government sees it.'

'Sure.' She looked sideways at him. 'Who better to ask than a government employee?'

'I wasn't expecting you, Mila. Someone with your passion and connectedness. I thought I was just getting a guide to show me around. I didn't mean to exploit your love for the reef.'

'Okay, so you're sorry. Is that what you came all this way to say?'

Rich frowned. 'You likened Wardoo to the *Portus*, that last day I saw you,' he said. 'And I spent a lot of time thinking about that, of all the reasons it wasn't true. Except that, eventually, I realised it was. I don't hesitate to let other areas of WestCorp's operations pay for maintaining and running the *Portus* because she's become a fundamental part of my survival. She makes me…happy. She's important.'

'Except the land isn't important to you,' she reminded him.

He found her eyes. Stared. 'It is to you.'

A whale shark bumping up against her legs couldn't have rocked her more. Cherry-flavoured confusion whirled in her head.

'You signed a fifty-year lease—' she grappled '—you're building an entire science and rescue facility. You're changing all your big corporate plans…to please *me*? Someone you've known for a few days at most?'

No. There had to be another angle here. Some kind of money trail at work.

Rich turned side on to face her.

'Mila, you have a handle on life that I'm only beginning to understand. You are just…in tune. You dive into life with full immersion. Before I met you I would have scoffed at how important that was in life. I'm pretty sure I did scoff at it, until I saw it in action. In *you*.' He brought them closer, but still didn't touch her. 'I envy what you have, Mila. And I absolutely don't want to be the one to take it from you.'

Uneasiness washed around them.

'You're not responsible for me, Rich,' she said tightly.

'I don't feel responsible, Mila. I feel…grateful.' He swung his legs up under him and pushed to standing. 'Come on, let's get warm.'

She was plenty warm looking up at all that hard flesh, thanks very much.

Without accepting his aid, she also stood and used the short, arduous climb up the *Portus'* steps to get her thoughts in order. On deck, Rich patted at his face and shoulders with one of the thick towels neatly piled there.

'I'm a king in the city, Mila. Well-connected, well-resourced. I have colleagues and respect and a diary full to overflowing with opportunity. Busy enough to mask any number of voids inside. But you called me empty and disconnected—' *and lonely* '—and you named all the things I'd started to feel so dramatically when I came here. To this place where none of those city achievements meant squat. A place that stripped me back to the essence of who I am. I hated being that exposed because it meant I couldn't kid myself any more.'

'About what?'

He tucked himself deeper into the massive towel.

'Losing my mother so young hit me hard, Mila. Being

sent away to school just added to that. I was convinced then that if I played by life's rules then I would be rewarded with the certainty that had just been stripped away from me. The rules said that if you worked hard you would be a success, and that with success came money and that people with money got the power.'

'And you wanted power?' she whispered.

'As a motherless eight-year-old abandoned in boarding school? Yes, I did. I never wanted life to happen *to* me again.'

Mila could only stand and stare. 'Did it work?'

'Yeah, everything was going great. All my sacrifices were paying off and I was rising through the ranks nicely. And then my father's heart ruptured one day while I was busy taking an international conference call and I couldn't get there in time and he died alone. Life stuck it to me, just to remind me it could. So I worked harder and I earned more. I forsook everything else and I stuck it back to life.'

'And did *that* work?' she breathed, knowing the answer already.

Rich slid her a sideways look and it was full of despair. 'I thought so. And then I came here. And I met you and I saw how you didn't need to compete with life because you just worked with it. Symbiotically. Like the creatures on the reef you told me about with all their diversity, working together, cooperatively. You *owned* life.'

Rich looked towards the coastline—burnished red against the electric blue of the coastal reef lagoons.

'I don't own it, Rich. I just live it. As best I can.'

'I'd worked my whole life to make sure that *I* got life's best, Mila. I upskilled and strategised and created this sanitised environment where everything that happened to me happened *because* of me. Not because of someone else and sure as heck not because of capricious life! And then

I discover that you're just getting it organically…just by being you.'

'Rich…'

'This is not a complaint, Mila. Just an explanation. I got back to Perth and I was all set to go ashore for that critical ten a.m., and then it hit me, right between my eyes.'

'What did?'

'That I didn't want to be a Grundy any more.'

Mila frowned. 'What do you want to be?'

His brows dipped and then straightened. His blue eyes cleared and widened with resolve. 'I think I want to be a Dawson.'

She gasped.

'*The* Dawson—the one you described to me that first day we met and spoke of with such respect. Protector of the reef. Part of the land up here. Part of the history. I want you to look at me like someone who built something here, not just…mined it for profits.'

She realised. 'That's why you wanted to keep the Wardoo lease?'

'Now I just have to learn how to run it.'

Mila thought through the ramifications of his words. 'You'd give up WestCorp?'

He shook his head. 'I'll transform it. Play to my own strengths and transition away from the rest. Get back to fundamentals.'

Nothing was quite as fundamental as grazing the animals that fed the country.

'You have zero expertise in running a cattle station,' she pointed out.

'I have expertise in buying floundering businesses and building them back up. That's how WestCorp got its start. About time I applied that to our oldest business, don't you think? See what it could be with some focus. Besides, as you so rightly pointed out, I have minions. Very talented minions.'

She could see it. Rich as a Dawson. Standing on Wardoo's wrap-around verandas, a slouch hat shielding him from the mid-morning sun, even if it was only once a month. But she wasn't in that picture. And, despite saying all the right things, he wasn't inviting her.

This was just a *mea culpa* for everything that had gone down between them. Nothing more.

'If anyone can do it,' she murmured, 'you can.'

Her heart squeezed just to say it. Having him be twelve hundred kilometres away was hard enough. Having him here in Coral Bay yet not *be* with him would be torture. But she'd done hard things before. And protecting herself was second nature.

'Nancy would be proud of you, Rich.'

It was impossible not to feel the upwelling of happiness for him; that this good man had found his way to such a good and optimistic place.

'I'm glad someone will because the rest of my world is going to be totally and utterly bemused. I'm going to need your help, Mila,' he said, eyes shining. 'To make a go of it.'

Earwax flooded her senses. She knew he didn't mean to be cruel, but what he asked… It was too much. Even for a woman who had hardened herself against so much in the past. She couldn't put herself through that.

She wouldn't.

He would have to find someone else to be his cheer squad as he upturned his life.

'You don't need me,' she said firmly. 'Now that you know what you want to do.'

Confusion stained his handsome face. 'But you're the one that inspired me.'

'I'm not some kind of muse,' she said, pulling her hair

up into something resembling a soggy ponytail. 'And I'm not your staff.'

He reeled back a little. 'No. Of course. That's not what I—'

Tying up her hair was like breathing to her—second nature. Yet she couldn't even manage that with her trembling hands. She abandoned her effort and clenched them as the smell of processed yeast overruled the heartbreak.

'I recognise that I'm a curiosity to you and that my *quirky* little life here is probably adorably idyllic from your perspective, particularly at a time when you're facing some major changes, but I never actually invited you to share it. And I'm not obliged to, simply because you've had an epiphany about your own life.'

Rich frowned. Stared. Realised.

'I've lost your faith,' he murmured.

'It's been nine weeks!' Anger made her rash but it was pain that made her spit. 'And you just roll up out of the blue wanting something from me yet again. Enough to even hunt me down two kilometres off—'

She cut herself off on a gasp. *Offshore...*

'You were in the deep!' she stammered. 'Way beyond the drop-off.'

Rich grimaced. 'I was trying not to think about it.'

'You came out into the open ocean to find me.' Where life was utterly uncontrollable. 'With sharks and whales and…and…'

'Sea monsters,' he added helpfully.

Maybe that was her cue to laugh. Maybe that would be the smart thing to do—laugh it off and move on with her life. But Rich had gone *into the deep*. Where he never, ever went.

The yeast entirely vanished, to make way for a strong thread of pineapple.

Love.

The thing she'd been struggling against since the day she'd sat, straddled between his thighs, on the sea kayak on Yardi Creek. The thing she'd very determinedly not let herself indulge since the night she'd motored away from him all those weeks ago.

No one had ever put themselves into danger for her. Or even vague discomfort. All her life *she* was the one who'd endured unease for the ease of others.

Yet Rich had climbed down into the vast unknown of open water and swum with a whale shark…

And he'd done it to get to *her*.

'Why are you really here, Rich?' she whispered.

He'd apologised.

He'd had an epiphany…all over the place.

But he hadn't told her why he'd come in person.

He studied her close, eyes tracking all over her face, and she became insanely self-conscious about what she must look like, fresh out of the water with a face full of mask pressure marks.

'I have something for you, Mila.' He reached for another towel and carefully draped it around her shoulders, tucking it into her cold hands. 'Come on.'

He discarded his own towel and Mila padded silently into the galley behind him as he crossed to a shelf beside the interior sofa and tucked something there into his fist. Gentle hands on her shoulders urged her down onto the sofa as he squatted in front of her. All that bare flesh and candyfloss was incredibly distracting.

'I should have reached out to you, Mila,' he started. 'Not left it nine weeks.' His eyes dropped to his fist momentarily, as though to check that whatever was in there was *still* in there. 'But it took me half of that to get my head around the things that you'd said. To get my head right.'

That still left several weeks…

'And then I didn't want to come back to you until I had something tangible to offer you. Development permission on the Northern Studies Centre. A plan. Something I could give you that would show how much I—'

His courage seemed to fail him just at the crucial moment. He blew a long, slow breath out and brought his gaze back to hers.

'This is harder than stepping into that ocean,' he murmured, but then he straightened. 'I don't have planning approval to give you, Mila. That's still a week or two away. But I have this. And it's something. A place-holder, if you like.'

He opened his white-knuckled hand to reveal a small silk pouch.

Mila stared at it and the tang of curiosity added itself to all the pineapple to create something almost like a delicious cocktail.

'What is it?'

'A gift. An apology.' He took a deep breath, hand outstretched. 'A promise.'

That word stalled her hand just as it hovered over the little pouch. But he didn't expand on it, just held his palm flat and not quite steady.

That made her own shake anew.

But the pouch opened easily and a pale necklace slid out. A wisp of white-gold chain and hanging from it…

'Is that your pearl?'

The one from the oyster stacks that day. The one she'd given him as a memento of the reef. The one that was small and a little bit too malformed to be of actual value.

It hung on its cobweb-fine chain as if it was as priceless as any of its more perfect spherical cousins.

More so because it came from Rich.

'It's your pearl,' he murmured. 'It always was.'

She lifted her eyes to his.

'I should have known better than to try and stage-manage this whole reunion,' he said. 'I guess I have a way to go in giving up control over uncontrollable things.'

Her heart thumped even harder.

This was a *reunion*?

Her eyes fell back to the pearl on its beautiful chain. 'But I gave this to you.'

He nodded. 'To remember you by. I would rather have the real deal.'

She stared at him, wordless.

'I know you've done it tough in the past,' he went on. 'That you consider yourself as much a misfit as your grand-mother. And I know that's made it hard for you to trust people. Or believe in them. But you believed in me when we met and I came to hope that maybe you trusted me a little bit too.'

Still she could do nothing but stare. And battle the myriad incompatible tastes swamping the back of her throat and nose.

'I'm hoping we can get that back. With time. And a fair amount of effort on my part.'

'You lied to me, Rich.' There was no getting around that.

'I was lying to me, too. You raised too many *what-ifs* in my nice ordered life, Mila. And I didn't deal in ifs, I only dealt in certainties.'

Did he mean to use the past tense?

'You threw into doubt everything I'd been raised to be-lieve, and I…panicked. I fell back on what I knew best. And what I started to feel for you… It was as uncontrollable as everything I'd ever fought against.'

'You said your world was in the city,' she whispered. Saying it aloud was too scary because what if she reminded him? What if she talked him out of what she was starting to think he was saying?

But she had to know.

And he had to say it.

'That's because I had no idea then that you were about to become my world,' he attested. 'My world is wherever you are.'

Pineapple suffused every other scent trying to get her attention. But every other scent had no chance. Not while she sat here, so near to a half-naked Rich with truth in his eyes and the most amazing miracle on his gorgeous lips.

'We barely know each other.'

Did she need to test him again? Or did she just not trust it?

Rich leaned closer. 'I know everything I need to know about you. And you have a lifetime to get to know me better.'

'What exactly are you saying?'

'I'm saying that you can swim Wardoo's sinkhole whenever you want. And you can use the *Portus* any time you need a ride somewhere. And you'll have your own swipe key for the Science Centre and sole management of the spawn bank.'

He forked his fingers through her hair either side of her face.

'I'm saying that you have a standing welcome in any part of my life. I'm through putting impediments of any kind between myself and the most spectacularly unique and beautiful woman I could ever imagine meeting. I'm saying that your synaesthesia does not entertain me or confuse me or challenge me. It delights me. It reminds me what I've been missing in this world.' His fingers curled gently against her scalp to punctuate his vow. 'I will make it my life's work to understand it—and you—because the Dawson kids are probably going to have it and I'd like them to always feel loved and supported, even by their poor, superpower-deficient dad.'

Dawson *kids*?

Her heart was out-and-out galloping now.

'I'm saying that all of this will happen on *your* schedule, as soon as I've won back your trust and faith in me. You and I are meant to be together, Mila. I don't think it's any coincidence that we first met at a place that was so special to my great-grandmother. Nancy had my back that day.'

He pressed his lips against hers briefly.

'I'm asking you to be with me, Mila Nakano. To help me navigate the great unknown waters ahead. To help me interpret them.' Then, when she just stared at him, still wordless, he added, 'I'm saying that I love you, Mermaid. Weirdness inclusive. In fact, especially for that.'

Mila just stared, overcome by his words, and by the pineapple onslaught that swamped her whole system. It seemed to finally dawn on Rich that she hadn't said a word in a while.

A very long while.

'Have I blown it?' he checked softly, setting himself back from her. 'Misjudged your interest?' She still didn't speak but he braved it out. 'Or am I the creepiest stalker ever to live, right now?'

Mila caressed the smooth undulations of the imperfect pearl resting in her fingers. Grounding herself. She traced the fine chain away from it and then back again. But the longer she did it, the clearer the pearl's personality became.

Rich's soft voice broke into her meditation.

'Is that a happy smile or a how-am-I-going-to-let-him-down-gently smile?'

She found his nervous eyes.

'It's the pearl,' she breathed. 'My subconscious has finally given them a personality.'

'Oh.' The topic change seemed to pain him, but he'd just promised not to rush her. 'What is it?'

Maybe her subconscious had been waiting for him all this time so that she'd know it when she saw it. 'Smitten.'

Her cotton candy stole back in as a cautious smile broke across Rich's face.

'Smitten is a good start,' he said, nodding his appraisal. 'I can work with smitten.'

'You won't need to. It's a small pearl,' she murmured on a deep, long breath. 'It only reflects a small percentage of what I'm feeling.'

This time, the hope in Rich's expression was so palpable it even engendered a burst of hot chocolate on his behalf.

Well, that was a first.

'Mila, you're killing me...'

'Payback.' She smiled, then slipped the pearl chain around her neck and fiddled with the clasp until it was secure. Made him wait. Made him sweat, just a little bit. After nine weeks, it was the least she could do.

And after a lifetime of strict caution, it was almost the best she could do.

'It killed me to walk away from you the last time I was on the *Portus*,' she said. 'I'm not doing it again. I may need to take things slow for a bit, but—' she took a deep breath '—yes, I would love to explore whatever lies ahead. With you,' she clarified, to be totally patent.

Rich hauled her to her feet and whipped the massive towel from around her until it circled him instead. Then he brought her right into its fluffy circle, hard up against him, and found her mouth with his own.

'I think I first fell for you during the coral spawn,' Rich murmured around their kisses. 'Literally in the middle of the snow globe. And then the truth slammed into me like you slammed into that dugong and I was a goner.'

'Yardi Creek for me,' she murmured. 'So I guess I've loved you longer.'

His smile took over his face. 'But I guarantee you I've loved you deeper.'

She curled her arms around his neck and kept him close. 'I guess we can call that a draw then. Although—' she fingered the little pearl on the chain '—I think the oyster might have known before either of us.'

He bent again for another kiss. 'Oysters always were astute.'

* * * * *